KU-764-023

TOMES OF THE DEAD

WAY OF THE
BAREFOOT ZOMBIE

The automatic locks on the security doors clicked open and they slid apart. The group moved out onto the sandy ground and into the blazing heat.

Benjamin's whole life had been leading up to this moment. There were real Zombies all around them. He stole sideways glances as they shuffled into the centre of the space with the rest of the party.

They were as magnificent as he'd imagined they would be. Shambling about in the noonday sun just as he'd pictured them a thousand times in his mind.

Noble Monsters, Death Defiers, Graveyard Rebels, none of the names he and his fellow Deathwalkers used to describe them did the awesome creatures justice. They were the ultimate passive-aggressive subversives.

They'd given death the middle finger and refused to lie down just because they weren't alive anymore. It was defiance that kept them up and running. Not hunger, like the idiots all around him thought. The pure defiance of anyone who tells them how to act or what to do. Defiance of the ridiculous hypocrisy of Western consumer culture and everyone who tries to uphold it.

WWW.ABADDONBOOKS.COM

An Abaddon Books™ Publication
www.abaddonbooks.com
abaddon@rebellion.co.uk

First published in 2009 by Abaddon Books™, Rebellion Intellectual
Property Limited, Riverside House, Osney Mead, Oxford, OX2 0ES, UK.

10 9 8 7 6 5 4 3 2 1

Editor: Jonathan Oliver
Cover: Mark Harrison
Design: Simon Parr & Luke Preece
Marketing and PR: Keith Richardson
Creative Director and CEO: Jason Kingsley
Chief Technical Officer: Chris Kingsley

ISBN: 978-1-906735-06-7

Printed in Denmark by Norhaven A/S

TOMES OF THE DEAD

Way of The Barefoot
ZOMBIE

Jasper Bark

Abaddon
Books

WWW.ABADDONBOOKS.COM

"Some can gaze and not be sick,
But I could never learn the trick.
There's this to say for blood and breath,
They give a man a taste for death."

A. E. Housman

"Nothing is more important than learning to think crudely. Crude thinking is the thinking of great men."

Bertolt Brecht

CHAPTER ONE

Is this where the adventure begins? thought Benjamin. *In the john on a private jet?*

His Uncle Brian once said there were no beginnings or endings in real life. Just a sequence of events from which we draw our own significance.

Brian, who was actually his step uncle, had been killed by a frozen turd. Benjamin wondered what significance Brian would have drawn from that. Personally, Benjamin couldn't take a dump on a long haul flight without thinking about it.

The homicidal turd had fallen off some bargain airline with a cracked sewage tank. The plane was so high up that the turd had frozen solid. It remained intact and rock hard as it plummeted the whole 35,000 feet.

It fell vertically and the wind resistance honed the end to a fine point. It had picked up quite a bit of speed by the time it hit Brian. It bored right through his skull and embedded itself in his brain. He died instantly.

This probably came as quite a relief to the Peruvian tour guides with Brian. He was lecturing them on why sanitation was so important to modern society and how this made New York far superior to anything the ancient Incas built.

He was on vacation in Peru at the time. Or rather he was indulging in a 'unique recreation experience' that his 'lifestyle-management expert' had organised for him. Brian indulged in these several times a year, just like all his super-rich buddies.

For seventy thousand bucks they'd do things like fly to South Africa and take pot shots at some endangered species the natives had tied down for them. Then over dinner, in a Michelin starred restaurant, some local celeb like Nelson Mandela would pretend their coked up rant about the importance of an unregulated market was full of profound insight.

This time around it was a guided tour of the ruined city of Gran Saposoa in the middle of the jungle. Brian's body had to be airlifted out and shipped home. The turd had thawed by the time the astonished medical examiner dug it out of his brain.There was a lawsuit of course, but it didn't go anywhere.

The most ironic thing for Benjamin was not how Brian died, but where the turd had come from. Brian was an insufferable snob. If there was one thing he hated worse than taxes and Democrats, it was the poor.

For Brian they were another species. They shared certain physical similarities with real humans but they were quite mentally inferior. That's why he crapped on them every opportunity he got. Waiters, parking attendants, hotel porters, all of them had to be put in their place.

It amused Benjamin no end to think that some immigrant flying coach had dropped his pants and done to Brian what Brian had been doing to the poor his whole life. That the frozen aftermath of one cheap airline meal had totalled the one thing Brian was most proud of – his cultivated brain.

That's where Brian's adventure ended. Benjamin's began here as he took the Zombie stud out of his ear. He'd kept it in as a final act of defiance, but that was stupid. He was trying to blend in. To look as though he was born to this and the earring didn't help that a bit. As he took it out he shed the last trapping of his old self, the transformation was complete.

Benjamin checked his reflection in the mirror to see how well he looked the part. His chestnut hair was cut short. The jet black dye had grown out. As had the ragged and uneven clumps into which his hair had previously been cut.

His blue eyes had quite an intensity. Especially as he no longer wore opalescent contacts and red eyeliner that made his eyes look like a dead man's.

He even noticed, with amusement, that he was getting a tan. It was strange how healthy his skin looked when it wasn't made up to look like a corpse. He wasn't used to seeing himself in an Oswald Boateng suit either, but it fitted his tall, thin frame alarmingly well.

One of the other passengers shot him a supercilious look as he headed back to his seat. A platinum blond in an Armani suit. She probably wasn't used to flying on a jet she didn't own.

Most of the passengers had arrived at the offshore meeting point in their own private jets. Others docked their 250 foot yachts in the adjacent marina and some landed in their helicopters so as not to appear too ostentatious.

The meeting point was a remote spot on the south coast of Texas. When Benjamin arrived some of the other guests were kicking up a fuss. There was a lot of discontent about the travel arrangements. People were incensed that after staking $5 million worth of assets on the course they were expected to fly together on a single luxury jet.

"Why not bump us down to coach with a bunch of peasants and be done with it?" said one man with a red neck and an English accent.

The staff handled the outrage professionally. They were courteous but insisted that the guests were contractually bound to abide by all the course rules. No privately owned jets could enter or leave the island's airspace. Failure to abide by any of the rules would result in a total loss of the attendants' stake.

The stake was what got the attendants a place on the course. It guaranteed that only the right kind of people would attend.

If they didn't have access to $5 million worth of assets then they weren't rich enough to be considered. And if they weren't prepared to stake that much then they didn't have enough conviction to study the Way of the Barefoot Zombie.

Richard's lawyer explained all this to Benjamin when his family agreed to make the stake in lieu of his inheritance. Upon completing the course the assets could be bought back at less than cost over a period of years, providing the attendant didn't break any conditions in the contract. This was all part of the 'incentive to succeed' that the course offered.

It was also an effective way of maintaining control over people who were not used to being controlled. Within only an hour or so of meeting, the guests were already jockeying for position. Some applied their charm and charisma, others flaunted their wealth and influence. All of them were trying to establish their supremacy.

These displays sickened Benjamin, but this time his disgust was tinged with panic. He was used to setting himself apart from such behaviour, but now he had to blend in with it.

He was gripped with self doubt. Would he really be able to pull this off? There was so much more at stake than $5 million.

They were already singling him out as someone who didn't belong. The platinum blond wasn't the only one to look down at him. How long before they found out why he was really here? What would they do to him when they did?

Benjamin could sense the undercurrent of animosity towards him. Beneath the civilised veneer of their thousand dollar hair cuts and their designer suits he was aware of the guests' true nature and their vicious intolerance of outsiders.

It's okay, he told himself, taking deep breaths. *You can do this. They're not on to you. You know these people. You were born for this.*

His breathing slowed and his heart stopped beating so fast. He glanced around him to make certain no-one had seen his moment of weakness, then he joined Tatyana and slid back into his seat.

Tatyana had transformed herself too. Her long blonde hair fell off her shoulders like she'd just stepped out of a salon. All the plastic bugs and stuffed rodents she'd once sewn into it had gone.

While her dark brown eyes and Slavic good looks stopped her looking like a typical WASP, when her face wasn't made up to resemble a decaying cadaver, she glowed with good health and affluence. Benjamin put his arm around her slender shoulders.

No-one would have picked them out as Deathwalkers now. There was nothing about their appearance that suggested they belonged to a cult that idolised the living dead.

"You okay?" said Tatyana, sensing he was on edge.

"Yeah," he lied. "What you doing?"

"Trying to find St Ignatius on Google Earth," she said, playing with her iPhone. "It just goes all blurry every time I go north of Haiti though."

"That's because they'll have blocked it. That's the kind of power they have. It's a totally private island. It's not on any maps or in any guidebooks."

"So how do we know that's where the plane's going?"

Benjamin pointed out the window at the small island below. "See for yourself. We're coming in to land."

Tatyana leaned into him "Nervous?"

"Nah. I'm pumped. Just think, in a few days we're going to see our first real live Zombie."

"Shouldn't that be real *dead* Zombie?"

"You know what I mean smart ass," he said and kissed her to hide his nerves.

CHAPTER TWO

"Are sir and madam travelling together?" the guy with the parasol asked them. All the passengers were met by a member of staff as soon as they stepped off the plane. "There is another vehicle allocated if you want to ride separately," he said, adjusting the parasol to make certain they were both sheltered.

"That's okay," said Tatyana. "We're fine together."

"This way then ma'am," the man indicated a fleet of Mercedes Maybachs. He escorted them to their car where a chauffeur stood ready with the door open. Benjamin followed Tatyana onto the huge leather backseat. More than twenty feet long and looking like something out of *The Great Gatsby* the Maybach was Mercedes' answer to Rolls Royce's Silver Phantom and a seriously impressive vehicle.

Benjamin's step cousin Brad had been showing his Maybach off at the Town and Country club a few months back. Brad had flaunted the fact that he'd paid way over the $385,000 price mark in order to jump the two year queue to buy one.

Benjamin was astonished that they had a fleet of them here on St Ignatius. Just another sign of how powerful they were. Of why he had to be so cautious.

"Is the temperature okay sir, ma'am?" the chauffeur asked. "I could cool the seats if you like, or even heat 'em. If you want to let go of any tension from the flight you can put the leg rests out and I can put the massage setting on."

"Everything's fine thanks," Tatyana said.

"There's Champagne, water and other refreshments in the refrigerator," said the chauffeur. "And there's glasses on the Champagne holder."

"Water's great," Tatyana said grabbing two bottles from the refrigerator and handing one to Benjamin.

"So," said the chauffeur as he pulled away. "Which way would you folks like to go? There's the main highway, the scenic route through the jungle or I can take this baby up to 155 along the coast road."

"Just take us where the least number of people are going to be," said Benjamin.

The chauffeur smiled "Scenic route it is then."

Benjamin stared at the back of the chauffeur's head and tried to make out whether he was smiling to himself. Benjamin had been waited on his whole life. He knew that the people who worked in service industries were often more judgemental than the people they served. Their deference was simply a way of hiding this.

This unspoken judgement, implied in a glance or a tone of voice, always stung Benjamin more than his peers' outspoken judgement. He didn't want to be held to their standards. He hated it when people who weren't a part of that world tried to put him in it, then secretly looked down on him because he didn't fit.

He should probably cut the guy some slack. He was only trying to do his job the best he could. Benjamin had to watch he didn't get paranoid. Even still, he knew that if he was going to pass for one of these people, convincing the service staff he belonged was a crucial part.

"Have you worked on the island long?" Tatyana said to the

chauffeur. It was one of her endearing little habits. She always spoke to cab drivers, receptionists and store clerks. Benjamin worried for a moment that the chauffeur would think it unusual or inappropriate behaviour. That Tatyana was about to blow their cover. But the guy seemed quite cool about it.

"About a year," he said. "I started on short term contracts and spent the rainy seasons driving limos in Florida."

"They have rainy seasons here?" said Tatyana.

"Sure. There's two, just like in Haiti. It's what keeps the weather so humid. Seeing as it's the end of October though, you got nothing to worry about."

"Is that why you've got so much jungle here?" Tatyana asked, looking out the window at the dense foliage that surrounded the road. True to his word the Chauffeur was taking them on the scenic route. The fierce afternoon sun struggled to break through a criss-crossing canopy of palm leaves and only just dappled the narrow road they drove along.

"I don't know if it's cos of the weather," said the chauffeur. "Course this was all sugar cane fields a hundred years ago, before they let it grow wild."

"Really?"

"Yeah, that was back when Mary Papamal owned it."

"Who?"

"Are you guys serious? You never heard of the Scarlet Witch of Mangrove Hall?"

"No," said Benjamin. "Should we have?"

"Well no, I'm not saying you should have heard of her. I was just surprised. She's the most famous person to have lived on St Ignatius, being a serial killer and all."

"A serial killer, for real?" said Tatyana. "And she came from St Ignatius?"

"Well she was born in France. Her parents moved to Haiti when she was four years old. They both died of typhoid when she was fourteen. She was raised by her Haitian maid who took her to Voodoo ceremonies and taught her magic. When she was eighteen she found her trust fund had been spent by the relatives put in charge of it. Her only hope was to marry some rich dude.

So she seduced Jean Papamal, the guy who owned Mangrove Hall. He was forty at the time and she was nineteen."

"Aw man that's gross," said Benjamin. "Imagine doing someone twice your age."

"Maybe he was cute," said Tatyana. "Besides, it wasn't like she had much choice. She'd lost both her parents and all her inheritance was stolen. I feel kind of sorry for her."

"Don't feel sorry for her," said the chauffeur. "She more than made up for the bad start she got in life. She murdered her first husband within a year of coming here and had his body bricked up in the wall of their bedroom. Then, when she discovered he was so in debt he was going to lose the whole plantation, she married a rich Admiral to save it."

"Did he last any longer than her first husband?" said Benjamin.

"Nope. By this point Mary had started to take lovers from the plantation slaves. So, one night she sneaks three of them into their bedroom and waits till the Admiral comes to bed. Then she has two of them hold him down and strangle the Admiral while she does the third slave and makes him watch. The last thing the guy sees before he dies is one of his slaves humping his wife. Then apparently she had a foursome with all three slaves while her husband's corpse was lying in the bed next to them."

"Whoa," said Benjamin. "She sounds like quite a chick."

"Oh yeah," said Tatyana. "*Now* you like her, soon as you find out she's into kinky stuff."

"She did a lot worse than that, " said the chauffeur. He enjoyed titillating them with this lurid local history. "Afterwards she had the three slaves stripped naked and tied them to the back of her carriage. Then she rode all over the island till the slaves were just bloody lumps of meat.

"Eew," said Tatyana. "And she got away with all this?"

"She ruled the whole plantation like a tyrant. Who was going to stop her? She used to take male and female slaves to her bed then have them killed the next morning. She would have other slaves whipped to death just for looking at her the wrong way. Everyone was terrified of her. Eventually she over stepped herself though."

"What happened?"

"There was a small colony of natives on the north side of the island who all practised Voodoo like she did. Mary took up with their Houngan, that's what they call a Voodoo high priest. They all have these rattles that hang round their necks that are called assons. No-one else is allowed to wear one, cos they're like a badge of office or something. This priest was a guy by the name of Toussaint. This was all fine until Mary gets the hots for the guy who was betrothed to Toussaint's daughter. When the guy turned her down she kidnapped Toussaint's daughter and planned to sacrifice her in some evil ceremony. So Toussaint led a revolt of the slaves. They stormed Mangrove Hall, murdered Mary and set light to the building. The whole plantation was in ruins for nearly a century until Doc Papa, the guy who runs this place, restored it two years ago."

"So what happened to all the slaves and their descendants?" said Tatyana. "Did they stay on the island?"

"Erm, I dunno. I guess they all went to Haiti or something."

The Chauffeur lapsed into silence. He looked uncomfortable. Probably because he didn't know as much as he made out. Tatyana felt bad about this and changed the subject.

"So are you still on short term contracts, or do you work here full time?"

"Full time now. Pay's phenomenal and so are the incentives."

"Incentives?"

"Let's just say I found a way to put all of my soul into my work."

"Ooh, sounds intriguing."

"Hey do you guys want to listen to some music?" said the chauffeur after another uncomfortable pause. "I got digital. You can get almost any station."

"That's okay man," said Benjamin. "Silence is good."

"Okay," said the chauffeur and put the visor up between them.

Tatyana looked at Benjamin as if to say 'what the fuck?'

Benjamin shrugged. They guy seemed to clam up pretty quickly. Had he rumbled them? Did he think Tatyana was coming on to him? She was pretty friendly. Some guys misread that.

Benjamin didn't think so. The chauffeur looked tense, a little nervous even. Like he'd let something slip. Said something he shouldn't have. But what? Was it all that stuff about Mary Papamal? If she was so well known why wouldn't he be allowed to tell them?

They were the last to arrive at Mangrove Hall. A beautiful three story stone and timber framed mansion from the eighteenth century. It sat at the top of a hill and was surrounded by beautifully kept terrace lawns with lush tropical plants in the borders.

To the left of the mansion was a complex of what looked like five-star apartments, which Benjamin gathered was the guests' accommodation. To the right was a building that looked like something out of Silicon Valley. God knows what went on in there.

From the moment they stepped through the doors of the restored mansion, a hundred sets of eyes were on Benjamin and Tatyana. All of them silently assessing how much they were worth.

Clothes, hair and jewellery, shoes, watches and handbags, all of it was given the once over by the staff and guests alike. The price of every item was being mentally calculated. Brand labels spotted and judgements made. The scrutiny was that much more intense for how casually and thoroughly everyone indulged in it.

Benjamin acted as though he was slumming it just to be seen in the place. Tatyana tried her best to follow suit. Inwardly he recoiled from identifying with these people, Secretly he suspected this had as much to do with wanting their acceptance as it did with despising them.

They checked in at the main desk and were shown through to a hospitality suite where a light buffet and drinks were laid on. The suite was in what would have been the mansion's old ballroom. It looked like something straight out of *Gone With the*

Wind. Benjamin wondered what sort of infernal gatherings Mary Papamal had presided over here.

Waiting staff circulated with bottles of vintage wine as the other guests picked over the exotic buffet like carrion birds. Pecking orders were already being established as they sized each other up.

A grey haired man with rattlesnake skin boots and a Texas drawl was holding court.

"So I get into the lift with this lawyer and she says to me: 'Mr McKane, can I give you a blow job?' And I say: 'Okay, but what's in it for me?'"

"Oh Sam McKane, you're too much," said the platinum blonde from the plane.

"Yeah. Too much for *your* price bracket."

Benjamin and Tatyana helped themselves to braised Guinea Hen with truffles and sipped glasses of Dom Perignon. They acted as though no-one dared talk to them to hide the fact that no-one could be bothered to talk to them. Most likely because no-one knew who they were.

Benjamin was just wondering if this could be used to their advantage when the room fell silent. The staff had placed a small podium in the centre of the room. Samuel Palmer, the CEO of St Ignatius, stepped up to it. He was a tall man in his early forties with a long face and a completely bald head. He had penetrating brown eyes and a predatory smile. You couldn't miss his natural presence and the commanding aura of power he gave off.

"Esteemed guests," he said. "I am delighted to welcome you to St Ignatius. I can promise you this, the next few days will be the single most important time of your lives. You are on your way to joining the world's one true elite. Sure you're rich. Some of you even have a little influence. You wouldn't be here otherwise. But you're looking for something more, something bigger and something better. And why not? You deserve it. You've all proven that.

"You've come here to find that extra something. And you won't be disappointed. You know there's more to be had, and you're people with a lot of initiative. If there was another way to get hold of it, you would have found out about it. But there isn't. Only we hold the key to success beyond success. Only we can point you down the path to wealth beyond reason and power beyond excess.

"What we're offering is more than any human can take. So we're going to make you more than human. Then you can take more than anyone's fair share. You will walk where most others fear to go. Your feet will tread the Way of the Barefoot Zombie."

There was huge applause and whoops of excitement from the guests. They devoured his words like cash starved banks in a government bail out.

"Tomorrow we begin the work in earnest. Tonight I suggest you take advantage of our hospitality and unwind a little." Palmer raised his wine glass to the guests and they returned the gesture.

A palpable thrill ran round the room. There was intense expectation. A sense that everyone was about to be let in on one of the most powerful secrets in existence. That there was no other place in world to be at that moment. That all the right people, and only the right people, were there.

A waitress moved past Benjamin, swerved to avoid another guest and bumped into Tatyana. She dropped the tray of half empty glasses she was carrying and they soaked Tatyana's shoes.

"I'm terribly sorry ma'am," the waitress said, kneeling to clear up the broken glass.

"That's quite alright. Here let me help you."

The room went quiet. Everyone turned to look at Benjamin and Tatyana. She'd broken a fundamental rule of conduct. You don't offer to help people who are paid to wait on you. Suddenly they began to suspect that it wasn't *only* the right people who were here.

Benjamin felt them circling. As though a room full of wolves had just discovered two sheep with the temerity to dress in their clothing.

He went cold. Sweat broke out on the back of his neck. Panic threatened to overwhelm him. They were going to be revealed. They'd only just got here and everything was falling apart. He had to do something. He had to do something right now.

Uncle Brian came to his rescue.

Benjamin emptied his glass over the waitress's head. "Yeah, let me help you bitch," he said and threw the glass on the floor next to her. The waitress gasped. "Let me help you clean this up properly."

He put his foot on the back of the waitress's neck and forced her face down into the broken glass and spilled alcohol. "You lick this shit up. Lick it up, because you're dumb and worthless and mopping the floor is the only thing your ugly face is good for."

He was channelling Brian now. Spitting out all the rage and disgust he'd seen his uncle heap on those beneath him. Had Brian been this frightened when he did it? Had he enjoyed it this much? Benjamin was disgusted with himself. Disgusted that it felt so good.

He looked up to see the other guests smiling with approval. A couple of them even applauded. He relaxed. Their cover wasn't blown. He'd passed the first test and they'd accepted him.

He belonged. They knew that now. But worst of all, so did he.

CHAPTER THREE

Tatyana was fixing her make up in the bathroom mirror. Applying another mask, creating another identity to hide behind.

Ironically it took her a lot longer to apply a little foundation, some mascara and lipstick than it did to apply all the make up she'd used as a Deathwalker. Then she'd been trying to make herself look like a walking corpse. Now she was trying to pass herself off as something even more hideous.

Benjamin came up behind her as she reached for some lip gloss. He put his hands on her hips and pulled her to him. She could feel his hard-on in the small of her back. He slid his hands around front and cupped her breasts.

"How about a little make up sex?"

She shrugged him off. "We don't have much time. We've got to be there at eight and I'm trying to fix my make up."

"That's what I'm trying to do. Fix us and make up. Shit, you're not still pissed about last night are you?"

"I'm not pissed, I'm just... I hated seeing you like that. I feel weird. Being around you right now brings up all kinds of memories."

"I'm not your father Tatyana."

"I know you're not."

She turned to face him. He was slumped against the polished marble wall. She thought about reaching out to him. Of maybe even dragging him onto the huge bed next door to make up. Then before she could stop herself she said: "But you did a pretty good impression of him last night."

Benjamin lost it. "Well I had to do something. They were on to us. You saw them. If I hadn't acted as quickly as I did we might have blown the whole thing. It's not my fault that you..."

"That I what?'

"Nothing."

"Go on say it. It's not your fault that I fucked up. That's what you think isn't it?"

Benjamin looked away. He stared at the floor and shrugged.

"Well, you did go to help that waitress. I mean what were you thinking? You know what these people are like. How they think and the way they treat staff. We're trying to blend in. To act and think like them, so they accept us as one of their own. I did what I did to look like one of them. To fit in. We've come too far to blow it all now."

Tatyana turned back to the mirror. She didn't want to look at herself so she gazed at the sink. "You're right," she said after a long pause. "It's just, well that wasn't *you* last night. And it scared me. It's a side of you I would never have guessed existed. And it did... well, it did bring back memories."

"I'm not your father."

"I know you're not, okay? You don't have to keep saying that. But that is just the sort of thing he would have done. And even now..."

"Even now what?"

"Look, I'm not accusing you, I'm not blaming you, but you sound just like him."

"Oh come on Tatyana!"

He was about to blow up again. She reached out and took hold of his hands. "Please, I'm trying to reach out here. I'm trying to explain how I feel."

"But saying that I sound just like him..."

"I'm not trying to pick a fight, but you *do*. That's exactly the sort of thing he used to say. 'You don't know the sort of people I have to mix with. I only do what I do to fit in with them'." Her light Russian accent became thicker as she impersonated her father. "That was always his excuse."

Benjamin let go of her hands and went to leave. She caught hold of his arm. "Wait. Look, we're both on edge. It's this place. It's doing things to us. But you're right we have come too far to blow it all now. There's too much at stake. We need each other. Please, let's not fight. You did what you had to do and I can't help feeling the way I do about it. But I love you and I need you now more than ever."

Benjamin stood with his shoulders slumped, staring at the floor. He sighed. "Okay"

"Love me?"

"Always."

Tatyana smiled and kissed him on the cheek. "We've only got a few minutes before we're due in the lecture theatre. Can we take a rain-check on that make up sex?"

"You bet."

CHAPTER FOUR

The lecture theatre was in the hi-tech annex on the other side of the mansion. Like everything else on St Ignatius it reeked of quality and taste. From the plush leather seating to the fully articulated screens around the stage, the attention to detail was flawless.

Tatyana wasn't the only one to be impressed. For all their sophistication, many of the other guests shot admiring glances at the facilities. Some caught each other's gaze and exchanged guilty smiles, as though caught out for not being jaded enough.

One guest stood out from the others the minute she walked into the room. She was a tall, elegant African American wearing a traditional African dress. She appeared to glide rather than walk and there was something very noble in the way she carried herself.

Two course officials pursued her into the theatre.

"Excuse me Ms Chevalier," said one, he was out of breath.

"Call me Miriam,"

"I'm terribly sorry. But there's a strict dress code for these lectures."

"There's nothing wrong with what I'm wearing."

"You have to wear a suit," said the other official. "Or some type of formal business wear. It is course policy I'm afraid."

Miriam straightened her back and pushed her shoulders back. Her voice took on a strange, hollow quality. Like it came from somewhere far away. "I said there's nothing wrong with what I'm wearing, it's perfectly suitable for the occasion."

The body language of the two officials completely changed. Their faces relaxed and they seemed to be looking far into the distance, paying no attention to what was going on around them.

"There's nothing wrong with what you're wearing," said the first official, in a deadpan tone.

"It's perfectly fitting," said the other.

"Thank you," said Miriam and the two officials drifted away in a trance.

Miriam became aware that Tatyana was watching her and looked her right in the eye. Miriam seemed quite shocked that anyone had seen what had just taken place.

Tatyana smiled in a nervous but friendly way. Miriam did not return the smile. She appeared cross. Tatyana's head started to spin. Her vision blurred and she slumped against Benjamin, who helped her sit down.

"You okay?" he said. "What happened?"

"I'm not sure. I... I can't seem to remember."

"Look," said Benjamin, helping her back to her feet. "We'll go sit at the back okay? So we don't draw any attention."

"Okay,"

He guided her into a seat. For a moment or two she couldn't remember where she was, or what she was doing here. Then it all came back in a sudden jolt that made her gasp.

Several guests turned to look at her.

"She's okay," said Benjamin, with his best winning smile. "Too much celebrating last night."

The lights dimmed then, taking attention away from her.

Tatyana knew where she was now and why she was here. But for the life of her she couldn't remember getting to the lecture theatre. The last thing she remembered was the fight she had with Benjamin that morning. Everything after that was a blank.

A single spotlight picked out a glass podium that rose out of the stage floor. Samuel Palmer stepped up to it.

"Good morning," Palmer said. "I trust you enjoyed our hospitality last night? I know some of you made very good use of it." Palmer smiled at this. A frightening smile that was more of a leer. The low chuckle that came from the audience was even more unsettling. Tatyana was thankful she'd gone to bed early.

"But that isn't what we're here to talk about. You're eager to meet the man behind this whole operation. How do I introduce a man like Doc Papa? I should probably turn to Shakespeare, because only the greatest writer in our language could do him justice. Shakespeare said: 'Some are born great, some achieve greatness and some have greatness thrust upon them'. There aren't many people for whom all three of those are true. But Doc Papa is that rare exception. A man who has gained power and knowledge beyond human reckoning."

A low rumble of drums started in the background, pounding out Voodoo rhythms that built to a crescendo as Palmer said: "Ladies and Gentlemen I give you Doc Papa."

The sound of the drums filled the hall. Tatyana felt them reverberate deep within her. Her body's natural rhythms synchronised themselves to the beat.

As they did she felt something ancient and primal awaken inside her. Like a distant memory from a time beyond recollection. It was as though there was another presence in her mind, whispering to her in a language she could neither hear nor understand. It felt alien from anything she'd encountered, but at the same time friendly and pure.

And then it was gone. It left like a lover withdrawing on the point of orgasm. She hadn't realised how intimate the presence was until it was gone. The lost memories of the last half hour flowed back into her mind in its place.

Before she had a chance to process the memories, two Haitian dancers entered the stage. A man and a woman, both dressed in traditional garb. The man carried a large boa constrictor on his shoulders. The woman had a long necklace of beads with seven rows in the colours of the rainbow. In one hand they both held a lit torch, in the other a bottle of rum. The six screens came together and began to show intricate symbols drawn on bare ground in white dust.

The drums got faster and the dancers became wilder and more frenetic. As the drums reached a rhythmic peak the dancers took a deep swig from the rum and then blew it in a fine spray at the torches.

The stage was shrouded by a curtain of flames. When they cleared, there stood Doc Papa. And as quickly and mysteriously as he seemed to have appeared, the dancers were gone.

Tatyana started when she saw him. As did everyone else. His mere presence seemed to have a physical impact on all of them. As though he had reached out and slapped or shaken them.

Tatyana could not take her eyes off him. She had never seen anyone with so much charisma. It emanated from him with all the force of an ocean breaking against the shore.

"Honneur la maison!" said Doc Papa in a rich deep voice that filled the hall. "Messieurs et Dames, bonswa." He held his arms open and smiled so broadly that everyone felt honoured to be greeted by him. He was a tall, imposing man with the light brown complexion of a Creole. Though he carried a lot of weight he moved with such an assured grace that you hardly noticed it.

He wore a dark blue suit and a white silk shirt that fitted him so perfectly they probably cost more than an average person made in a year. Around his neck, on a golden chain, hung a rattle covered with a network of what looked snake vertebrae. That must be the asson that the chauffeur had told them about, Tatyana realised.

"Congratulations on becoming one of the true elite," Doc Papa said. "As a breed apart you are used to making good decisions. This is your best one yet. To walk with me along the Way of the Barefoot Zombie is to transcend your humanity. To become one of the masters, not one of the prey.

"Under my tutelage you will learn to use great powers. You may not realise it but you have already learned to use one of the prime magical systems of our age. I am talking about money.

"We in the Western world are not conditioned to think of money as magic. But that is what it is. I amassed a fortune in hedge funds before I realised this. Before I saw money for what it is. A spirit that mediates in the affairs of men. One that assures people reach agreement when buying and selling. One that decides who profits and who loses. A spirit that establishes the natural order of society, raising up some to great heights of power and laying others low.

"'Ah yes,' you might say to me. 'But that is not the way that money works. Money is not an immaterial spirit. It sits here in my wallet, it lies in my bank account and it pays for my homes.'" He took a hundred dollar bill from his pocket. "What is this note though? It is not the things you can buy with it. It is a promise to pay the bearer on demand an agreed sum. But what is the bearer being paid on demand? Where does this sum come from?

"Anyone with even a pedestrian knowledge of banking will tell you that money is created with a push of a button every time some poor slob takes out a loan. That loan itself becomes an asset to be sold on by the bank.

"The price of the asset is based on the amount of interest the moron will be paying for the rest of his life. Yet any economist will tell you that this system of monetary creation is incapable of generating enough capital to repay any of this interest.

"Yet if the pathetic slob fails to repay the same interest that our economy is incapable of generating, we come and take his car, his house and all of his dignity while we're at it. Because he failed to give back to us something that never existed in the first place. By taking the guy's house in lieu of the loan, which as I've established never existed in the first place, the bank literally gets something for nothing.

"Smoke and mirrors, it's the ultimate conjuring trick, creating something out of nothing. Magic my friends. Magic pure and simple.

"Still don't believe me? Then let us look at what magic is. Consider Voodoo and the service of the Loa. What is the magical system that a Houngan uses? It is simply a means to impose his will upon the world using a series of symbols imbued with power through ritual and ceremony. A Houngan draws symbols called Vévés on the ground to conjure up the Loa, the spirits that will do his bidding.

"He then bargains with the Loa to impart power to the symbols he makes or draws on paper. How does he bargain? Through ritual and ceremony. A group of believers come together at a preordained place to act in a preordained manner in order to bring power to their symbols so that they can invisibly affect the world to their benefit.

"Now let us look at the stock market. Consider what happens when some klepto-communist gets elected leader of some third world country then starts to threaten land reform and nationalisation. The first thing we do on the stock market is speculate against their currency to drive down its value. Then when the country is on its knees with hyper inflation and spiralling unemployment, where does it turn but the IMF, desperate for a loan.

"The IMF agrees the loan on the condition that the country implements stringent economic measures. These of course will include abolishing minimum wage and mass privatisations, allowing Western companies to move in and snap up local resources at bargain prices.

"This has been accomplished many times from Latin America to South Africa without any show of force. How is this done? Quite simply, a group of people known as traders come together at a preordained place known as the stock market and act in a preordained manner. They do this to bring power to a group of symbols known as the currency index so that they can invisibly affect another nation's economy to their benefit.

"A hand is raised on a stock market floor. A series of symbols appear on a screen and a whole nation is placed in complete thrall to another. Magic plain and simple."

Doc Papa spread his arms wide and smiled. The audience were transfixed by his words.

"Like all magic however, money is purely a means to an ends and not, as many peasants believe, an end in itself. Like all magic it also takes a little while to master, but with the right teacher you can use it to accomplish anything. To change the world in any way you want"

Tatyana felt a thrill run through the audience at the prospect of attaining such knowledge. They were sitting up in their seats, rapt with attention.

"Before you can change the world," said Doc Papa. "You have to change yourself. You have to shed the last vestiges of that enfeebling impediment we like to call our humanity. You must be reborn as something more than human. Something shorn of all the frailties and defects that confine the others to the common herd. Something a little like this..."

Doc Papa bent down and picked up a large metal ring that was attached to two heavy chains. The chains ran into two trapdoors that had opened in the stage. They were attached to two metal collars around the necks of two figures that rose up from inside the trapdoors.

Tatyana's felt a jolt of anticipation when she realised what they were. She turned to Benjamin. He grinned back with excitement and grabbed her hand. This was the reason they came to St Ignatius. For the first time they got to see the noble monsters they had travelled so far to save.

The figures were motionless. Their bodies were limp and their eyes lifeless. Their skin had the pallid texture of a corpse. Doc Papa clicked his fingers. With a shudder that ran the length of their bodies, the figures started to move.

Their nostrils started working first. They flared them like animals scenting the breeze. They bared their teeth and started to gnash them. Mouths that didn't look capable of eating showed a grim parody of hunger.

Their muscles began to twitch and twist their bodies into clumsy postures of menace. Both figures crouched low, then, with an unexpected burst of speed, they sprang at the audience.

Doc Papa yanked on the chains and they stopped just short of the front row. Their heads jerked about as they caught the scent of flesh. Like wild animals they snapped at the prey that was just out of reach.

Their decaying bodies could not accommodate the ferocity of their appetites. The violence of their actions strained the tendons and ligatures of their arms as they flailed and clawed at the living.

The skin across the cheek of one began to tear as the jaws worked ferociously. A loose tooth flew out of the ragged hole as its jaws clamped down on empty air.

The people in the front row scrambled out of their seats. While those in the back rows craned forward to get a better look. There was an intense excitement in the room. A grim fascination that came from witnessing a very real threat to their lives.

"Magnificent aren't they?" Doc Papa said as he tugged the chains they were straining at. "Look at how they thirst for your blood. How can you not admire that single minded sense of purpose? That hunger so great they would destroy their bodies just to feed it. Is there anyone here who thinks they would survive an encounter with them? Anyone care to brave it if I let one off the leash? No? I thought as much.

"What it is that makes them dangerous? Unlike them, your bodies work and your brains function? So why could they physically overcome any of you?

"Because they want it more. They are not confused by the things that inhibit you, like a conscience or social custom. Their hunger is raw and real and quite, quite prefect."

"Rete!," Doc Papa commanded. "Dans le nom des Gédés, Rete!" The figures dropped their arms to their sides and became perfectly still. "Isit." The figures turned their backs on the audience and walked towards him. At his signal they turned to face the audience once more, placid and still.

"If there are any among you who still doubt the existence of magic, look now upon the proof. I instilled that terrifying drive in them and I alone control it. You can instil it in yourselves without having to give up your lives as they have. That is what you came here to learn.

"It is this drive that I am referring to when I speak of your 'Inner

Zombie'. It is the first of many powerful secrets you will discover when you walk in the footsteps of the Barefoot Zombie.

"This is how you dominate the market and impose your will upon it. This is how you become its master, not one of the timid quislings who are prey to its fluctuations.

"Any decent economist will tell you that the market works best when it's free of government intervention or regulation. This is the nature of the beast you must tame. To take hold of it and make it submit to your bidding, you must let go of anything that confines you. Any cloying weakness with which society has tied your hands. Once you have released your Inner Zombie you have the power to enslave the wildest of free markets.

"Before you can release your Inner Zombie and instil your own terrifying drive you have to encounter it. You have to meet it head on and find out what it is. You must discover what you are truly capable of being.

"These will be the first steps you take along the Way of the Barefoot Zombie. They will be the most terrifying and the most empowering thing you have ever done with your lives. You have spoken many times about 'making a killing on the markets' without once getting blood on your hands. It is time to learn what killing is really about.

"These two Zombies are far from the only two specimens here on the island. Any cheap necromancer can raise a couple of corpses and command them. I have created the world's first and only captive colony of Zombies.

"There has never been a better opportunity for studying the Zombie. For living with them, acting like them and learning to become one of them. That is what you are going to do over the coming weeks."

CHAPTER FIVE

Once Doc Papa's lecture was over, the head Group Encounter leader came on and told them what to expect over the next few days. Tatyana's mind drifted off. She was far more interested in the half hour of memory she had suddenly lost and then regained.

That woman Miriam Chevalier was responsible. She'd done something to her mind. Tatyana was sure of it.

Tatyana looked over to where Miriam was seated. There was a strange, hazy field all around her. It was hard to look at Miriam and Tatyana's eyes kept wanting to slide away and look else where. This only intrigued Tatyana more, and she concentrated harder on looking at Miriam, fighting the impulse to look away and forget all about her.

Why had this woman reached into Tatyana's mind and taken away her memory? More importantly, how had she done that?

Tatyana watched as Miriam stood and left her seat. Partly because of the field around her, and partly because everyone was paying attention to the stage, Miriam was able to slip away without anyone noticing.

Tatyana knew she had to follow. She slipped out of her seat and headed to the back of the theatre.

Unlike Miriam, she didn't have any field around her to deflect scrutiny. Several heads turned as she sneaked away. Tatyana tried her best not to catch anyone's eye.

Benjamin had gone on for ages about how important it was not to draw attention to themselves. She knew he was right. But she also knew this was more important.

Miriam turned her head, aware she was being followed. Tatyana bent down behind a row of chairs and pretended to adjust the Jimmy Choo shoes Benjamin had insisted she buy.

When she looked back up Miriam didn't seem to have spotted her. Tatyana had spotted something of interest though. Miriam's field left a ghost trail behind her. If she looked carefully, Tatyana could just catch sight of it out of the corner of her eye.

She slipped off the shoes so her heels didn't clatter on the floor. Then, acting on an instinct that surprised her, she chased after Miriam, stepping inside the ghost trail.

She had no idea why, but the trail lent her the same ability to deflect attention as Miriam's field. Not even Miriam noticed her so long as she stayed within it. This wasn't always easy though. The trail had a tendency to waft in an out of Miriam's footsteps as if an invisible breeze was blowing it. Tatyana had to side step quite a bit to stay inside it.

She followed Miriam out of the lecture theatre and around a corner into a corridor she hadn't seen before. Miriam raced along at a pace Tatyana found hard to match. Even at such speed she moved with a grace that was effortless.

Miriam opened a service door at the end of the long corridor and snuck through it. Tatyana ran to catch the door before it swung shut. The narrow passageway beyond wasn't as opulent as the rest of the annex. Bare pipes and electric wires ran along the unpainted concrete walls.

At the end of the passageway a metal staircase descended into a large service bay. Food goods and domestic products were stacked against concrete pillars in large polythene wrapped palettes.

Miriam moved through the bay onto a large walkway. At the end of this was a hi-tech security door with long corridors running off to the left and right. Miriam stopped at the door and took out a piece of red chalk. She drew several symbols on the wall around a card-swipe mechanism that looked like an electronic lock. The symbols looked similar to those she'd seen on the screens drawn in white powder.

Tatyana stood in the shadows and watched as Miriam prayed under her breath. She seemed to be in a trance. Miriam took out a card and ran it through the swipe on the wall.

The lights went out. Tatyana couldn't see a thing. She wedged herself into a corner as the sound of running feet hurtled towards them.

"This is a restricted area Ma'am," said a man's voice. "You just tripped the alarm. I'm going to have to ask you to stand still with your hands on your head."

Two torch beams clicked on. Both beams were directed at Miriam and Tatyana could see the torches were mounted on the automatic weapons of two guards.

Tatyana was very nervous. She'd seen the guards all over the island. They tried to maintain a discreet presence in front of the guests but now they were pointing guns at a guest Tatyana had followed into a restricted area.

Way to go not calling attention to yourself, she thought.

The guards clicked off their night-vision goggles.

"You're not supposed to be down here Ma'am. You're life is in danger. Not just from us. There's an army of the undead on the other side of that door. I'm going to have to ask you to lie face down with your hands behind your back."

Instead of doing what the guards told her, Miriam looked up at the ceiling and began to mutter something in a whispered voice.

"Ma'am get on the floor please," said the guard, his tone more urgent now.

"On the floor Bitch! Now!" shouted the other guard, taking a step closer to her.

Tatyana's heart was pounding in her chest. She hardly dared breathe and one of her legs shook so hard she couldn't stop it. They were going to shoot her. Tatyana knew they were and Miriam wasn't doing a thing about it.

Tatyana closed her eyes and waited for the shot. She wished she wasn't an atheist. That she believed in anything enough to pray to it right now. She pictured a stained glass window of the Virgin Mary she'd once seen that had changed the way she felt about religion. It was the closest she'd ever come to having faith in something. She held the image in her mind like an invisible guardian and begged it to stop the guards finding her.

Instead of hearing a shot Tatyana felt a calm and loving presence all around her. Was this the Virgin Mary?

Don't worry, I won't let any harm befall those who love me.

Tatyana was confused. *But I'm an atheist*, she thought. The tone of the presence changed at this. It was still warm and loving but she could swear it was laughing. The same way her mother would laugh when, as a little girl, Tatyana had said something cute without realising it. Then the presence faded.

Tatyana looked around the corner and saw something even weirder. The guards weren't moving. They stood staring straight ahead without any expression.

Miriam was reaching her fingers out to the air either side of the guards' temples and coaxing what looked like a fine black mist out of their heads. Tatyana blinked and looked again, sure that she hadn't seen what she thought she was seeing.

But there it was. The black mist and Miriam's fingers. What was she doing to them? Why weren't they moving? Was that their memories Miriam was taking? Was that what Miriam had done to her earlier?

Before Tatyana could come to any conclusions, Miriam shook her hands and seemed to banish the memory mist. The guards didn't move as she walked past Tatyana and back down the walkway.

Tatyana watched her disappear into the darkness and then glanced back at the guards. They weren't even blinking.

She had no idea what had just happened, but she knew she had to get out of there quick.

It was already beginning to seem like a dream as she stumbled back down the walkway. She kept hoping she was going to wake up as she felt her way along the wall and tried to remember the way back in the pitch dark.

She couldn't repress the feeling that she'd just had an entirely different sort of awakening though.

CHAPTER SIX

"So, where did you go?"

"Oh you know, just around." She was deliberately being evasive. This set off all his old paranoia.

Benjamin had been trying to get Tatyana to talk about where she went since he found her up in their room hours later. He was curious what she saw when she skipped out. She seemed shaken and said she was tired, so he'd let her get some sleep without bothering her.

Now she'd had a good night's sleep he tried again, rolling over to hold her beneath the sheets of their king size bed.

"No I don't know," he said. "That's why I'm asking."

"Why is it so important to you?"

"Well for one thing you might have seen something that could be vital to our mission. Even the tiniest detail might have a significance you haven't realised yet. I can't understand why you don't want to tell me all about it."

"Look, I'm still processing it all okay. I'm not even sure what happened myself. I just need a bit of time."

"Won't it help to talk about it?"

"Can we just drop it please?" She reached under the covers and took him in her hand. "Maybe we could have that make up sex you've been promising me?"

He grew hard the minute she touched him but he couldn't keep the nagging suspicions out of his mind. "Is it because you were with someone you don't want me to know about? Did you sneak off with someone?"

"One of the guests you mean? Come on give me some credit."

"I did give you credit before remember, and look what happened then."

"Do you have to keep bringing that up? Can't you cut me a little slack and maybe just trust me for once?"

"How can I trust you when you won't talk to me?" He pushed her hand away and slid out of bed. "I'm going for a shower."

Tatyana rolled over and stared up at the ceiling with an angry sigh.

Benjamin punched the shower control and hurt his hand. The hot water relaxed him as he rubbed his sore fingers. He was more angry at himself than Tatyana. Partly because he'd just turned down the opportunity to have sex and partly because he hadn't gotten over that business with her old boyfriend.

It was stupid really. It had happened six months ago. They'd been going steady for a while when Tatyana told him she was going to see an old boyfriend who happened to be in town. He'd been perfectly cool with it at first. But there was something about the way she'd said the guy's name that kept eating away at him.

On the day in question he took Richard's Bentley and followed her. He knew it was stupid but he couldn't stop himself. He pulled up next to the park where she met the guy and kept tabs on them through field binoculars. He felt kind of creepy doing it and he had no idea what he'd say if some cop saw him.

Nothing happened for ages. They wandered about, chatted and ate ice cream. Then, just when Benjamin was feeling like a total putz and was about to slope off, they kissed. He nearly dropped his binoculars.

The guy moved in on her. They were laughing and she gave him a look that Benjamin knew all too well. The guy leaned in and she turned her head. He took her face in his hands, turned it to him and kissed her. They really went for it, tongues and everything.

Benjamin couldn't believe it. He was so mad he was shaking. He threw the binoculars on the floor and battered the dashboard with his fists. He should have left right there and then but he wasn't thinking rationally anymore. He waited until they parted and confronted Tatyana.

She couldn't believe he'd followed her. She was incensed at the way he'd behaved. Imagine the gall. After what she'd just done she had the nerve to get mad with him. They had a blazing row right there in the park and she stormed off.

It was two weeks before he heard from her again. She sent him a couple of texts which he ignored. Then a week or so later he finally gave in to his Mom's nagging and tidied his room.

At the bottom of a pile of dirty briefs and magazines he came across the DVD of Zombie *Flesh Eaters* that she'd bought him for his birthday. Inside the case was the note she'd written him:

> Yours are the hands that pulled my eye onto the splinter of love and embedded it in my brain. Yours are the teeth that gnaw on my guts every time I think about life without you. You are the Zombie that wrestles with the sharks of my fear and shines the sunlight of love on my despairing sea.

He broke down and bawled like a kid when he read it.

Their first date had been a midnight screening of Zombie *Flesh Eaters*. The scene where the Zombie fights the shark. That was their scene. They had their first kiss during it. Then, during the infamous scene where the splinter is driven into the eyeball of the Doctor's wife, she gave him the best hand job he'd ever had.

Holding the note, he knew right there and then, that he would never find anyone to write him a more tender and touching love letter.

They got back together the next day. He forgave her of course, but he could never bring himself to forget.

He kept playing the image of her kissing the other guy over and over in his mind. It was like a scab that he couldn't help picking. It wasn't just his jealousy and insecurity that drove him to keep going over it. If he was honest, he realised that it turned him on.

Every time he thought about their kiss he took it that little bit further. He imagined the other guy's hands roaming over Tatyana's body. Taking her dress off. Pinning her down to the park bench...

Even now, just thinking about it in the shower made him harder than when she'd held his penis. He poured the shower gel onto his palm and took hold of himself.

"Enjoying yourself?" said Tatyana. He dropped the shower gel and spun round to see her standing by the door in her robe. "It's okay. I only came to say sorry. You're right, I should have opened up to you. I've remembered something I saw. Something that could be really useful to our plans. I know a way to get into the compound where the Zombies are."

CHAPTER SEVEN

The dress code for the first encounter session was smart casual. Benjamin wore his Yves Saint Laurent shirt with a pair of Ralph Lauren jeans and his limited edition Nike trainers. He helped Tatyana pick out a long sleeved Gucci top with slacks and pair of Manolo Blahnik Slingbacks.

He still felt sore at her even though she'd told him about the basement and the hidden door to the compound. She hadn't told him what she was doing down there. Still, they were making an effort to get along and be civil, for the sake of the mission if nothing else.

Coffee and *petit fours* were being served in a room just off the mansion's entrance hall. They were among the last to arrive. The platinum blonde sashayed up to Benjamin the minute she saw him.

"If it isn't the handsome young man who knows how to treat a lady," she said. "So long as she's staff that is. I'm Lavinia Ponsonby, I don't think we've been introduced." She flashed him her teeth, her cleavage and her jewellery as she offered him her hand. They all cost a fortune, Benjamin was sure.

"I'm Benjamin Hollinger. This is..."

"Your charming young friend," Lavinia said to Tatyana. "Love the slacks dearie. How brave of you to wear them."

Tatyana bristled at this. Benjamin had never seen her do that before. "There's some people here I really must introduce you to," Lavinia said, taking Benjamin's arm and leading him off. "Hope you don't mind me stealing your man away." Lavinia said to Tatyana over her shoulder.

Tatyana shot Benjamin an angry look that said 'don't leave me alone here'. He shrugged and shot one back to say 'sorry, got to fit in, you know that'. Out of the corner of his eye he saw Lavinia flash Tatyana the sort smile a lioness would give a young cub whose prey she'd just stolen.

They were totally fighting over him. He couldn't believe how much that turned him on. Seems Tatyana wasn't the only one with options.

Lavinia steered him over to a group of three men and a woman. "This is Benjamin Hollinger," she said, displaying him on her arm like she'd just landed him. "I simply had to bring him over. This is Sam McKane." Lavinia pushed him towards the grey haired Texan he'd spotted on the first night.

"Good to meet you," said Sam, crushing Benjamin's hand in his huge mitt.

"Is that a Frank Muller Aeternitas?" said Benjamin pointing at Sam's watch.

"Why yes it is young man," said Sam pulling back his sleeve to show it off. "Accurate to within one hundredth of a second. Tells the day, date, months and moon phases for the next thousand years, even takes leap years into account. You wear a Frank Muller yourself?"

"Got one for my Dad's last birthday," said Benjamin, not mentioning that it was lost at a crap table in Vegas the next month. "People with a Frank Muller on their wrist, they're an elite. Like an exclusive club, you see someone wearing one, you know they've got class."

Sam McKane threw his arm around Benjamin's shoulders and punched him affectionately in the chest. "I like this kid! He's got taste and character. C'mere you gotta meet these yahoos. This here's Arthur Sonnenfeldt. He owns a lot of real estate." A short, plump man shook Benjamin's hand. "George Griffin here founded a few investment groups," Benjamin shook hands with a tall, thin man who wore glasses and an air of smug superiority. "And Bessie here runs a shop or two."

"Oh don't listen to him," said Bessie rolling her eyes in mock outrage. "I own several chains of exclusive boutiques." She was a redhead in a power suit who looked around thirty, but that was probably because she had a good surgeon. Bessie air kissed him and squeezed his biceps. "Someone works out," she said with a wink.

"Hands off," said Lavinia. "I saw him first." She snaked her arm around Benjamin's waist and pulled him to her. It felt good. A few weeks ago these people wouldn't have given him the steam off their lattés, now they were slapping him on the back and praising his opinions. He was alarmed by how much he liked this.

"Ladies and Gentlemen my name is Dr Susan Chen," said an Asian woman mounting a dais at the far end of the room. She was wearing a white coat and a headset mic. "I'm going to be leading your first encounter session. If you'd all kindly follow me we can begin."

Tatyana tapped him on the shoulder. "Can I have a word?" she said, glowering.

"Sorry sweetie," said Lavinia, with a menacing smile. "But he's promised he'll walk *me* to the compound and I won't hear of letting him go."

"I should probably meet you in there," said Benjamin in an attempt to relieve the tension. Lavinia whisked him away leaving Tatyana looking far from happy.

"You're all mine today," said Lavinia in a voice that made him nervous and excited. "One thing you'll learn about Lavinia Ponsonby, she never lets go of what's hers."

Dr Chen led them all the way through the annex and up

several flights of stairs to a state-of-the-art observation corridor. It was constructed entirely from glass and gave an incredible aerial view of the Zombie enclosures. Immediately below them Benjamin could see at least eight Zombies milling around the grass huts and crumbling concrete walls of their specially constructed environment.

There was a cold knot of anticipation in his stomach as it dawned on him. This was for real. He'd pictured this encounter so many times and here he was. About to get up close and personal with the noble monster for the first time. Un-freaking believable.

"There's a few things I need to take you through before we can expose you to the undead," said Dr Chen as the guests gathered round her. "I'm a scientist not a magician. I can't tell you anything about how these corpses came to life but I've been studying the undead on St Ignatius for over a year now. That's why, after a careful series of observations, I'm authorised to advise the following precautionary measures. We are not legally responsible for your safety in any way. If you want to stay alive it is essential that you bear them in mind at all times.

"The golden rule in any encounter with the undead is to remain calm at all times. Just like dogs they can smell when you're afraid. Most of their other senses are as good as dead. But the lack of them seems to have sharpened their sense of smell.

"They can scent blood and adrenalin from up to ten feet away. If your heart is pumping and your adrenalin is high they will be driven to attack." Dr Chen tapped the glass behind her and a screen appeared showing a CGI model of a Zombie.

"The Zombie's bloodlust comes from a very basic survival instinct. It would appear that an infusion of human flesh and blood can slow down their body's decay." Dr Chen tapped the stomach of the Zombie image and the screen zoomed in on a shot of its insides. "The undead don't feed like normal living creatures. However, just as their muscles can replicate basic motor functions, it would appear that their guts can also perform a type of basic digestion. They can't ingest normal food but they can break down living human blood and tissue to replenish themselves."

She changed the screen again. It split in two and showed accelerated footage of two different Zombies. Both of them strapped to an operating table. One was decaying rapidly the other remained unchanged. "The undead that we starved decayed at the normal rate of an unpreserved corpse. While those that received a regular diet of blood remain unchanged for an indefinite period."

It was worse than Benjamin thought. Here they were openly flaunting the fact they were starving these proud monsters to death.

"Is that where their hunger comes from?" said George Griffin.

"Yes it is," said Dr Chen. "What makes it so pure is that it's the only basic drive the undead have. It's what sets them apart from any other predator. They have no fear of death or injury and no biological imperatives such as the need to procreate and protect their young. They've nothing to lose and everything to gain. Hunger is what they're all about."

The screen changed again. This time it showed footage of a Zombie in a cage. Benjamin hid his fists in his pockets.

"Never show any emotion or make any sudden movements in the presence of the undead. These are the things that identify you as prey. When people are first exposed to the undead they tend to exhibit hysteria or try and run. This is why they are attacked. As the following footage shows."

The screen showed a clip of a woman in a white coat sobbing as another researcher shouted: "You're an idiot, an idiot!" at her. The caged Zombie flew at the bars.

Next it cut to a young researcher with a pony tail. He was dancing to his ipod. The Zombie's arm reached through the bars and grabbed the researcher's hair. Another arm came into shot wielding a machete. It hacked off several of the Zombie's fingers and the researcher's pony tail setting him free.

Incredibly, the final clip showed a guy on a surf simulator next to the cage. Surf music played as the guy wobbled about on the board. He turned and screamed as the Zombie smashed into the bars and grabbed the board. The Zombie pulled the board and the guy fell off. He ran as the Zombie cracked the board and threw it aside, grasping after him through the bars.

It would have been comical if it wasn't so wrong. They were taunting the Zombies. Torturing them and pretending it was science. Benjamin felt his excitement sour. Several of the guest laughed and many smiled. He remembered why he hated them. Fuck their attention and approval. They didn't understand. They weren't capable of understanding anything he held dear.

He wasn't a part of their world. He couldn't be part of any world that treated the noble monster in this way. He looked for Tatyana. She caught his eye and nodded to show she shared his sadness and anger.

He realised what a jerk he was being. Lavinia had let go off his arm and was staring avidly at the window. He sidled away from her over to Tatyana. The look on her face reflected her relief and anger at him.

"Whenever you are exposed to the undead you need to keep in mind five basic rules," said Dr Chen. "These are the 'Five Rules of Interaction.'" The screen flashed up these rules as she spoke.

"Number One: Show no signs of life. Take small shallow breaths, try not to twitch or scratch yourself and keep your expression blank.

"Number Two: Move in slow motion. Keep every movement extremely slow and deliberate. The longer it takes for you to do something the less likely the undead are to notice you. Only sudden movements draw their attention.

"Number Three: It doesn't matter and you don't care. Nothing here is personal, the less you care about the Zombies and what's happening around you the less likely you are to show an emotion. The less emotion you show the less likely you are to be attacked.

"Number Four: Follow the herd but think ahead of it. In the case of the undead two heads really are better than one. They tend to form packs quite quickly. The more undead there are, the closer they come to exhibiting something approaching thought. Whatever tiny brain functions they have seem to increase *en masse*. Always act how the majority of the undead are acting, but concentrate on their reasons for acting the way they do so you can pre-empt them if you need to. When you are more advanced this technique can be developed to control or shepherd them.

"And, finally, Number Five: Master yourself and nothing can threaten you. Self awareness and self control will allow you to interact with the undead in perfect safety.

"If you keep these rules in mind at all times you will be able to observe the undead from an unprecedented perspective. You will be able to study them and become like them. You will face certain death every day and become stronger for surviving it."

Dr Chen switched off the screen and led the group down the observation corridor. "Now if you'll follow me I'll show you to the changing rooms where you'll be fitted with the appropriate garments."

CHAPTER EIGHT

"Ugh, why'd they give me this shirt?" said Tatyana. "It stinks like a corpse."

"That's the whole point," Benjamin said. "They're clothes people died or were buried in. It makes us smell like the Zombies."

They were standing outside the security doors to the compound. They'd been through the changing area where they were measured and fitted with damp, encrusted clothes.

They'd been split into two parties of ten. Benjamin and Tatyana were thrilled to be in the first group chosen for an encounter. Dr Chen entered with four others all dressed and made up to resemble Zombies. Benjamin was instantly jealous. He'd never been able to get the look down as good as they had. He took mental notes for future use.

"These are your encounter group leaders," said Dr Chen. "They're going to spend a bit of time teaching you to move properly then they'll take you in. This is a controlled environment and these are entry level undead. They've been chosen for their docility and their familiarity with the living. So long as you stick to the Five Rules of Interaction you'll be perfectly safe your first time out."

Dr Chen stepped back and the four guides moved in on them. A Latino guy came over to Benjamin and Tatyana. He was tall and good looking and moved like a dancer. His manner was camp but relaxed and commanding.

"Okay guys my name's Raoul," he said. "I'm going to be taking you through a few moves. Let's start with your posture. I want you to stand with your feet apart like this. Now relax your shoulders and let your arms hang down by your sides. Okay that's good, now I want you to let your head roll forward onto your chest."

Raoul checked they were doing it properly and adjusted Benjamin's posture, pulling his shoulders down to relax them more. "Good, now when you move you have to use as few muscles as possible. So shift the weight from foot to foot like this, using only your leg muscles, and let the rest of your body move by itself."

Raoul lurched forward, looking exactly like the Zombies Benjamin had seen. His legs moved spasmodically and his feet shuffled side to side while the rest of his body hung limp and swayed.

Tatyana had a go and Benjamin followed. Neither of them were any good. Raoul had made it look so easy and they were messing up.

I should be better at this, Benjamin thought. *How many Zombie flicks have I watched? I should nail this first time.*

They tried a couple more times. Raoul gave them a few pointers and then they were good to go.

"Okay everyone," Raoul said to the whole party. "This is what we're going to do. As a group we're going to move slowly into the centre of the space. We're going to stay there, standing very still until I give you the signal it's safe to move. I'll roll my head side to side like this. At that point you're free to walk off and explore. Take a look at the Zombies and try and copy them. Don't go close until you're absolutely sure you're safe. If any of you get nervous move slowly back to join the four of us in the centre. You're safer in a group and we'll protect you. When I do this," Raoul shuffled back and forth in a particular manner. "I want you all to come back and join me. That's when we'll leave at a slow and measured pace. Has everyone got that?" Everyone nodded, doing their best Zombie impression. "Okay. Time to dance."

The automatic locks on the security doors clicked open and slid apart. The group moved out onto the sandy ground and into the blazing heat.

Benjamin's whole life had been leading up to this moment. There were real Zombies all around them. He stole sideways glances as they shuffled into the centre of the space with the rest of the party.

They were as magnificent as he'd imagined they would be. Shambling about in the noonday sun just as he'd pictured them a thousand times in his mind.

Noble Monsters, Death Defiers, Graveyard Rebels, none of the names he and his fellow Deathwalkers used to describe them did the awesome creatures justice. They were the ultimate passive-aggressive subversives.

They'd given death the middle finger and refused to lie down just because they weren't alive anymore. It was defiance that kept them up and running. Not hunger, like the idiots all around him thought. The pure defiance of anyone who tells them how to act or what to do. Defiance of the ridiculous hypocrisy of Western consumer culture and everyone who tries to uphold it.

Rule Number Three: It doesn't matter and you don't care.

That had been his daily mantra for the last ten years. Ever since his Mom left his Dad for a blue blood banker and thrust him into a world of false appearances and phoney standards. He'd stumbled through each day wanting to eat the brains and tear the guts out of everyone he met. That was why he understood the Zombie better than anyone on this island.

Here he was face to face with his idols. And suddenly it did matter, and he couldn't help but care. He cared about what they were doing to these proud monsters. It mattered that they were being locked up and exploited like this.

That's why he was here, pretending to be like these despicable cretins.

Rule Number Four: Follow the herd but think ahead of it.

That was exactly what he was doing. He was biding his time until the right moment came to strike. When it did, he'd make them all pay.

They stood in the centre of the space for what seemed like ages. Hardly anyone dared move. They were huddled together in a group with four guides circling them for protection.

Finally Raoul gave the signal for them to move off and start exploring.

Benjamin headed very slowly over to a group of four Zombies crouched over a carcass. They were gnawing the last of the meat off its bones as the flies buzzed around them.

Benjamin wasn't sure where the corpse had come from. He rather hoped it had been donated to the island. In the same way that some people leave their bodies to medical science.

Lavinia sidled over and circled the group of Zombies. She winked suggestively at him. He should've snubbed her. Instead he smiled sheepishly. God he was shallow. But she gave him a hard on. What could he do?

They were supposed to be copying the Zombies actions. Benjamin just stood very still and watched them. He was fighting to keep his excitement under control. And though he didn't want to admit it, his fear too.

Lavinia was a lot bolder than he. She knelt ever so carefully down next to the feeding Zombies and stuck her head into the carcass. Benjamin was impressed. She had guts. With great care and patience Lavinia reached into the carcass and took out a thigh bone.

She brought the bone up to her lips and began to nibble at it. She was slow to begin with, running her teeth and her tongue along it. Then she attacked it with more relish, mimicking the Zombies' mindless way of gnawing.

Benjamin couldn't take his eyes off her. He really was getting a boner at the sight of her with the bone. Christ he was a sick puppy.

A female Zombie looked up and put her hand on the bone Lavinia was gnawing. Lavinia snarled at the Zombie but it only tightened its grip on the bone.

Lavinia wouldn't let go. The Zombie put its other hand on the bone and began to pull harder. Lavinia tugged right back and bared her teeth.

"Mine bitch, it's mine," she shouted and yanked the bone out of the Zombie's hands. Benjamin winced as he heard one of its fingers break.

There was an ominous moment of silence as everyone turned to look at her, including the other Zombies. From the look on her face Lavinia knew that she'd just fucked up.

The female Zombie started to make a weird noise in the back of its throat that increased in volume. Then it sprang at Lavinia.

Lavinia was just as quick to her feet and brought the thigh bone down on its head. Benjamin heard bone fracture but the Zombie was undeterred and kept coming for her.

Lavinia swung twice more beating the Zombie back a few steps. The bone splintered against the Zombie's skull.

The Zombie lurched at her and grabbed her shoulders. Lavinia put her hand on its forehead to hold it back and stabbed at its face with the splintered end of the bone.

She rammed the bone into the Zombie's eye socket. The force of this caused its other eyeball to pop out of its head and slither down its cheek. Blood and brain tissue bubbled out of the Zombie's empty eye socket and nasal cavities.

"Die you fucking whore!" Lavinia shrieked.

Without thinking Benjamin stepped forward to protect the Zombie and tripped over the carcass. Too late he realised his mistake.

The other three Zombies got to their feet and started to make the same guttural noise the female Zombie had. All the Zombies in the compound were making it.

Lavinia pushed the motionless female Zombie away and bolted for the exit. Most of the other guests were running too. The Zombies charged after them.

Benjamin stood absolutely still as alarms started to blare.

A Zombie hobbled right up to him. He tried not to breath or shake as it stared him directly in the face. The front of his pants became warm and damp.

Oh God I'm going to die, he thought. His heart was battering at the inside of his chest. *I don't want to die. Not here like this.*

For some reason he thought of his mother. More than anything, he wanted her to hold him and make everything better.

Time stopped altogether. He waited for the Zombie to strike. To tear open his throat with its teeth. He wondered if it would hurt as much as he feared.

The killing blow never came. The Zombie simply turned away and shambled off.

Benjamin was elated. It knew. It could sense there was something different about him. That he had a rapport with them. That he understood. It could tell he had a special connection to the undead.

Several secret doors opened and guards ran in with flame throwers. They used controlled bursts to drive the Zombies back without actually harming them.

They corralled the Zombies as the security doors slid open and the guest were ushered through. Benjamin sauntered up to the doors without any sign of panic. He had nothing to fear from the undead.

He walked up to the other guests with a cool air of superiority. They were all staring at him. Was that awe in their eyes or admiration? Then he realised his pants were wet. They could all see that he'd pissed himself.

"One thing I learned about Lavinia Ponsonby," said Benjamin. "She never lets go of what's hers."

They were standing in one of the large reception rooms off the lobby.

"You meant nothing more to her than that bone you know," Tatyana said.

"And what were you?" he said. "Another Zombie?"

"I was just in her way. You're lucky she didn't try and break you over my head."

"You're right. I was a jerk."

"Jerk doesn't begin to cover it."

The other guests were cackling and gossiping. Schadenfreude was the order of the day.

"That five mil she put down," Benjamin heard Arthur Sonnenfeldt say. "That was more than she had. She was maxed out on credit just to get that."

"Never venture what you can't afford to lose," said George Griffin. "It's a basic law of finance. Risk doesn't drive your bottom line. It merely adds to it."

"She's lost it all now," Bessie chimed in. "Some people never learn. You never touch your reserve. You only spend the interest."

They'd been called down as soon as they'd showered and changed. Samuel Palmer made a brief address claiming no responsibility for the incident. Instead he chided them like school kids. "The lesson to be learned from this is that when you're dealing with Zombies, don't make it personal. With the undead, just as in business, nothing is personal."

Lavinia was being sent home, under guard, and she'd lost her deposit. Not only had she disobeyed the rules and broken the terms of her contract, according to Palmer she had also destroyed valuable property.

The nerve of the guy referring to the noble monster as a piece of property.

A door opened on the other side of the room and Lavinia strode in with her luggage. She held her head high. The armed guards at her side completely failed to intimidate her.

Benjamin realised she'd purposefully chosen to walk through the room where all the guest were gathered. No sneaking shamefully out the back entrance for her. You had to admire her spirit. She was a formidable woman and she was going to let everyone know it.

Some of the guests turned away as she walked the length of the room. Others nodded in respect. Sam McKane stepped up to take her hand. "Lavinia," he said with affection.

"Sam."

"These galoots treating you right?" he said pointing to the guards.

"I've got them under control."

"You need anything?"

"I'm a big girl Sam. I can look after myself. But thanks for asking."

They smiled and she walked on. As she was about to leave Benjamin stopped her. "Listen Lavinia," he said. "I just wanted to say how sorry I am about the way everything turned out. And if things had been different then, y'know, maybe..."

Lavinia looked at him with ice cold contempt. "Maybe what? We'd ride off into the sunset together, hand in hand? Do me a favour. Get over yourself and grow up." With that she swept out of his life forever.

Benjamin glanced over at Tatyana. She wasn't impressed. She raised an eyebrow as if to say 'what did you expect?'

"You're right. Jerk doesn't begin to cover it."

CHAPTER NINE

Three Months Ago

A message popped up on Benjamin's screen.

2:03pm
Lucío
Dude, you doin Zombie Crawl this wknd? Shd be a blast. lol.
2:03pm
Ben
Sorry, got bigger fish to fry. ;-)
2:04pm
Lucío
klkl, it's gonna be a gd 1 tho.

Yeah right. Zombie Crawl was okay for bored teenagers who enjoyed parading through town with a bunch of friends dressed as Zombies. But it was no place for a serious Deathwalker. He was about to take things to a whole new level.

"Benjamin, have you tidied your room like you promised?" his Mom shouted.

"Yes Mom." he lied. He'd stuff everything into a bag and jam it under his bed later.

His Mom always went into meltdown whenever she was throwing some lame social event for Richard. A whole army of cleaners and gardeners descended on the house. His room was on the third floor anyway. It's not like any guests were going to see it. Even those that were sneaking off to schtupp someone else's wife.

He signed out and closed his laptop. He had guests of his own coming. Better get the basement ready for them.

He spotted Richard as he stepped out onto the landing. Automatically he put his head down and tried to walk past without being seen.

"I thought we weren't doing this anymore," said Richard in his usual whiny voice.

"Uh, yeah, hi," Benjamin grunted, still looking at the floor.

"Are you helping your mother get ready for the party?"

"Uh, yeah," said Benjamin. Then added. "Just going to tidy the basement."

"That's right you've got your own... friends coming. They do know to use the side entrance don't they?"

"Uh, think so."

"Think so?"

"No, they do."

"Good."

There was an uncomfortable silence then Richard said. "Is that a scar on your cheek?"

"It's an open pus wound. I just made it."

"An open pus wound," Richard shook his head and sighed. The dickwad. Why'd he have to act like that? Always putting Benjamin down. Never coming right out and saying it but acting like Benjamin was this weight around his neck that he had to drag around everywhere.

It's not like *he* was perfect. With his goofy Hawaian shirts and sandals. *And his golfing sweaters*, thought Benjamin. *Don't get me started on those.*

Richard looked like he wanted to say something, thought better of it and walked off. Lucky escape then.

An hour or so later Benjamin left the basement and headed to his room. The guests were starting to arrive. A few minutes tidying would keep his Mom off his back. He was just making his way across the hall to the stairs when he heard a familiar voice.

"Hey Sports Fans!"

Oh shit.

"Hi Mr Petersen," Benjamin turned to see a fat guy with a ginger buzz cut bearing down on him.

"Benjamin, I got three words for ya," said Petersen clapping him on the back. "Sub Prime Mortgage! It's the future of finance my boy. Now a bright boy like you is bound to want to follow his old man into the profession."

"What, Richard?" said Benjamin, unable to hide his contempt.

"Hey don't knock 'im, guy's a shark. Mind like a bear trap. You wanna take on your old man though, ya gotta know where the action is. See, the way this thing works, it's beautiful. Now ya can't have a growth economy without debt, but sooner or later every schmuck who can afford it is gonna be maxed out. Ya gotta have new frontiers see. That's where the CDO comes in. That's a collateralised debt obligation, work of genius. Ya take a bunch a debts from a bunch of schlubbs that no bank's ever gonna subsidise and you mix 'em up with a bunch of legit credit, takes all the risk out of the deal. The toxic debt gets a triple A rating and the profits are through the roof. Through the roof, ya follow me?"

"I think so."

"Good man! See ya get rid of the toxic debt same way ya get rid of toxic waste, ya dump it into a fresh reservoir and all the risk gets flushed downstream and disperses naturally. Genius! Remember ya heard it here first."

"Okay, thanks Mr Petersen, I'll bear that in mind."

"Where'd ya get the scar? That a sports injury?"

"Something like that."

Benjamin wrestled himself free and made a bolt for the stairs.

"Sub Prime Mortgage!" Petersen called after him. "It's a source of profit that ain't ever gonna dry up."

Benjamin smiled and ran. Sheesh, had the guy never heard of Listerine? Toxic debt? More like toxic breath.

"Just a minute young man." Benjamin was on the second floor when a hand grabbed him and dragged him into one of the guest rooms.

"Mom," said Benjamin, with more than a hint of complaint in his voice.

"Don't you 'Mom' me," she said. She was holding a large vodka Martini. "You promised me you'd tidy your room. I've just been in your room and if that's your idea of tidy you might as well live on the street."

"You're soused."

"I'm nothing of the sort. And this isn't about me, it's about you. I thought things were going to change. I thought you promised to start making an effort from now on."

"Could we do this later? I've got people coming."

"And I've got people here already. Your room is a pig sty and I've just laid out five million dollars so you can run off and play at being a vampire. Is it too much to ask that you uphold your side of the bargain?"

"It's Zombies Mom, not vampires, Zombies. And you didn't lay out five million. Richard agreed to put it up to prove to you what a fuck up I am, because he expects me to fail."

"Don't you go disparaging Richard."

"Why not? That's all he does to me."

"He's been very generous to the both of us. He's opened his heart and his home to us and we owe him for that."

"That's bullshit Mom! Richard bought you to have something beautiful to show off on his arm. Just like those Picassos and the Matisse he has downstairs. He's not an art lover, he just wants to show people what he can afford to buy."

His Mom went really quiet. She was real mad. No she was beyond mad. He'd said too much, way too much. Suddenly he was a little boy again, caught playing with matches and the world was about to fall on his head. Shit, was he going to cry?

No, his Mom beat him to it. A huge, great tear ran down her cheek and took a gob of mascara with it. She knocked back the Martini and sat down on the bed.

"Look Mom, I'm sorry, I shouldn't have..."

"No, no, you're right," she said, opening a draw in the bedside table and pulling out a pack of Winstons.

"I didn't know you smoked," he said as she lit one.

"I could fill a book with what you don't know," she said, blowing out smoke. He felt very small and foolish. "I know this hasn't been easy on you. I know you miss your father. Hell, there are times when I miss him, even after everything he put me through. He was so handsome. You look so much like him too, even with all your Frankenstein make up."

"It's Zombie Mom."

"He was great in the sack too. Probably the best I ever had."

"Mom, too much information."

"What? You think because you're young you've got the market on sex cornered? Why do you think Richard took us in? Do you think anyone's ever done him better than I have?"

"Eew, gross Mom, that's an image I don't want."

"It might surprise you to find that quite a few men still find me attractive," she paused and gave him a serious look. "When did I lose you Benjamin? We used to be so close. We used to tell each other everything. Do you have any idea how much I miss that?"

Benjamin didn't say anything. He felt embarrassed and uncomfortable. Why was she suddenly getting all *Melrose Place* on him?

"There was this one time, you were only seven years old, but you were so wise and brave you nearly broke my heart. I'd just found out that your father had pawned all my jewellery. Everything that my mother had left to me. She died when I was eighteen and that's all I had to remember her by. There was stuff in there that went back to my great, great grandmother. Things she'd had made personally, unique and irreplaceable. He pawned them and blew everything in a crap game. I wasn't ever going to see any of it again.

"I was kneeling on the kitchen floor and I was sobbing my heart out. For the jewellery that I'd lost. The mother that I'd lost and for the whole marriage your father had thrown away on countless card tables and horse races. Then I hear your little feet come up behind me. You put your hands on my shoulders and you lead me to the table. Then you fished your Mickey Mouse handkerchief out your pocket and you handed it to me and do you remember what you said. Do you remember? You said... you said: 'Dry your eyes Princess. Cos I'm here now and I won't let anything bad happen to you.'

"And I flung my arms around you and I cried even more. But not for what I'd lost. For what I'd found. I realised that what I had in my arms was a million times more precious than any stupid jewellery. *And he'll never take this away from me,* I thought. *He'll never take this away.* But I was wrong.

"It was the vase wasn't it? That damned Lalique that Richard was so proud of." She stopped and dabbed her eyes with a tissue. Benjamin hung his head with a shame that was eight years old and still powerful.

He hadn't known his Dad like he did now. He used to save up the weekly allowance Richard gave him for his Dad's monthly visits. That way they'd have money for all the things his father would take him out to, funfairs, meals out, ice cream parlours. He even paid for the gas to drive them there.

His Dad would always go on about how much money Richard had. And how he'd have that much money one day, Benjamin would see. All it took was one winning streak. Then he'd buy the hot dogs. You could be sure he would.

He started to ask Benjamin about all the nice things Richard had about the house. Asked him if there were any items that Richard wouldn't miss. Expensive things that his Dad could loan to his friends for safe keeping. Only there was this horse and it couldn't miss and when it came in the two of them could go on holiday together. All he needed was to raise enough cash.

Benjamin took the vase and gave it to his Dad. He knew it was precious because Richard had said so. His Dad said he'd give it back to him before anyone even noticed. That was the last he saw of the vase. And his Dad for a long while.

"I told Richard I'd broken it while dusting you know," his Mom said. "He was furious. He wanted to know what I was doing demeaning myself when he paid a staff of cleaners to do the dusting. He actually sold some of the jewellery he bought me to recoup the loss of the vase. Can you believe that? What is it about men and my jewellery?

"I confronted your father of course. Told him if he ever did that again I'd have him thrown in jail and he'd never see you again. He got so mad at me he refused to see you for years. And who did you hold responsible? After I'd lied to protect you.

"You stopped speaking to me. You were the only man I ever loved who didn't shit all over me. My father did, he was a bastard, and both my husbands have had their moments. There was only you and yet we drift further and further apart every day. Why am I always in the wrong? Why don't you ever cut me some slack? What's so bad about the life I've given you? What do you want that you don't have?"

"A life that I actually like for a start," He shouldn't have said that. "Look Mom I don't want to fight. I still love you, but you know I'm not seven now. I'm sorry if I don't give you my Mickey Mouse handkerchief anymore, but I've got my own things going on."

"Just tell me what I need to say Benjamin. Tell me what I need to do to make it all better. Mommy always used to make it all better, remember? Once upon a time there wasn't anything I couldn't fix."

He could feel his eyes filling up with tears. She had a way of doing that to him. No matter how old or independent he got there were buttons only she could push.

"Mom. Can we please not do this now, I've got people on the way and you've..."

There was a knock at the door. "Who is it?" said his Mom.

"Sorry to disturb you Ma'am," said one of the staff. "But there's been a disturbance downstairs with one of Master Benjamin's guests."

"I'll be right there."

"No Mom, it's okay, I'll go. It's my friend. You fix your make-up and go look after your guests."

A couple of hours later Tatyana arrived. She was the last to get there. She phoned Benjamin on his mobile and he went to meet her at the side entrance.

She looked fabulous. Everyone had pushed the boat out with their Zombie make up but he'd never seen her go to such trouble. She could have been the real thing.

She winced as he kissed her. "Wait a minute. That split lip and those bruises are real aren't they?"

"Some of them," she admitted.

"It's your father isn't it?" he could feel his rage rising like mercury in a thermometer. "Motherfucker!" He punched the security pad by the side gate and felt a stabbing pain shoot up his arm. Tatyana led him towards the house.

"He's not himself lately," she said. She was always making excuses for her father, in spite of what a bastard he was. "He's being threatened with extradition. President Putin wants to prosecute him for tax evasion. He could go to prison. He's worried about becoming another Mikhail Khodorovsky."

"Who?"

"You're so American some times. If it doesn't happen in your backyard then you don't want to know about it. Don't you ever watch CNN?"

"Richard does, I prefer to be out the room when he's around."

"Mikhail Khodorovsky used to be the wealthiest man in my country. He was an oil tycoon who was charged with fraud by the Prosecutor General's office and sent to prison for nine years. Things are not good in my country and Putin likes to throw the masses an oligarch's head now and again to keep them quiet. Now he's got my father in his sights."

"Well if you ask me your father deserves to go to prison."

"Thanks, and where does that leave me and my Mother? We'll have to go back to Russia with him. He'll lose most of his money and that means I won't be able to come on the mission with you."

"Oh."

"Oh indeed."

"That still doesn't give him the right to knock you around."

"Okay, can we drop it now. Are the others here?"

"They're in the den. Klaus got here first. He parked his old truck on Richard's ornamental lawn. When I got there he was calling the staff fascists and pawns of capitalist exploitation."

"Hah! That sounds like Klaus. Doesn't stop him enjoying the benefits of your step dad's capitalist exploitation."

"First thing he did when he got in was grab a bottle of Dom Perignon and a jar of Beluga."

They headed down the basement stairs and into the den. "*White Zombie*?" he heard Dan say. "I don't get it?"

"Ja," said Klaus. "If you're wanting a black and white movie why aren't you picking *I Walked with a Zombie*?"

"No. You're not getting it," said Andy. "It's the birth of the genre. The first Zombie film ever made. What better film to have playing as your child comes into the world?"

"Nein," said Klaus. "I am still casting my vote for *Brain Dead*. It has the first scene of Zombies giving birth."

"In a Zombie's case," said Andy. "I think technically it's called 'giving death'."

Tatyana didn't tend to join in with the guys' debates. She went and gave Tweakie a hug.

"I love your new hair," she said running her fingers through Tweakie's bright red locks.

"Thanks," said Tweakie. " I was going for a Linnea Quigley in *Return of the Living Dead* look. Hey check it out, have you seen my new eye?"

"Oh my God that's so cool," said Tatyana, touching the prosthetic eyeball that dangled out of Tweakie's socket. "Did you make it yourself?"

"Yeah, I did it at work. Told them I was trying out some new effects. We're waiting to see if we get this gig with HBO."

"Doing make-up or effects?" said Benjamin.

"Both," Tweakie said. "Should be a blast. *Six Feet Under* but with Zombies. That's the pitch."

"Awesome," said Benjamin.

"What are the boys arguing about?" said Tatyana.

"Dan wants to know what film he should have playing as his kid is born," said Tweakie.

"How long to go now?" Tatyana asked Dan.

"Six weeks. Hey, check it out, I've got this birthing pool for Sarah right, she's gonna have a home birth. We're gonna spray it black and have eyeballs and severed arms floating in the water when Sarah gets in. Man, the midwife's gonna shit! Loving your make-up incidentally, how'd you get that grey mottled skin?"

"That's an air brush job, right?" said Tweakie.

"Right," said Tatyana. "Is that, like, a shroud you're wearing?"

"It's a smock," said Dan. "I'm going for a classic *Living Dead at the Manchester Morgue* look. I've been watching it a lot recently. They have it playing on a loop at Romero's when I'm behind the bar."

"Ja," said Klaus. "That's why you never get any work done."

"Least I don't clean the toilet with my head. When you gonna get a proper haircut?"

"The Mohican is a classic look," said Klaus running his hand over the stiff purple hair. He was a tiny guy with a big beak of a nose and small round glasses. "Zombies are the ultimate Punks. The two looks go perfectly. The Zombie rebels against the graveyard. The punk rebels against society. I am being the ultimate rebel against the living death of capitalism. Hey that reminds me Benjamin, did you find that old Rolex you were going to be lending me?"

"No I gave it to Andy. He's using it to house some of the radio equipment we'll need."

"What, we're gonna have wristwatch radios?" said Dan. "Just like Dick Tracy?"

"Err, no," said Andy. "That's science-fiction. This is the real world, where the dead walk."

Benjamin loved Andy. A lot of people found him hard to take cos of his Asperger's Syndrome. But once you got past his odd manner and his freakish intelligence he was one of the sweetest guys you could meet.

Andy dropped his knapsack on the card table and pulled out Benjamin's Rolex, a pair of limited edition Reeboks and an aerosol.

"This is what I wanted to show you two," he said to Benjamin and Tatyana. "This is how we're going to stay in touch."

"Why can't we just text?" said Tweakie.

"There's no mobile reception or internet access," said Benjamin. "They block it all to keep you isolated."

"Which is why we're going to communicate with miniaturised long wave radios," said Andy. "I've disguised it so you can carry it in without being detected." He folded an aerial out of the aerosol, took the soles off the shoes to reveal the receivers and showed them how to assemble the disguised equipment.

"Whoa, that is totally old school James Bond," said Dan. "You're like the undead Q, Andy."

"Yes I am. Licensed to chill. And there's more." Andy held up the Rolex. "I've replaced the workings of the watch with a device capable of releasing an electro magnetic pulse. This will overload the circuits of any security lock. There won't be anywhere you won't be able to enter."

"That is so cool Andy," said Benjamin.

He put his arm around Andy's shoulder to congratulate him. Andy stiffened and put his hands up. "No touching!"

Benjamin backed away. "Sorry bro, I forgot."

"That's perfectly alright. Worse things happen at sea."

"Yeah, speaking of which," said Tweakie, wearing a bemused expression. "What's the latest on your Dad's yacht?"

"Richard's yacht," Benjamin corrected her. "I've had keys copied without Richard knowing. I'll give them to you before you head off to the marina. Remember to board when its dark and to sail at first light."

"Yeah, yeah, okay dog, we know the plan," said Dan. "What's with all this 'sail at first light' shit? What are you, the Ancient Mariner?"

"It's the safest time to leave the marina without being seen," said Benjamin. "Andy, do you think you can handle the sat-nav?"

"If I can handle advanced calculus with a migraine and severe allergies, I don't think a little thing like a sat-nav is going to phase me."

"Probably not," said Benjamin. "Follow the coast down to Florida but stay in open water. You don't want the coast guard coming down on your ass. Then it's straight across the Gulf of Mexico."

"I am loving this," said Klaus. "We are using the using the trappings of Western consumerism as a weapon to undo it. Hey, we can still get cable while we're out in open water can't we? I will be dying if I miss *Wheel of Fortune*."

"I dunno Klaus," said Benjamin. "I'll get it taped for you if you can't. Now you'll be okay to locate the island won't you? Cos you know it's not on any maps."

"We'll be okay Ben," said Tweakie, putting her hands on his shoulders. She turned to Tatyana. "Does he always fuss like an old woman?"

"He hasn't even started yet," said Tatyana with a smile.

"So it's for real then?" said Dan. "We're actually doing this. We're going to put the Zombie Liberation Front on the map and wake up all the Deathwalkers."

"Hey, ja," said Klaus. "You know what we should do? When we free all the Zombies we should be taking one to Romero's. Give him a plate of brains and leave him at the bar."

"That'd put the shits up all those teeny Deathwalkers who hang out there" said Dan. "They think they're so radical cos they go on Zombie Crawl once a month."

"No I'm having it even better," said Klaus. "We take a bunch of them to Zombiestock. Not even Burning Man has a pack of real Zombies. We'll become the top festival."

"You could get some to perform onstage with your band," Dan said to Tweakie. "That'll get you on the main stage."

"Are you dumbasses for real?" said Tweakie, shaking her head. "Have you forgotten why we're doing this? If we try and turn these noble monsters into some side show attraction we're no better than the rich bastards who are exploiting them."

"We're going to release them into a safe jungle environment," said Tatyana. "Somewhere where they're beyond the reach of civilised man and his exploitative ways."

"Like the Bronx you mean?" said Dan.

"Not the Bronx wise ass," Tweakie smacked the back of his head then turned to Benjamin. "Where *are* we taking them exactly?"

That was the tiny flaw in his plan. "I'm still working on that," he admitted. "Don't worry I'll find somewhere before we leave though."

"You better," Tweakie warned him. "Cos it's your butt it's gonna come out of if you don't."

"We're going to be out in open water with a hold full of noble monsters," said Tatyana. "I don't think it's just Benjamin's pert little butt that it's gonna come out of."

"Listen guys," said Benjamin. "I don't want to get all sentimental on you or nothing. But I just want to say thanks. For ages I've been looking for a group of committed individuals to take Deathwalking to the next logical level. Now that I've found you, well, I couldn't be happier."

"Hey, don't sweat it dog," said Dan. "We got your back. We're family."

"Here's to the ZLF," said Andy raising his soda in a toast.

Everyone raised their drinks. "To the ZLF."

"Ja," said Klaus raising the half empty champagne bottle. "We are tearing down the beliefs of the Bourgeoisie and trampling the opiate of the masses. Hey, do you think anyone upstairs can get me some coke?"

CHAPTER TEN

"What are you doing?"

Benjamin was bugging her again. He was like a little kid sometimes. Always wanting her attention. If he wasn't so cute she'd have given up ages ago.

It's like her Aunt said though. You don't meet the perfect man – you make him. You start with the best raw material you can get and you sculpt it into something worth having.

Not that it had worked too well for her Aunt. She was constantly improving men only to have them stolen away by younger, slimmer women.

"Are you okay? C'mon speak to me."

"I was practising my Zombie breathing dumb ass," Tatyana said, sitting up in bed. It was the first time she'd moved in thirty minutes. "You know, like they told us to do – at least three times a day."

"Oh yeah, guess I should probably be joining in. You're getting rather good though. Had me worried for a second. You had almost no vital signs. For a moment, I thought you'd actually died."

"I find it weirdly relaxing actually. Just letting go of everything and resting, taking a break from actually living. It's like a drug you know, sort of addictive."

Benjamin got excited at this. He jumped off the bed and started gesticulating. "I know exactly what you mean. I find encounters with the noble monster totally addictive. I'm in the zone out there. I'm at one with them and they can sense it. I've definitely got the most developed Inner Zombie on the island."

"Steady on genius. We've only been at it a week. Don't get ahead of yourself."

"I'm not getting ahead of myself. I'm good at this. Things are starting to make sense for the first time. Even you and me are getting along better."

"Now there's no women flirting with you."

"Aw c'mon, cheap shot."

"Okay, you're right. I am happier, about us, about everything. It is beneficial. I guess that's why they charge so much for the course."

"They said they've got something special planned for us today. Time to take the next big step. I am *so* ready for it."

"Well you better get showered and changed then. We're supposed to be down there in ten."

"Oh shit!"

Today's encounter was in a different part of the compound. They assembled in an observation room overlooking a large enclosed arena. Tatyana shared the anticipation she could see on the faces of the guests. They could all tell that something different and special was going to happen.

Raoul, their movement coach and encounter leader, came in to address them. "As I told you yesterday, today we're going to move you on to the next stage of your training. As this is a moment of significance, someone of great consequence is going to address you."

Tatyana felt an immense presence behind her. Without thinking, everyone in the group turned at the same time. Standing behind them was Doc Papa. He smiled with satisfaction at their shock and awe.

"Good morning," he said. "A pleasure to see you all again. I understand from my staff that you've been doing rather well. Now it's time to do rather better. So far we have shown you the Way of the Barefoot Zombie. But there is a difference between knowing the Way and *walking* the Way.

"Tomorrow night I am hosting a dinner for some special guests. We are going to be joined by St Ignatius's Board of Directors and the previous graduates of my course. It's fair to say that between them they control most of the wealth on the planet." Tatyana saw the excitement and anticipation on the faces of the guests at the mention of this. They were like a bunch of groupies who've just been told their favourite band were oiled, naked and waiting in the next room.

"Whether or not you join us will depend on how well you perform today. If you fail, you are going home. To survive in the company of merciless killers is not enough. You must learn to become like them in order to dominate them. To become like them you must kill as they kill – without thought or compunction. Observe."

Doc Papa pointed to the window and they all turned at the same time to look out of it. They were like living puppets. He just had to pull their strings and they did whatever he wanted.

A cage descended into the centre of the arena. It was held by a heavy chain and stopped about twelve feet above the ground. Inside was a man with a thick black moustache, wearing a Hawaiian shirt. He looked Latin American. He was frightened and disoriented. He moved about the cage, testing the bars and trying to see what was going on in the arena below.

"This pathetic specimen is a militant trade unionist from Venezuela," said Doc Papa.

A set of gates opened onto the arena and two women, also Latino, stumbled. They blinked and shaded their eyes from the sunlight. The man in the cage called out to them and they went to stand beneath him.

"His wife and sister are also in the same union," said Doc Papa. "They've been causing a lot of problems for Western clothing companies. Instead of being thankful for the work their benefactors provide, they've been spreading scurrilous lies about the state of their factories. Calling them sweatshops and trying to bully the companies into paying higher wages. They've even gone as far as trying to hamstring these legitimate operations by demanding an end to child labour."

Tatyana saw many of the guests sneer, shake their heads and make disparaging noises.

"Instead we called an end to their activities. Observe how to deal with labour relations the Barefoot Zombie way."

Two more gates opened on to the arena. Speakers clicked on in the observation room so they could hear what was happening in the arena.

"Madre de Dios," said one of the women and clung to the other. The man in the cage started shouting to the women and pointing at the gates.

Around twenty Zombies shambled into the arena. One of the women started crying and wailing at the sight of them. The Zombies scented the air then began to lurch towards the women.

The man in the cage reached down through bars. The slimmer of the two women tried to jump up and catch hold of his hands. The other woman ran back towards the gates they'd come though.

Four Zombies gave chase as the woman hit the gates. They were locked and the woman battered on them as the Zombies bore down on her.

A scrawny female Zombie got to her first. The woman tried to push the Zombie away. It caught hold of her hair and the woman put her hand against its face to hold it off.

The Zombie opened its mouth wide and bit down on the woman's hand. The woman shrieked in pain and yanked herself away, leaving the Zombie with great clumps of hair in its hands.

Two of the woman's fingers were missing. Blood poured out of the stumps, covering her hand and the sleeve of her blouse. The woman gasped in shock. Staring in disbelief at her hand.

She backed into a fat Zombie who came up behind her. The Zombie caught her by the shoulders and lunged for her neck. She managed to twist free from its grip and it fastened its teeth on her shoulder instead.

The woman screamed and punched the Zombie in the head with her uninjured hand. The Zombie bit harder but she managed to tear herself away. The Zombie chewed on a big chunk of skin and fabric from her blouse as it lumbered after her.

Three more Zombies loomed up in front of the woman as she fled her attackers. They were maddened by the smell of the blood that was gushing out of her shoulder wound and finger stumps.

They encircled her and dragged her to the ground. Tatyana could see the woman's legs kicking as the three Zombies began to feed. She was still sobbing with pain as the other two joined them and yet more scrambled over for a taste of flesh.

The slimmer woman had managed to catch hold of the hands of the man in the cage. He was trying to pull her to safety as the Zombies circled below.

The woman's legs flailed as she tried to pull herself up onto the cage. A tall male Zombie caught hold of her foot. The woman kicked at it and her shoe came off.

The Zombie chewed on the shoe for a few seconds then threw it away. It stretched up its arm and grabbed her naked foot. The woman cried out in terror as the Zombie tried to drag her back down. The man in the cage tried to pull her up but he wasn't strong enough.

The Zombie bit into her foot, tearing off a huge chunk of skin and cartilage. The woman howled in pain and let go of the cage. It was only the man's hands on her wrists that stopped her falling.

The woman thrashed sending droplets of blood raining down on the Zombies that were gathering beneath her. They looked up towards the source of the blood. Their jaws working hungrily.

The tall Zombie got hold of her foot again and yanked again. A tug of war ensued between the Zombie and the man in the cage. The woman's screams of panic became shriller and shriller until the man lost his grip.

She hit the floor and the Zombies pounced. The man in the cage let out a howl of dismay. He beat his fists against the bars and spat angry curses at the Zombies. Then he curled up into a ball and sobbed his heart out as he watched what they were doing to the woman he obviously loved.

Tatyana buried her face in Benjamin's chest and tried to block out the woman's screams. Everyone else leaned forward to get a better view of the feeding. Benjamin was torn between comforting her and watching himself.

She'd seen thousands of Zombie movies before. Seen them pull people apart and cheered with her friends. This was different. This was really happening. These were real Zombies and real people, not bad Italian actors and cheap special effects.

These women had been sacrificed for trying to help children. She couldn't bear to listen to their screams of torment. She felt physically sick as the other guests cheered their slow agonising deaths.

Benjamin pushed her gently away and turned her head to the observation window. His eyes implored her not to lose it. She knew what he was doing. This was all part of the test Doc Papa had mentioned. If they didn't play along, if they showed any signs of weakness, they'd be sent home. The mission would be aborted and it would all have been for nothing.

She looked out over the carnage, the Zombies feeding and the caged man's tears. She looked but she tried not to see or hear. She remembered the last time she'd felt like this. She was ten years old. She was having dinner with her parents.

Her mother had over-cooked the roast. Her father was angry about his job and was looking for someone to take it out on. He picked her mother as usual. He'd thrown the gravy at her and then punched her to the ground.

Tatyana had dropped her cutlery and moved to help her Mother. Terrified for her welfare, Tatyana's mother had told her to sit and to keep on eating. Told her to mind her manners or her Father would become even more angry.

She had to sit at the table and carry on as if nothing was happening. As if they were a normal family having a normal lunch. As if she couldn't hear her mother's cries and the sound of her father beating her until his arms ached.

Tatyana slowed her breathing to almost nothing. She let her limbs relax until all the energy drained out of them. Let her heart rate drop until it was hardly beating at all. She was tired of living right now. Tired of all the pain it brought.

She wanted a break. They'd told her to practise her Zombie breathing. Well now she was.

CHAPTER ELEVEN

"Now it is your turn," Doc Papa said. The Zombies had picked the corpses clean and had shuffled off to find other distractions. "Now you must hunt in a pack. You must kill as they kill with bare hands and teeth. You must gorge yourselves on raw human flesh."

There was a collective in-take of breath among the guests. Tatyana could see the looks of apprehension and anticipation that they shared.

"You have a small window of opportunity in which to attack. It is imperative that you strike swiftly and decisively. The victim is traumatised and disoriented. He does not understand what is happening to him. Nothing in his life so far has prepared him for this.

"He is like a faltering national economy in the aftermath of a calamity. A struggling country hit by hyper-inflation, natural disaster or years of war. Ripe for exploitation!

"It is in these times that multi billionaires are made. When, disguised as foreign aid, the IMF is able to demand economic shock therapy. Privatising public industries, slashing public services, raising taxes on the poor while systematically cutting their wages. Because the populace is too shocked to even realise what is happening to them, let alone resist or fight back.

"You must be like a multi-national descending on a weak nation. Just as they strip the country of its public coffers and natural resources, you must strip him of everything. Tear out his guts, gorge yourself on his life blood and suck the marrow from his bones. Squeeze the life out of him like it was the last penny of an impoverished people.

"Because he is in a position of weakness and you are in a position of strength. Because you are clever enough to have seen the opportunity and to have found the means to exploit it. That is what creating wealth is all about. That is the Way of the Barefoot Zombie. The lessons you learn in the arena today will determine if you are fit enough to be among the world's most rich and powerful."

Doc Papa's words had an invigorating effect on the guests. Tatyana could feel the hunger growing in them. A deep seated hunger for blood, and for the wealth and influence they realised was within reach. She felt like she was standing in a pack of starving jackals.

Raoul and the other encounter leaders took them down as the Zombies were cleared from the arena. They were told to strip to their underwear and then led to a set of gates.

As the gates opened they spilled out into the arena. Most of the guests were pumped, filled with excitement and blood lust. Others were apprehensive but, from the looks on their faces, Tatyana could tell they were ready to kill.

The bottom of the cage opened and the man tumbled onto the arena floor. Five of them were on top of him before he even had time to stand. They tore off his shirt and sunk their teeth into his neck and arms but found it difficult to even break his skin, let alone tear it.

"¡No, no, parada! ¿Qué usted está haciendo? ¡Párela, en nombre de Dios parada!" the man called out.

An Asian woman tugged the man's hair to keep his head still and bit his cheek. The man screamed in pain as she managed not only to draw blood, but to peel off a chunk of his face.

At the sight of blood the other guests went wild. Four of them lunged at his face with open mouths. Tatyana heard the man's nose break. Someone else tore off part of his bottom lip, exposing his teeth.

The man kicked his legs violently and thrashed around. He almost succeeded in getting away from them. His foot connected with one guy's mouth who reeled back and spat blood.

"Oh my God he just broke my crown!" the guy said. "Do you have any idea how much that dental work cost you little shit?" He went to kick the man, missed and hit one of the guests. He lifted his foot to try and stomp on the man but Raoul and another encounter leader stopped him and led him out of the arena. Someone wasn't going to make the dinner tomorrow night.

Benjamin was kneeling next to the man's midriff. He grabbed Tatyana and pulled her down next to him. The man was naked now, still writhing and screaming but that only seemed to get the guests more excited.

All of them were chewing on parts of his body, trying to shred his flesh. Bessie, the ageing redhead, was trying to tear his penis off with her teeth. Tatyana could see the years of bitterness and broken marriages coming out in the vicious way she gnawed on his flaccid member.

Using both their teeth and fingernails, someone managed to part the man's stomach wall. Benjamin saw his chance and stuck his hand in. He pulled out a section of the man's intestinal tract.

He turned and offered a section to Tatyana. He seemed almost pleased with himself. He waved the intestines under her nose but they were too gross to even touch. He implored her with his eyes, saying 'please don't fuck this up.'

He was right. She took the pink and bloody tube in her hands. It was hot and heavier than she thought it would be. She put it slowly to her lips and gagged at the smell. Benjamin bit into his section and Tatyana tried to do the same.

The wall of the intestine was thick and rubbery and slick with blood. Her teeth just slipped off. Benjamin had more success than her. The intestines tore and a thick liquid poured out. Benjamin wretched as it spilled into his mouth and tried not to vomit.

Tatyana could hear the man moan in pain. He was still alive and she was trying to eat his innards. Tears ran down her cheeks and mingled with the human blood dripping from her chin.

Make this end, Tatyana thought. *Oh God please, please make this end.*

She looked up and, out of the corner of her eye, she suddenly became aware of Miriam. She had that hazy field around her again. Maybe it was only because Tatyana's eyes were full of tears that she could see her.

Miriam was moving her hands about in a series of precise movements and muttering what looked like some sort of incantation. She was doing it so she didn't have to join in with the carnage, Tatyana realised.

Tatyana reached out a hand to her. She wanted nothing more than to disappear into that hazy field. To find the blind spot and just fade from view.

Her hand was slick with blood though. Miriam and her field disappeared the minute she reached out for her.

What was she reaching out for?

She'd been thinking about something... fading from... what was it?

No, it was gone.

She looked down at herself. Her face and chest were smeared with blood.

The stains would never come out.

CHAPTER TWELVE

Shit, would the taste never come out? Tatyana had brushed her teeth like twenty times now. Her gums were bleeding and her mouth was raw. She couldn't tell if she was tasting her own blood or the man's.

The man. That's all she could think of him as. The man' That's all he was. She didn't know his name or anything about him other than he was once in a union. That's how they wanted it. The less she knew about him the easier he was to kill.

That was the whole point of it she supposed. The Zombies who tore those women apart didn't know anything about them and weren't capable of caring if they did. That was how she was supposed to be, uncaring and insensible. But there was a point that she couldn't go beyond. And she couldn't help but care.

She scrubbed the back of her tongue. Maybe that's where the taste was. The toothbrush hit the back of her throat and she retched. Thank goodness she wasn't going to be... *Oh no, here it comes.*

She bent forward and threw up into the sink. Her vomit was pink and speckled with shreds of undigested flesh. She hoped to God it was her own guts she'd just puked up.

Guts. Oh God.

She threw up again. And again. And again, until her stomach was empty and even then she kept retching. Bile burned the back of her throat and the inside of her mouth. She let go of the sink, slid to the floor and started to cry.

"Shit are you alright?" Benjamin said. He was standing in the bathroom doorway.

"No I'm not alright. I've just puked someone else's guts into the sink. What the fuck makes you think I'm alright?"

"Alright, calm down. Don't take it out on me. What did I do?"

"What did you do? What did you do? You took me to this island. You fed me human flesh and tried to turn me into a fucking Zombie. And that's just for starters!"

"So you just want to give it all up and go home, is that? You just want to turn your back on these noble monsters after everything you've seen. You know what they're doing to them here. Can you just turn your back on that?"

"Right now Benjamin, I don't give a shit about some murderous corpses."

"I don't believe I'm hearing this. How could you say that? How could you?"

"How could you feed me some guy's guts as he lay there on the ground screaming in pain? Answer me that, huh?"

"You know why I had to do that. Do you think I liked doing it anymore than you?"

"I don't know Benjamin, I don't know. And right now I don't fucking care. I'm sorry but that's just the way I feel. No, fuck that. I'm not sorry. I'm sick of saying that." She put on a ditzy voice, parodying herself. "'I'm sorry, it's just this place. C'mon let's have sex and make up.' Fuck that. Fuck the Zombies and fuck you!"

There was an ominous silence. Benjamin just stood there looking stunned. Tatyana felt sick. Not from what she'd eaten, but from what she felt. These emotions didn't agree with her.

There was laughter in the corridor outside their room.

"What's going on?" Tatyana said.

"There's a party going on downstairs. They want to celebrate... y'know."

"They would wouldn't they?" Tatyana said. "Do you want to use the bathroom? Is that why you came in?"

"Erm, no, I was going to use the radio to contact the guys. They should have reached the Gulf of Mexico by now. That's if they haven't killed each other yet."

"Yeah," Tatyana tried to smile but failed.

"Don't s'pose you want to come and help me?"

"No, don't s'pose I do."

"Okay. Only I found somewhere for them to dock. It's on the south side of the island so they can probably get there without being detected."

"Oh," she said, trying to sound interested.

"I found it on the map of the island that's in the lobby and I think I've worked out the exact co-ordinates."

"Good for you."

Benjamin left and returned with a blanket. "Thought you might need this," he said putting it around her shoulders. "You were shivering."

She felt tears in her eyes as she looked up at him. He was trying. He had no idea how to handle her like this but he was trying, bless his heart.

"Thanks" she said.

He nodded and pulled his cute little half smile. She almost forgave him.

"I love you," he said.

"I know."

He stood in the doorway without moving. She looked up and caught his gaze. There didn't seem to be any words to bridge the gap between them. And if there were, neither of them were clever enough to find them.

CHAPTER THIRTEEN

Newbies were so dull once they'd popped their murder cherry. You'd think they were the first people to ever tear someone apart with their bare hands and teeth.

Samuel Palmer raised a glass to a group by the bar who caught his eye. They were flexing their muscles and pulling their guts in to impress some Swedish escorts.

He was obligated to attend these functions as part of his job. Another fifteen minutes and he'd have done his time. Then he could slip away for a little celebrating of his own.

The strangest thing about killing someone is the huge appetites it awakes in you. To begin with a lot of people throw up. But when the nausea wears off the hunger kicks in. You want to eat and fuck like they were Olympic events.

It was probably something primal, Palmer had decided. Some throw back to Cro-Magnon times when killing your opponent meant you got to fuck his women and steal his food. It meant you were a victor and not a victim. That you deserved to propagate your genes and gorge yourself on the fruits of your kill.

Whatever the reason, St Ignatius made certain to cater to those appetites. It was all part of the process and it made what came later that much more effective.

So they laid on a buffet of the rarest delicacies, prepared by chefs so talented they wouldn't demean themselves by appearing in a Michelin guide. For desert they flew in an army of high class escorts trained to cater to every taste and persuasion.

There was even a dispensary providing designer drugs. From the finest Colombian coke to Viagra, E and narcotics that weren't available on any open market. All washed down with vintage Champagne.

God he found these events tedious.

Bessie Smetherington, the boutique queen, sauntered past him and winked. The dyed red hair and the expensive boob job weren't fooling the two Brazilian hunks she had on either arm. Palmer saw her stop and chat to an Amalgamated Plastics heiress – what was her name again? Moira Jacobs, that was it.

"Fabulous arm candy darling," said Moira. "Where did you pick up such exquisite ornaments?"

"Aren't they great? I think they'll look fabulous in my room. I'm surprised you haven't picked out a bargain for yourself yet."

"Well the night is young and I'm feeling a little curious this evening. Think I might choose myself a his and hers set, if you catch my drift."

"Taking the rough with the smooth are you?"

"Darling, I'm taking more than my fair share, like I always do," Moira said and went to ogle some Thai women. Bessie left with her hands on two perfect Brazilian butts.

Palmer did one more circuit of the room. He slapped backs, kissed cheeks and generally pressed the flesh. The party was beginning to move up stairs. He wouldn't be missed when he left.

He went through the kitchen and out into a service corridor. At the end was a goods elevator. He rode that down to a sub-basement.

No-one else came down this far. He was the only one on the

island with the access codes. He punched them into the keypad and the reinforced steel door slid open.

The room beyond was lined with huge metal draws like the ones found in a morgue. He breathed in the sweet mortuary smell – disinfectant and dead flesh.

It always triggered the same memory in him. The first time he'd ever smelled it. His third year at Harvard. He'd been drinking with one of the med students, James something-or-other.

When they were good and tight James revealed he had the key to the place where they stored the cadavers for the students' exams. He invited Palmer to come take a look, just for kicks. It sounded fun so Palmer agreed.

It was the second time he'd ever seen a corpse. James pulled out several for him to see. One of them was hot. A girl in her twenties who'd choked on a doughnut when her boyfriend did the Heimlich manoeuvre wrong.

"Hey, you wanna see something cool?" said James. He picked up a large hollow needle. "This is a trocar, they use it to get fluid out the corpses." He slipped it down the end of one corpse's penis, making it stand up. "Look. He has a boner."

"Hey, you know what we oughta do?" said Palmer. "We should get the hot chick out of her draw and make him bone her."

"Man, that would be awesome. Wait, wait we're gonna need this." James opened a draw and took out a tube. "It's lube."

Palmer didn't ask what it was doing in the morgue.

He got incredibly excited as they lifted the hot chick's corpse out of her drawer. The smell of her dead flesh, the pliant way her body moved in his arms, it turned him on.

A tiny sliver of blood escaped from her mouth as they slid her onto the dead guy. Palmer had never seen anything so beautiful in his life. The sagging flesh of the dead guy just sank beneath her weight.

Look at the useless prick just lying there, not even knowing how lucky he is, thought Palmer. He realised he was eaten up with jealousy.

James was giggling fit to bust. Palmer was pissed at him. He was having an erotic revelation and James was killing the romance. He was about to pop him one right in the mouth when they heard footsteps.

"Shit it's the guard," said James. "We gotta get outta here."

"Wait, shouldn't we put the corpses back?"

"There isn't time, c'mon man we gotta leave *now*!"

Palmer took one last look at the hot chick's corpse. He was filled with longing as James grabbed him by the collar and dragged him out of the room. They got out of the building without being caught and went back to their frat house.

There was a minor scandal on campus when the bodies were found. However it was soon put down to a student prank and the faculty preferred to brush the matter aside to avoid bad publicity.

Palmer always avoided James after that. James didn't make any effort to see him either. The two shared a guilty secret that they'd both as soon forget.

What Palmer couldn't forget was the hot chick's corpse. The way it felt in his arms. The odours it gave off. How cold it felt against his skin.

He'd lie in bed at night and fantasise about breaking into the morgue on a white charger and rescuing the corpse from its slab. He'd picture himself riding off into the sunset with the corpse in his arms. Her mouldering head resting gently on his shoulder. His nostrils filled with the sweet scent of her decay.

He even found out where they'd buried her remains, after she'd been dissected by some student. He used to visit the grave and dream about digging her up. Stitching her body parts back together. The ultimate act of love and devotion to the object of his desire.

After a while he realised his obsession was never going to come to anything. So he put it out of his mind and shifted his desires elsewhere. But the fantasy never went away. Like a tap that drips just as you're about to sleep, it would wake him up in the middle of the night. It was getting so he couldn't ignore his desire for the dead any longer.

Leaving college, he found he had a talent for playing the market. It was like a beautiful and harmonious machine to him.

It operated according to perfect laws that carried people and nations along in its wake. Its workings beguiled and enchanted him. Everything was ordered according to bottom lines and balance sheets.

His star rose on Wall Street and so did his portfolio of holdings. As a treat on his thirtieth birthday, when he'd amassed more wealth than he could ever spend, he bought himself a chain of morticians.

He took to making surprise inspections of these establishments. Late at night, when the staff had gone home. That was when his second life began. When he found the space to be the person he truly was. Where he could indulge all those fantasies he hadn't dared admit before.

As befitted someone with his wealth and ability, Palmer did everything with class. He chose his lovers very carefully. He didn't want just any old cadaver. He went for a certain type. She had to have a hot body. He preferred blondes, but he could always have the hair dyed or buy a wig. And she had to be under thirty, preferably twenty five or younger.

This made his quest for love a little more tricky, but he was a resourceful man. He expanded the chain of morticians into twelve more states and instigated an aggressive campaign for new business. As a result his investment thrived. And so did his opportunities for romance.

He scoured the obituaries for new conquests. When he found one he would take personal charge of the burial. He even liaised with the family and helped them through their time of grief. He would comfort a mother at a graveside while he was secretly preparing her daughter for a passionate encounter.

He would start by buying her gifts. A Prada evening dress, with matching heels or a set of diamond earrings. She had to be properly kitted out before she could be wooed.

He had a private room built into each of his mortuaries. He prided himself on the decor of all of them. Each was unique and done out with perfect taste.

He would have a meal sent over from the area's finest restaurant and set a table for himself and his date. Only when the correct rituals of courtship had been observed would he think of touching her.

It made the whole experience that much more exquisite. He would luxuriate in his new love for days on end. Hardly leaving her, except to deal with pressing business. But eventually the blossom of his passion would fade as her flesh began to decompose.

By their very nature, his romances were fleeting. At times his heart would be broken. But there was always the obituary page. Another sad loss would catch his eye and the thrill of the chase would begin again.

As his mortician empire grew so did the occasional problem with staff. It seemed men and women of his persuasion were often drawn to the profession. In much greater numbers than most people suspected. Palmer would be especially vigilant for the tell tale signs. No-one knew them better than he.

He couldn't be everywhere though and he couldn't check every person who worked for him. It never crossed his mind that they would be just as wise to him. He had been so careful for so many years that he was surprised when he received the first e-mails.

They were from an online group called the American Necromantic Adventurer's League. They had set up a forum and were campaigning to rehabilitate necrophilia. They aimed to change its public image from a sociopathic act to a lifestyle choice. They claimed necromantics were using their sexuality to come to an emotional and spiritual understanding with death.

The e-mails revealed that certain anonymous employees had highlighted him as a possible patron for their activities. They suggested that he shared certain values with the group and that sponsoring them would be the best way to maintain the secrecy surrounding his own love life.

Palmer was not intimidated by their veiled threats. He defended himself by going on the attack. He led a prominent campaign against League members within the industry as a way of deflecting attention from himself. He paid private investigators to hunt them all down and had them arrested. His wealth and influence guaranteed stiff sentences for them all. Then he sold his holdings in the mortuary business.

Palmer was in his forties by this point and had begun to tire of the bachelor life. He started to long for a more permanent relationship. His dilemma was that he didn't feel any attraction towards living women and he didn't want to give up the variety of bodies and experiences he was used to.

That's when he was approached by Doc Papa. It seemed another group of people, with whom he shared common interests, had been watching him – the super rich. They were head hunting a CEO for a private enterprise in the Caribbean. One that would cater exclusively to the monetary elite.

When they described the proposition to him in full, he was struck by two things. It had a sound business model and it would transport his love life to a whole new level.

Palmer savoured the mortuary aroma for a few seconds longer. Then he opened the door of a large refrigerator and took out a bucket of fresh human brains.

He pulled open a drawer from the middle row. Inside his current favourite concubine strained against her straps and snapped her teeth at him in greeting.

"Hello my sweet," Palmer said stroking her bleached, straightened hair. "I know, I know I've missed you too, but Daddy has to work, yes he does."

Palmer reached into the bucket and chose a ripe brain. The concubine's nose twitched as she smelled it. She rolled her milky white eyes in their encrusted sockets. She was coming on to him. She was such a minx.

"Patience my sweet," Palmer said, dangling the brain over her mouth like a bunch of grapes. "Eat your brain first. They're good for you. The doctor told me so. They're the best thing to slow your decomposition, yes they are."

The concubine tore the spongy, pink tissue of the brain with her dead teeth, swallowing each mouthful as quickly as she could. Palmer dabbed the blood and brain tissue away from her mouth with his handkerchief.

"There that's better isn't it? You're all hot for Daddy now aren't you? I can tell you are."

Palmer unbuckled his belt. The other concubines caught the scent of the brains. They got excited inside their drawers. They writhed and kicked in excitement.

"Wait my angels, wait. I don't have anywhere to be until five am. I will see to all of you soon enough."

CHAPTER FOURTEEN

"Ow! what are you some kind of fascist?" Klaus winced from the slap she gave him upside the head. He sloped off rubbing his scalp. "Are you having your period or something?"

Tweakie raised her hand again and he cowered. "I told you to put the champagne and caviar on ice. Since when did 'on ice' mean pour it down your scrawny gullet? We were saving that to celebrate once we make off with the Zombies."

"It was an act of love," said Klaus, he tried to look wounded and indignant. "A supreme sacrifice. I was saving Ben and Tatyana from the trap of their pampered upbringing. Too much decadence can sap the revolutionary spirit. I was keeping them pure for the cause by taking all temptation out of their way."

"Say what?"

"You don't think I am enjoying stuffing myself with expensive delicacies do you? Of course not. But I'm prepared to be doing anything to further the cause."

"Un-fucking-believable!"

Tweakie turned away from him for fear of what she might do if he got too close. They'd been out on the open sea for two weeks now and she was beginning to wish Benjamin's folks had bought a bigger yacht. Two hundred feet seemed tiny when she had to share it with these three guys.

It had been fun for the first few days. Stealing the yacht had given her a rush. Like jacking cars back in middle school. Only this thrill was a hundred times bigger. The yacht was awesome and took off at an incredible rate of knots.

For a few hours she felt thirteen again. Drinking cheap wine in the back of an old convertible they'd lifted from the front of the trailer park. Those were some of her happiest memories. Driving around all day getting bombed. Forgetting all about school or having to go back to her Mom's trailer and the wandering hands of whatever drunken dumbass she'd dragged home.

"Now don't yuh say nuthin' to yore Momma little gurl, it'll only go worse on yuh."

Course the yacht was a serious step up from a broken down old Dodge. It had a king sized jacuzzi, seven cabins, retractable plasma TV screen, twin jet skis and its own helicopter pad. And that was just the upper deck. The lower deck had a fully equipped gym, a swimming pool and a dance floor with a well-stocked bar.

From what she'd seen of Benjamin's folks, she couldn't imagine them busting any moves though. Or using what she swore was a stripper pole in the middle of the dance floor. Still, there was no telling what some people got up to in the privacy of the Mid-Atlantic.

The trip started out with calm waters, blue skies and glorious sunshine. By the second day, thanks to her boat-mates, it turned into a perfect storm of hissy fits and fall outs.

Straight after breakfast Klaus annexed the lounge bar with almost military precision. That was where the plasma TV was. He seized control of the remote on behalf of the people.

They weighed anchor after lunch and Dan and Andy stormed the gates of the lounge bar. They demanded a vote on which channel to watch and overruled Klaus on the viewing schedule.

Klaus called them all fascists for bringing democracy into the lounge bar 'against the will of the people'. He became as welcome in the lounge then as a hurricane in Haiti and he stormed out.

The next morning Dan had finally charged the batteries on his camcorder. Something he'd forgotten to do before they left. Just in time to film Klaus as he seized control of the means of producing breakfast.

A heated debate ensued over whether the worker's council they'd formed to run the kitchen should get an equal say in the food they prepared and who washed the dishes.

Klaus argued that he should lead the kitchen on behalf of the masses because only he was qualified to say what a real revolutionary menu looked like. Besides, he had a skin complaint that made him allergic to detergents and he was requisitioning the maple syrup because he was diabetic and if his insulin levels dropped he could die.

Tweakie stayed mostly in her cabin after that. Klaus and Andy debated whether she was more like Trotsky for deserting the revolution or Che Guevara for taking the struggle on to new territories. It was no skin off her butt. So long as she didn't have to listen to them argue.

She only came out to take her turn at the wheel or to help Andy navigate. So long as she made allowances for his weird behaviour he was easier to get along with than the others. Andy seemed quite glad of her company too. He called her 'quite useful to have about.' Like the servobot he'd always wanted, 'only with slightly smaller breasts'. She guessed that was a compliment in his bizarre world.

Dan did try and get her to talk to camera as part of the documentary he was making of their 'ground breaking voyage'. She wasn't into it but she agreed to keep a video diary just to get him off her back. He lent her his spare camera but she never got round to recording anything.

She was just on her way to return it when she'd run into Klaus finishing the last of the caviar. She headed up a flight of stairs to the control deck. Dan had the camera on. He was interviewing Andy at the wheel.

"Do think we'll pick up the techniques pretty quickly?" said Dan. "Or do you think we'll have to hang back for the first few days?"

"Well that all depends on how good Benjamin and Tatyana prove to be as teachers," said Andy. "I imagine we'll get better at interacting with the undead once they pass on what they've learned, and we've had a chance to try it out. I don't think we'll have much of a choice about learning quickly when the whole boat's stuffed full of noble monsters though."

"Yeah I don't s'pose we will. Do you think you'll be able to build a rapport with the noble monsters?"

"I think I'll build a better rapport with them than I have with most humans."

"Why's that?"

"Well, for a start," said Andy, pushing his glasses back and nodding at Tweakie in the doorway. "They're not encumbered with emotions like humans are."

"Encumbered with emotions?" said Tweakie. "You going all Mr Spock on us Andy?" She handed Dan the spare camera. "Here this is yours."

"Did you shoot anything?"

Tweakie shrugged. "I'll get around to it later."

"Well I don't see any practical purpose to most peoples' emotions," said Andy. "Except to confuse genuinely intelligent people like me. There's no problem trying to read Zombies like there is with people. You don't have to decipher their emotions by the weird faces they pull or the inexplicable way they suddenly start to act. Like if their faces gets red and they start shouting loudly then they're probably angry. Or if their mouths turn down and their eyes get watery then you know they're sad. But even then that could also mean they're happy and proud, like when you graduate MIT with the highest grade in your class at only fifteen. Then they want to tell you how proud they are, when you still think you've upset them in some way and they try and hug and kiss you. *Blech!* Zombies don't kiss. That's the best bit about them. You don't have to worry about smelling their spit on your cheek."

"So you understand them better," said Dan. "Is that it?"

"Yes I would say it is. You know where you are with a Zombie. The way they act makes sense. That's why they're so noble."

"How about you Tweakie?" Dan turned the camera on her. "Zombies and their lack of emotion, is that what does it for you?"

Tweakie considered giving him the finger but thought better of it. "It's not the fact that they don't feel emotions. They don't feel anything, period. That's the attraction. Nothing hurts them. They're invulnerable."

"And that's a good thing?" said Andy.

"Growing up how I did. It's a Godsend," said Tweakie, chewing on a fingernail. "I had to learn that. Took me years to get to there and I'm still not always safe. Nothing touches them. That's what I admire. What I long for myself."

"Yeah, they're bad assess," said Dan. "Like me."

"Oh, and you're a bad ass all of a sudden?" said Andy with a smirk. "Because you got kicked out of UCLA for dealing drugs?"

"Better believe it," said Dan taking the camera from his eye and flexing his biceps. "Bad to the bone. You wanna try me?"

"Your make-up's smudged," said Andy.

"Is it?" Dan turned to Tweakie. "I've been meaning to ask you about that. Am I using the right foundation? Only all the sun and sea air is playing havoc with my pallor. I keep sweating and then it streaks and I swear I start looking like Alice frigging Cooper."

"You want something with a powder base that absorbs moisture."

Everyone jumped when the radio crackled to life. "This is Agent Z to Deathship 1. Are you receiving me?"

"Shit, that's Benjamin," said Dan. "He got through. Your freaking contraption worked."

"Of course it did," said Andy, looking affronted.

"I repeat, Deathship 1, are you receiving me?"

"What's happening? Are you having secret meetings without me?" Klaus appeared in the doorway.

"It's Benjamin," said Andy. "He's just made radio contact."

"Reading you loud and clear good buddy," said Dan. "You nailed any noble monsters yet?"

"Only your Momma," said Benjamin. "Betcha didn't know she was here did you?"

"Was *your* Momma who invited her if I recall."

"Listen, we're days away from liberating the noble monsters. And I've found somewhere on the island you can dock without being seen. Was used by smugglers back in the day."

"Sounds awesome."

"It's perfect," said Benjamin.

CHAPTER FIFTEEN

"So does every temple..."

"Ounfó."

"Sorry Ounfó, have one of those poles in the centre?"

"Yes it does," Doc Papa said. He put down the knife and wiped his fingers. The blood was making them slippery. The three drummers increased the tempo. "That's a Poteau Mitan. It's a link between the worlds below and the worlds above. Like a great tree of life with its branches in the heavens and its roots in the waters below the Earth. It represents the royal path taken by the Loa to meet with humanity. "

"And these Loa are like spirits right?"

"They are supernatural beings who act as intermediaries between God and His creation. They are present in all realms of nature and create the structure of time and space. They preside over all areas of human activity from agriculture to war. They also guide those who serve them, sometimes they intervene in our lives. We summon them in our ceremonies and they take possession of their servants when they have important news to impart."

"I see, and the colours and marking on this Pot... erm..."

"Poteau Mitan."

"Yes, Poteau Mitan, sorry. Do they have a special significance?"

"They represent the Serpent and Rainbow. The sacred symbols of the Loa Dambala and his consort Ayida Wédo. They symbolise the essence of creation and the sacred link between land, sea and sky."

"Fascinating, fascinating, I heard a lot about Voodoo last year when I shot a film in Haiti about the aftermath of the hurricanes. You might have seen it."

"I'm afraid I don't care much for your work."

"No, no, I don't suppose you do, given your... err, political leanings. It was about the ecological disaster in Haiti that's killed thousands of people and left millions homeless. The US and the World Bank pressured Haiti into opening its markets to US imports. This ruined local agriculture. The unemployed peasant farmers were driven into city slums with no food or fuel. That's what drove the deforestation. Haiti has less than two per cent of forest cover. When the hurricanes hit last year they destroyed most of the country's harvest and left all but a few areas uninhabitable. If Haiti had had more forests the damage wouldn't have been so great and less people would have died as a direct result of US intervention."

"Well that's one opinion," said Doc Papa slicing through a layer of subcutaneous fat.

"Sorry I was getting on my soap box a bit there. I tend to do that when I'm nervous. What I meant to say was I heard a lot about Voodoo while I was out there, but this is the first actual rite I've seen. What is that pattern you made on the floor with the white powder?"

"It's a Vèvè," said Doc Papa. "A mystic symbol intended to invoke the presence of a Loa. Like a sacred access code to call them down."

"Okay, and which Loa is this for?"

"We're conducting a Petro rite to invoke Erzulie Zantor."

"Petro, now forgive me if I'm wrong, but isn't that like the dark side of Voodoo? And Rada I think it's called, is like the light side?"

"That's a rather simplified western view," Doc Papa said and began to remove the first of the vital organs. "The original rites that evolved into Voodoo come from several different parts of Africa. They were brought over to Haiti by the tribes that were conquered and sold into slavery. Petro, Rada, Kongo, Nago these are names of nanchons or nations. They refer to the rites used to invoke certain Loa. It so happens that if you use certain rites the Loa you call upon may come in their mean or vengeful form. This rite for instance is outlawed among most practitioners and conducted only by those of the red sect."

"Why is that?"

"All Loa demand a sacrifice. They must be fed before they manifest themselves and enter the bodies of their followers. This rite demands a Cochon sans poils."

"And what's that?"

"A human sacrifice.

"Is that my liver?"

"Yes it is. It's actually very healthy for a man of your age."

"Oh God, I'm going to die aren't I?"

"I would say that's inevitable"

Doc Papa stepped back and looked over his handiwork. The sacrifice was staked out on the ground. His middle was split from stomach to sternum like the subject of an autopsy. All of his vital organs had been removed with great precision and laid out on the ground around him according to tradition. They glistened in the light of the ritual fires. Like their owner, they still throbbed with an unnatural life.

"Look Mr Papa, or whatever your name is, if you put me back together again and let me go I swear I won't tell a soul about the island. I could even be useful to you. I've got contacts. I could get you some really good publicity."

"You have nothing I want. Don't try and bargain."

"I've got money, if that's what you want. I have independent means. It's how I fund all my films. It's yours, all of it. All you have to do is stitch me up and send me home."

"You're being kept alive through magical labours because it is necessary to the ceremony. To resurrect you though, that is beyond even my powers."

"I'll be missed you know. I'm a public figure. Questions will be asked. You'll be called to answer for what you're doing."

"Your body has already been found and your obituaries written. No-one will question a thing."

"Why? Why are you doing this to me? Why me? What have I ever done to you?"

"You produce irresponsible films that interfere with the business of myself and my colleagues. Your so-called exposés of human rights infractions cost us money. You are an overhead we cannot afford and so you have been silenced."

"You can't do this. You can't. It's not fair. It's not humane. Please, I beg of you, please..."

"Hush now, can't you hear she comes? And she is so very, very hungry."

Doc Papa reached into the sacrifice's chest and pulled out his heart. He kissed it and held it aloft. Vincenzo, his Commandant Général de la Place, gave the signal and the flag bearers began to parade around the Peristyle, the area of the Ounfó prescribed for dancing. They were followed by the Ounsi, his female followers. Clad not in the traditional white, but red as befitted the rite. The drummers changed the beat to a call and response between the Manman, the largest drum, and the two smaller drums the Grondez and the Ka Tha Bou.

The sacrifice began to scream as Doc Papa chanted over his heart.

"Ahi coeur de Cochon gris!

"Tambour moin rélé.

"Jou-t' allongé... Ahi!

"Ahi! Erzulie Zandor... Ahi!"

The heart in Doc Papa's hands stopped beating. The sacrifice was accepted and his spirit consumed.

The Loa Erzulie Zandor gripped Vincenzo and shook him violently. Vincenzo's body convulsed and he threw himself to the ground before leaping into the air and then hitting the ground again. He looked like a rag doll in the hands of a malevolent child.

As an initiated Houngan, Doc Papa had undergone the rite of the Pris de Yeux. This allowed him to see into the invisible world of the Loa. He allowed himself, for just the briefest of moments, to view Erzulie Zandor in her actual form. She was a being of impossible angles spilling into dimensions he couldn't comprehend, surrounded by an aura full of colours no human eye can see or brain process. It hurt him to his very core to even try and behold her.

For the sake of his sanity he shifted his konesans into a different conception of her. She was the very essence of every mother who had ever killed to protect her young or murdered a rival in a fit of jealousy. She was the ultimate female of her species and more deadly than any male. Her beauty was terrible to behold.

Erzulie Zandor had taken full possession of Vincenzo now. She grabbed one of the female followers and beat her viciously till she bled, then flung the woman to one side. She knocked a flag bearer to the floor, sat astride him and rode the man like a bitch in heat. She spat on him as she did and cursed him for the miserable piece of filth he was.

Then she turned her attention to Doc Papa and stalked towards him. He held up his asson as a sign of his authority.

She sneered at him. "Do you think that pathetic child's toy can protect you from me?"

He ignored her taunt. "I have need of your wisdom and your special knowledge. Grant me your insight Erzulie Zandor, most deadly and magnificent of all the Loa."

"And why would I speak with a speck of shit like you?"

"I have fed you great Loa and I have called you here into my Ounfó when few others would dare. I have given you flesh to wear and blood to drink. I ask only that you confer on me that which costs you nothing to share. There is an artefact in the invisible world that I need to locate, will you help me?"

"Mmm, that costs me nothing does it, little piss-pot? How poorly you value my blessings."

"They are of inestimable value to me great Loa. That is why I have gone to such pains to prepare an audience with you. Have my labours fallen short of your expectations? Is my hospitality lacking? Just tell me and I will rectify it."

"You've gone to great pains to use me for your own ends you little shit-bag. And don't think I don't know it."

"And you have only come because it suits *your* purpose great Loa."

"Don't think to second guess me you little piss-stain. I've come because it amuses me to watch you grovel. All tall and proud like a blood stiffened cock you are. And how you wilt before me. How you crawl back into your scrotum. What would you have of me man child?"

"As I said before, I need your assistance locating an artefact. It's known as the Gateway of the Souls, it is crucial to my plans."

"And you can't find it anywhere can you?"

"No, Erzulie Zandor."

"And without it all these webs you've been weaving will come unstuck. Can't have that can we? Can't lose all those fat juicy flies you've captured."

"No."

"No indeed. And what prizes these flies are, how fat and juicy. And yet your plans are so much more than any of them suspect. So audacious, so bold, no-one has ever aimed for such power and control."

"Will it work? Will I gain what I seek? Will you help me find the Gateway of the Souls?"

"So many questions, like an eager hatchling you are, grabbing for worms at his mother's beak."

Erzulie Zandor eyed him for a long while without talking. She was weighing something up. Doc Papa felt the sweat trickle down the back of his neck. Finally she spoke. "Will I help you find it? Will I? Will I? Will I? Why yes I think I will. It amuses me greatly. I think there is a beautiful irony about it. So many souls harnessed to the tyranny of one mind. No-one has achieved that before. It will be a lesson to many. I will lead you to the Gateway of the Souls, but it won't be where you expect. This is your very last chance to step away from this path. If you have any doubts, heed them now."

"I have no doubts. I am committed to this."

"Good, that's what I was hoping you would say."

This was more than he could have hoped. He maintained his calm demeanour, but inside his spirit leapt with elation. He was quite sure Erzulie Zandor could see this. She cackled indulgently.

"This is not a simple matter though," she said. "The Gateway is tied up in a blood feud. And a curse that, after all these centuries, remains unresolved. It emanates from the same source as the Gateway."

"I have dealt with that already."

"Have you? Have you really? There are ancestors present who say otherwise. Dead who are unfed and hungry for revenge. Who cry out for retribution to any Loa who will listen."

"They petition against a crime I had no part in," said Doc Papa.

Erzulie Zandor threw back Vincenzo's head and laughed from inside him. "That is not the way it works little shit smear. You have inherited this blood debt and the dead say it is due for payment."

"I thank you for the warning then. I will take steps to ensure it's dealt with."

"Be sure that you do little man. Be sure that you do."

Erzulie Zandor threw Vincenzo back and left his body before it hit the ground. From the vicious thump it made, Doc Papa imagined Vincenzo would be lucky to escape with just heavy bruising.

The female followers ran to help Vincenzo and their sister who had been had beaten. Doc Papa turned away as they bent and attended to the two of them on the ground.

He was on the verge of controlling more wealth and power than any human being had ever had. Of Fashioning a future for humanity like nothing it had ever seen.

Yet deeds from the past had been put around his neck like

millstones. Events that took place centuries before he was born threatened to jeopardise it all.

There was nothing he wouldn't do to prevent that from happening.

CHAPTER SIXTEEN

Nine Months Ago

Tatyana was petrified.

The day had started out so well. Everything had been so perfect. It could only go hideously wrong from now on.

She was riding with her mother in the back of the Rolls. Her mother had promised to let her ride back alone, but she wanted to savour this moment with her daughter. Tatyana could hardly begrudge her that.

When she was Tatyana's age, her mother could only dream about going to a ball thrown by the Daughters of the American Revolution. Nothing like it ever took place in Stalingrad. She would read about these events in the glossy magazines she found at her uncle's dacha. He was a diplomat and the Party gave him a nice house in the country for his services to the Soviet state.

He brought the magazines back for his wife, but Tatyana's mother was allowed to flick through them when her family came to visit. She was studying English at school and it was thought to be good practise for her to read them. What she recalled most when she told Tatyana about it were the pictures.

They were so full of colour and excitement. The men looked so dashing in their tuxedos, and the women so glamorous and fashionable in their gowns. The colour and the opulence of the society events in the magazines seemed so thrilling and forbidden compared to Stalingrad with it's drab clothes and Soviet architecture.

Tatyana's mother would fantasise about attending one of the balls she'd read about as she stood in line for hours to buy bread or potatoes. Now here she was, riding through Manhattan with her only daughter in the back of a Rolls Royce, on the way to the Waldorf-Astoria.

Her mother had chosen the Vera Wang gown she was wearing. Tatyana had to admit she looked good in it. Much better than she ever thought she would. She'd been surprised when she saw herself in her bedroom mirror.

Her mother had cried when she saw Tatyana. Her father came in to see what all the fuss was about and even he smiled when he laid eyes on her. He put his hands on her shoulders, kissed her and told her she looked beautiful.

Getting an invitation to the DAR Debutantes Ball for his daughter was a big deal for him too. It meant that all the money he was spreading about to gain acceptance in the Fortune 500 circles was working. Tatyana was going to be presented to the cream of New York society.

For that moment, at least, things felt right for them. Her father wasn't brooding or flying into dark rages. He was proud of his wife and daughter. They didn't have to tiptoe round him for fear of his temper. He loved them both and wanted to let them know it. He even waved goodbye to them as they drove off.

That's why Tatyana was so terrified now. Surely things couldn't remain this good for long?

They didn't. Cross town traffic was appalling and they arrived late. Tatyana was met by Ingrid Hedberg, the chair of the ball committee, as she arrived in the lobby and was whisked away to take her place by the stage.

Tatyana had to run the gauntlet of the whole committee on her way. Elderly women with expensive jewellery and puckered up faces who tutted their disapproval as she walked past.

As her father wasn't permitted to present her, a special chaperone had been found for just that purpose.

"This is Frank Tufts," said Ingrid, introducing Tatyana to a tall portly guy in his late fifties. "He's a stockbroker now but he used to play baseball for the San Francisco Giants."

"Well now that was a good few years ago," said Frank with a genial smile. "It's a pleasure to meet you young lady."

"Thanks. You too."

The formal presentation had already begun by the time she was positioned at the end of the receiving line on the main stage in the ballroom. She was hidden in the wings for most of the ceremony, which suited her fine.

Frank took her arm when it came time for her to be presented. The announcer mispronounced her name, calling her Tatania Bulgakov.

Frank walked her around the stage and stopped in the centre. "This is the part where you curtsey dear," he whispered.

Tatyana hadn't curtsied since her childhood ballet class. She could just about remember how to do it. She put one foot behind the other and bent her knees. The heel on her left shoe skidded out from under her as she did and she nearly fell.

"That's okay, I've got you," said Frank helping her back up.

A bunch of the other debs giggled at this, until Ingrid silenced them with a stern stare. Tatyana was blushing so much she could have heated the whole ballroom. Her escort joined them on stage. He was a short frat boy who was rather full of himself called Thomas Miller the Third. He escorted her off the stage, tried to feel her up as they approached the dance floor, then promptly dumped her to join his friends at the bar.

Tatyana wandered around, feeling a little aimless. She didn't know a soul there and wasn't a part of any of the cliques. She spotted the girl she'd stood next to in the receiving line. She was over by the punch bowl.

Tatyana walked over to join her.

"Hi," she said.

"Hi," said the girl, then turned back to the two girls she'd been chatting to.

"We're like best friends at the ball," said one of the other girls.

"Yeah," said the other. "We, like, met at Bergdorf Goodman's. I was, like, about to buy this one dress and I looked over and saw Patricia."

"And I was, like, trying on exactly the same dress as Abigail."

"And we were both, like, 'Oh My God!'"

"So neither of us, like, bought it."

"But then the weird thing is, when we arrived we saw this other girl wearing the same dress."

"And she looked, like, really fat in it."

"Yeah, and we were, like, 'hasn't she ever heard of the South Beach Diet?'"

"So you had a lucky escape then," said Tatyana. The three girls turned to look at her. Their expressions weren't friendly. "I mean, not buying the dress."

"I'm sorry," said Patricia. "Did you, like, want something?"

"Yeah," said Abigail. "Cos you're, like, blocking the punch bowl."

"Oh, I'm sorry," said Tatyana and sloped away.

She didn't feel much like dancing and no-one had asked her anyway so she snuck outside and stood on the balcony. She was gazing out at the Manhattan skyline, wondering if she could spend the whole ball out there and not supposing she'd be missed, when a young man joined her.

"Nice to see someone else who loves these events as much as I do," he said.

"I'm sorry. It's just rather hot in there and..."

"Stuffy?"

"Stuffy doesn't begin to cover it."

He smiled at her remark. He had a really cute smile. She felt a little nervous flutter in her stomach. He looked kind of out of place though. He was wearing an expensive tuxedo but it was covered in soil and the sleeves were torn. His face was white with make-up and he had lots of fake blood on him.

"Are you a Goth or something?"

"A Goth?" he snorted with derision. "A Goth, gimme a break, that's so like last millennium. I'm a Deathwalker."

"A Deathwalker, is that some sort of emo thing?"

"An emo thing." He said with a look of amused horror. "You really don't get out much do you?"

"Probably more than you do. You look like you've just dug your way out of a grave."

"Exactly. That's totally what I want to look like. Deathwalking, it's not a Goth or an emo thing, it's way more punk than that. Deathwalkers revere the living dead, corpses who've risen from the grave."

"You mean like Zombies?"

"Yeah, only we like to call them the Noble Monster or the Graveyard Rebel. They're the ultimate passive aggressive icon of rebellion against society. There's no hypocrisy or phoniness with a noble monster, like there is with all those jerk offs in there."

"I'd certainly love to see a load of Zombies go apeshit on them."

"Now you're talking. Wouldn't that be awesome. I'm Benjamin by the way."

"Tatyana. Did they let you on stage like that?"

"No, and the debutante I was supposed to escort was pissed I can tell you."

"I bet she was. I'm surprised they even let you in the building."

"Oh they didn't want to, believe me, but my step-dad made the second highest contribution to the ball so they had to."

"Second highest?"

"Yeah it would have been the highest but, at the last minute, some Russian gangster spunked like half a mil so his little daughter could play at being a debutante.

"That would be my father."

"Oops," he said and smiled bashfully. "I'm sorry, I thought you were French or something."

"French?" now she pretended to be outraged.

"Well I heard your accent was European and I knew it wasn't English so I just assumed you were French or something."

"That's so typically American."

"You must think I'm such a dick."

She didn't actually. She thought he was rather cute. She was also fairly sure he was checking her out. She didn't really get checked out by many cute guys. Except for those who came on to her just to see if she would put out on the first night. When they found out she didn't they lost interest.

It wasn't that she was bad looking. She didn't have the classical waspish good looks, but she wasn't unattractive, at least she didn't think so. It was more that she was a bit socially awkward. They could tell she didn't fit in easily. They usually wanted some cheerleader type so they could show their friends they were 'The Man' when it came to macking and all that.

"Hey," Benjamin said. "Do you wanna get out of here and go somewhere really cool?"

"Okay."

"Great, let's bounce."

"This is somewhere really cool is it?" she said as they got out of the taxi at Church Street between Fulton and Vesey.

"What do you mean? This is awesome."

Benjamin jumped the rails and helped her over. Tatyana looked around at the sycamore trees and the ancient marble tombstones.

"This your home away from home is it?" she said.

"This is the oldest graveyard in Manhattan," he said and pointed at the chapel up ahead. "Do you know how many Presidents have worshipped at that chapel?"

"Do you?"

"Erm, it's four or five I think. I wasn't paying that much attention. But I know George Washington did something here on Inauguration Day and even ol' Dubya's shown his face."

"Should I be impressed?"

"By Bush or my knowledge?"

"By your idea of how to show a gal a good time."

"Hey, you ain't seen nothing yet. Come with me."

He took her hand and led her over to the chapel. She got another flutter of excitement as his fingers closed about hers. They stopped at a back door.

"Wait here," he said.

He disappeared and left Tatyana standing in the cold air wondering why she'd left the ball with a complete stranger. Was she really that reckless? After about five minutes there was a faint click and the door opened.

"How did you get in?" she said.

"You don't want to know."

They walked through a porch in total darkness. Then they passed through a storage room and into a larger room.

"This is the vestry," Benjamin said. He lit a zippo and held it up to get a better look at the place. There was a coffin over in the corner, propped up on a table. He went and took a look inside.

"Is it?" Tatyana said.

Benjamin shook his head. "There's no-one in there."

They left the vestry and went through what looked like a hand-carved door into the main building. It was a bit too gloomy to see the interior of the church properly. The streetlights spilled in through the stained glass windows and lit up different details of the brownstone architecture and the woodwork.

"Shouldn't there be benches or something for people to sit on?" she said.

"You mean pews? They had them all taken out a little while ago. To cope with all the visitors. This place has been kind of popular recently."

She couldn't believe she was standing here with some guy she'd only just met. Being here gave her a double kick. Not only was she breaking and entering, she was inside a religious building.

As a former officer of the KGB, Tatyana's father was a devout atheist. He had always taken a Marxist approach to the evils of religion. Even after he became a capitalist. He swapped 'scientific rationalism' for 'dialectical materialism' but his basic opinion remained the same.

It was a "superstitious throw back to a less enlightened time". Now they lived in the west he claimed to see "that it had certain uses for controlling the stupider sections of society". But it wasn't for him and his family.

Churches were forbidden, even exotic, spaces to Tatyana. Somewhere that people from different countries and cultures went. She'd never been to a wedding or a funeral in a church. That was something other people did on the TV and in the movies. Her grandfather had been buried in a municipal cemetery and her cousins had been married in state offices.

For as long as Tatyana could remember she'd had a strange fascination with religion. It was like her mother's fascination with western high society, or the fascination she, and the other girls at her private school, used to have with sex.

It was the pomp and ceremony of it. All those rituals churchgoers use to mark the different stages of their lives. The way it brought families together to celebrate the most diverse things like rejoicing in marriages and mourning the death of those they loved.

She still wondered what it felt like to believe in something that sounded so impossible, and to be filled by so much hope because it *was* impossible yet you knew it was true. She couldn't think of a single thing she believed in that much. She wasn't sure she even wanted to.

"So, what do you think?" said Benjamin.

"Actually you're right," Tatyana said. "This *is* really cool."

"Come with me," he took her hand again, much to her delight. He guided her over to a window that was right by a street lamp. The light struck the stained glass and hit the floor in a mosaic of colours.

Benjamin stepped into the multi coloured rays and his white, pallid face became a harlequin's mask. Tatyana did the same and the colours lit up her perfect white ball gown like it was a patchwork quilt. She laughed and twirled round, sending her dress spinning out to catch the different colours.

Tatyana stopped and looked up at the window. It showed the Virgin Mary in a classic pose with the young Christ Child on her lap. She was surrounded by angels singing her praises. The light coming from the halo around her head was the brightest. Its rays fell on Tatyana and seemed to fill her with the same light.

Is this what it feels like to believe?

"Who's there?" said a voice from the nave. "Don't move, I've got a gun."

"Shit," said Benjamin. "It must be a security guard. Come with me."

He grabbed her arm and dragged her towards the vestry. They ran past the pulpit on the way. He charged up to the altar and lifted a bottle of wine. "What are you doing wasting time?" she hissed.

"It's okay. I've got a plan."

They stumbled into the vestry but couldn't see a thing. Their eyes hadn't adjusted to the dark. They ran to where they thought the door was and hit the coffin. The footsteps behind them sounded like they were catching up.

"Quick, hide in there" Benjamin said and directed her into a broom closet as he clambered into the coffin.

Tatyana watched through a crack in the door as the security guard burst into the vestry and shone his torch around the room. He was a large guy, who could stand to lose a few pounds. Not to mention the ridiculous walrus moustache on his top lip.

She really *was* petrified now. Getting caught or arrested didn't worry her. She was terrified of what she was going to say to her father when she arrived back home in a police car with a criminal record for breaking and entering. How was she going to explain to him why she'd left a ball he had paid a small fortune for her to attend, to break into a church with a guy she'd never met before who was dressed like a Zombie?

"You punks are in trouble now," the guard said. "I'm warning you, come on out and don't try anything funny." His torch beam stopped on the coffin.

Benjamin's fingers appeared on the side of the coffin. He let out a deep groan and sat up. Really slowly like he was in some corny old horror movie. His skin looked extra white in the torch beam. The bloody wounds stood out on his face, as did the soil on his tuxedo.

He turned to the guard and opened his mouth. A gout of wine spilled out like blood. "I... want... to... eat... your... brains!" he croaked, like he was coughing up loose earth.

The security guard let out a high pitched scream. He sounded like a scared little girl. Tatyana had never heard a grown man make a noise like it. He threw his torch at the coffin and ran, full pelt, out of the vestry.

Tatyana waited until the sound of his footsteps faded, before she stepped out of the closet. She was so relieved she was shaking. She started to laugh hysterically as Benjamin grinned at her out of the coffin.

"That is the coolest fucking thing I have ever seen," she said.

Benjamin winked and she almost jumped on him right there. "Do I know how to show a gal a good time, or do I know how to show a gal a good time?" Benjamin climbed out of the coffin and found the guard's torch. "Now we can see to get out of here."

People were starting to head home when they got back to the ball. Gregor, her father's chauffeur, was waiting behind the wheel of the Rolls. He didn't take too kindly to Benjamin when he saw him.

"We better say goodnight here," Tatyana said at the top of the hotel steps.

"Okay," said Benjamin and took both her hands in his.

Shit he wasn't going to try and kiss her was he? Actually, she rather hoped he was.

"Listen," he said. "I had a really good time tonight."

"So did I." She licked her lips to make sure they weren't dry.

"I thought this whole ball was going to be one long drag but you made it really special."

"Thanks, you kinda picked things up for me too." She looked at his lips. They were red with wine and fake blood. She wondered what they'd feel like pressed against hers.

"I'd really like to see you again," he said.

She put her head to one side and moved a little closer.

Come on, what was stopping him? Couldn't he see she wanted to?

"I'd like that too," she said.

Benjamin glanced past her. "I think your driver's coming over."

"Oh yeah, sorry about that," she glanced behind her to see Gregor advancing on them. "He's kind of protective. It's my father's orders."

"He's a lot bigger than me. I better go. Can I get your number?"

"Sure," she fumbled in her purse and dropped it on the steps. Its contents rolled out at her feet. "Shit, sorry," she said as she stuffed them back in. Damn, she felt stupid and clumsy. She found a card and gave it him. "My mobile number. Call me."

"Will do," Benjamin said. He smiled at Gregor and disappeared into the lobby.

"Everything alright Miss Bulgakov?" Gregor asked. She was annoyed by him being there and embarrassed by his heavy Russian accent.

"Yes, yes. I'm fine, just take me home."

Why didn't he kiss me? she thought as she lay back against the hand-stitched leather upholstery of the Rolls. Did her breath smell? Did she do something wrong? Maybe she should change her deodorant. She sniffed discreetly at her pits.

Maybe he was just a gentleman. A walking dead gentleman, now that was a turn up for the books. He had asked for her number though, *and* he'd said he wanted to see her again. She better charge the battery on her mobile.

What if he didn't call? She knew what she was like. She was going to be checking her phone every five minutes now until he did.

What a night though. Who would have thought? The only way it could have been any more perfect was if they *had* kissed. Still that was something to look forward to.

She wondered what she'd tell her mother in the morning.

So dear, did you have a good time last night?

Yes mother I met a charming young Zombie. He had the cutest smile and a butt you could eat your breakfast off. That reminds me, we must have him over for morning coffee. Oh you'll laugh when you hear this, we broke into a graveyard together and terrified a security guard. You must be so glad you paid for all that private education.

She hoped he did call. He was cute and dangerous and he had this lost, sensitive look in his eyes that made her ache when she thought about it.

If they did get it together, he was a keeper. She knew that already. Once they were together she couldn't imagine anything that could come between them.

CHAPTER SEVENTEEN

Palmer had showered, changed and shaved by five am. The guests would all be sleeping off the effects of the night's celebrations.

In a few hours, when they woke, he would have the staff round up all the escorts. Then he'd have them ferried to a sound proof room where Doc Papa would put them into a trance and remove all memory of the last twenty-four hours. This was a precaution against careless guests who let too much slip during pillow talk.

There was nothing like a good orgasm to stir up a loose tongue or prick a conscience. Many high class hookers were as much confessors as they were bed partners. He couldn't have them leaving the island with tales of murder and mutilation playing on their minds.

Doc Papa was already at the runway when Palmer got there. Palmer cursed himself that he'd been beaten on punctuality. Doc Papa looked at him and grinned in satisfaction. That was the unnerving thing about him. He seemed to see the thoughts as they formed right there in your mind.

He took his place at Doc Papa's side as the island's private jet came in to land. The steps were wheeled into place by the ground crew. A hand woven red carpet, trimmed with ermine, was rolled out to meet it.

A meat truck pulled up. The driver opened the doors and a group of miserable specimens trudged out. They wore dreadlocks, nose rings and sou'westers. They had badges pinned to their waterproofs and slogans painted on them. All in all there was about thirty of them.

At a signal from Doc Papa they lined up either side of the carpet and took carving knives out of their pockets. He had them in a trance. They were completely prey to his will.

The sheer power Doc Papa wielded over other humans never failed to excite Palmer. Just being in his company made the most audacious and remarkable things seem possible. Nothing and nobody was an obstacle to him. Everything he said and did was all about enforcing that.

The pathetic, bleeding hearts lining the carpet called themselves environmental activists. They'd been taken in Japanese waters, aboard a boat with the cringe-worthy title of *Sunshine Superman*. They were interfering with international trade by sabotaging whaling ships.

Just because the idiots at the UN had decided to place an international ban on those waters, these contemptible meddlers thought it gave them the right to intervene in the whaler's activities. Hundreds of thousands of dollars worth of trade was being wasted through their actions. All to save some species that was near extinction anyway.

Because they refused to accept the economics of non-renewable resources like the whale, they had been rounded up and taken to St Ignatius. Palmer himself had overseen the operation. Doc Papa was very pleased with the result. He hadn't said what the purpose of extraditing them was, but Palmer knew he had something spectacular in mind to greet the share holders.

The door of the jet opened and the shareholders stepped out.

Doc Papa shook his asson twice and the activists fell to their knees, raised their knives with both hands and held them over their faces. The shareholders didn't descend, but looked on with wry fascination to see what Doc Papa would have them do next.

At another shake of the asson the activists plunged the knives into their left eye sockets. With precision they twisted the knives so they sliced through the cornea and severed the ocular muscles holding the eye in place.

Using their left hands, each activist then reached into their sockets and pulled their eyeball out of its orbit. Blood trickled from the sockets as the activists took the carving knives and sliced through the thin red optic nerves at the back of the eyeball that connected it to the brain.

The activists tossed their severed eyeballs onto the red carpet and repeated the process with their right eye. The shareholders responded with sardonic smiles and a smatter of applause. Doc Papa had rolled out a carpet of human eyeballs to welcome them.

As the shareholders descended the steps Doc Papa shook his asson one last time. The eyeballs started to squirm about of their own accord and arrange themselves into their original pairs.

The activists dropped their knives and started groaning and waving their hands in front of them as though they were trying to ward something off. They were still frozen to the spot but Doc Papa had returned the power of speech and limited movement. Why were they responding like this though?

Then Palmer realised. They could still see out of the severed eyes squirming on the carpet.

The shareholders realised it too as they began to walk over the carpet of eyes. The eyeballs popped with a satisfying, wet squelch when they trod on them. The shareholders ground the vitreous humour into the carpet with their hand-stitched leather shoes.

The activists screamed with pain and fear as their eyeballs were trampled. They implored the shareholders to stop. Calling out for mercy.

"No, don't, please no..."

"Stop, don't, stop please I'm begging you..."

"Oh God, why are you doing this? Dear Lord why?"

It amused Palmer that self professed atheists and pagans always invoked God when they were about to die. They didn't call on the Great Mother or logical reason. Oh no, they all shouted for God without fail. And they all asked why.

If they couldn't see the point Doc Papa was making here then they were beyond tedious explanations. It was simple. They had to be reminded of how powerless they were.

The world was run a certain way by a certain breed of men and there was nothing they could do about it. Palmer and his kind would do whatever they pleased whenever it pleased them and nothing would stand in their way. All these bleeding hearts could do was sit at the sidelines and look on as the ruling elite trampled over them.

In his novel *1984*, George Orwell had said 'if you want a vision of the future, imagine a boot stamping on a human face - forever.' He was partly right. Except it wasn't a boot it was a $4,000 shoe, and it wasn't a face it was an eyeball. A powerless eyeball that could only look up as the shoe came down and ground it into lifeless jelly.

Of course, that wasn't the only point that Doc Papa was making. He was also displaying the full extent of his power to the shareholders. He was letting them know who was fully in charge.

The men trampling the eyes into the ground were the richest and most ruthless operators in the world. They were without mercy or compunction. You never underestimated or turned your back on them and you showed them no weakness at any time.

This was also what Doc Papa was testing with his welcoming stunt. The limits of their cruelty and viciousness. He was probing them to see how far they would go. Whether any of them would show a sign of squeamishness or compassion. Not one of them did.

As the shareholders reached the end of the carpet Doc Papa clapped his hands and the activist keeled over. Having broken their hearts, he now stopped them.

"Impressive," said Walden Truffét, the majority shareholder. "What do you do for an encore?"

"Bring them back to life," said Doc Papa shaking Truffét's hand. Truffét was a portly man with silver hair and large horn rimmed glasses.

"So you got the new recruits primed?" said Frank Evans, a short, stocky man with died black hair and a craggy face.

"Oh yes," said Doc Papa. "All it will take is one little push and they will be right where we want them."

"Well," said O'Shaugnessy, a tall, freckled Irish man. "That's what *we're* here for."

CHAPTER EIGHTEEN

There was a new mood among the guests in the morning. Benjamin could see it in their eyes. The way they moved. The way they greeted one another. All of it was downbeat.

There was something muted in the way they filed into the lecture hall. An air of gloom hung over everyone. The triumph of the night before had been replaced by something a lot like regret. It felt like the bill for the orgy had just come and it looked to bankrupt them all.

No-one made small talk. Everyone avoided eye contact. It wasn't just that they were hung over or tired from their late nights. It seemed like it had suddenly dawned on them, in the unforgiving light of morning, just what they had done the previous day. And, in spite of everything they had been taught, they couldn't shake off the guilt it caused them.

Benjamin felt it too. He couldn't quite face up to what they had done yet. He didn't want to admit to himself that he'd played a part in it. That *he* was the sort of person who could commit such acts. Or force others, like Tatyana, to commit them.

She still wasn't talking to him, not properly. They had conversations and stuff, like what to order for breakfast and which draw she put his spare socks in. But she hadn't opened up to him about what she was feeling.

They were drifting away from each other and there was nothing he could do to stop it. It was like watching some dreadful accident in slow motion. He could see everything that was going to happen but he just couldn't move fast enough to avoid it.

He didn't want to lose her. But he couldn't do anything until she told him what was going on inside her. He was numb from all the fear he ought to be feeling. Fear of losing Tatyana. Fear of being revealed as an outsider. Fear of what he was becoming and having to admit what he'd always been. No wonder he could identify with the gloom that had soured everyone's mood.

You wouldn't know it to look at the guests, but today was supposed to be special. The beginning of the pay off for all their training. There were guest lecturers for the morning and hints of some special ceremony that night. If it was anything like the 'special' surprise they had yesterday, then Benjamin wasn't looking forward to it.

Palmer announced the first lecturer. It was Eamonn O'Shaugnessy. Benjamin was surprised to find even he knew who that was. He was a hero of Richard's and a cult figure on Wall Street. He commanded seven figure sums for public speaking and those appearances that he made were always sold out.

He was tall with sandy brown hair that was greying at the temples. He looked like the sort of guy you'd see hosting an infomercial for the Irish Tourist Board. Benjamin half expected him to raise a pint of Guiness and start singing the praises of the Emerald Isle.

Instead the man shot them a smile that was half lovable patriarch and half man-eating shark.

"Good morning," he said as he took to the podium. "How are you all? I hear there was a good craic last night. Anyone nursing a hangover?" There was no response and he smiled a knowing smile. "No? No-one who cares to admit it anyway. And who could blame you? You're not going to admit a weakness sitting here surrounded by your peers. I can tell by the bloodshot eyes I'm seeing round the room that more than a few you are feeling rough though. And that's not all you're feeling.

"You know what got me ahead in business? Not my ability to read the market. Though that's netted me a billion or more, to be sure. What's really clinched it for me is my ability to read people. To look into the other feller's eyes and see what he's thinking and feeling before even he realises it. That's what's been invaluable to me. That's why I'm standing here now worth more than the lot of you put together.

"Do you want to know what I see when I'm looking at all of you? I see guilt, and I see doubt."

There was a murmur of dissent from the guests. Eamonn raised his hand to still it. "No, no, I do. I know you're less likely to admit to that than being hung over, but it's written on every one of your faces. Once you know what the signs are you can spot it a mile off. Do you know how I know what the signs are? Cos I've been there myself.

"You've just signed over a fortune to be here. And for what? To murder some poor guy? To act like a vicious animal? No – worse, to act like an undead monster. Is that what you came here for? And what if someone finds out? What if word is leaked to the press or the authorities? What will you do then?

"What you're feeling is only natural. You wouldn't be human if you didn't feel a tiny bit of remorse. After what you've just done, anyone would. You're only human. And that's the problem. That's what we're here to rectify.

"You see, the regret you're feeling now, can make you prone to the terrible allure of altruism. But, you have to watch out for that, because it's a trap. You know the first thing you find when you make more money than you can ever spend? It doesn't make you happy. In fact, I'll go farther than that. You find you start to despise money. Because it's worthless. You went to so much time and trouble to make it and then you find it doesn't do a thing for you. And you're right to despise it. It's only when you hate it and you spit on it that it clings to you like a dog that's been kicked and is desperate for your affection. It's why poor people love money so much. Cos you have to hate money if you want to make a serious amount of it.

"But don't mistake this hatred for the source of your unhappiness. Just because it feels good to give your money away doesn't mean you're doing the right thing. And yes, I will admit that building a few schools in some African backwater feels better than building a new wing on your mansion. But doing your secretary over her desk also feels good, and that can get you into a whole heap of trouble with alimony I can tell you."

The guests laughed at this. O'Shaugnessy acknowledged this with a nod of the head and then put on a serious expression. "Don't let your ego get ahead of you. Just because you control more wealth than most first world countries doesn't mean you need to start running them. You might be more competent than the people they voted in, but it's not your affair. If you start handing out cash to people who haven't got the sense or guts to make their own they won't thank you for it.

"At best they'll see you as a big tit that they can suck on any time they need it. At worst they'll start thinking the reason they haven't got any money is not because they're stupid and lazy, but because you stole it all from them in the first place.

"Build them a welfare state and what happens? They stop working. It's the same with philanthropy. It takes away incentive and it turns grown men and women into little children waiting for Daddy to give them a hand out. And all because you were feeling a bit blue and wanted to stroke your own ego.

"Remorse, guilt, regret, it's a slippery road. And it leads to ruin. There is a way to avoid all this though. As I said, it's a natural human failing. The way to get around that is to become more than human.

"'Now how do I do that?' You might be asking yourself? Well now, I'm not the feller to be telling you. So let me give the stage over to our host here on St Ignatius. My esteemed colleague – Doc Papa!"

There was a huge round of applause from the guests. There

was something almost obscene about the way O'Shaugnessy had worked the audience. Playing on their doubts and their prejudices to work them into a frenzy. It had worked though. Boy had it worked. The mood in the room had gone from despondency to eager anticipation.

Doc Papa shook O'Shaugnessy's hand and took the podium. "Thank you Eamonn for those insightful words. You are perfectly right of course, in everything you said. Indeed it does fall to me to reveal one of the most powerful secrets that we guard here on St Ignatius. I am talking about the process of transcending your humanity.

"Before you can achieve that, however, you have to consider what it is that makes you truly human. What is it that hangs a conscience around your neck to keep you down and hold you back from all you could be? I will tell you. It is that most misunderstood of all human commodities – your soul.

"It is your soul that now torments you. That plagues you with remorse even as you take the first steps towards greatness. No matter how hard you try to evade it. Your soul will find a way to retard your development. Do not underestimate its strength or tenacity. It is the one part of you that is immortal and it knows more about you than you yourself know.

"Why do you think there are so many tales of men and women who sell their souls for success? Because that is what it takes to truly succeed.

"Let me draw you an analogy. Consider the gold standard. Until very recently the limits of a country's currency were dictated by the amount of gold in its coffers. The worth of every note its economy issued was controlled by the amount of interest it could raise on its gold reserves. Imagine the summit of man's imagination, the peak of his potential to shape the world in his image, all of it was tied to how much yellow metal he could scratch out of the ground.

"When we abandoned the gold standard we created an unlimited expansion of credit. There was no horizon beyond which we couldn't sail. No end to the territory we could conquer and call our own. The potential for our endeavours was ours to create, and ours alone.

"Western alchemists, were the earliest of what I call 'Econo-mystics.' They searched for the philosopher's stone that would turn base metal into gold. That would breathe life into dead matter. And what was this gold they sought to wring from the meanest substance?

"Why it was the human soul. The soul is the gold standard by which all human endeavour and achievement is measured.

"Once you have abandoned it there is no end to what you can achieve. But that doesn't mean your soul has no value. It is worth more than your success, believe me. As a great philosopher once said 'what does it profit a man to gain the world if he lose his soul?'

"Gold did not lose its value when we suspended the gold standard. Neither will your soul. Countries did not sell off their gold reserves. And you no longer have to sell your soul in order to succeed. You can simply lease it.

"Voodoo teaches that there are two component parts to the soul. The Gros Bon Ange and the Ti Bon Ange. It is the Gros Bon Ange that keeps track of every misdemeanour you commit. When you go to meet your maker and you're judged on whether you can enter paradise, it is your Gros Bon Ange who will argue on your behalf.

"When a person dies, the Gros Bon Ange does not move far from the body. There is a rite that captures the Gros Bon Ange and contains it in a vessel called a Pot-tet. This is essential for passage into the afterlife.

"Through my superior knowledge of Voodoo I have perfected a means of removing the Gros Bon Ange from a person's body before they are even dead. In a unique marriage of science and Voodoo I can lift the main portion of the living soul out a person's body and maintain it in a state of suspended animation until it is ready to be returned to its owner.

"Think of us as a bank where you can safely store what is at once your most valuable possession and your biggest impediment. A bank that allows you to achieve huge success by removing the biggest obstacle from your path.

"Like all banks, you can make withdrawals as well as deposits. Once you've made your billions your soul can be returned to you completely unsullied by everything you've done. Not one of your sins will have touched it. Your Gros Bon Ange will have no knowledge of your crimes and will be as pristine as the day you banked it. All you need do is pay the release fee plus compound interest.

"This is a one-time offer. Tomorrow we begin the Festival of the Gédé, the only time of year when this rite can be performed. Any guests not wishing to participate are free to leave the island now, your deposit will be forfeit however. Are there any questions?"

George Griffin raised his hand. "You mentioned there were two parts to the soul. What happens to the other part, this Ti Bon something?"

"Ti Bon Ange," said Doc Papa. "That's a very good question, thank you. The Ti Bon Ange governs your higher faculties and your capacity to reason. It looks after the mind in other words. It is not bothered by your conscience. This will remain with your body. In fact when it is freed from the shackles of the Gros Bon Ange you will find that the Ti Bon Ange actually sharpens your mental faculties.

"Now, if you're all satisfied we can move on to the paperwork. There are legal disclaimers, NDAs and contracts to be drawn up. These will all have to be signed in blood. Please let the administrators know if that is going to be a problem. There are no more seminars for the day. We'll see you this evening at the celebratory dinner where you'll get a chance to meet the shareholders and the previous course graduates."

Doc Papa left the stage and the guests rushed to sign up. The only people who lagged behind were Benjamin, Tatyana and the African American woman Tatyana was fascinated with, Miriam. Tatyana hadn't said anything specific about her, but Benjamin kept catching her glancing over at the woman. She had something to do with Tatyana's mysterious disappearance a few days ago, Benjamin knew she did.

He was having a hard time working out what was going on with Tatyana. Maybe she had the hots for this Miriam. There would have been a time when that thought would have excited him. Now he just wanted to get a handle on what she was thinking or feeling.

He stood up and turned to Tatyana. "Are you coming?

"Don't hate me. But I don't think I can do this."

"What? But..."

"Please don't Benjamin. I know what you're going to say, okay? We go through this every time. I get worried and you bully me into it so I don't let the cause down. This is different though. This is some seriously heavy shit going down. They're talking about taking our souls away. How scary is that? I mean how much further do we have to go? I'm frightened I'm going to lose myself entirely."

He felt a cold knot of fear in his gut. "Do you want to go home?" he said, praying she would say no.

"I don't know."

"Maybe we could do something. Y'know like switch bloods when we sign. Or write our names wrong, so the documents don't mean anything."

"How would that help?"

"It might. I don't know. Help me out here. At least I'm trying."

Tatyana looked him straight in the eyes. "You are trying aren't you? Bless you for that at least."

"Tatyana, I... I don't..."

"I know. Okay I'll stay. But it has to be tomorrow night. When all the guests are going to the rite we'll sneak away and do it. I don't want any part of losing my soul."

"Sheesh I thought you were an atheist."

"Well maybe you thought wrong. Tomorrow night or I'm gone."

"Okay, tomorrow night it is then. I'll radio the guys to make sure they're ready."

CHAPTER NINETEEN

"Are you sure this is the right corridor?"

"Look you asked me that the last two times and I already told you, I'm not sure," Tatyana was about to blow. "It's got to be one of these three."

"Well it wasn't the last two."

"So it's probably this one. Will you just give it a rest?"

"They've bound to have noticed we've gone by now. They could come looking at any minute."

Tatyana found the service door she was looking for. They headed through into the bare passageway and Benjamin finally shut up. He had no idea how close he'd come to a fist in the face. She shouldn't think like that, but he could be really annoying at times.

She was sweating from all the running. It made her scalp itch. She scratched her freshly cropped hair. She was going to miss her old locks.

They'd lined up all the guests first thing in the morning and cut their hair. Women's down to two inches, men's to an inch. The hair was collected and stuck inside the earthenware containers called Pot-tets where their souls would be kept.

It was really gross and eerie. The guests had to put their toe nails and finger nails into the pot too. They even made everyone spit in the Pot-tet and pee in a jar so they could add that to the mix.

But that wasn't as bad as the poultice they made them wear. They slapped cornmeal, goat dung, chicken blood, feathers, herbs and raw eggs on to their foreheads and wrapped a big white linen bandage round it to hold it in place. They were supposed to leave it on until the ceremony.

Apparently each of these ingredients would feed their Gros Bon Ange and prepare it to leave their bodies through their foreheads. Tatyana didn't know about her soul, but last night's dinner wanted to leave her guts every time she caught a whiff of the stuff.

After that they'd been taken outside in the blazing heat and made to lie down on the floor of a mud hut. They were packed in together and told to lie on their sides, pressed up against each other as though they were spooning.

A creepy looking guy called Vincenzo, who was some sort of assistant priest, came in. He told them to practise their Zombie breathing and still their vital signs. Tatyana was quite glad of this. The heat, the smell and the physical discomfort were unbearable. Zombie breathing was her way of escaping.

As they lay on the floor barely breathing, women who were all dressed in white, entered the hut. A single drum beat out a rhythm as the women sang high wailing songs in what they called Langay. This was some secret African language that the spirits they called the Loa spoke.

Vincenzo shook his rattle in time to the drum and every three hours he clapped his hands. This was a sign that everyone should turn on to their other side.

The purpose of this ceremony, it was explained to them, was to fool their Gros Bon Anges into thinking that they were dying. The songs were from the underworld of the Gédé, the Loa of the dead whose festival it was. They called to the Gros Bon Anges to leave their bodies and return to the afterlife.

It was dark by the time the ceremony finished. Tatyana ached all over but she hardly noticed. She was totally out of it. The breathing, the drumming and the songs had put her into some sort of trance.

They left the hut and went on a procession into the jungle. Tatyana floated along the small dirt track with the other guests. She barely registered the tall trees and the dense undergrowth all around her.

A group of men she hadn't seen before led the procession. They were blowing strange multi-coloured bamboo trumpets. A group of drummers marched in back of them.

They were quite far in when Benjamin grabbed her arm and pulled her into some prickly bushes. She tripped on a vine and thorns tore her skin. Benjamin put his hand over her mouth to stop her crying out.

Tatyana tried to wriggle free of him but Benjamin held her tight. She wanted to carry on with the other guests. To follow them into the dark heart of the lush, tropical landscape. To give over her soul for the secrets the ceremony promised.

As the procession moved on, it's hold on Tatyana faded as the thick ferns and creepers of the jungle swallowed it up. Luckily Benjamin hadn't been so caught up as her. He'd seen a chance to get them out and jumped at it. They traced their steps back through the dense jungle and returned to the mansion.

They had to be super careful getting back in. The apartment complex was crawling with the new arrivals. The previous course graduates who had bored everyone rigid with how rich and successful they now were at the dinner the previous night. Keeping out of their way hadn't been easy.

Once they'd got back to their room they'd both showered and changed into some corpse clothes they'd stolen. Then they'd made their way to the annex on the other side of the mansion and Tatyana had tried to retrace the route she took when she followed Miriam.

At the bottom of the metal steps Tatyana tried to remember

which way they'd gone through the service bay.

Benjamin lit his zippo. "Does this help?"

"Thanks. I think it's over this way."

She was surprised to find that she had less problem finding the compound than she thought. They got to the hi-tech security doors without being seen and Benjamin pulled out the Rolex Andy had fixed up for them.

"Do you think it'll work?" she said as Benjamin hooked it up like Andy had shown him.

"We're fucked if it doesn't. 'Sides, you gotta have faith in the Andy-droid. He's never let us down before."

There was a high-pitched whine followed by a low hum and, with a click, the doors opened.

"We're in," Benjamin said.

They stepped through the doors and dropped into their best Zombie shuffles.

This was the first time they'd ever encountered the noble monsters unsupervised. Tatyana was struggling to keep her heartbeat down and her breathing shallow. She was excited and nervous. This was what all the months of planning had been about. This was the ultimate test of everything she stood for. There was no room for fuck-ups.

It took a little while for their eyes to adjust to the darkness. There was no lighting and they couldn't carry a torch or use a naked flame. Vague shapes loomed out of the darkness making Tatyana's heart race. Most of them turned out to be inanimate objects. All the same it was dangerous to have a high pulse rate.

The plan was to round up the biggest group of Zombies then head round the compound picking up any stragglers. Once they'd gotten all the noble monsters together they were going to head out to the harbour on the south side of the island, where Benjamin had instructed the guys to wait.

The Fourth Rule of Interaction was 'Follow the herd but think ahead of it.' Apparently this would eventually allow them to take control of large groups of Zombies. Sort of like undead sheepdogs was how Tatyana pictured it.

Dr Chen had said that it was only in large groups that Zombies started to exhibit any sort of intelligence. Almost as if they developed a group mind that got cleverer the more of them there were. She and Benjamin figured the bigger the group got, the more conscious they'd be. The more conscious they became, the easier it would be for them to understand that Benjamin and Tatyana were there to help them.

"It's like any revolutionary activity when you think about it," Benjamin said. "The more you raise the consciousness of the masses, who are like the noble monsters, the easier it is to get them together in greater numbers so they can, like, throw off the shackles of their oppressors."

Tatyana nodded because she didn't want another argument. She agreed with the aims and principals of the ZLF, but it always worried her when they started talking about being revolutionary.

Her father had used the 'cause of the glorious revolution' to justify all the things he did for the KGB. She also knew that, deep in his heart, he regretted every one of those things. He took that regret out on Tatyana and her mother. She didn't want Benjamin to end up regretting what he did in the name of being 'revolutionary'. She wasn't going to bear the brunt of that as well.

They lumbered into the main area of the compound at a snail's pace.

Rule Number Two: 'Move in Slow Motion. Keep every movement extremely slow and deliberate'. This gave Tatyana time to scope out the layout.

The compound was mainly scrub land with patches of grass and stretches of sand. Ruined stone buildings, with crumbling walls and no roofs, dotted the area. For the most part the noble monsters just shambled aimlessly around.

It was the middle of the night but there didn't seem to be any change in the noble monsters' behaviour. Tatyana wondered if Zombies ever slept. What would a Zombie dream of if it did?

Over towards one of the electrified fences was a building that looked newly built. It was different from every other structure in the compound. It had a steel roof and its doors and windows were reinforced. Tatyana was quite sure there was something important inside.

Benjamin ambled over to a set of stone steps. They led up to a raised concrete floor that might have been part of a building once. At the top of the steps Benjamin turned and struck a pose like he was Lenin addressing the masses. None of the noble monsters paid him any attention.

So Benjamin raised his fist in a 'Black Power' salute and let out a long, low groan. A few Zombies turned to look at him. Benjamin pointed towards the exit and then raised his fist again. What was he playing at? Did he honestly think he was going to get them to revolt? Who did he think he was, some sort of undead Che Guevara?

Most of the Zombies ignored him. A small number stood and watched him for a moment. They sniffed the air for blood. When they realised there was nothing to feed on they too turned away.

Time to give Benjamin a reality check. Tatyana signalled that she was going to check out the new building and that he ought to follow her. He tried a few more grunts and poses and then admitted defeat. Sadly, the oppressed Zombies just weren't swayed by his revolutionary stance.

Tatyana remembered that one of Benjamin's favourite 'really bad Zombie movies' was *Revolt of the Zombies*. It was a shame for him that he didn't get to play it out in real life, but someone had to get on with the serious business of freeing the noble monsters.

Besides, he'd get over it so long as he remembered Rule Number Three: 'It doesn't matter and you don't care'.

The door to the building was locked. Luckily the lock was electronic. The Rolex Andy had fixed up did the business and got them in.

CHAPTER TWENTY

It didn't smell right.

They'd never been far from the smell of death from the moment they had arrived on the island. Not surprising when you spend all day with walking corpses. But the smell inside the building wasn't like the mortuary smell of the noble monsters. It was much worse. It was like rotting meat mixed with chronic BO.

They walked through into a room that looked like an abattoir. There was a large stone block in the centre that was covered in congealed blood. Two metal drains ran along the floor either side of the block, both caked with dried blood.

Along the wall was a long row of knives and saws, many of which were covered in gore. In the far corner of the room was a pile of sou'westers next to another pile of dungarees and other clothes, a lot of which had badges and slogans painted on them.

"This doesn't feel right," said Benjamin. "We don't have time to go exploring. We need to round up the noble monsters before they come looking for us."

"Wait," Tatyana said. "This is important. There's something here that can help us. I know there is."

They moved into an adjacent room.

"Oh shit," said Benjamin and threw up.

Hanging from two rows of meat hooks in the ceiling were around twenty headless bodies with their hands and feet removed. To one side was a huge plastic container filled with human heads. All of them were missing their brains and the tops of their skulls.

Lined up against the far wall were three meat racks that looked like cages with wheels attached to their bases.

"You okay?" Tatyana said putting a hand on Benjamin's shoulder.

"Yeah, yeah fine. I think it's the smell. Caught me by surprise."

"After everything you've seen and done, *this* makes you puke?"

"Okay, don't go on about it."

"This must be how they feed the Zombies. I don't even want to think about where they get these bodies from."

Tatyana went to examine the cages against the wall. She reached through the bars experimentally.

"Okay we've seen what's inside here," said Benjamin. "Can we get back to rounding up the Zombies? That is what we're here for, in case you'd forgotten."

"This is how we're going to round them up," Tatyana said grabbing a large pole with a hook on the end. "Here, give me a hand getting one of these stiffs down."

The bodies hanging from the ceiling were heavier than they looked. Even with both of them holding the pole it took them four attempts to get one down.

Benjamin staggered backwards and the headless corpse landed on his foot. He yelped and fell on his butt. Tatyana put her hand over her mouth to stop from laughing.

"I'm glad you find this funny," he said.

"I'm sorry," she said trying to look sympathetic. "Here, we've got to get this body into one of those cages."

They lugged the headless corpse over to the cage. With a little effort and a lot of cussing they hung it from the middle bar. Tatyana shut and bolted the cage.

"Try reaching the corpse through the bars," she said. Benjamin stuck his arm through the bars. "You can't can you?"

"So?"

"So we can use it as bait to lure the Zombies. As soon as they smell the body they'll come running. But they won't be able to get at it."

"How's that gonna help us?"

"This cage thing is on wheels. If we keep pushing it round the compound they'll keep chasing it and we can round them all up. It's like the old carrot on a piece of string trick. Except this time it's a rotting corpse."

Benjamin shrugged. "It might work"

"If your Jedi mind powers fail, you mean?"

"There's no need to get snippy."

"You're right. Let's get this out of here. Don't know about you but I'll be glad to get away from this smell."

They pushed the cage with the body in it out of the building and into the compound. The rattling of the bars and the squeak of the wheels caused a few noble monsters to prick up their undead ears.

The stench of the rotting corpse soon began to waft out on the humid night air. Tatyana watched as the noble monsters caught its scent. It was like a transformation. Suddenly they had a purpose.

They stopped ambling and made straight for the corpse. Some of them began to chew in anticipation, grinding their dead teeth together. Others raised their arms and began grasping for the flesh they could smell.

The noble monsters got to the cage and pressed themselves up against the bars. The corpse was out of their reach. They groaned in frustration, pushing stale air up through dead throats.

Benjamin and Tatyana started to move the rack forward as more and more of the living dead joined them. They had to keep turning it to make certain the Zombies didn't crowd round all four sides and stop it moving.

As more Zombies joined the throng Tatyana found herself crushed up against the bars. All around her the walking dead were straining for the corpse that was just out of reach. They jostled her, groaning, flailing and gnashing their rotten teeth.

It took a lot of self control to keep from freaking out. One wrong move from her or Benjamin and the Zombies pressed up against them would realise they were right next to two living bodies and would forget the dead one in the cage.

Rule Number Five: 'Master yourself and nothing can threaten you'.

Tatyana kept up her Zombie breathing. Rule Number One: 'Show no signs of life'. In this situation playing dead was the best way to stay alive.

As more and more Zombies joined the throng something weird started to happen. Tatyana was sure she could sense them all thinking. Not proper thoughts, but they seemed to arrive at some sort of instinctive consensus that got stronger as more of them joined the throng.

The more Tatyana acted like one of them the more she was aware of this group mind at the fringes of her own. If she thought as slowly and deliberately as she was moving, she found she could nudge the group mind in the direction she wanted.

She and Benjamin no longer had to steer the cage around the compound, the whole group just did it by instinct. Noble monsters started joining the group because it was a group, not just because they could smell the corpse.

The more they started acting in unison, the less frantic and purposeless the Zombies seemed. Benjamin and Tatyana were directing them. This was what Rule Number Four meant. They were following the herd but thinking ahead of it. They'd developed to such a degree they could take control of the noble monsters.

Eventually they reached the main gates to the compound. The group stopped. Tatyana willed them to step aside and let Benjamin get to the lock.

There was a slight pause then the Zombies stared to move out of his way. Shuffling a few steps at a time. Making just enough room for Benjamin to squeeze past them. He got away from the group and used the Rolex to unlock the huge security doors.

The gates slid back to reveal a dirt track that wound off into the scrubland surrounding the compound. This was it. The plan was working. They were practically out of there.

"What the fuck? Jesus Christ there's hundreds of them!"

Tatyana glanced up and saw two armed guards standing in front of the open gates. One of them spoke into his radio. "Central, this is Operative 154 come in Central. We have a Code Red security breach in Sector 1. I repeat, we have a Code Red security breach in Sector 1. There's hundreds of the fuckers. Send back up immediately!"

One of the guards raised his weapon and let off a few rounds. His fellow guard stopped the man.

"Are you fucking crazy?" he said. "Do you want to get us both killed? Do you know what they'd do to us if we harmed one of those things?" He turned and spotted Benjamin over by the gate. "Hey you! What the fuck are you playing at?"

"It's just one of the monsters," said the other guard. "What you talking to it for?"

"No it's not. I recognise that kid. He's one of the guests." The guard pointed his weapon at Benjamin. "Hey you, yes you, what the fuck are you playing at? Shut that fucking gate now. I said shut it!"

Benjamin froze. He looked over at Tatyana for help. She had no idea what to do either. The noble monsters were starting to get agitated. Tatyana could feel their group mind starting to fracture and come apart. The guard dropped a bullet into his barrel and aimed at Benjamin. "If you don't shut that gate I will shoot you, now do it!"

Tatyana reacted without thinking. The sight of someone threatening Benjamin's life enraged her. She pushed the cage and sent it careening into the guard.

The cage crashed into the man and sent him sprawling. He let off a shot as he fell. Benjamin screamed with pain and held his shoulder.

Tatyana felt a huge pang of grief. This wasn't happening. Benjamin couldn't be hurt. He couldn't. She ran to him without any thought for her own safety.

As she did, she felt the Zombies' group mind shatter. The noble monsters fell on the guards like a tidal wave.

Tatyana was oblivious to the guards' screams of pain and terror as she reached Benjamin. He was lying on the ground holding a bloody shoulder and whimpering.

Tatyana helped him to his feet.

"He shot me," Benjamin said.

Tatyana removed his hand from his shoulder and inspected the damage. "He just grazed the skin. I think you'll live." Then she threw her arms around him. "Thank God you're alright. Thank God, thank God, thank..." Did she really just thank God?

Benjamin stiffened. Tatyana let go of him. He was shaking. She turned to see what had scared him. Thirty or more of the Zombies were bearing down on them.

They could smell the blood. Tatyana stepped in front of Benjamin to protect him. She tried to do her Zombie breathing. Her heart was beating too fast. She was afraid for their safety. It wasn't working.

She grabbed Benjamin's hand and tried to run for it. They were surrounded. There were too many of them. There was no way through.

They were seconds away from being torn apart. Tatyana gripped Benjamin's hand. "I love you. You're a dickhead, but I love you."

She closed her eyes but she couldn't hold back the tears. She didn't want to die. *Oh God please don't make it hurt.* She was sorry for everything. She was so fucking sorry.

She felt a dead hand grip her arm. *Will I come back as one of them?* she thought. She pulled herself loose and buried her face in Benjamin's chest.

This was it. This was the end. This was...

"Rete," someone shouted. "Dans le nom de Baron Samedi rete!"

Tatyana clung to Benjamin. She waited for the teeth and the

clawing fingers and the dead bodies to overwhelm her. But they never came.

She opened her eyes. The Zombies weren't moving. They were standing dead still.

"What's going on?" Tatyana said.

"I don't know," said Benjamin. "They just kinda stopped after that woman shouted something."

"What woman?"

The Zombies began to shuffle. Some to the left, others to the right until they formed a small path down the middle.

Walking towards them along the path, Tatyana was astonished to see Miriam Chevalier.

CHAPTER TWENTY-ONE

"Just what do you think you're doing?" Miriam said.

"We were... err, trying to free the noble monsters," Benjamin said.

Miriam looked puzzled. "You were trying to free what?"

"He means the Zombies." Tatyana said.

Miriam threw back her head and laughed. "Noble monsters, is that what you call these poor creatures? After all the time you've spent with them, seeing what they've become. Do you honestly think they're noble?"

"Well no, not when you put it like that," said Benjamin. "But you don't understand. It's not what they've become it's what they represent, they..."

"Be quiet," said Miriam. She turned to Tatyana. "You haven't answered my question. What do you think you're doing?"

"We were trying to free them. Like Benjamin said."

"Free them? You mean you were just going to let them loose on this island. Do you have any idea how stupid that is?"

"No. We have a plan. We were going to guide them to the other side of the island. We've got a boat, I mean a yacht, waiting offshore. A big one, it's a hundred foot."

"Two hundred foot," said Benjamin.

"And what were you going to do with them once you got them aboard this boat?"

"We were, erm, going to set them free in the wild, I think," said Tatyana. "Somewhere where they couldn't do any harm."

Miriam shook her head in disbelief. "You mean you were going to let most of them rot away to nothing. And those that did survive would have attacked innocent people."

"Look we weren't trying to do anything bad," Benjamin said. "You don't mean to tell me you think they should be locked up like this and exploited by these people? And what are you doing here anyway? Aren't you supposed to be at that ceremony with the rest of them?"

"That ceremony is a blasphemy and a perversion of Voodoo. I wouldn't have anything to do with it. And to answer your other question, no I don't think these victims should be locked up and exploited like this."

"Whoa, victims, that's a pretty harsh word," said Tatyana staring at the motionless Zombies. "What did you do to them? Those words that you shouted, that was some kind of spell right?"

"That's one way of describing it. I have stilled what Doc Papa calls their 'perfect hunger'. You are safe around them for the time being, but it is only temporary. You mentioned you have a yacht. Does it have a crew?"

"Yes it does and I've told them to meet us at the little harbour on the other side of the island. It's about five miles south west of here."

"I know where it is," said Miriam. "Ultimately, these victims cannot leave the island and I won't allow you to release them elsewhere. In the short term however, I think it would be useful to remove them from harm's way. I'll let you take them on board the yacht for a brief period."

"Wait a minute," said Benjamin. "We don't even know who

you are and suddenly you turn up, start giving orders and try to take over our mission. Why the hell should we listen to you?"

"Do you want me to leave and let these poor wretches tear you apart?"

"No," said Tatyana. "We don't want that. I'm sorry, we seem to have gotten off on the wrong foot. We're very grateful that you saved us and I think we want the same things. Maybe we can work together on this?"

"I'm prepared to let you come along on a temporary basis. So long as you do exactly as I tell you."

"Well that's mighty big of you," said Benjamin.

"Shut up," said Tatyana. "What he means is, just let us know how we can help."

Miriam nodded and turned away from them. She clicked her fingers and the Zombies began to follow her down the dirt track.

"What are you taking her side for?" said Benjamin. "And why did you tell me to shut up?"

"Because you were being a dick," Tatyana said. "C'mon they're going to leave us behind."

"You mean you're just going to follow her?"

"Well duh."

"How do we know she's not in league with Doc Papa? What if she's leading us straight into a trap?"

"Benjamin she's not leading us into a trap. She saved our lives. You heard how she speaks about the people that run this place. She doesn't like them anymore than we do and she cares about these Zombies."

"So she says. But she called them victims. They're not victims."

"They're being exploited and locked up. How are they not victims?"

"Well okay, they're victims of exploitation. But she's making out like it's a bad thing that they're noble monsters. You heard how she spoke about them. I just don't trust her."

"You know, I can hear every word you're saying," said Miriam. "For your own safety you should stay with me here at the front."

Tatyana started walking to catch her up. Benjamin stayed where he was. She turned and gave him a look. He stuck his hands in his pockets and skulked after them.

"Wait you're going the wrong way," said Benjamin, after five minutes of silence. "This isn't the road. I memorised the map."

"The one in the foyer?" said Miriam. "That's not a map. That's a pretty picture for tourists."

"So I suppose you know better?"

"I ought to. I've lived here most of my life."

Tatyana was stunned. "I thought this was a private island. I didn't know anyone still lived here."

"St Ignatius has been inhabited for as long as Haiti. Where do you think all these Zombies came from? How do you think they got here?"

Tatyana was stunned. "You mean all these Zombies..."

"Are my brothers and sisters, aunts and uncles, friends and lovers. They're the people I grew up with. The people I have sworn, as a holy duty, to protect."

CHAPTER TWENTY-TWO

The guests were right where Doc Papa wanted them. They lay prone on the floor of the Peristyle, the holy space where the ceremony was conducted. Their souls were banked in the Pot-tets. The drummers beat on the stretched skins of their Asòtòs. The rhythms kept the guests in their deep trance. They also kept his acolytes in a heightened state of consciousness.

They mirrored the pulse of the ancient energy lines that flowed down the Poteau Mitan in the centre of the temple. Drawn from the invisible world, these lines spread out across the Ounfó like a snare. A net to capture the souls of the world's richest people. With the blessing of the Loa his Ounfó would become a temple to the economic dominance of the world.

The ceremony was past its peak. All that remained was to seal the Pot-tet with their Bakas. This sacred talisman trapped the Gross Bon Ange in the Pot-tets and stopped it from returning to the invisible world where the Loa dwelt. This was where the Gros Bon Ange had come from and where it wanted to return.

The symbols of the Baka were carved onto pieces of ivory and stained with the blood of a particular guest. They were magically designed to hold each guest's Gros Bon Ange captive and to stop them leaving the earthly plane.

Once they were on the containers the deal was ratified and they belonged to Doc Papa. The guests didn't realise that yet, but they would soon enough.

There was a cryogenics centre built out back of the temple. With the Gros Bon Anges imprisoned, the Pot-tets would be taken there and deep frozen. They were the only truly recession-proof assets Doc Papa had ever encountered. Because they were the true source of value in the world.

As the beat of the drums reached the right pitch, Doc Papa raised the sacred rattle that signified his office as Houngan. Dark energies crackled down the Poteau Mitan and moved through his body, filling the rattle like a malevolent beacon.

Doc Papa's body shook with the transference of this energy as though hit by lightning. He could feel the awe this inspired in his acolytes every time he performed the act. Then he shook the Asson over the Bakas and let the energy leap out of it and infuse them all. Empowering each one with the dark blessing of the Loa.

Something was wrong.

As the last of the dark energy moved from him into the Bakas Doc Papa felt a presence at the outskirts of the Peristyle. A presence that shouldn't be there.

He looked across the space and saw Tomlinson, the Commander of the Armed Guards. What was he doing here? Doc Papa didn't bother hiding his fury. He turned to Vincenzo, and signalled for him to gather up the Bakas and place them on the Pot-tets arranged on the stone altar.

Tomlinson was a big man and heavily armed but Doc Papa could see him shaking as he approached. Doc Papa pointed to the door to the courtyard and Tomlinson followed him. As soon as they were through Tomlinson knelt.

"Sir. I apologise for the interruption. I know it's unwarranted but we've had a Code Red security breach."

"What?"

"The Zombies, they've escaped and killed two of my men."

"How did this happen?"

"I don't know yet sir," Tomlinson un-holstered his pistol and offered it to Doc Papa. "I take full responsibility."

"Put that away you idiot. If I wanted to kill you I have far better means. And don't think you'll get off that lightly if I do. Where are they now?"

"They're heading south towards the coast. We've got a chopper following them. We also have reports of a vessel off the southern coast."

"Do not move from this spot until I tell you," said Doc Papa. Tomlinson saluted and bowed. Doc Papa left him and returned to the Peristyle.

He took Vincenzo to one side. "There are matters that need my attention. You will have to finish conducting the ceremony. If anything goes wrong I will hold you entirely responsible. Do you understand?" Vincenzo nodded. Doc Papa could see that he was fearful yet surprised.

Doc Papa didn't bother to explain. He left Vincenzo and had Felippe, the largest of his acolytes, accompany him and Tomlinson to his jeep.

The jeep pulled up at the edge of a rise overlooking the harbour. Doc Papa and Felippe got out. He told the guards with them to lift down the two sheep he'd brought. He and Felippe led the animals away and left the guards with the jeep.

The chopper following the group of Zombies had given them continual updates on the group's position as they'd driven over. Doc Papa didn't need to be told where they were going though. He gave the guards precise orders where to head.

There was only one natural harbour on the island. A vessel had been spotted. The Zombies must be heading for it. They couldn't be acting alone. Someone was guiding them.

Someone was trying to steal his second biggest asset. Three of the guests were missing. He'd despatched guards to find them as soon as their absence was spotted. Now he knew where they'd gone.

He didn't know whose pay they were in but they would suffer as they told him. No-one tried to take what was his. He was going to send a message. Written in blood on their broken bodies.

There was a tiny beach below. A large promontory hid it from the harbour. They took the sheep down the steep path. This was the very beach where Doc Papa's body had washed up several years ago. It had significance for him. Therefore it had power.

He tethered the sheep to a tree at the edge of the beach. Their eyes were tinged with green and this was why he had chosen them. They were the perfect offering.

Doc Papa removed the knife from his belt. He took hold of the first sheep by its horns and said a prayer to Saint Ulrich, known as Agwe in Voodoo, sovereign Loa of the sea.

When the prayer was done he slit the sheep's throats and caught the blood in two white cups, Agwe's favourite colour. He then slit the sheep's stomachs, cracked open their chests and removed their hearts.

Felippe placed a miniature flat bottomed boat on the ground and Doc Papa placed both the hearts in it. Felippe added gunpowder, dried fish, white chocolate, a bottle of champagne and one cup of sheep's blood.

Doc Papa drank the other cup. Then he took a handful of corn flour and, letting it trickle through his fingers in a steady stream, drew Agwe's Vévé around the boat. When this was done he lit an oil lamp in a white cup and placed that on the boat as Felippe started to beat on a drum.

Doc Papa spoke an invocation to Agwe. Then he raised a conch shell to his lips and blew. He placed the boat on to his head and began to wade, with great care, into the sea.

He drew one last breath as the sea covered his head. The boat floated away. Doc Papa watched it from below as the waves carried it. It sailed some distance and then sank. This showed it had been accepted and the ceremony was a success.

He felt something grip his legs and begin to shake him. It enclosed his body and squeezed the air out of his lungs. His body sank to the floor like a discarded skin as he was lifted out of it.

It was Agwe. The Loa had come in his most vengeful form. He was the crushing bleakness of the ocean floor, where no light ever shines. He was the boiling anger of the storm that capsizes stricken ships. He was the decimating force of the tidal wave, destroying coastal dwellings.

Though Doc Papa left his body Agwe didn't take it over and ride him. Instead Doc Papa mounted Agwe and rode him like the foam on the crest of a wave. Doc Papa's spirit skimmed along the surface with Agwe, as Felippe waded into the sea and pulled his body back to the shore.

Agwe took him to the yacht that was pulling into the harbour. There were four people aboard – a woman and three men, all in their early twenties. Borrowing the energy of the Loa, Doc Papa explored the yacht in his incorporeal form. He also explored the occupants.

One in particular caught his attention. He was a little younger than the others, but his mental faculties were far more developed. That was his weakness.

There was a huge imbalance in his psychic energy. A disproportionate amount was invested in certain cognitive functions. This placed him far above most normal intellects, at the expense of other aspects of his consciousness, namely his emotional and spiritual sides.

As his reasoning and intelligence had grown and blossomed, the other aspects of his conscious had withered on the vine. This was like an open door to Doc Papa. He had none of the usual defences an average person has. Nothing stood in his way as Doc Papa moved into the young man's mind.

Andy was his name. Doc Papa began to pick over his memories as he seeped into the young man's mind and took control. Andy was so lacking in self awareness that he didn't notice he was being possessed. Way past the point when a normal individual would have noticed something was amiss and tried to fight it, he was still unaware. It was a *fait accompli*.

His memories were not like other people's. Anything to do with feelings or empathy was repressed or discarded due to his inability to process it. Instead there was an endless array of facts and raw data, more than the average mind could hold.

Doc Papa found it overwhelming at first. With a little methodical sifting however, he found what he needed. It surprised him.

His estimation of the situation was wrong. These four were not in the employ of any rival. They, and two of the missing guests, were part of some guerrilla organisation. They viewed the theft of his property as some sort of political act.

How truly pathetic. They seriously thought the corpses he had animated were some sort of noble monstrosity. Never in his life had Doc Papa seen a more miserable and ridiculous attempt at subversion.

They were about to see the error of their ways. They wouldn't enjoy it. But he would.

CHAPTER TWENTY-THREE

"Andy, have you seen Klaus anywhere?" It was the one called Dan clattering down the stairs to the engine room. "That engine is sounding seriously unhealthy, are you sure you know what's up with it?"

Doc Papa met him at the bottom of the stairs. "Oh yes," he said through Andy's mouth. "I know exactly why it's making that noise. Come and see."

Dan followed him without a second thought. He was looking at the camcorder he carried everywhere.

None of the others aboard the boat suspected a thing. They were used to Andy acting in a weird manner. They didn't notice any of the tell-tale signs of possession. The vacant stare, the hollow voice, the weird movements, that was just business as usual for Andy as far as they were concerned. It was too perfect.

"We're supposed to be docking now," said Dan. "They're gonna be waiting for us. It won't be cool if we just leave them hanging. Was Klaus any use to you or did he just get in the way?"

Doc Papa led him round the corner and showed him Klaus. "Actually," he said. "Klaus proved to be very useful. I learned a lot."

Dan reacted exactly as Doc Papa hoped he would. He was appalled and nearly hysterical with grief. It was good to have his work appreciated.

Dan dropped the camcorder, fell to his knees and vomited. Doc Papa was very pleased. He couldn't help but admire his handiwork It hadn't been easy with Andy's puny frame, even though Klaus wasn't very big himself.

Klaus was stretched out like a dissected frog. His feet had been nailed to the floor and his hands were nailed to a low ceiling beam above the engine. There was a bloody hole in his throat where Doc Papa had removed his vocal chords. He hadn't wanted Klaus's screams to alert the others.

He'd needed information from Klaus, but it wasn't necessary for him to talk. Doc Papa had found other ways to interrogate him. Ways he was rather proud of, even though he'd had to improvise.

Klaus's stomach was slit wide open. Doc Papa had removed his intestinal tract and tied it to the propeller shaft. As the propeller spun it had tugged Klaus's innards from his body.

While Klaus twitched and writhed in pain and tried to scream out of the bubbling, red hole in his throat, his life had flashed before his eyes. Doc Papa had watched with him. Lifting the succession of memories, like a thin film, from Klaus's mind.

It was surprising how total someone's recall was at the point of death. The whole of Klaus's pointless little life was laid bare. Doc Papa saw his lawyer parents neglect him in favour of their careers, packing him off to boarding school at the first opportunity. He witnessed the older boys punch and taunt him relentlessly for being scrawny with a big nose. He watched what the games master did in the showers when he kept Klaus behind after the lesson.

Doc Papa sneered as Klaus built the brittle facade of his character to protect himself from the betrayals and injustice he'd suffered. He sighed with boredom as the anger Klaus felt at his school and his parents became a general anger at authority and the state. He knew this anger was really fear. The fear of a little boy, who never got over being bullied, dressed up in left-wing rhetoric.

Doc Papa brought this fear to perfect fruition in the last moments of Klaus's life. As the last memory faded and the breath slipped from Klaus's body, Doc Papa let him know that all his fears had come true.

He was dying at the hands of everything he hated most. The corrupt capitalist system had finally come and tortured him to death. Just as he always feared it would.

Doc Papa had also learned everything he needed to know about the ZLF and their pitiable attempt at direct action. Benjamin and Tatyana were the ringleaders. He had been wary of them, for reasons he couldn't explain, since the first background check. Now he knew why.

Miriam Chevalier was still a mystery to him. Why was she helping them? Did they have something over her? There was nothing in her background to explain it.

Doc Papa would find out soon enough. Just as soon as he had destroyed this yacht and killed its occupants. He flooded the fuel tanks and reached for a lighter.

Dan was still crawling around on all fours in front of Klaus, vomiting and weeping.

"Jesus Christ Andy," he said. "Why? I mean Klaus was a pain in the ass but he didn't deserve this. No-one deserves this."

Doc Papa picked up a shovel with Andy's hands.

"Wait Andy, wait," said Dan. "I don't want to die. I want to see my child grow up. What the fuck are you playing at?"

"Call it a counter revolution," said Doc Papa as he split Dan's head open.

CHAPTER TWENTY-FOUR

What the fuck was happening?

Benjamin had been standing on the shore for nearly two hours now. There was a big black stealth chopper circling overhead and an army of guards likely to turn up any minute.

The yacht was only a small distance from the shore. They could see it clearly but it hadn't moved an inch since they got to the harbour.

"Can Zombies swim?" he asked Miriam.

She sighed and rolled her eyes. What the fuck was her problem? What had he ever done to her? She said the noble monsters were her fellow islanders and she wanted to help them. Well who rescued them from the compound? He did. So why was she giving him such a hard time?

"Could we send out a flare?" said Tatyana. "Or light a fire?"

"Have you got a flare?" said Benjamin. "Cos I haven't. Or any wood for that matter and, in case you've forgotten, Zombies are afraid of fire."

"I'm only trying to help. I don't see you coming up with any ideas. We need to find some way to talk with the guys on the yacht. Why didn't you think to bring the radio Andy made?"

"Where was I supposed to carry it? Up my ass?"

A couple of the Zombies near them started to get restless.

"Stop arguing," said Miriam. "It makes them harder to control. You must remain calm at all times."

"Oh yeah," said Benjamin. "Like the First Rule of Interaction. 'Show no signs of life'."

"If you want to put it that way," said Miriam, turning away from him. What, was it her time of the month or something?

"Seriously though," said Tatyana, taking shallow breaths and hardly moving. "We need to get in contact with them. Do you think they can see we're here from the deck?"

"I don't know," said Benjamin, trying to sound as emotionless as possible. He had a sudden flash of Richard and his Mom when they were really pissed at each other but were trying not to argue in front of him. This must be what they felt like. "Maybe they can't see us cos it's dark. I can't understand why they've just stopped."

Benjamin stared at the yacht. It was Richard's pride and joy. When Benjamin was younger Richard had dragged him and his Mom away on trips several times a year.

Benjamin could remember standing in the marina with his Mom watching the yacht come in, willing it not to arrive. Trying to put off the moment when he'd have to get on board and watch Richard strut about and play captain. Benjamin was expected to act as an unpaid crew member which meant Richard got to order him around the whole time.

Now, in a complete reversal he was standing on the shore willing the yacht to come in. Willing it to move or at least do something other than sit there dead in the water.

Then it exploded.

A giant ball of fire burst out of the stern of the yacht tearing it into a thousand flaming fragments. Benjamin could feel the heat of the explosion from the shore. The noise was deafening. He felt a stabbing pain in his inner ear.

The front of the yacht keeled over into the water and started to sink. Burning debris rained down, sending the Zombies into a panic.

Oh shit! What was Richard going to say? Benjamin was a dead man if he ever got out of this alive.

Miriam began chanting in a weird voice to subdue the Zombies. She was having a hard time of it with flaming chunks of yacht falling all around them.

Benjamin felt numb with shock. Then he saw something moving across the water away from the yacht. Someone had gotten away on one of the jet skis. It was Tweakie. Thank God she was alright. Maybe the others had got out too. She was charging across the water at full throttle. As she came into view Benjamin could see she was terrified. He'd never seen Tweakie so scared before.

He waded into the water to get her attention. Before he could shout to her, Tweakie hit a wave and took off into the air. She lost control of the jet ski and it flipped right over, smashing into her in mid air.

It hit the water upside down and sank. So did Tweakie.

This wasn't happening. They couldn't be dead. They just couldn't.

Benjamin started wading into the sea. He was going to swim out and pull them free. All four of them. They weren't going to die on his watch. No sir.

Tatyana grabbed him. She tried to pull him back to the shore. He shrugged her off and kept on going. But she wouldn't let up.

"Let me go," he said. "I've got to go save them. Let me go."

"You're not thinking straight. You're not going to save them. You're going to kill yourself."

"Get off of me. I can save them. I can!"

"They're dead Benjamin, dead. You can't save them!"

She was crying. Benjamin realised he was too. Great heaving sobs of grief broke out of him and he hugged Tatyana tight. They were quite far out and the waves were knocking them back and forth. They turned and struggled back to the shore.

"Stay in the sea," Miriam shouted. "You're safer there. They won't follow you in."

The Zombies still weren't under control. They were highly agitated. Some looked seriously dangerous, like cornered beasts, ready to spring.

The sea was cold and Benjamin was only wearing a dead man's shirt and slacks. The salt water stung his shoulder wound. His feet were numb and so were his nuts. He and Tatyana started to shiver. Even so there was no way either of them were going to leave the water and face the Zombies right now.

The chopper moved out over the water to where the yacht had sunk then headed inland. This almost seemed like a signal. All the debris had stopped burning and Miriam's incantation began to work. The Zombies became quiet and subdued again.

Benjamin's teeth were chattering as he waded back to the shore. There was a real chill in the night wind. He and Tatyana clung on to each other not just for warmth, but also out of fear and grief. The two things that united them most at that moment.

There was a sudden burst of gunfire followed by controlled jets of flame from two flame throwers. A squadron of armed guards came into view. They were surrounded. The Zombies started flailing and groaning again.

"Do not attempt to move," a voice called out through a megaphone. "We're authorised to use extreme force. We know there's three of you trying to steal the Zombies. Lie face down on the ground and do not move until we've rounded them all up."

"Steal the Zombies?" said Benjamin. "Do you believe these guys?"

"Be quiet and do as they say," said Miriam.

Benjamin turned to argue with her but he couldn't find her. He kept looking at where she ought to be but he couldn't see her. It felt as though his sight kept being pushed to one side.

Tatyana grabbed him and pulled him to the ground.

"Hey," he complained, but she pushed his head down. Miriam started chanting something in the strange language of the spirits.

"Hey, they're all moving," said a voice.

"Hold your fire," said another. "They're coming peacefully."

"What is this?" said someone else. "They ain't attacking or

nothing? Look at them, they're just walking."

"Is it a trap?"

"Nah, it's gotta be somethin' the boss man's done. That's Voodoo that is. He's hexed 'em or somethin'."

"Well I ain't gonna complain. Last thing I want is to tussle with a flesh eater."

Benjamin glanced around him. The Zombies weren't moving. They were all standing still or rocking from side to side.

"I don't see anyone in among the Zombies either."

"They must've run off and ditched them. Thought I heard something in the water."

"Or maybe the Zombies got out by themselves."

"Could be."

Benjamin listened as the footsteps of the guards receded. He got to his feet and helped Tatyana up.

"Was that you?" Tatyana said to Miriam. "Did you do that?"

"It was a simple illusion to get them out the way," Miriam said. "It won't hold for long though. And if they run into anyone else it will be broken. We need to get out of here."

"Where are we going to go?" said Tatyana. "We can't get off the island now."

"Do you know where this Voodoo temple is?" said Benjamin. "The one where they're doing the ceremony?"

"The *Ounfó*," said Miriam. "Of course I do. But we can't go there."

"Why not? It's the last place they'll expect us to go. Which means we'll have the element of surprise."

"Yeah," said Tatyana. "But aren't we trying to escape them? I mean, why would we want to go to the one place where the most people are gathered?"

"Cos it'll scare the shit out of them," said Benjamin. "Think about it, most of them are in a big daze from the ceremony. Now imagine a great horde of blood thirsty Zombies suddenly appearing out of nowhere, with no cages to hold them in and no encounter leaders to help them out. Everyone's going to freak out. There'll be panic and confusion. No-one will know what's going on."

"Okay," said Tatyana. "I guess that'll give a temporary advantage. But what about afterwards? What happens then?"

"Well no-one's going to hang around in the temple are they? Not with an army of Zombies milling around. So we'll have it to ourselves. It's right in the middle of the island right, surrounded by jungle so it's going to be really hard to get troops in to attack the place. They won't be able to track us in the chopper cos the vegetation's too dense. And... wait I've just realised, that's where all the souls are kept right?"

"Right."

"So aren't they like the most valuable things on the island? If we're occupying the Ounfó, we can hold them to ransom. We'll have something to bargain with. Maybe enough to get us off the island."

"Do you know," said Miriam. "That is the first and only intelligent thing I've heard you say. Come, let's go."

With that she turned and led the Zombies away from the shore. Benjamin wasn't certain whether she was being complimentary or if she'd just insulted him again.

Tatyana held his hand. "Well done," she said. "You're not such a dickhead after all."

"What the fuck is her problem?"

"I don't know," said Tatyana, smiling at him. "It's dark y'know. Maybe she hasn't seen how cute you are yet."

Now it was his turn to smile. "Thanks. We better catch her up. We've still got a ways to go."

CHAPTER TWENTY-FIVE

Doc Papa had swallowed a lot of salt water. He coughed and wretched it up onto the sand while Felippe stood guard to make sure no-one saw.

He was pleased with his work on the yacht. Though he was aware that he now owed Agwe a great favour. He owed many of the Loa. Like an entrepreneur notching up debts as he builds an empire, Doc Papa had promised much to a whole pantheon of Loa. More than any Houngan could ever pay back in a normal lifetime. When his plans came to fruition however, he would more than wipe the slate clean.

Felippe handed him a bottle of water. He rinsed his mouth and spat. He composed himself and returned to the jeep. Tomlinson looked worried. "I'm afraid there's another problem sir." he said.

"I've just finished sorting out your last problem. What's happened now?"

"It's the Zombies sir, they've... well they've disappeared."

"Disappeared! What do you mean?"

"The men rounded them up from the harbour as you ordered. But as they were escorting them back to base they vanished. One minute they could see them all. The next minute they couldn't. I don't understand it myself."

"That's because you're an idiot. What about the three rogue guests. Do you have them in custody?"

"No sir."

Doc Papa bristled. Tomlinson fought to keep his composure in front of his men. "The men never apprehended the guests. They weren't there when they recaptured the Zombies. They reported some commotion in the water as they arrived. They assumed the guests had deserted the Zombies and tried to swim for the yacht. I imagine they were killed when it exploded."

"You don't have any imagination. And your assumption is almost as stupid as your men's. Has the chopper been able to locate them?"

"No sir, I've had it circling the area but I haven't heard anything yet."

Doc Papa turned away from the idiot. He let his mind roam out into the invisible world, tracing the paths of the spirits and the demons.

"Sir, if I could just..." Tomlinson said behind him.

Doc Papa raised his hand to silence the man.

"But sir..." Tomlinson persisted.

Doc Papa brought his thumb and middle finger together and Tomlinson's wind pipe constricted. As Tomlinson choked with his hands to his throat, Doc Papa let his mind roam once again.

Out in the jungles, where the spirits of the trees and the demons of the hunt roamed free, he found a collective Zombie mind. It was a strong one. He had never encountered one so united. There were almost traces of innate intelligence in it. No wait, there was more. There was a human mind guiding them, one that knew Voodoo.

So that's why they hadn't been spotted. They were hiding in the jungle. But who was controlling them? Doc Papa edged closer to the Zombies' group mind, homing in on their guide. Before he could get any closer he was out. The mind he had been looking for had detected him and pushed him away.

He tried to find them again but he couldn't get anywhere near. Whoever was controlling them was obviously skilled and powerful. But who were they? It couldn't be either of the trust fund babies. They were too young and feckless and there was nothing in their backgrounds to suggest they'd had any exposure to Voodoo.

It had to be the Chevalier woman. Her husband's family originally came from St Ignatius, but he was in real estate and her family were Catholics. Could she have been secretly trained? Surely he would have detected it if she had. Why had she come here. What was she doing with the undead?

Doc Papa slipped out of the invisible world and released Tomlinson from the choking spell. He waited while the man gasped for air and regained his composure.

"The Zombies are in the jungle," Doc Papa said. "They're staying away from the paths and are hidden by the undergrowth. That's why the chopper didn't spot them. Your men never captured them. They were most likely taken in by an illusion."

"But who's doing this sir? My men claim the three guests weren't with them. You're not suggesting they're acting by themselves?"

"Don't embarrass yourself more than you already have. Of course one of the guests is controlling them. Your men didn't see them because that was all part of the illusion. One of the guests is skilled in the service of the Loa."

"I'm sorry sir?"

"They know Voodoo you fool and somehow they managed to evade my detection."

"I'll send every available guard into the jungle to round the Zombies up sir."

"To be honest, I'm more worried about the guests. I need them under strict control. Send a squadron of your men into the jungle to track down the Zombies. I'll aid them through invisible means a little later. In the meantime I want all available men posted to the harbour, the air field and the guest's quarters. I don't want anyone getting off this island. The whole of St Ignatius is on lockdown. Do you understand?"

"Perfectly sir."

"Do not let me down again Tomlinson. This is your very last opportunity to get off this island alive. Am I making myself clear?"

"Crystal sir."

"Good."

CHAPTER TWENTY-SIX

Benjamin had a fucking hard on. This was the ultimate. This was what it was all about. He had never been so pumped in his life.

This was everything he'd been fantasising about since he first saw *Dawn of the Dead*. He was turning up with a whole posse of noble monsters to crash a party stuffed full of the type of dead-eyed phonies and snobs his step father hung out with. He was about to tear down the whole stifling world he'd grown up in.

Every fantasy he'd ever had about letting a horde of Zombies loose among the privileged elite was about to come true. Let's see who didn't fit in now. He couldn't believe his luck. This was real payback.

The Ounfó, as Miriam called the temple, was in sight. The sound of the drums was furious. It helped to cover the noise they were making as they approached.

"What are we waiting for?" Benjamin said. "Let's charge the place."

"Wait," said Miriam. "We have to do this carefully. I don't want anyone to get hurt."

"Why'd you care about not hurting these people? You've seen what they're capable of."

"And I've also seen what you're capable of in their company."

"Oh come on, that's totally different. That's not me. I only did those things to infiltrate them. I'm not part of their world."

"How can you afford to come here if you're not part of their world?" said Miriam. She really knew how to kill his buzz.

He turned to Tatyana. "Tell her. Tell her I'm not like them."

"It's cos you're *not* like them that you *won't* want anyone to get hurt," said Tatyana. "It's only when you try and fit in with them that you're not yourself. When you're not with them you puke at the sight of corpses, you don't try and make more."

The two of them were determined to bring him down. His stomach turned over at the thought of the corpses hanging in the compound. He thought about the things he'd done to blend in with the guests and he felt a stab of anger and hatred.

He wanted to punish them for what they'd made him become. His whole life they'd been trying to turn him into someone he wasn't. On this island they'd finally succeeded.

He imagined charging into the place with the Zombies, locking the doors and letting them feed. He remembered all the horrific things he'd seen the Zombies do while on the island. Then he pictured the guests suffering at their undead hands.

He saw Richard in the midst of his fantasy, trapped with all the other guests. He lingered on Richard's face as the Zombies struck and wiped the smugness and superiority off it for good.

Then he imagined his mother next to Richard. He thought of the terror and pain that would be on her face. He felt a pang of raw emotion at the thought of his mother in peril. He wanted to protect her at all costs. He wanted to kill anything that came near her. He hated anything that would hurt her. He hated... he...

Surely not, he didn't... he couldn't hate... For a minute there he had though. He had *hated* the Zombies. When he thought of what they might do to someone he loved he saw them as monsters. Pure killing machines with nothing noble about them.

Miriam turned and looked him straight in the eyes. "You are carrying too much pain and hatred inside you," she said. "The weight of it is bruising your soul. I sense you are close to realising this. Let that pain go."

That pain had defined him. His hatred and his anger had fed him, given him strength. If he let them go then he wouldn't be himself. Who would he be?

"Look there isn't time for this," he said. "We've got to get these nobl... I mean these undead to safety."

"It is not for you or I to decide the appropriate time," she said. "That is God's prerogative. He has instructed His Loa and they move through me. Give me your hands."

He held out his hands and Miriam took them in her own. Her hands were warm and soft and pulsed with energy.

"It's okay," she said and smiled.

God she had a beautiful smile. He could forgive her anything when she smiled like that. All the put downs and the ball busting, everything.

She chanted soft words in Creole that sounded like music being poured out of a crystal container. He heard a name repeated over and over – Erzulie Dantò. He focused on the name and it seemed to resonate within him. As though someone had struck a tuning fork and his soul was vibrating in sympathy.

He was aware of a huge painful weight on his chest. It was stopping him breathing. He felt like he was going to fall backwards it was so heavy. Then invisible arms caught him, encircled him and lifted him back up.

They were like the arms of his mother, everyone's mother and the mother of everyone. There was peace, serenity and most of all love in them. A love that gave and accepted without measure or compunction.

As Miriam held his hands and continued to chant, the arms moved through him and took hold of the weight on his chest. Then slowly, as though they were removing a foreign object embedded in his flesh, the hands began to remove the weight.

As it was lifted from him, Benjamin felt the memories flood back in and he saw where the pain and the anger came from. Benjamin hated Richard because he blamed him for everything his Dad had done to hurt his Mom. He couldn't blame his Dad because he loved him, so he blamed Richard. He also feared Richard would hurt his Mom.

He hated Richard's world because he couldn't live up to what it expected of him. He had failed. No, there was more to it than that. He *had* failed, but *what* had he failed?

As the weight on his chest got less and less, he found himself back in the kitchen with his mother sobbing on the floor. He realised then it was his mother he had failed. He hadn't protected her as he promised he would.

He really meant it when he handed her his handkerchief. He'd wanted to look after her. To rescue her. But he hadn't. He'd let Richard take her and make her unhappy. He'd never forgiven himself and he'd blamed her for that.

That was what had driven a wedge between them. That was where his pain came from and why he was so angry.

Then he felt a presence in his mind. It was foreign but totally familiar, wise but innocent and ancient but fresh. It was the mother, the sister and the lover he had always yearned for. It was a Loa, he realised. The one Miriam had named: Erzulie Dantò.

She spoke to him without using words. She told him the pain was no longer his and he was to let it go. Then she passed through him, took the pain, and was gone.

He felt so much loss when she left. Suddenly, more than anything in the world, he wanted his mother.

He broke down and cried like a little boy. Like his mother that day on the kitchen floor. Like a young man confronting himself for the first time.

Two sets of arms encircled him, real arms, Miriam's and Tatyana's. He rested his head on their shoulders and sobbed.

All around them the Zombies rocked from foot to foot and began a low moan, like the wind keening round the corner of a building. Benjamin couldn't be certain, but it felt like they were sympathising.

The drums ceased as he stopped crying.

"It's time," Miriam said. "Are you okay to do this?"

He nodded and wiped his eyes on his sleeve. "Let's go."

CHAPTER TWENTY-SEVEN

It was pandemonium. Tatyana thought it would be. Zombies jostled her on all sides. She was practising Zombie breathing and moving with care. She was under Miriam's protection but she wasn't going to take risks.

The Zombies were excited. They could smell fresh blood and fear. The instinct to feed was beginning to override their behaviour. Tatyana could sense their group mind splintering. Only Miriam was holding it together. Her mind straddled the group mind, guiding it like a rider steers a horse.

Miriam was conducting the whole operation from outside the Ounfó. Before she sent in the Zombies they had cased the place. There was a yard out front full of trees, some of which were painted bright colours. Miriam explained that they were sanctuaries for the Loas.

Beyond the yard was a walled courtyard with a high roof and a bare earth floor. This was the Peristyle, where all the major ceremonies took place. To the rear of that was a small square building. This was the Holy of Holies. Miriam explained that only the Houngan (the high priest) or Mambo (high priestess) and their close circle of acolytes could enter there.

Tatyana was enthralled. She felt something deep inside herself open up as Miriam spoke about Voodoo and serving the Loa, something she hadn't thought existed. Like a hunger for something she'd never tasted.

It seemed more than just a fascination with the forbidden topic of religion. She was genuinely excited about seeing everything inside the Ounfó. Miriam's descriptions and explanations left her exhilarated and confused. Was it Miriam? Did she just have a crush on her, or was there more to it?

Tacked on the back of the Holy of Holies was a building Miriam knew nothing about. It was all hi-tech chrome and glass. It looked totally out of place and there was a bad feeling coming off it. They all felt it, Miriam especially.

Miriam went back round to the yard out front. She tapped the lower branches of a tree and a snake appeared. She held out her hand and it curled around her arm.

Miriam whispered to the snake and Tatyana heard her say "Dambala Wédo Yé-H-we" several times.

The snake seemed hypnotised by Miriam's words. She placed it on the ground and it slithered towards the side entrance of the Peristyle at a rapid pace. The Zombies followed it.

Miriam told Tatyana to go in with them and not be afraid, she would be protected. Her job was to make sure that the guests all got out unharmed. Miriam would remain outside with Benjamin until the Ounfó was cleared.

Tatyana was surprised that Benjamin didn't make any objections to this. He still seemed spaced out after the healing Miriam had performed on him. He was definitely changed. He seemed sweeter and less likely to fly into a rage.

The guests were still groggy from the ceremony as Tatyana and the Zombies entered. The sight of so many unsupervised Zombies pouring into the place soon woke them up.

They couldn't have looked more horrified if their whole stock portfolio had just been wiped out.

"Jesus fucking Christ?" Sam McKane, the grey haired Texan, said jumping to his feet. "It's an invasion. We're being invaded."

"Where the hell did they come from?" Arthur Sonnenfeldt said, trying to dive behind Sam. "There's so many of them, how'd they get out of the compound?"

More and more Zombies filled the Peristyle which was still littered with the remnants of the ceremony. Several Zombies skidded in the animal blood on the earthen floor. Their feet trampled the intricate patterns drawn in powder on the ground. The clouds of white dust they kicked up added to the confusion.

Tatyana saw Bessie, the red-headed woman she last saw trying to gnaw some guy's penis off, go into hysterics. She screamed, an honest to goodness scream of terror just like in the movies.

This was the cue for the rest of the guests to bolt for the entrance. Too many people hit the doorway at once. There was a jam and they began to push and shove each other.

One young guy punched an elderly male Zombie in the face. Tatyana heard bones crack and saw dead skin tear. The Zombie hardly moved though. It just bit at his fist when it smelled the fresh blood on his scraped knuckles.

It reached out to get hold of the young guy. He kicked the Zombie in the midriff to keep it away and he fell over on his back. When he saw how ravenous the Zombie had become the man scrambled to his feet and scampered away.

A stocky guy with sandy brown hair picked up a censer full of flaming oil and tried to ward them off. The oil spilled onto his shirt and set it alight. The man panicked and ran for the door. He collided with the tall guy, George Griffin. George pushed him away and he and two others got the man down and rolled him on the ground as he howled in pain.

Tatyana wended her way through the Zombies as the last of the guests spilled into the yard outside. She watched from the doorway as they spread out and ran between the trees.

Snakes dropped out of the lower branches. Some dangled by their tails and hissed with menace. Others landed on the ground in front of the fleeing guests.

The guests changed direction and ran through the middle

of the yard where there were no deadly snakes. This must be Miriam's doing. She was shepherding the guests, making certain they went where she wanted.

Tatyana heard a scuffle over at the other end of the Peristyle. The creepy priest Vincenzo and some other men dressed in white came out of the Holy of Holies. The guys in white must be the acolytes Miriam had mentioned.

One of the acolytes raced through the Zombies, waving a ceremonial flag and chanting. He got to the multi coloured pole in the centre of the Peristyle. What had Miriam called it? The Poteau Mitain.

There was a coiled leather whip hanging from the side of the Poteau Mitain. It obviously had some sort of spiritual significance. The acolyte climbed on the pedestal at the base of the Poteau Mitain and took the whip down. He began to crack it over the heads of the Zombies.

The Zombies all stopped and turned to look at him. He waved his flag back and forth and used the whip to corral the Zombies.

"Rete. Dans le nom des Gédé – Rete!"

He was calling the Zombies to heel and it was working.

Shit, what was going to happen if they lost control of the Zombies? Tatyana started to edge towards the entrance so she could slip out unseen. As she did, she looked up and saw a giant constrictor curling its way down the Poteau Mitain.

The acolyte with the whip hadn't seen it. As he barked orders at the Zombies in Creole it wound its way closer to him. He didn't see the snake until it slipped round his neck. His hands went up to it, but its coils were too strong and it crushed his windpipe.

The acolyte's face turned purple. He dropped the flag and the whip and clawed at the constrictor as his eyes bulged. Tatyana heard the crack of his neck breaking and the man fell to the floor.

The Zombies nearest him smelled the fresh corpse. They closed in on the dead body. Their jaws working in anticipation, they knelt and began to tear strips off him.

At the sight of this, Vincenzo and the other acolytes turned and ran back into the Holy of Holies. Tatyana heard their footsteps race through the Ounfó and into the hi-tech building behind it.

"Let them go," said Miriam. "The Ounfó is ours."

She looked around at the Peristyle. Some of the Zombies were fighting over the corpse, scrabbling for the last few shreds. Others were milling around inspecting the space, staring at it as though they were trying to recapture some distant memory of their former life.

"I grew up attending this Ounfó," Miriam said. "I was initiated here, I became its Mambo and led the congregation for years. Yet now it seems as foreign to me as it does to both of you."

CHAPTER TWENTY-EIGHT

They left the Zombies in the Peristyle and went into the Holy of Holies, looking for Vincenzo and the others. Tatyana felt honoured. She could see Benjamin was curious and excited to be allowed into the inner-sanctum too.

The entrance chamber was lit by candles and had crude paintings of Catholic icons on the walls. Miriam explained that these were representations of the Loa that blessed the temple. On one wall was a picture of a dark skinned St Patrick chasing the snakes out of Ireland. This represented Dambala the snake Loa of the heavens. On the opposite wall was a painting of Our Lady of the Immaculate Conception, who was the Catholic equivalent of Ayida Wédo, the rainbow Loa married to Dambala.

"Wait I don't understand," said Tatyana. "How can you be a Catholic when you practice magic?"

"Voodoo is not magic," Miriam said. "It is a religion with a complex theology. One that embraces Catholicism."

"So you believe in God, but you worship spirits, how can that be?"

"God is in all things, all places and all times. People often ask how He can allow a thing to happen. They do not understand that He allows all things to happen out of His love for us. However, because He knows we look for divine guidance and intervention in our lives at a level He is too great to provide, he created the Loa to be his intermediaries. We serve the Loa because they fulfil the greater will of God."

"Wow, that's quite mind blowing," said Tatyana as they passed through a coloured hanging into the main chamber. "But it makes a lot of sense."

At the far end of the chamber was a stone altar. There was a huge assortment of objects on it. There were dolls in ceremonial dress, Catholic icons, ritual rattles, jars and pots containing strange herbs, flags, amulets and charms and several representations of serpents, including a large stuffed snake.

"That is the Pé," said Miriam. "The name comes from the old African word 'kpé' meaning stone. This one is sanctified to the Loa Dambala. The other two chambers through there have their own Pés blessed by Ayida Wédo and Erzulie Dantò."

They didn't go through these other chambers. Miriam took them, instead, into another room. "This is the *Djévo* where the initiations take place. Normally you would never be allowed in here, but these are exceptional times. The Ounfó has been desecrated and I believe the Loas have brought you into their service." Miriam peered through the gloom. "That door should not be there."

On the other side of the room, standing open, was a solid steel security door. It had a huge circular handle in the middle, like the door of a bank vault.

Tatyana walked over and peered through it. "This must lead to that hi-tech building we saw."

Benjamin put his hand on her shoulder. "Careful. They could still be in there."

"I'm pretty sure I heard them running out," said Tatyana. They heard the engine of a jeep start up outside. "I think that means they're going."

They walked through an empty entrance chamber into a room that was filled with banks of computer screens.

"This doesn't look like Voodoo to me," said Benjamin.

"No," said Miriam. "This is anything but Voodoo."

On the other side of the room, the walls were lined with row after row of sealed glass compartments. Inside the compartments were the earthenware containers Doc Papa had called Pot-tets. A fine white mist swirled around each container and frost ferns were forming on the inside of many of the compartments. A gauge on the front showed the temperature inside the compartments was way below freezing.

At the opposite end of the long room were several huge tanks of liquid nitrogen. A network of tubes ran along the walls from the tanks to the compartments.

"Cryogenics," said Benjamin. "This is a cryogenics facility. They're freezing all the souls once they capture them, but why?"

"To numb them," said Miriam. "To put them to sleep and tie them to the earthly plane."

"So, does Voodoo include science as well as Christianity?" said Tatyana.

"Not this type of science," said Miriam. "Doc Papa has displaced the Loa of this Ounfó and made bargains with many other Loa who do not look kindly on St Ignatius or its people. Dambala and Ayida Wedo are not pleased with him or what he has done to their Ounfó."

"Like building this soul bank," said Benjamin. "And using it to freeze people's souls and stuff?"

"Precisely. He has desecrated this Ounfó and he has perverted our most sacred ceremonies."

"You mean that ceremony we took part in, to remove our souls?" said Tatyana. "That wasn't proper Voodoo?"

"There is no right or wrong Voodoo. But there is Voodoo that harms and Voodoo that heals and strengthens. The ceremony that you took part in was a twisted version of a ceremony that has been central to our worship for years."

"But you don't want to remove people's souls and capture them, right?" said Tatyana.

"No. The ceremony is called the Lave Tet it means the 'washing of the head'. It is a ceremony in which the initiate is married to their patron Loa. The Pot-tet is prepared as a place for their Gros Bon Ange to reside while their Met Tet, or patron Loa is inside them. When they die their soul will also return to the Pot-tet on the way to the afterlife. This is meant to strengthen the soul and allow it to grow. Not to imprison it and hold it to ransom."

"No wonder the Loa are pissed off with him then."

"Indeed."

"There's loads of souls though," said Benjamin. "Just about everyone on the island must have banked their soul here."

"It looks that way doesn't it?" said Miriam.

A sudden burst of gunfire made them all jump.

"We know you're in there," said a voice from outside. "We have you surrounded. There's no use trying to run. Come out of the building and leave the Zombies behind."

"What are we going to do?" said Tatyana.

"They won't try and storm the place," said Benjamin. "They can't risk damaging the soul bank or harming the Zombies."

"Yeah, but we can't get out of here either," said Tatyana. "They've got us trapped."

"Their presence here is completely immaterial," said Miriam. "The Loa wish us to leave, but before we do we must perform a service for them."

"How can we leave when the place is surrounded?" said Tatyana.

"I thought we were going to use the souls to bargain our way out," said Benjamin.

"All will become clear in a little while," said Miriam. "First we need to shut down the power to this building."

"I can do that," said Benjamin. "There's got to be fuse box, or a breaker board around here. I'm sure I can find it."

"Good. Please do that quickly."

Benjamin scampered off while Miriam took Tatyana back through to the Holy of Holies. She picked up a pole and used it to open a trapdoor in the ceiling of one of the chambers. Then she stood on a box and pulled herself up through the trapdoor. She reached out a hand for Tatyana. "Here, come on up."

Tatyana climbed into a narrow crawl space. Miriam led her to a tiny room just large enough for the two of them to sit up in. It had six large windows with no glass in them, only angled wooden slats.

"This is an old observatory," whispered Miriam. "It was built in the days when we had foreign missionaries and soldiers on St Ignatius. They feared our religion and tried to suppress it. At times the congregation had to keep watch for them. You can see the surrounding jungle from here without being seen."

Tatyana peered through the slats. She could see about ten men stationed around the Ounfó. Many were hiding behind trees and the large leaves of tropical plants. They looked hot and scared.

"I thought you said that Voodoo accepted Christianity," said Tatyana in a low whisper. "How come the missionaries wanted to persecute you?"

"Sadly they still see our religion as superstition and devil worship, no matter what we believe. Voodoo has also played a big part in the struggle against foreign oppression. So whether the occupiers are French or American they have always tried to suppress us."

Tatyana jumped as the slats in the window she was leaning against started to rattle as though a fierce wind was blowing them. Three other sets of slats did the same, even though there wasn't the slightest breeze.

"Get down!" said Miriam. She pulled Tatyana to the floor as the slats splintered.

Gunfire raked the small observation room as Tatyana and Miriam pressed themselves to the floor with their hands over their heads. Tatyana could hear the bullets whistle and crack as they hit the wood inches above her head. They began to wriggle down the crawlspace as the whole observatory fell apart and blew away in a bodiless wind.

"What's happening?" said Tatyana as they dropped back into the chamber.

"I believe it's Doc Papa," Miriam said. "He's attacking us through the invisible world." A commotion broke out in the Peristyle. Tatyana could hear the Zombies bellow and moan as she and Miriam ran to see what it was.

Tatyana watched as Miriam strode into the Peristyle and began chanting something. Some of the Zombies became quiet and placid straight away. Other continued to rage and fight among themselves.

Miriam's voice grew weaker and she put her hands to her head as though in great pain. She stumbled and fell to her knees. Tatyana went to help her but Miriam waved her away. She was holding her throat and coughing. The Zombies nearest Tatyana turned towards her. Scenting her blood they began to advance. With great care Tatyana stepped back inside the Holy of Holies. She was in danger but she couldn't leave Miriam.

Miriam rallied. She stopped coughing and seemed to gather herself. She got to her feet and sang out her incantation in a voice so clear and loud it seemed to still every other sound in the jungle.

The Zombies fell silent. There was no sound for a moment and not even the air moved. Miriam strode back inside the Holy of Holies with her head high.

"We do not have much time."

The lights went out as soon as they stepped into the hi-tech building. The computers died and, with a click and a hiss, the cryogenic units stopped humming.

Benjamin appeared carrying a lit candle. "Told you it wouldn't be a problem. I found these in a cupboard." He handed candles to Tatyana and Miriam and lit them from his. "What was happening outside?"

"We were under magical attack," said Miriam. "Doc Papa was trying to neutralise us so his men could move in and round up the Zombies. We're safe for the time being but we need to work fast. We have to get all the Pot-tets out of their compartments and arrange them on the floor."

"We'll have break the glass to get them out," said Benjamin. "But we can't touch them. They'll take the skin off our hands they're so cold."

They hunted around the room in the candlelight. Benjamin found a couple of pairs of large steel tongs that must have been used to lift the Pot-tets into the compartments. He handed one to Tatyana then swung his into the door of a compartment. The glass shattered.

"Come on," said Benjamin. "There's loads of them and we don't have long."

When they were done Miriam returned, holding a large flask of oil and a broom. She told Benjamin to clear away all the glass while she and Tatyana arranged the Pot-tets in a particular formation on the floor.

Once the floor was clear and the containers were in place Miriam uncorked the flask of oil. With the oil she drew an intricate pattern around the Pot-tets.

"You're drawing one of those patterns I keep seeing everywhere," said Tatyana. "What are they called?"

"Vèvès," said Miriam. "They're used in most ceremonies. They represent a sacred geometry that creates a space for heavenly bodies to dwell. They reproduce the astral forces of the Loa and act as a beacon that calls them to our world."

"Do you have like, different Vèvès for every Loa then?"

"And every ceremony, yes. This is the Vèvè for the ritual of the Boulez-Zain-Les-Mort."

"I'm sorry to keep coming out with questions, but I am so fascinated I can't tell you. Do you mind if ask what that is?" Tatyana said.

"No, I don't mind. You do not realise it yet but there are forces at work here that compel you to ask those questions, and oblige me to answer them. You remember I told you that for a while the souls of the dead initiates return to their Pot-tets? They do this to shelter from the immense cold they feel after their earthly body has died. The Pot-tets is filled with remnants of their earthly form so they feel safe there.

"We must feed and nurture the deceased souls so they're strong enough to walk the roads of the dead and join the Loas in heaven. The Boulez-Zain-Les-Mort is a fire rite to warm the dead souls and set them on their way to heaven. Because the souls in these

Pot-tets are not initiates and aren't dead it won't have that effect on them. It *will* break the spell they are under though and that will sabotage this whole soul bank."

"What will happen to all the souls?"

"Unless they return to their living bodies they'll be trapped on the earthly plane, unable to leave the Pot-tets. Without any strength or sustenance they'll begin to wither and slowly fade, denying their owners any chance of immortality in the afterlife."

"Whoa, that's harsh."

"Not as harsh as the fate to which these people condemned my fellow islanders," said Miriam, finishing off the Vèvè. "And it doesn't deny them the possibility of redemption."

She bent and set a candle to the oil. The flames raced round the Vèvè and crackled around the Pot-tets.

Miriam raised her arms in a gesture of great reverence and began to chant. "O vèvè Voudoun vè, Bon Dié O! O vélà Kounn tié. Vélà Kounn tié! Dambala Wédo Kounn tié!"

The flames leapt higher. The heat was immense. Tatyana and Benjamin had to retreat. Miriam seemed unaffected. The seals on the Pot-tets began to melt with the heat.

Tatyana heard a scream that seemed to come from as far away in time as it did in space. As it got closer, she felt it not just with her ears but with her whole mind and body. As the scream got louder it drowned out every other sensation until it was too painful to bear. For the sake of her mind and her sanity she let go of her consciousness.

CHAPTER TWENTY-NINE

Cold. Something was cold. His cheek. The side of his face. Benjamin's mind drifted back to his body. The cold sensation was like an anchor that dragged him back to the present.

He became aware of his body. His shoulder hurt. He was lying on his side on a hard floor. He opened his eyes and sat up. Where was he? He didn't recognise the room. It was dark and shadows flickered warily across the broken glass boxes on the walls, as though afraid of cutting themselves.

A woman was standing in front of him holding a candle. Tatyana moved next to him. Tatyana, he recognised her, his first concrete memory. It stirred up others.

He was on an island – St Ignatius, in a cryogenics lab. There were souls in those pots. The spell that held them had been broken.

There was more. His Mom – he'd let go of the pain. He felt a sense of loss at this memory. No, not loss, lightness. The loss was for his Mom – the closeness they no longer felt. He missed that. He missed his Mom.

The woman offered him her hand. Miriam, that was her name. It didn't suit her. It was wrong somehow. He stood with her help.

"Miriam," he said. "That's not your real name is it?"

"It's the name I wear with this body."

She was being mysterious again. She was like that. She'd trust them with a little bit of information then she'd pull back. He bent down and helped Tatyana to her feet. Miriam gave them candles.

"That was intense," Tatyana said. "Was I out for long?"

"Only a matter of minutes," said Miriam. "It was only because you were so close to the point of release that you passed out at all. The others will be unconscious for a long time."

"The others?" said Benjamin. "You mean the people whose souls were banked?"

"Yes, the ritual set off quite a shockwave and it will have hit them hardest. I think it's time for us to leave."

"Where are we going to go?" said Tatyana.

"We need somewhere more fortified. I can't keep us all safe in the Ounfó. There's an abandoned copper mine about twenty minutes from here. We can hide out there until the time is right."

"Right for what?"

"To bring my people back."

"And how long will that be?" said Benjamin.

"Less than a day now. But come, we need to get going before the guards come round."

She left the cryogenics room and Tatyana went with her. Benjamin took one last look at the rows of shattered glass compartments and the blistered Pot-tets.

The seals on the charred earthenware containers were broken. In the wavering candlelight, Benjamin was sure the Pot-tets were making a noise. Not one he could hear directly. If he listened for it, it wasn't there. It was like those things that you only saw out of the corner of your eye. Except you could only hear this out of the corner of your ear, if there was such a thing.

It wasn't a good noise. It was mournful and full of regret, like a wail of loss or a scream of self-hatred. He suddenly felt extremely unnerved and realised that he didn't want to be in this room anymore. In fact he never wanted to be in there again.

Benjamin joined Miriam and Tatyana in the main chamber of the Holy of Holies. They were watching an elderly female Zombie standing in front of the Pé. The Zombie was trying to pick up some of the pots on the stone altar and open them, but her dead fingers fumbled with the lids.

The Zombie was transfixed by the stuffed snake on the altar. She put out her hand and her fingers brushed against the scales of the serpent. Benjamin had never seen a Zombie do anything with such gentleness and care.

Her hand fell on a bowl full of white powder. She lifted it to her face and sniffed. Some of the powder stuck to the dry wrinkled skin of her face, giving it an almost comical look.

With even more care than before, she put her hand into the bowl. Benjamin could see her hands twitch as the wasted and rotting muscles of her arm fought to fulfil a simple task. Even still she was able to lift some of the powder between her fingers and shake it onto the floor.

"She remembers," said Tatyana. "It's like she's drawing one of those things, a Vèvè. "

"In her day she was one of the most skilled and proficient of the Ounsi," said Miriam. "Her work was spectacular. No Ounfó was ever blessed with a better artist."

"So you know her then?"

"I ought to, she gave birth to and raised me."

"That's your mother?" said Benjamin.

He was suddenly moved by what Miriam must be going through. She was surrounded by the walking corpses of all the people she cared most for. He couldn't imagine how she felt. He remembered how he felt watching his Mom change when she married Richard. She'd been so full of fun when it was just the two of them. She was as much his best buddy as his Mom.

Then Richard came along and she totally altered to fit in with what he expected from a wife. As she became more formal and joyless each day, it was like something inside her died. But that was nothing like what Miriam was facing.

If anything it was similar to what his great aunt had gone through when her second husband lost his mind. She had to watch him become a shell of his former self. There was nothing left of him at the end.

That was only *one* loved one. Miriam had to cope with her whole community becoming less than human. Benjamin began to feel ashamed that he'd actually referred to them as noble monsters. He had no idea at the time, but even still, no wonder she was such a bitch to him.

Miriam led her mother out into the Peristyle where they collected the other Zombies and left the Ounfó. As they walked past the unconscious soldiers slumped over their weapons among the foliage the sky began to lighten. It would be morning soon.

"Were you close to your mother?" Benjamin asked.

Miriam shook her head. "We fought constantly. We were too alike, both headstrong. The last time we spoke I told her I never wanted to see her again. I wish I could take those words back."

"What did you fight about?" said Tatyana.

"A man. She never approved of my lovers. And it pains me to say it, but this time she was right."

"Was it one of the men here?" said Tatyana. "I mean, you know..."

"Yes I know what you mean. And no he isn't undead, but he is here on the island. In fact he now runs it."

"What?" said Benjamin. "You mean Doc Papa was your lover? I don't believe it."

"I'm afraid it's true."

"But that can't be. I don't understand. How come he didn't recognise you the minute he saw you? Why didn't he guess what you were going to do?"

"For a start he thinks I'm dead and that he was the one who

killed me. Secondly, as you quite rightly guessed back there in the Ounfó, Miriam isn't my real name, and this isn't the body I was born with."

"Now you've really lost me."

"What is your real name then?" said Tatyana.

"It's Brigitte. Brigitte Laveau."

CHAPTER THIRTY

A Year Ago

"Behold, I tell you a mystery. We shall all indeed rise again: but we shall not all be changed. In a moment, in the twinkling of an eye, at the last trumpet: for the trumpet shall sound and the dead shall rise again incorruptible. And we shall be changed..."

Oliver gripped Brigitte's hand as the priest droned on. It was the first sign that he was letting go of his emotions, like a sudden drop in temperature signals a coming storm. His shoulders started to shake. She put her arm around his waist. He dropped his head on her shoulder and began to sob. "Oh, Miriam, Miriam, Miriam," was all he could say.

"Anima ejus, et ánimæ ómnium fidélium defunctórum, per misericórdiam Dei requiéscant in pace. Amen," the priest intoned as the coffin was lowered into the grave.

The air was still and the sun shone bright. It was unseasonably warm even for New Orleans, as though the weather was trying to make reparations for the fury it had unleashed so recently.

The familiarity her new body felt with Oliver's touch only distanced her from it. Though he had come to loom so large in her life, he was still a relative stranger. The handful of mourners who stood by the graveside and placed consoling hands on Oliver's shoulder were friends of his and Miriam's. Brigitte had never met any of them. From the grief Oliver showed, they all supposed that it was a close family friend he was grieving. None of them guessed it was really his wife.

It was a strange thing to attend your own funeral in a foreign land. Brigitte had to keep the range of emotions she felt at bay, so she could be strong for Oliver. Seeing the coffin in the ground was not as unnerving as seeing her corpse in an open casket at the vigil the night before.

Her old body had seemed so alien to her as it lay in a coffin surrounded by candles. There was the old scar on her hand. There was the face she had seen in the mirror, whose changes she had tracked since childhood. Yet it no longer belonged to her. It was separate from her and she felt disdain for it.

"Take us home," Oliver told the driver as they climbed into the limo. "I want to be alone with my..." he hesitated to say the word 'wife', settling on, "... we want to be alone with each other."

"What about your guests?" said Brigitte.

"They'll understand. Why, did you want to spend time with them?"

"No, it's alright. I'm happy to do what you want. You're the one in mourning."

"Funny, I thought we were both grieving our loss."

The last remark was surprisingly thoughtful of him, to think of *her* loss in *his* hour of grief. Maybe the next nine or ten months with him wouldn't be as difficult as Brigitte feared. She was not seeing him at his best. This was a difficult time for both of them.

Oliver put his arm around Brigitte and pulled her close. She might have objected another time but she knew he needed the comfort. As his hand slipped from her shoulder to her hip she could tell that comfort wasn't all he wanted.

She told herself that this was okay. He was in a difficult place at the moment and his feelings were confused. Actually she recalled reading that it was a natural part of the grieving process to feel strong desire soon after losing a partner.

She was also aware that she had an obligation to Oliver and Miriam. An obligation that, once fulfilled, would ensure the lives of everyone on St Ignatius. Brigitte rested her head on Oliver's shoulder and gazed out of the window. Her mind went back over her first months in the city.

Brigitte had first met Oliver Chevalier in a trailer park for evacuees in the Lower Ninth Ward of New Orleans. She was staying with a group of ex-pats from St Ignatius who had all lost their homes in the flood.

Oliver had been helping with the reconstruction of the Lower Ninth. This area of the city had been hit hardest by the hurricanes and he had set up a foundation to raise money to restore and rebuild it. The people she was staying with knew Oliver's family came from St Ignatius and he still had an interest in the island. They were also aware that his wife was very sick.

Oliver did not serve the Loa. He was Catholic, but he had a great respect for the religion of his ancestors. He had been raised by his grandmother who grew up on St Ignatius and told him stories of the Voodoo ceremonies of her youth.

Brigitte was introduced to Oliver as a Mambo, a powerful Voodoo priestess. Her fellow islanders were sure she could help with Oliver's wife Miriam. Oliver was very wealthy. He had paid for the best medical care available, but nothing was working. He was ready to try anything, including the Voodoo his grandmother had told him so much about.

Brigitte agreed to help Miriam but she was keen to limit both Miriam and Oliver's expectations. Oliver said he understood and offered Brigitte a guest cottage on his estate in the Garden District. This was how Brigitte came to meet Miriam Chevalier, the woman whose body and identity she would eventually assume.

They did not hit it off straight away. Miriam was a devout

Catholic and did not want some "medicine woman" trying to cure her with "evil spirits". Brigitte was careful to reassure her that she had no truck with evil forces. Instead she spoke about her own belief in God and her relationship with the saints.

Brigitte also provided a sympathetic ear to Miriam as she spoke of what troubled her most. Her anger at the disease that was killing her. Her regret for all the things she wouldn't get to do. Her dismay that she would never be able to give Oliver what he wanted most of all from their marriage.

More than anything, Miriam confided, she was afraid of the months of pain and wasting that were to come. So afraid that she was strongly considering euthanasia. She knew of clinics in Europe that could provide the service simply and painlessly. Miriam wanted to die with dignity and without suffering, but she was afraid of how this would endanger her immortal soul. She could not reconcile her wishes with her belief that suicide was a sin.

A deep affection grew between them as they prayed and spoke and wept together. They shared stories of growing up and Miriam became as fascinated with Brigitte's heritage as her husband was with his grandmother's tales of Voodoo.

Brigitte also told Miriam of the dreadful plight that had befallen her fellow islanders. Miriam could not quite believe Brigitte at first. Nothing like that happened in the privileged world she lived in.

She knew that Brigitte wouldn't lie though. And the Bible spoke of the dead returning to life so she could believe that, if she stretched her imagination. What Miriam had most problem in accepting was the thought that someone could actually reduce an entire community to nothing more than walking corpses in order to enslave them. She couldn't conceive of human beings reduced to monstrosities so that that rich Westerners could study them and learn to become crueler and more exploitative.

In a way Brigitte shared her disbelief. It was hard to believe that any human being was capable of such measures. But with patience and tact, Brigitte pointed out to Miriam that it wasn't so far removed from how the West already treated much of the Third World.

After all, Brigitte argued, the sweat shops that supply the West with cheap consumer goods reduce the men, women and children who work in them into disposable labour. When the bottom line is driven by how cheap the cost of labour is then labour becomes a mere commodity and so do the human beings providing it. Taking away someone's life and turning them into a Zombie is simply the logical conclusion of an economic system that takes away people's working rights and turns them into units of labour in order to enslave them in poverty.

Miriam was uncertain about this. She thought Brigitte might have a point but it sounded to her like she was preaching socialism, so Brigitte let the matter drop. It wasn't until Brigitte broke down and spoke of the guilt she felt for the part she'd played in what happened that Miriam truly came around.

Brigitte had trained the man who'd enslaved her island and given him the tools he used to do it. What's more she'd saved his life when he was first washed up on its shores, the only survivor of a dreadful accident. She'd nursed him back to health and they'd become lovers.

The idyll was broken when Brigitte was visited by the spirit of her ancestor who told her of the curse he'd placed on her lover's family. A curse that she was expected to fulfill.

Brigitte sought to break the curse through love. She went against the wills of both their ancestors and the Loa, and everyone she ever loved had paid the price.

Brigitte hadn't mentioned the magical artefact that her ancestor had entrusted to her however. This was secret. Even when her lover had tricked and captured her she hadn't revealed where it was, desperate as her lover was to know. She would dearly have loved to confide this in Miriam though, for the burden of the artefact weighed heavily on Brigitte's soul.

When Brigitte spoke of the horrors of her escape, the truth of it finally came home to Miriam. Brigitte told how she had been buried alive by her lover, who had started calling himself Doc Papa.

She described how, as the air in the coffin ran out, she had sent her soul out of her body and taken over one of the Zombies. A strong young man who was also her second cousin. Inside the young man's walking corpse she had given her captors the slip and sought out her grave. With less than an hour left to live she had dug up the earth of the grave with the young man's dead hands. As she dug she had also neutralised the wards and spells Doc Papa had placed upon the grave.

When she was finally free Brigitte's soul returned to her body and she sent the young Zombie back to join the others so his absence wouldn't be spotted. Then she replaced all the earth and reset the spells so Doc Papa wouldn't realise she was gone.

She stole away from the island in an abandoned fishing boat and made her way to Haiti. From there she eventually found her way to the US. No matter how far she traveled she couldn't shake her guilt. Guilt for escaping while the rest of her community still suffered and guilt for having brought that suffering on them.

Miriam's bedside became a private space of absolution for both of them. Between the endless stream of specialists examining Miriam, she and Brigitte became the confessors each of them so badly needed. The bond of trust between them became so strong that Miriam finally felt able to ask Brigitte for the help of the Loa.

In the dead of night they held a rite. Brigitte called upon the Loa and Ayida Wédo mounted her. Brigitte lost all consciousness as the Ayida Wédo took over her body. When she came around Miriam was in tears.

She recounted her vision to Brigitte. Miriam said the Virgin Mary had visited and spoken to her through Brigitte. She'd told Miriam that God had a plan for her and that there was a place for her in heaven, with her father and her aunt. They had visited too and had told her she would soon be with them in her eternal reward.

The Virgin Mary had told Miriam there was a way to relieve her suffering and to save the people of Brigitte's island. Brigitte had to use the rites known to her as a Voodoo priestess to help Miriam's soul leave its dying body and make its way to heaven before the illness claimed her. With her soul gone the illness would lose its hold on her.

Miriam's body would then become a living vessel for Brigitte's soul. She could send it out of her body and into Miriam's as she'd done when she possessed the young male Zombie. This would allow Brigitte to pose as Miriam.

Brigitte could return to St Ignatius using Miriam's identity. Miriam would put her half of Oliver's fortune at Brigitte's disposal so she could buy her way onto the course and pretend to be one of Doc Papa's students. No-one would recognise her so she would be free to infiltrate Doc Papa's organisation and save her people.

Brigitte did not know what to say. She recognised Ayida Wédo's hand in the plan. The Loa had appeared to Miriam in her aspect as Our Lady of the Immaculate Conception. Nevertheless, Brigitte was over-awed by the generosity and bravery Miriam showed in offering to do this for her and her people.

She reached out and put her arms round Miriam and the two of them wept on the hospital bed. Tears of grief mingled with joy. Grief for everything they had lost in their lives and joy for the blessings they could bring one another. They wept with gratitude for having found a sister in each other. For the joy that sisterhood brought and the grief it would mean when they parted.

Brigitte had then left Miriam's side for the first time in weeks so Miriam could tell Oliver about her plans. Oliver was not pleased to begin with. When he saw how much it meant to Miriam, though, he began to come round. Miriam finally won him over when she explained how it would allow her to give him the one thing they'd always wanted.

Brigitte gazed out of the limousine's window at the ornate Victorian houses of the Garden District, with their perfect lawns and wrought-iron fences. Her mind was still in the past, reliving her last days with Miriam.

"You've been quiet for a long time," said Oliver. "What are you thinking about?"

"Miriam," said Brigitte. "How much I'm going to miss her. How grateful I am to you and her, for everything you've done."

Oliver took her hands in his. "I'm grateful to you too. Watching Miriam lying there in that bed, dying a little more each day, felt like a part of me was dying with her. The part of me that could be happy and feel hope and enjoy life. I thought that would go forever when she went. But you're giving me something to live for again and I can't thank you enough."

Brigitte smiled a sad smile and squeezed Oliver's hands. They pulled past a mansion as Brigitte recalled the last time Oliver had said that to her.

It was just before the final ceremony. Oliver had taken her hands just he did in the car and thanked her. They were standing on the second storey landing outside the master bedroom. There were tears streaming down his cheeks. He had just said goodbye to his wife. Miriam had returned to the mansion. She wanted to spend her last earthly hours in the comfort and privacy of her home.

Brigitte had called on certain special traders down on South Rampart Street to buy the materials she needed for the ceremony. The room had been prepared in accordance with the Loa's wishes. Oliver left them alone.

The full ceremony took over two days to complete. There were so many gates Brigitte had to open to the afterlife. So many Loa had to be called on to ensure the safe passage of Miriam's soul and the health of her body when Brigitte entered it. Brigitte couldn't afford to let her concentration lapse for a second. Her life and Miriam's soul depended on it.

Finally, Brigitte opened Miriam's eyes and looked out of them for the first time. She saw her old body sitting in a chair next to the bed. She called Oliver back in. They placed Brigitte's old body on the bed and called the undertaker and a priest. Then they set about planning Brigitte's funeral. A funeral that only they knew was secretly to honour Miriam.

"I don't know about you, but I need a drink," said Oliver as Brigitte sank into a leather sofa in the library back at the mansion. "Here take a look at this." He threw her a brochure for an exclusive hotel in the Maldives while he fixed them both a drink.

"What's this?"

"It's where we're going on vacation next week. I just ordered the tickets."

"And you didn't think to ask me?"

"I thought we needed a break. Don't you like the Maldives?"

"It would have been nice if you'd asked me whether I wanted to go before you booked the tickets."

Oliver sighed and looked at the floor. "Okay, there's going to be difficulties with this that I didn't foresee." He took a slug of his drink and handed Brigitte hers. "Miriam used to like it when I took charge. She liked surprises too, so I'd tend to spring things on her. I'm a take charge kind of a guy and I like to move quickly. You have to be that way when you manage a large portfolio of investments. That's how I manage things and that's how I manage people."

"I'm not one of the people you manage."

"You're right," Oliver said, changing his tone. "Would you like to come away with me to the Maldives? You've been through a lot. We both have. I think the break would do us both some good."

Miriam flicked through the glossy brochure. The rooms were immense, the facilities incredible. It reeked of a luxury that made Brigitte uncomfortable.

"I don't know if I could relax in a place like this while so many people here are still homeless. While the people from my island are still suffering."

"You're suffering from too much guilt," said Oliver. "You still have survivor's guilt and you're adding new wealth guilt to that. It's natural to feel that way for a while but you have to come to terms with it or it wears you down and depresses you."

"How can you come to terms with it? How can you live like this when so many other people live in poverty?"

"By helping those people. By using the wealth and the talents I've been blessed with to tackle some of the problems they're facing."

"I thought rich people and their greed were the *main* problem the poor are facing."

"There's nothing wrong with being rich Brigitte, any more than being poor. Rich people don't necessarily create poor ones. "

"If there were less rich people there'd be less poor."

"There's always going to be rich people though. I'm totally in favour of equal opportunities for everyone. But not everyone is equal. That's the way the world is. Some people are just smarter than others or more driven. Some people can jump higher, run faster or draw better than most other people. It's only fair they should be rewarded for this. Any system that punishes them and stifles their talent isn't creating equality. It's just denying the world the benefit of those talents and the wealth they could have created. Being rich doesn't mean you have to be a bad person."

"No, but most rich people are. That's why they turn innocent people into monsters so they can learn to become worse monsters themselves."

"And most black people are poor, but that doesn't mean that every black person has to be poor and it doesn't mean every rich person has to be bad. I'm living proof of both those assertions. You don't have to brutalise and exploit other people in order to get rich. Even if some people do get rich that way – a lot of people don't. Their brutality and exploitation can be their undoing. It's not the only way to make or use a fortune. But come, I don't want to argue on a night like this."

"I don't know," said Brigitte, uncrossing her legs. "I find it quite stimulating."

"Good, finish your drink."

Oliver put his hand on her thigh and her heart beat faster. She felt a jolt of nervous anticipation and a deep yearning her new body had been waiting a long time to unleash. Did the passion belong entirely to Miriam's body? A body that knew Oliver's so well. If it didn't, was it wrong of Brigitte to desire him?

Oliver led her to the master bedroom. She found she rather

liked him being masterful in this instance. Oliver put his arm round her waist and pulled her to him. She could smell his aftershave and the fresh sweat breaking on his skin. His scent was as familiar as it was exciting and new to her.

He ran his hand over her breast. Brigitte flinched and stepped back from him.

"I'm sorry," Oliver said. "Miriam used to really like that."

"And so do I. But this is the first time I've done this with you. I need you to go a little slower."

"I'm sorry, of course you do."

Brigitte suddenly became aware of a warm golden light at the foot of the bed they were standing by. She turned her head to look at the source.

"What's the matter?" said Oliver. "Did I do something else wrong?"

"No, it's Miriam. She's with us. She's come to say her final goodbye."

"She's not mad at us is she?"

"No, she's happy. She's here to give us her blessing."

Brigitte could feel Miriam's happiness coming off her in waves and radiating through the room. She fancied even Oliver could feel it.

Miriam was overjoyed that she and Oliver would soon have what they'd always wanted from their marriage. A child.

CHAPTER THIRTY-ONE

Doc Papa thrived on crisis management. It was a circumstance to which his temperament and skill set were best suited. He always did best in those situations where other, weaker types failed.

That's why he wasn't the least bit fazed when Truffet and the rest of the shareholders stormed into his office on the top floor of the mansion.

"Just what the fuck is going on around here?" Lyon's growled in his deep southern drawl. He'd made his fortune selling arms and ammunition to the domestic market and liked to portray himself as an old time gunslinger. At only five foot five with balding ginger hair, he didn't cut too imposing a figure however.

"One minute I'm getting blown in a hot tub. The next I'm lying on the floor and someone's giving me CPR," Lyons said. "Apparently, practically everyone on the island was knocked unconscious. If that Thai hooker hadn't dragged me out of the tub I would've drowned."

"There are some distressing rumours going around," Truffet said. He peered down at Doc Papa through his horn-rimmed spectacles. "I understand that our two biggest assets have been stolen."

"The assets are perfectly safe," said Doc Papa. "Someone did try to get the undead off the island but I dealt with the problem and my men are currently rounding them up."

"Someone, *who*?" said Lyons.

Doc Papa smiled. "A pitiful, little collection of wannabe terrorists calling themselves the Zombie Liberation Front."

The shareholders laughed with disbelief.

"Just when you think you've heard of every nut-job," said Simons.

"What about the soul bank?" said Frank Evans.

"All the Pot-tets are still in the soul bank and the area has been secured," said Doc Papa. "Everything is under control."

"So why do I feel so cold inside?" said Evans. "Why am I losing the feeling in my hands and feet? Why is my heart beating slower and slower?"

"The soul bank has been sabotaged," said Doc Papa. "As I said, all the Pot-tets are in our possession, but their seals have been corrupted."

"What does that mean?" barked Lyons.

"The souls are no longer fixed in their Pot-tets. The spells surrounding the containers have been reversed and the souls are slowly leaking out."

"Does that include our souls?"

"Yes it does. The unconsciousness that you all experienced was a side effect of this. When the spells were reversed this sent a psychic shockwave across the island."

"Who did this and why?" said O'Shaugnessy.

"I believe it was one of the current crop of guests. A lady calling herself Miriam Chavalier."

"One of the guests," said Lyon. "How the fuck did she manage that?"

"Apparently she knows Voodoo. A fact our extensive background check failed to turn up. I believe she did it in order to create a diversion so she could escape from the Ounfó with the Zombies."

"I thought you said your men were rounding the Zombies up," said O'Shaugnessy. "Now you're saying they've escaped. Do you have the Zombies or not?"

"It is merely a matter of time."

"Never mind about the Zombies," said Evans. "What about our souls? What's going to happen to them? What's going to happen to us?"

"Without the correct vessel to hold them the souls will slowly fade out of existence. They are denied access to the afterlife and they can't remain intact unless they have something to house them."

"Can't you just put them back inside us?" said Lyons.

"I'm afraid the stars aren't in the right alignment to return the souls to their bodies. I can't perform that ceremony for a while."

"What does that mean to us?" said O'Shaugnessy. "If you can't put them back in us, what's going to happen?"

"The worst case scenario is that as your Gros Bon Ange, the part of your soul that's in the Pot-tet, slowly withers away, your Ti Bon Ange, the soul that's still with you, will also go. This will mean that your intelligence will disappear along with all vital signs of life and you'll become a Zombie."

Evans banged his fist on the desk. His craggy face was even redder than usual. "God damn it! Do you mean to tell me that we're all going to become Zombies because you can't organise proper fucking security?"

"No. That isn't what I mean to tell you at all." Doc Papa leaned back in his chair and smiled. His movements were precise and controlled. "You are all going to be fine. I have allowed for just such a contingency." He pressed the button on his intercom. "You can come in now."

The door opened and Palmer and Vincenzo entered. Palmer was carrying a briefcase which he handed to Doc Papa. Doc Papa opened the briefcase and showed the contents to the shareholders.

On a velvet cushion were five talismans carved in ivory and stained with blood. "These gentlemen are Bakas," said Doc Papa. "I think you'll remember them from the ceremony I performed. They're special talismans that hold your souls to the earthly plane. They are also beacons that light the way for your soul. You have but to place them on a suitable vessel and your soul will make its new home there."

"What suitable vessel," said O'Shaugnessy. "I thought you said all the Pot-tets were corrupted."

"They are," said Doc Papa. "But they aren't the only vessel in which a dispossessed soul can live. A Zombie is a perfect vessel for just such a soul, because they're nothing more than human bodies with no soul or intellect. All the guests will be issued with their Bakas and a Zombie will be provided as soon as they are back in our custody."

"Why can't you just use the Baka's to put our souls back in our own bodies? Why do we have to stick it in some walking corpse?"

"While your soul is in your body it has the opportunity to move on to the afterlife. The Baka is designed to hold the soul to this plane of existence, so it can't transfer the soul into anything living that will allow the soul to move on. Don't worry, your soul will be completely safe in the Zombie we find for it."

"Fuck that," said Lyons. "I'm not waiting around for you to round up some Zombies while my life is on the line!"

"You won't have to wait around. In fact Palmer has five beautiful little Zombies all tied up and waiting to house your souls right here in the centre."

Palmer turned bright red. "I, err... don't know what you're talking about."

"Oh come now Palmer," said Doc Papa. "Do you seriously think I don't know all about your little harem? Nothing that goes on here escapes my attention. Now kindly escort the shareholders to your underground lair so they can save their souls."

"But there's only five Zombies down there," said Palmer. "What about *my* soul?"

"That's hardly one of my more pressing problems. I'll attend to that in time."

"But..."

"I said go!"

Palmer left with his tail between his legs, closely followed by the shareholders.

Doc Papa stood and walked to the window. Vincenzo remained standing quietly by the desk.

"You know what I learned from my days as a trader?" Doc Papa said. Vincenzo knew better than to answer. "That every catastrophe is an opportunity for great profit. Those men haven't the vision to see this, that's why I've got them just where I want them. Like all small minded fools they see only a crisis, where I see greater forces at work – forces of opportunity. When these forces strike, it doesn't matter if they're a market correcting itself, an ecological disaster or the Loa exerting their will, there is always a great profit to be made. When people are panicked and uncertain of what's happening they're vulnerable. And when they're vulnerable you can profit from them."

"You were toying with them, weren't you?" said Vincenzo.

"I see you've been paying attention for once. They're not aware of it of course, but whoever sabotaged the soul bank did us a favour. With the souls released from their Pot-tets they're that much easier to reap and to dominate."

"Do you know who sabotaged the soul bank yet?"

"I have my suspicions, now I just have to go and confirm them. If I'm right then Erzulie Zandor has made good on her word."

CHAPTER THIRTY-TWO

Sam McKane was fighting mad. He was ready to hog-tie that Doc Papa son-of-a-bitch and put one right between his eyes. As soon as he got off this God-forsaken island he was going to put together an army of lawyers so big these motherfuckers would be shitting writs for the rest of their lives.

Goddamn it, there was blood on his alligator boots. The cut on his hand was dripping again. Problem was he couldn't hardly feel a thing in either of his hands anymore. He cut the hand this morning on a cologne bottle. Dropped it on the bathroom floor trying to get rid of the smell.

He was starting to stink like one of them damned walking corpses. Every one of the guests was. He didn't know what they'd done to him but, by God, they were going to pay.

He wrapped his kerchief round his hand. He really should go to the infirmary and get it seen to but he couldn't afford to leave the mansion. They were about to make some sort of announcement and he needed to know what was going on.

All the guests were packed in there, as well as those cocksuckers they'd flown in who'd already done the course. No-one knew what was going on. Everyone was nervous and confused, milling around and waiting for something to happen. All of 'em looking like spare pricks at a party for unemployed whores. Finally Palmer appeared. He looked in poor shape and he was obviously as pissed as the rest of them. He was flanked by a squadron of guards who set up a podium for him. He was mobbed before he even opened his mouth.

Everyone charged him, shouting questions, waving fists, making demands. The guards shielded Palmer as he raised his hands to quiet the clamour of raised voices.

"Alright, alright that's enough," Palmer said. "Let's have a bit of order. I'm not going to take individual questions at this juncture. To begin with the management on St Ignatius would like to apologise for the disruption in our services and any inconvenience this has caused you." There was a chorus of jeers and catcalls. Palmer shook his head. "Okay, if you want to find out what's going on, you're going to have to let me get through this. Now some of you might have noticed some changes in the way you feel. This is a perfectly natural part of the process you're going through. It'll all become clear in a little while.

"We're always striving to increase the parameters of the course here on St Ignatius and to improve the scope of your learning. That's why I'm excited to announce the next stage in your journey along the Way of the Barefoot Zombie. This part of the course will be new to all of you. Due to the nature of what we had planned and the timing in unveiling it we couldn't make any pre-announcements. But we can now promise you an even greater degree of intimacy with your Inner Zombie and an increased level of power and understanding."

There were disgruntled murmurings among the guests. Sam knew bullshit when he smelt it, and he could smell it now. Palmer held up an ivory disk with some Voodoo markings on it.

"Now you should all remember this from the soul transference ceremony. It's a Baka. It's a Voodoo talisman that keeps your soul safe. You should think of it as a credit card for the soul bank. It allows you to deposit your soul and withdraw it. Now we've added a new facility which allows you to transfer your soul between vessels.

"Up until now we've only offered you the opportunity to store your soul in a Pot-tet. But now you can upgrade to one of the Living Dead. Once you've been issued with your personal Baka we'll find a time in the next few days when you can choose a Zombie from our colony to house your soul.

"Now some of you might have noticed they've left the compound at present. I also understand that our newest graduates encountered them at the Ounfó last night. This is all part of the process of readying them for your souls. To get the Zombies properly receptive we had to allow them to roam free for a while. But let me assure you they have been under supervision at all times and will be returned to the compound shortly."

There was a huge uproar at this. Whatever it was Palmer was selling, no-one was buying it.

"I've already said I won't take individual questions. Now the guards are going to pass among you with your personalised Bakas. I suggest you try and receive them in as orderly a fashion as possible. Once you've been issued with your Baka you merely have to place it on the forehead of a Zombie, right between the eyes where the third eye is, to transfer your soul into it."

Two guards stepped around the front of the podium as Palmer beat a hasty retreat. They opened two security cases. Inside were the Bakas. Everyone rushed them.

"What do you think of what Palmer just said?" George Griffin asked Sam.

"I think it's horse shit is what it is."

"I hear that terrorists have kidnapped the Zombies," said Arthur Sonnenfeldt. "And they blew up the soul bank, used some kind of gas to knock us all out. That's why they're giving us these Bakas, because the soul bank doesn't work anymore."

"But why would terrorists want to kidnap the Zombies?" said Bessie. "What are they going to do with them?"

"Let 'em loose in some public place, use 'em to torture prisoners," said Sam. "Who knows what these whack-jobs will get up to? They're motivated by envy and dogma. They hate us cos of the things we have and they don't."

"More importantly," said George, "what does this mean to us? What's going to happen to us if our souls aren't safe?"

"I think it's obvious isn't it?" said Sam. "We're turning into one of them. We're becoming walking corpses."

"Oh my," said Bessie.

"How could we be this stupid?" said Arthur. "I mean to just hand over our souls to them. What were we thinking?"

"We weren't thinking," said George. "We were so caught up in what we could gain we didn't assess the risks properly. Why does anyone make a stupid investment? Because they don't want to lose out when it looks as though everyone else is profiting. If an investment keeps paying off we all want to jump on. We don't want to think about what might happen if the bubble bursts, because no-one else is. We're a herd animal. We run with the pack, even when it's charging off a steep cliff. You've only got to look at the current financial crisis to see that."

"Yeah, well the current financial crisis is the least of my worries," said Sam. "How're we going to get our hands on a Zombie to keep our souls safe?"

"Don't you trust the centre to round them up for us?" said Bessie.

"Not one bit. We're going to have to take matters into our own hands, before time runs out."

Without any warning everyone started to pile out of the lobby, pushing past Sam and the others. Sam grabbed the arm of the young guy he'd seen taking a swing at a Zombie back in the Ounfó. "Hey buddy. Where's everyone going?"

"Into the jungle. Someone's found out where all the Zombies are."

"Oh yeah, and where's that?"

"There's an abandoned copper mine about twenty minutes down the track from the temple."

"Much obliged," said Sam and let the young guy go.

"Listen," said Arthur, getting antsy. "I don't mean to be rude or nothing, but I don't want to miss out on this."

"Me neither," said Bessie and followed Arthur.

"Just like I told you," said George. "We're a herd animal. Always will be. Be seeing you Sam."

"Bye George. You take care going over them cliffs now."

Sam sauntered over to the guards posted by the entrance to the office suite.

"Sir," said one of the youngest to his superior. "Shouldn't we be doing something?"

"My orders are to guard the mansion," said his superior. "And that's what I'm doing. I wasn't told nothing 'bout keeping no guests in the building."

"Morning boys." Sam said.

"Sir," said the guard. "We're not permitted to fraternise with guests of the establishment."

"Well now son, I appreciate that, but fraternising wasn't quite what I had in mind. I'll come straight to the point. I've got a business proposition for y'all."

CHAPTER THIRTY-THREE

"This nail isn't long enough," Benjamin said. "See, it only just goes though the plank? You need to get me some longer ones."

"There aren't any longer ones," Tatyana said. "We've got to make do with what we can find."

Benjamin punched the wall in frustration. He always got bullish and overbearing when he tried to do any kind of DIY. Maybe he thought it made him look more manly. Tatyana didn't care. He was pissing her off, acting like a brute.

"I still don't see why Miria ... I mean Brigitte couldn't get a bunch of the Zombies to help out," he said.

"Because they wouldn't be any use to us. Can you image one of them trying to use a hammer?"

"Ow," he said, accidentally hitting his thumb. "Well they couldn't do a much worse job than me."

Tatyana smiled, she liked him better when he kept his sense of humour.

They were both tense and exhausted. They hadn't slept since

the night before. Their muscles ached from barricading the doors and windows of the old copper mine's offices. The smelled of damp and decay. Bits of machinery and office supplies from the sixties lay in dusty corners.

"Does that look as though it'll hold?" said Benjamin looking at the last of the planks he'd nailed to the main window.

"I guess."

"Y'know. I can't work out whether this is more like the beginning of *Night of the Living Dead*, where Duane Jones and Judith O'Dea are boarding up the windows of the house they're trapped in. Or *Day of the Dead*, where everyone's holed up in that military bunker next to the abandoned mine."

"Oh for God's sake Benjamin, will you give it a rest with the Zombie movies What is up with you? This isn't some dumb movie, this is really happening to us."

"I know it's not a movie okay? I am painfully aware there are men out there with guns that are coming to kill us and we're barricaded in here with a bunch of walking corpses that could tear us to pieces at any moment. And that is scaring me shitless right now. The only way I have of dealing with that is by viewing the whole thing as a movie. So that way I can kid myself that if anything goes wrong I can just hit pause and rewind. Is that okay with you?"

Now it was Tatyana's turn to feel like a brute. "Yeah, that's just fine with me. We've all got our ways of coping. Sorry for busting your balls."

"That's okay, we're both on edge."

"I guess it's your way of sticking to the Third Rule of Interaction: 'It doesn't matter and you don't care'."

"Or Rule Number Five."

'Master yourself and nothing can threaten you.'

"Yeah, I wish that was the case. Right now everything seems threatening. No matter what side of the barricades we're on. Speaking of which, all we've got to do is block up that last door. We're out of planks. Do you think a couple of filing cabinets and a desk will hold it?"

"It's worth a try."

They'd just shoved the desk up against the two filing cabinets when they heard it.

"Does that sound like someone running to you?" said Benjamin.

It did. Tatyana could hear several sets of footsteps in the undergrowth outside the office. Then she heard someone shout, though they were too far away for her to make out what they said.

"Is that the guards again?" Tatyana said. She walked round to one of the windows they'd just boarded up and peered through a gap in the planks.

Benjamin joined her. "Can't see anything. How 'bout you?"

A sudden sharp tap on the window pane made them both jump.

"Hey Benjamin, is that you? It is. It is you. Hey let me in kid."

Tatyana looked at Benjamin, who just shrugged. It was Arthur Sonnenfeldt. He was red faced from running and he was motioning to them to let him in.

"Err, Arthur I think you ought to get out of here," Benjamin called out to him. "This place is full of Zombies and the guards are on their way."

"I know, I know that's why you've got to let me in quick. Hey how'd you get in there with them anyway? You've got to tell me the way in."

Benjamin looked at Tatyana. "Do you think we should let him in?"

"I don't know. What if he's a spy or something? Maybe they've sent him to try and get in so he can let the guards in."

Benjamin called out to Arthur again. "I don't think that's a good idea. We're going to go now Arthur. You really ought to get out of here."

"Hey, hey! Don't you walk away from me." Arthur shouted. "Don't you walk away from me you little pissant! Come back here, you've got to let me in, you've got to. I don't have much longer, I can feel it. It's alright for you, you're young. Don't go, I said don't..."

"What the hell is he talking about?" said Benjamin.

"I have no idea," said Tatyana.

She heard more commotion in the jungle outside and Arthur called out: "Hey, hey, over here, they're in here, quick!"

Tatyana heard what sounded like a stampede charging towards them. Then the sound of thirty or forty pairs of hands began banging on the windows, the doors and the walls. The two filing cabinets it had taken them ages to move began to shake as someone battered on the door.

People were shouting "open up," and "let us in" and "you get those boards down right now, you hear, right now!"

The panes in the windows shattered and the planks over them started to shake. Someone found the board Benjamin hadn't entirely nailed in place and pushed it off. It crashed to the floor. Five or six arms reached through the gap, grasping at the air and tearing at the other boards.

It was the other guests, they were trying to get in, but why? Tatyana could see the expressions on their faces, desperate, angry full of fear and need. These weren't marauding creatures, they were human beings, panicked and nearly hysterical. Even with everything she'd been through it was one of the most frightening things she'd ever seen.

Brigitte came through from the next room where she'd been looking after the Zombies. Tatyana could hear they were getting agitated.

"What's going on?" Brigitte said.

"I have no idea," Benjamin said. "They all turned up and demanded we let them in."

"Are they crazy?" Tatyana said. "Why would they want to get in here with all these Zombies?"

"I think I know," said Brigitte.

They all looked up as they heard footsteps on the roof.

"Can they get in that way?" said Benjamin.

The noise of breaking glass reached them as the skylight in the other room broke.

"I think they just have," Tatyana said.

Tatyana followed the others in time to see three guests she didn't recognise jump down among the Zombies. One of them had cut her hand on the skylight. She landed badly and yowled in pain.

Four Zombies closed in. The woman got to her feet and held out her hands to ward them off. The smell of the blood drove them wild.

She tried backing, stumbled and fell. The Zombies fell on her. The woman screamed in agony as their dead, decaying teeth tore into her.

Tatyana looked to Brigitte, who shook her head. "It's too late to intervene," she said. "It would just get more of them riled up."

The other two intruders fared better. They got to their feet and dropped straight into Zombie mode, obeying the first two Rules of Interaction.

More and more of the Zombies crowded round the body of the dead guest, trying to tear a scrap of flesh or bone loose. Brigitte couldn't push through throng to get to the intruders.

Through the bustle of the Zombies Tatyana saw one of the intruders pull out an ivory disk. He held it at arms length and moved in a slow, predatory manner towards one of the Zombies scrabbling for the woman's flesh.

When he got close enough the man placed the ivory talisman on the Zombie's forehead. Both of them shook as though several thousand volts went through them the minute the talisman touched the Zombie.

This caused the man to stumble and fall over two Zombies who were feeding. They dropped the bones they were gnawing and grabbed him. The man tried to wrestle them off but his sudden movements jostled other Zombies who moved in on him.

The man managed to sit upright before a young female Zombie with beads in its hair sunk its teeth into his neck. The man roared as the Zombie came away with a huge chunk of his flesh in its mouth. Blood pumped in great gouts from the ragged hole. It spilled down his chest and soaked into his shirt as he started to hyperventilate. Excited by the freshly spilled blood the other Zombies sunk their teeth into him.

As this was happening the Zombie he had touched with the talisman began to shout and scream in distress. It was the first time Tatyana had heard one of them try to speak. It was hard to understand at first. Its vocal chords had not been used in a while and there wasn't much air coming from its lungs.

Tatyana was surprised when she realised it was shouting: "No! Stop it, stop it, get off you're killing me!" The screaming Zombie tried pulling the other Zombies off the man but didn't succeed.

Brigitte waded into the middle of the undead and raised her arms. She shouted something in the tongue of the dead and the Zombies became more docile. They parted to form a space around Brigitte and the screaming Zombie, slinking off to chew on their stolen morsels like scolded children.

The other intruder hung back and watched as Brigitte bent down and picked up the ivory talisman the man had dropped. She glanced at it and shook her head in disgust.

"Get out of him!" she said to the screaming Zombie.

"Please," said the Zombie. "This is all I've got, please let me stay. I'll leave right away. I won't bother you."

"Get out now!" Brigitte raised her arm and made a sign in the air.

"But I've got nowhere to go. I can't pass over now. I'll die completely and totally."

"You already have," said Brigitte and clicked her fingers.

The Zombie went rigid and fell, face first, to the ground.

Brigitte crouched and checked the unmoving body. She let out a wail of anguish and dismay. "You've killed him," she cried beating the dead body with her fists. "I can't save him now you've killed him!"

Brigitte glanced up at the other intruder. She was shaking with anger as she stood and confronted him. "Give me the Baka."

"But..." said the man. "It's my only hope. It's all I've got."

"I wasn't asking you. I said give it to me!"

The man handed it over. Miriam held the talisman to her lips and whispered to it. The man clutched at his chest and his stomach as though something was missing from him. "What... did... you... what... did... you... do?"

"I sent your Gros Bon Ange on to the crossroads of the worlds, to wait with the souls of all the others. If I am successful it will

be returned to you when all the others are reunited with theirs."
The man put his hands to his head as though he had a splitting
headache. "I cant... think. Why... happen... that...?"

"Now your Gros Bon Ange is no longer on this plane, your Ti
Bon Ange has gone to join it. You're changing."

The man's eyes rolled up into his head and his body shuddered.
He had obviously died but he didn't fall to the ground. His
body twitched and jerked. It began to walk as though it didn't
understand why it was still moving, going nowhere and bumping
in to the other Zombies.

"What's happened to him?" said Tatyana.

"He has become the same as the islanders." said Brigitte.

"A Zombie?"

"If you want to call it that, yes. The souls of my islanders are
trapped at the crossroads of the astral worlds. Their souls cannot
carry on into the afterlife so their bodies cannot rest. I have sent
his soul to be with theirs. If I can return their souls to them his
will also be returned."

"How will you do that?"

"Tonight is the last night of the Festival of the Gédé, the one
night of the year when I can perform the ceremony that will
return their souls to them. I need to get them to a crossroads
at the centre of St Ignatius to do this. Until then I need to keep
them safe."

"What's with these weird disks they're carrying?" said
Benjamin.

"They're called Bakas. They were created for the ceremony
Doc Papa performed last night. They hold the soul to the earthly
plane and they can also direct it into other vessels. Now we've
destroyed their soul bank, the only place they can store their
souls is inside a living corpse."

"So that's what happened when he put his Baka thing on the
Zombie's forehead? He was transferring his soul into it? Then
you drove his soul out of the Zombie's body. But why did you
get upset about killing him?"

"Way to go with the sensitive questions," said Tatyana.

"That's okay," said Brigitte. "I wasn't upset about killing him.

What upset me was that the body he was possessing died."

"The body," said Tatyana. "Was that someone you knew well?"

"It was my brother. We were very close. And I failed him."

Tatyana couldn't think of anything else to say after that. Neither could Benjamin. They left Brigitte alone to mourn her loss.

Tatyana wanted to check the barricades in the office were still up. To her alarm half of them were down and the guests outside were almost able to climb in.

"There's a large basement downstairs that connects to the mine shaft," Brigitte said. "It's one of the main entrances to the mine. It has a metal door we can bolt. We have to get down there quickly."

Brigitte led them through the room and down several flights of stairs. Watching the Zombies stumbling progress down the concrete steps was painful.

There were several falls with every flight. The Zombies who fell had to be encouraged back to their feet. All the while they could hear the guests getting closer to finally breaking in.

Finally they got the last of the Zombies into the basement and bolted the heavy iron door. They could hear the guests' feet clattering on the concrete steps as they did.

The basement was pitch black with the door closed. Tatyana couldn't see a thing. All she could hear was the sound of the Zombies shuffling feet and their strange groaning breath.

She reached out for Benjamin and found him in the dark. She slipped her arms round his waist and pulled him close. He seemed a little surprised. They hadn't been physically close since she'd held him while he cried outside the Ounfó. He put his arms round her for comfort all the same.

Tatyana heard a match strike and saw a flickering light come closer. It was Brigitte carrying an oil lamp.

"This was left behind here," she said. "Lucky I have good night vision."

"Can I talk Zombie movies for a minute?" said Benjamin.

"Sure," said Tatyana. "Knock yourself out."

"Well it just occurred to me that what's happening here is like the complete opposite of more or less any Zombie movie. Sooner or later pretty much all of them boil down to a siege situation. A group of living people find themselves inside an enclosed space surrounded by Zombies trying to break in. The Zombies want to bite the people so they'll die and come back as Zombies."

"Okay, I watched a lot of these movies with you don't forget. So tell me something I don't know."

"Haven't you noticed it's the Zombies who are under siege here? The living are the ones trying to break in and get to *them*. Not to kill them but to bring them back to life by injecting their souls into them with those weird Baka things. It's a complete reversal of the formula."

"That's because there's no formula here, " said Tatyana. "This isn't fiction. Welcome to real life. This isn't like any Zombie movie you've ever seen."

CHAPTER THIRTY-FOUR

"Got you." The little vixen was coming out from behind the trees. Palmer had her just where he wanted her.

He'd picked her up on the island's CCTV. He'd had a huge row with Doc Papa about getting the camera's installed around the island. Doc Papa had claimed he didn't need them. That he could access the "invisible world" using his Voodoo and that was much better.

Palmer had pointed out that Doc Papa had better things to do with his time than monitor the entire island via the 'invisible world', and that the people they'd have to pay to do the monitoring wouldn't know Voodoo. Doc Papa eventually conceded, but only after he found a way to make it look as though it had been his idea all along. Simply to remind Palmer who was really in control.

That's what Doc Papa was doing when he handed all of Palmer's lovelies over to those cock sucking shareholders. He was trying to put Palmer in his place. He was also trying to incentivise him, so that Palmer would ensure the Zombies were rounded up at all costs in order to save his own soul.

Doc Papa had reckoned without Palmer's resourcefulness though. None of the guests, or even the shareholders, were ever told, but there were quite a few stray Zombies roaming the island. Usually they were in the remoter areas which is why they hadn't been rounded up.

The first thing Palmer did after handing his lovers over to the shareholders was head straight for the control room to check the CCTV cameras for these strays. After an hour of searching he finally saw something he liked. A hot little number wandering round the jungle on the other side of the island.

Which is how he came to be sitting in a jeep, stalking her a couple of hours later. As she came into view Palmer picked up the snare and slipped out of the jeep. He snuck up to a tree she was shambling towards and waited.

As she passed the tree Palmer stepped out behind her and slipped the snare around her neck. The Zombie began to thrash about as soon he caught her. Her teeth gnashed and her arms grasped for him. Oh she was a feisty little one indeed.

Probably hadn't eaten in a while by the look of her. She wasn't in the best shape. Still he couldn't afford to be choosy in the circumstances. She was the closest thing to his type that he could find.

He pushed her up against a tree with the snare, then walked around back of her so she couldn't grab him. Holding the Baka in his free hand he placed it on her forehead right where her third eye ought to be.

What happened next felt a lot like an ejaculation that started several miles away and rushed right through him and into the Zombie. Both of them shook so hard that Palmer dropped the snare and fell backwards. Strangely he felt colder and more empty than ever when it was over. Even though he had found a vessel for his dispossessed soul.

Palmer got to his feet and rested against the tree. He felt shaken and drained as though he had just undergone a huge emotional outburst. He looked over at the Zombie. It was no longer flailing about like a wild creature. That was the only visible change in its appearance apart from the eyes.

The eyes were alight with an awareness and intelligence she hadn't possessed before. A cold, prying intelligence that Palmer recognised as his own. It was a strange sensation to see himself staring out of someone else's eyes. He didn't care much for it. It made him feel judged. There was a silent condemnation coming from behind those newly awoken eyes.

"Alright," he said. "I presume you can understand me?"

The Zombie made to speak but her mouth wasn't able make any words. She put her hand to her throat as though something was blocking it.

"You need to get in the jeep. We're getting off the island. Things are falling apart. It's time to cut our losses and run before the bottom falls out of the whole enterprise. Do you hear me?"

The Zombie nodded and followed Palmer to the jeep.

"I've got to get you back inside me before I get off the island," said Palmer. "Today is the final day of the Festival of the Gédé. In spite of what Doc Papa told those idiot shareholders, this is the last day that souls *can* be transferred. He's obviously playing some power game with them. Manipulating them like he does everyone else. But not me, oh no, if he thinks he's got my measure then he's sorely mistaken. He thinks he's the only one who really knows what's going on round here, but he's wrong. I've picked up a thing or two in my time on this island. I know we need to take you to a glade in the centre of the island. And we need to sacrifice a black goat and a black hen. That's why we've got to make a quick pit stop back at the compound to pick them up."

Palmer glanced over at the Zombie. She was looking intently at him, almost through him. "For Christ's sake will you stop staring like that? You're making me uncomfortable."

The Zombie coughed violently. It looked like she was choking. Eventually she spat a great mouthful of soil and dead leaves into her hand. Then a giant, chestnut brown beetle crawled out of her mouth, opened its carapace and flew away.

"I'm sorry," she said in a gravelly voice, that came from vocal chords that hadn't been used in a while. "That was stopping me from talking."

Palmer turned away to concentrate on the track as he started up the jeep. He found the sight of the Zombie coughing up soil and insects so repulsive that he was seriously turned on. He tried to ignore the huge erection he was getting as he drove off.

"It's not the staring."

"What?"

"It's not the staring that makes you uncomfortable," said the Zombie. Her voice sounded unusually masculine. "It's that fact that you can't ignore me any longer. You've been ignoring the existence of your soul for most of your life. Now you're faced with the incontrovertible proof that you have a soul, you don't like it. You can't neglect me anymore. I'm right in your face."

She really knew how to kill the mood.

"I know you exist," said Palmer. "I've seen too much in my time here to think otherwise."

"Yes but I'm an inconvenient truth to you. A guilty secret you have to keep hidden from others, like a weakness."

"Look, I'm doing everything in my power to get you back inside me. I can't be that ashamed of you."

"You're only hanging on to me because of what I mean to your survival. I'm just an asset to you. Something to stop you turning into a Zombie."

"You're the most precious asset I have. Isn't that obvious from the lengths I'm going to just to hang on to you?"

"I've got to argue your case before God when we die you know?" said Palmer's soul. "Convince Him not to toss you into the abyss. That's what a Gros Bon Ange does. You haven't given me much to work with so far though have you? What am I going to say in your defence? That I was the most precious thing on your balance sheet. So that cancels out all the people you've hurt with the things that you've done?"

Palmer stared straight ahead at the jungle. "You sound just like my father."

"Yes," said the Zombie. "I suppose I do. That's why I judge you so harshly. Because that's how your father judged you. That's how you were taught to judge yourself. Nothing you ever did was good enough. That's how he made you feel all the time. And your mother, she may as well have been dead to you for all the comfort and love she showed. All of that was reserved for your sister not you. Then when you were twelve she did die. You got to spend a whole hour with the corpse, do you remember? That was the longest you'd spent in her company since you were a baby. Just before you had to go, when you knew no-one was looking, you bent and gave her cold lips a goodbye kiss, do you recall? You probably don't realise it, but that's where this whole necrophilia thing started."

"I don't know what you're talking about."

"Don't try putting me on. I am you, remember. I know more of your guilty secrets than you do. Don't go pretending this doesn't turn you on. You've finally done what you've wanted to do your whole life. You've impregnated a corpse with your soul. Most men get to see bits of themselves inside the children they beget on women. But you, you got to impregnate the object of your desire with nothing more than your own life. When you look into the eyes of this corpse you see only yourself staring back. Isn't that what every narcissist like you dreams of in a lover?"

Palmer put his foot down in annoyance. "You're just a tease. That's all you are. A filthy tease."

"I'm not stopping you lover. I've never stopped you indulging your desires, have I? You wouldn't listen to me anyway. I know all about that hard on you're trying to hide. I know where you'd like to put it. This corpse is pretty ripe isn't it, all rotting and decayed. I know what that smell's doing to you. Why resist anymore?"

"There isn't time."

"There won't be any time soon. This might be your only opportunity."

Palmer stopped the jeep. He leant over and put his hands on the Zombie's hips. She moved closer to him. He pressed his lips to her cheek. The skin felt rotten and soft, it was on the point of putrefaction. He could see the maggots crawling around underneath it.

Palmer couldn't believe how much this aroused him. He slid

his hand up the Zombie's thigh, lifted her tattered dress and slipped his fingers into her fraying knickers.

Then he froze. He felt sickened and repulsed by what he felt inside her underwear. He pulled his hand away in revulsion. "You tricked me. You knew."

"Oh, did I forget to tell you?" said his soul laughing inside the Zombie. She slipped down her knickers and revealed the largest penis Palmer had ever seen, on the living or the dead. "You just picked up the island's only Zombie lady-boy."

CHAPTER THIRTY-FIVE

Sam McKane was ready to kick ass. This was where people started paying. He was taking control and he was getting his due.

The jeep he was riding was off-road. It kept swerving to avoid palm trees and rocks. He and the guards were thrown about in the back.

He seemed to be losing all sensation of pain. His back would usually be in agony after this much punishment, not to mention his ass. It didn't bother him at all though. He wondered if this was a drawback or a bonus of the changes he was going through. He didn't care to find out what would happen if he changed much further. That was why he was taking action.

The jeep pulled up in a clearing and the men jumped out. Sam climbed out after them. "Why are we stopping? he demanded. "This isn't the mine."

"No sir," said Donovan, the Head Guard. "The mine's about ten minutes down that track. This is the best wi-fi connection in this part of the island."

"Wi-fi? I thought there wasn't any internet here?"

"Not for the private use of guests there isn't sir. But the guards and the management have access. There's a transmitter in the security post, behind us."

"Security post?"

"They're all over the island sir, tiny bases where two or three men can hole up for security and defence purposes."

A thickset guard with a moustache handed Donovan a silver laptop, which he opened and gave to Sam. "Now about the small matter of payment," Donovan said.

Sam grunted. "Playing hardball huh? Where'd you get the laptop?"

"One of my men stole it sir. You said you'd transfer two million dollars into an account we could all access. You'll be able to do that on this machine."

"We're getting a little ahead of ourselves aren't we son? I'm paying you to do a job. So far all you've done is get my ass sore by driving me into the middle of nowhere."

"Sir, the mine is just around the corner. We're ahead of any other troops that they've sent. But my men need assurances if they're going to disobey direct orders and put their lives in danger."

"You'll get paid, soon as you've got me a Zombie. Don't you worry about that."

"Sir, we need to get paid now or you can take your chances getting your own damn Zombie."

Sam logged on to one of his three private banks and brought up his account details. "I'm going to create an account for you. I'll transfer a million into it now and I'll transfer the rest once I'm off the island."

"Make it a million and a half."

"Make it suck my dick." Sam handed the laptop back to Donovan. "That's the account I've created for you, all the security and access details are on the screen and you can see the balance."

"One million dollars," said Donovan. A guard looking over his shoulder whistled. Donovan put his elbow in the guard's ribs.

"Shut up Kavanaugh."

Kavanaugh was as tall as Donovan but not as broad and, judging from his pizza face, a decade younger. He sloped off.

"Yates stick this back in the truck." Donovan handed the laptop to the guard with the moustache.

"Now this is what you're going to do," said Sam. "Two of you will stay and guard me in the jeep, the rest of you will break into the that mine and get me the three fittest male Zombies you can find. When I've transferred my soul into the Zombie I want you're going to drive me to the harbour, commandeer a boat to escort me to mainland Haiti. When I'm safe, and I've got hold of my own witchdoctor who can get me back my soul, you can have the rest of the money."

"Sir, what about Zombies for myself and my men?" said Donovan. "Our souls were in that bank too."

"There won't be room in the jeep for that many Zombies and there wont be time for all of you to cherry pick your favourite ones. You go straight in, get my Zombies and come straight out. Is that clear?"

"With respect sir, time is of the essence for all of us. If I send men to Haiti with you they won't get a chance to save their souls. And judging from the rate we're all changing that means they won't be of much use to when you hit Haiti."

"That's your problem son, not mine. When I pay someone to do a job, I don't expect to have to hold their hand every damn step of the way. That's something you've got to sort out in your own time, not while you're working for me."

"Thanks Sam," said Donovan. "That makes this a lot easier." He pulled out his pistol.

"What the fuck? Boy do you want me to take that thing off you and shove it up your ass?"

"Old man, you're too frail to even shove it up your own ass."

"Hey Donovan man," said Yates. "Are you sure you know what you're doing?"

"I know exactly what I'm doing."

"You ain't gonna shoot him now are ya?" said Kavanaugh. "Cos if you do, then we won't get paid t'other million."

"We ain't ever going to get paid the other million," Donovan said. "This wily old cunt'd fuck us six ways to Sunday before he ever paid us that. We've got all we're going to get out of him."

"Now son, that ain't exactly true," Sam said. "Why I've always been strictly honest and above board in all my dealings. You ask anyone I've done business with. I'm a man of my word and when I give it, by heck I keep it."

"Like fuck you do," said Donovan. "I'm sorry Sam but I'm just not buying your act."

Sam felt his heart start to beat faster. He could even feel sweat on his brow. He was wrangling for his life and soul now.

"Now hold on a moment. You're turning down a lot of money here boys. You could all be set up for life with what I'm offering. Now you guys like to bargain hard, I respect that. I tell you what, as a show of good faith I'll even throw in an extra half million when we get to Haiti. What do you say?"

"Not interested Sam," said Donovan.

Yates stepped up to him. "Whoa, whoa hold on Donovan. You didn't consult us about this. What if we want to take him up on his offer?"

"He's right boys," said Sam. "You ought to listen to this man."

"Shut your fucking face Sam," said Donovan. "I'm your commanding officer Yates. Since when did I consult you about what I'm going to do?"

"I'm just saying we could make a lot more money if you don't shoot him now. We might not get a chance at this much money ever again in our lives."

"I'm with Yates," said Kavanaugh.

"Another word from you dickwad," said Donovan. "And you're next for a bullet. We can make a lot more money than he's offering, or probably even got. Here's what we're going to do. When I've shot him we're going to go down to that mine and take control of all those Zombies. We're going to hole up with them nice and secure so no-one can get in and then we're going to auction them off, one at time, to those rich bastards. If he's prepared to pay us two million for one of 'em, then they all will.

There's at least fifty of them on this island. You do the math."

"Now that's just plain crazy boy," said Sam. "There's a hundred guards on this island they'll never let you get away with that."

"If we take the Zombies down into the mine they won't be able to find us. We'll control the one thing on the island everyone wants, including the guards. They'll *have* to do business with us."

"Look son, let me give you a piece of business advice. I've been in business a long time and I've learned a thing or two. You stick with the deal you've got in your hand, you don't go endangering it by chasing off after some half-baked, cockamamie scheme. I'm prepared to go higher if the price is an issue. How does three and a half million sound?"

"Not interested."

"Why don't we make it four million?"

"Why don't we make it suck my dick." Donovan said and fired three times.

Sam felt like he'd been punched three times in the stomach and back. He looked down at the holes the bullet had left in his gut and wondered why it didn't hurt as much as it ought to. Blood began to trickle out but not as fast or as much as he expected. His body was even getting slow at dying now.

"He's still standing," said Kavanaugh. "Why is he standing?"

Donovan raised his pistol and aimed at Sam's head.

Sam cowered and held out his hand to protect his face. The last thing he saw, in the split second before his brains blew out of the back of his head, was the bullet slicing off his middle finger.

CHAPTER THIRTY-SIX

"That's impossible," said Vincenzo.

Doc Papa looked at the freshly dug soil of the grave and the long empty box at the bottom of it. "Apparently not."

"But you put her in that box," Vincenzo said. "I saw you nail it shut. I helped you bury her. We did the ceremony, the wards and charms are all still working. How did she get out if they're all still working? They should have warned us."

"And yet they didn't. It seems we underestimated her. And babbling like an idiot isn't going to help."

"What *is* going to help?"

"Following my orders to the letter. Giving yourself over entirely to my will. I am divinely ordained by the Loas. To follow me is to follow them."

"Right now I'm following you down the road to ruin."

Doc Papa drew himself up and glowered at Vincenzo. The sheer force of his stare was enough to make Vincenzo wilt.

Doc Papa dismissed the two acolytes who had dug up the grave.

They went back to wait by the vehicle. The light was dimming, evening was coming on. The clock was ticking and he had much to achieve before the Festival of the Gédé drew to a close.

"Describing our current situation as 'the road to ruin' only shows how little you understand," said Doc Papa. "This is confirmation that the Loa have blessed my plans. For a start we've settled the little matter of who our rouge Mambo is. I should have recognised her handiwork the minute all this started."

"You can't seriously be suggesting that Brigitte Laveau is back on St Ignatius? We created a living death for her. How did she escape that? How did she get back on the island without us knowing about it?"

"My guess is that she never died. She found some way to circumvent our spell and got off the island without us finding out. Then she either created an entirely new identity, complete with a new body and a new fortune, or she found a way to borrow one. You have to admire her prowess if nothing else."

"You still have the hots for her," said Vincenzo with a smirk.

Doc Papa drew a symbol in the air and Vincenzo collapsed in agony. He had been overstepping himself a lot lately and needed to be reminded just how in thrall he was to Doc Papa. With a supreme effort of will Vincenzo held up a hand in surrender. As he was in a good mood Doc Papa only let him suffer a little while longer.

"Can I get up now?" said Vincenzo.

"Why don't you try?"

Vincenzo shook as he got to his feet. He stared down at the empty grave so as not to look Doc Papa in the eye. "You really think Brigitte Laveau is back on the island?"

"I'm certain of it. Erzulie Zandor is putting all the pieces into place for me just as she promised."

"By sending this accursed woman back to stop you?"

"Not to stop me. To help me."

"Help you?"

"She's the only one who knows where the Gateway of the Souls is."

"You really think it exists?" Vincenzo held up his hands

in deference. "I don't mean any disrespect but we've looked everywhere in the Invisible World and we never found even a trace of it. The only proof we've found of it's existence are a few rumours and the word of a woman we tried to kill."

"I know it exists. Don't mistake your ignorance for lack of proof. You know only as much as I allow you to, that's why I'm permanently ahead of you. You can't even see the pattern here. At the very moment when I need the Gateway most Erzulie Zandor sends me the one person who knows its location, just as she said she would."

"How are you going to get it from her? She wouldn't tell you the last time, even to save herself from a living death. Now we're not even sure where she is, let alone the Gateway of the Souls. All we know is she's down a mine somewhere."

"I am disappointed that you show so little faith in my abilities Vincenzo. Maybe I was wrong to give you so much responsibility. Perhaps another of my acolytes would assist me better."

"I wasn't saying I don't have faith in you. I just wanted to know what you were planning so I could assist you in the best possible way."

"The best way you can assist me is to do exactly as you're told when you're told. I don't need to know her exact physical location. Now I know who she is I can find her through the Invisible World. I can tear the knowledge from her mind. As I'm fairly certain she doesn't know I've discovered who she really is, that gives me the advantage of surprise. An advantage I intend to fully exploit."

Doc Papa turned his back on Vincenzo and walked back to the jeep. Vincenzo followed at a respectful distance. Doc Papa wasn't buying his fake deference. Vincenzo was asking too many questions. Why was he so keen to know Doc Papa's plans and motives all of a sudden? It smacked of duplicity.

Doc Papa didn't think Vincenzo had the intelligence or the initiative to challenge him alone. Someone else must have made him a counter offer and Doc Papa knew just who. It stood to reason really. Doc Papa would have done the same thing in their position. It was simply good business sense and he would have been disappointed in his associates if they hadn't attempted something. That's why he hadn't let Vincenzo out of his sight since the shareholders had stormed into his office.

He was even a little impressed by Vincenzo's treacherousness. Still they had all made the mistake of underestimating him. Doc Papa was more than prepared for them when they made their move.

He stopped when they reached the jeep and let Vincenzo get in first, smiling innocently to hide his true thoughts. Vincenzo smiled humbly back, hiding his true feelings almost as expertly. He hadn't realised he'd been rumbled yet.

"To the mansion," Doc Papa instructed the driver. It was time to visit his ceremony room. The most secret and highly guarded room of the mansion, where the endgame would be played out.

CHAPTER THIRTY-SEVEN

Two Years Ago

Doc stood at the bottom of the stone steps. Above him the burnt out shell of Mangrove Hall caught the crimson twilight of the setting sun. Moss and lichen covered the steps and tufts of grass pushed their way out of the cracks. The terraced lawns were given over to weeds and creepers.

This was a palace once. Look at what they've done to it. This is why they have to pay, Emil. You have to make them pay and you have to rebuild it. Restore this estate to its former glory Emil.

Emil, the name didn't feel appropriate anymore. That was the name of another man from another world. A man of wealth and influence. The man he had nearly forgotten he once was.

Doc was the name of the person who had stood in for that man when he had no memory. Neither name sat comfortably with him anymore. Neither of them represented what he had become. He needed a better mantle. One that befitted a man uniquely placed to re-make the world.

The name Doc came from his title. He couldn't be a Houngan in spite of his accomplishments, so they'd called him Doctor as was customary. As no-one knew his real name the islanders shortened Doctor to Doc and that's how he became known.

You're a Papamal Emil, any new name you choose must take that into account.

Doc shook his head to quiet the voice. It was becoming tiresome now. The spirit knew this and clung to him tighter as a consequence. That was how ghosts were when they got their claws into you.

He had to admit she'd been useful to him though. She knew where his lost memories lay. She could trace them along the ancestral bloodlines. She re-taught him his whole past and much more besides.

Doc had known nothing of his past before that. His memories started when he was washed ashore the small beach. He knew now that his charter plane, on its way to Rio, had crashed into the waters off St Ignatius. The engines failed according to the pilot. It was the last thing he said. Doc wondered if there weren't other forces at work.

Doc had total amnesia when the natives found him and brought him to Brigitte. Brigitte tended his wounds, brought his fever down and nursed him back to health. Every time she touched him she set off a different fever, deep inside him. He saw it burn in her eyes too. As his health returned this fever grew hotter in both of them. Eventually they were forced to succumb and it claimed them.

It wasn't the only thing to claim Doc. When he was well enough, Doc asked to be taken to a Voodoo ceremony. Brigitte was happy to oblige and introduced him to her congregation at the Ounfó. As the ceremony reached its peak, to everyone's surprise, the Loa Baron Samedi, ruler of the Gédé, chose to mount Doc and ride him.

As he lurched about in a macabre and obscene manner, Baron Samedi told the congregation that Doc had a special significance to the Loa. Baron Samedi commanded that Doc be initiated into the deepest mysteries of Voodoo.

So Doc became Brigitte's student as well as her lover. Under her tutelage he rose up through the stages of initiation faster than anyone had ever seen. He was joined with his patron Loa, or Met-tet, Baron Samedi in the ritual of the lave tet. Then he walked through fire in the kanzo rite. Finally he became a houn'ior and took the asson, his mystic rattle and badge of office, after walking the Poun'goueh – the waters of the abyss.

With no recollections of his former life he was an empty vessel ready to be filled with the knowledge of Voodoo. He went from being a broken castaway to a powerful Vodouisant, second only to Brigitte in the standing of the Ounfó, loved, feared and respected by the inhabitants of the island that had become his home.

Even still there was an aching hole in his life, like a wound that wouldn't heal. Nothing about his life or personality seemed fixed or permanent until he could anchor it to his past. But that past was missing. Without memories he felt insubstantial and insufficient. So much of him remained a question, so little provided answers.

It pained Brigitte to see her lover so troubled. To help him she suggested a special rite in which they would invoke his ancestors. As his memories were now like lost family members, the powers they should consult were his ancestors.

They had watched over him all his life. They knew the man he'd been, was and would be. They held all his memories in trust, so they could return them at the point of death. Your life did indeed flash before your eyes just before you died. Your ancestors saw to that.

Two weeks ago they'd held the rite inside the Djévo, the private chamber of the Ounfó. It had not gone as planned. Someone had come through, but not who they expected. Brigitte had been visited, not Doc.

She seemed confused as the spirit of her own ancestor came upon her. She wouldn't tell Doc what the ancestor was saying but it troubled her greatly. She fled the Ounfó without speaking to him and disappeared into the night.

He hadn't seen her since.

You're better off without her. You lost her but you gained me, and I can teach you so much more.

Doc had indeed gained the presence of perhaps his most famous ancestor. As soon as Brigitte left the temple his ancestor came upon him and revealed herself. She'd been waiting for his lover to leave.

His ancestor brought his lost memories with her and something even more valuable. A new sense of purpose.

As he experienced the succession of memories once more it was like living his life all over again, only this time as a different person. He had to introduce the person he'd become to the person he used to be. And in spite of the giant gulf between their worlds, he had to integrate them into one working personality.

His old self was appalled and amused to discover that he'd been living like a peasant on a tiny island near a third world country. The occult power that his new self wielded impressed him though.

His new self was astounded to find he used to own and control more wealth than he knew existed. The sheer number of material possessions he used to have overwhelmed him. He liked the influence and control this wealth could buy however.

One thing that united both selves was a lust for power. It was around this trait that he built his new character.

And I brought you power didn't I? I showed you a way to rule this island and to raise a fortune bigger than anything your forefathers dreamed.

Doc was careful to hide the thought that he found his ancestor's ambitions to be hopelessly limited in comparison to his own.

While Brigitte was away he took the time to plot his next move. He made covert contacts and new allies and waited for the right time to strike. That time had now arrived.

She'd sent word to him earlier today that she wanted to speak. He was to meet her in the ruins of Mangrove hall.

So now he climbed the steps of a building that had meant so much to his forefathers. That he had seen practically every day since coming to the island. Yet had never once explored.

He thought it fitting that Brigitte had chosen to meet him here. In this crumbling ruin that haunted the skyline of the entire island. He wondered if she was aware of the irony.

Despite all the things he planned to do, he was excited about seeing her again. There was a primordial attraction between them, like some unstoppable natural force.

Pah, men! Stop thinking with your cock and start thinking with your head for a change. She's a pathetic peasant girl descended from slave stock. You could do a lot better. I admit I enjoyed a few of them myself, that's what they're there for. But I never got attached to one.

Doc walked between the pillars that held up the stone porch and through the burnt archway from which the doors had once hung. His footsteps echoed round the blackened stone walls as he crossed the tiled floor. Good thing he wasn't trying to sneak up on her.

Brigitte was standing in front of a window at the rear of the property. He could see her silhouette against the fading evening light. She turned as she heard him coming and shot him a welcoming smile. Her face was half in shadow and twice as lovely for it.

"You came," she said.

"How could I stay away?"

Brigitte was wearing a simple pink dress and had tucked a blossom behind her ear. She couldn't have looked more desirable.

"Look who's all dressed up."

"I thought I'd make an effort," she said. "I haven't seen you in a while."

"I missed you," he said slipping his arm around her waist almost without thinking. She put her hand on his chest, to stop him moving closer. He could see that she liked touching him though.

Pull yourself together, you're like a dog on heat. You catch one whiff of cunny and you fall to pieces.

Doc let go of Brigitte.

"I'm sorry that I haven't been in touch," she said. "I had a lot to think about and now I've got a lot to tell you."

"I'm all ears."

"You've probably guessed by now that it was me who was visited by an ancestor. The rite didn't go wrong, there was a good reason for this. It concerns your ancestors and mine. I was contacted by my ancestor Toussaint Laveau who's daughter Millicent was my great, great grandmother. He told me your name, you're Emil Papamal, your ancestor is the woman who used to live in this house Mary April Papamal. Before he died Toussaint placed a curse on Mary's bloodline. One of her ancestors would suffer a hideous death at the hands of a Laveau. That's you my love."

"Go on."

"You're not shocked by this?"

You're the one who has the shock coming my dear.

"I'm still processing it. Why did he place the curse on my ancestor? What was so bad about her?"

"You've heard the stories. You must know."

"Those stories are just rumours and legends. The things mothers make up to scare their children."

"No, they're all true. Toussaint showed me everything. How she married Jean Papamal for his money and then murdered him. Then after she inherited everything, this house and his sugar plantation, she discovered he was bankrupt."

The man was a fool who lived beyond his means. He would have lost the whole estate if I hadn't acted when I did.

Be quiet, Doc thought. *She has powers. She'll hear you. You'll ruin everything.*

"Are you alright my love?" Brigitte put her hand on his shoulder. "You seem distant, distracted."

"This is a lot to take in. I'm having a bit of trouble. I wanted to regain my past, and you're telling me you're going to kill me because of things that happened over a century ago."

"I'm sorry, I know it's a lot to take in. It took me a while to come to terms with it all. But it's important that you know this."

"Okay. So, if her husband went bankrupt, is that how this place became a ruin?"

"No that was much later, she saved the plantation by marrying a rich Admiral about a year later. She didn't like him any better than her first husband though. That's when she started taking lovers from among her slaves. When her new husband found out he threatened to divorce her and dispossess her of everything. His money and the plantation, which he now legally owned."

"What did she do?"

"She hid three of her lovers in his bedroom. When he retired she had one of them hold him down while another throttled him and the third took her right there on the bed in front of him. He died watching his wife coupling with one of the slaves. She spent the night with all three of them while her husband's corpse lay next to them in the bed.

"That's when your great grandfather was conceived. She never knew who his true father was. For reasons known only to her self she carried the baby to term and handed him over to her slaves to rear. She let him keep her name though, which is why you now bear it."

"I still don't see what all this has to do with you and me?"

"It has everything to do with you and me. What happened to our ancestors continues to affect us today. There was a settlement of free islanders on the south side of the island, a small fishing village where the harbour is. Toussaint was their Houngan. Mary wanted his power and tried to join his Ounfó. He resisted at first, but she held a lot of power. In the end, for the sake of his congregation he thought it better to be allied to her than against her so he let her join."

That's a lie! He lusted after me from the minute he saw me. He was as eager for my body as you are for this bitch's flesh. He would have done anything to get me and, after leading him on for a while, I obliged.

"They were lovers?"

"Yes, how did you know that?" Brigitte was silent for a moment and looked about her. "Is there something here with us? I'm sure I can detect something."

"It's this place. It must be filled with ghosts. You were telling me about our ancestors."

"That's right, Mary used all her feminine wiles to seduce Toussaint. She was very beautiful and very cunning and, in spite of his wisdom, Toussaint gave in. But she took against my great, great grandmother. Millicent was betrothed to a young man who had caught Mary's eye. When the young man spurned her Mary was determined to have her revenge.

"Mary kidnapped Millicent and planned to sacrifice her in a hideous ceremony she had planned. She'd come across a spell that would steal the souls of every one of her slaves and turn them all into walking corpses that would do her absolute bidding. She planned to set them to work on the plantation."

It was an economic decision. It would have slashed my overheads. Do you have any idea how much it costs to feed and clothe the amount of slaves needed to run a plantation that size? A third of my profits went to looking after them. Think of how rich I'd have been if not for her stinking ancestor.

"Toussaint only discovered her plans once the ceremony was underway. He confronted her as she began to siphon off the souls of the slaves. To save the slaves and his daughter Toussaint invoked and opened the Gateway of the Souls."

"The Gateway of the Souls," said Doc. "That's like some sort of black hole isn't it? An artefact that draws lost souls to it from anywhere in the Invisible World. That really exists?"

"It exists and Toussaint opened it. He drew the souls of the slaves back from the crossroads where they were trapped and returned them to their bodies. But once created the Gateway can never be destroyed and Mary hungered for its power. Toussaint was too exhausted from conjuring up the Gateway to fight Mary for control of it. To stop her from seizing it he transported it inside himself."

"That can be done? How? You must tell me."

"There are things that you must wait to learn."

"So what happened to Toussaint then?"

"In a fit of anger Mary tried to finish the sacrifice and stab Toussaint's daughter. He threw himself in the way and was killed instead. As he died he uttered the curse that we've now got to deal with."

Curse, more like a pathetic grudge. Feeble sorcery that won't come to anything, I'll see to that.

"You said that the Gateway of the Souls can't be destroyed, so I'm guessing it didn't disappear when Toussaint died. Does that mean it still exists?"

"It does."

"Where is it, you have to tell me?"

"It is safe, that's all you need to know."

"And what about Mary Papamal? What did your ancestor say happened to her?"

"There was a revolt. The slaves grabbed their farm tools and stormed the house as Toussaint died. They murdered Mary and her henchmen and set light to the plantation."

"And they got away with that? Why didn't the authorities do anything?"

"I don't know. Things were pretty volatile on mainland Haiti then I suppose."

"What about the plantation?"

"Well neither Mary or Jean Papamal had any relatives, so the slaves took it over, turned most of it into small holdings and farmed it."

"Incredible that no-one exploited the potential in such a huge estate. That they let it go to waste."

"That's a strange thing to say."

"Sorry I was just thinking aloud." Doc took Brigitte's hands and looked into her eyes. "So what about this curse, am I going to suffer a hideous death at your hands?"

Doc's tone was playful and mocking, but Brigitte's expression was serious.

"That's what I've been thinking about while I was away," she said. "That's why I ran that night in the Djevo and hid from you. I didn't want you to be that woman's ancestor. I didn't want the curse hanging over our heads for the rest of our lives. I didn't want to kill you."

"But the curse is there and we both know about it now, we can't avoid that."

"We can't avoid it but we don't need to fulfill it. It doesn't have to rule our lives. It was dark, hateful Voodoo, spoken by a dying man who wanted to make his murderer pay. She did pay, so why should I have to suffer because of his death? I'm not a murderer and you're innocent. Why should you have to pay for something your ancestor did?"

"So how do you suggest we get around this?"

"Love."

"Love?"

"Yes, it's that simple."

"We've never spoken about love before."

"You're not a man who speaks about his emotions. You never tell me what you're feeling."

"But love?"

"It doesn't have to be romantic love, if that scares you. It can be the love you have for your friends or your partner in crime. Love is how you beat hate and dispel dark Voodoo like this."

Brigitte's became flirtatious. "I've certainly loved you with my body many times."

Doc grinned. She'd given him an idea. She was playing to her strengths to win him over. But she'd betrayed her weakness and, if he used it right, this would all go a lot quicker and easier.

"I have to admit I *do* love your body," he said. "I've had an idea. If love dispels dark Voodoo then what about a love spell? Why don't we forge a love knot?"

"A love knot? That's for binding a couple together forever. That's a big step."

"One that will save us both. You said so yourself. You're not afraid of commitment are you?"

"No, but I... I mean, you never..."

"Speak about my feelings? Perhaps it's time I did, especially when my life depends on it." Doc produced a nylon scarf from his pocket. "I believe we need one of these for the spell. And a small clipping from an intimate area." He took a penknife from his pocket, reached into the front of his trousers and cut some of his public hair.

Brigitte looked surprised. "Why are you carrying a knife and scarves around?"

"I just had a feeling that I might need them. I think the Loa were guiding my actions. I'll need a clipping from you as well, if this is going to work." Doc placed his hand on Brigitte's thigh and gently lifted her dress.

Brigitte held his wrist and stopped him. "You're getting rather forward aren't you?"

"And you're getting rather coy, that isn't like you."

"Maybe I like to be asked properly."

"Would you be so kind?"

"Maybe I will." She slipped her panties off. He took a clipping of her hair. He was close enough to smell her body. Her scent was intoxicating. He was completely hard. Did he have time for one last tryst?

Don't be an idiot! Strike now before she realises, while she's vulnerable.

However much she annoyed him, his ancestor was right. Palming his own hair, he split Brigitte's into two clipping and tied the scarf around them. Then he tied seven more knots, each one more intricate than the last.

"Be careful," Brigitte said. "If you make a mistake with one of the knots you could..."

"Paralyse you?" Doc said.

Brigitte sat rigid on the crumbling window sill. Only her eyes showed any sign of life.

"That was the whole idea. I wasn't making a love knot. I was creating a spell to snare you. Of course the effect is only temporary, as you know. Unless the knots are sealed with goofer dust and burned."

Doc took a snakeskin pouch from his pocket. It contained the goofer dust, a fine powder of ground rattlesnake skulls and graveyard dust mixed with salt and brimstone. He sprinkled the dust over the knotted scarf then placed the scarf in the pouch.

This is the Mambo who trained you? I'm not impressed. I thought you said she had power, yet you tricked her so easily.

Brigitte's eyes widened in alarm as she finally felt the presence of Doc's ancestor.

"Yes she's been with me for quite a while," Doc said. "You weren't the only one to get visited that night. She's taught me a lot as well. Not only have I regained my past, I've also planned out my future. I'm afraid you're not in it. I already knew about the curse but I have a different solution. I'm going to take you out of the picture. You can't inflict a hideous death on me if I get to you first. I plan a living death though. If I killed you outright your spirit could wreak vengeance on me. If I trap your soul in the grave with your corpse there's nothing you can do.

"You see I've realised there's a huge natural resource on this island that's ripe for exploitation. You may not be aware of this but I'm rather wealthy. Having just remembered this I'm rather keen to find new ventures to invest in. Thanks to my ancestor I now know how to conduct the ceremony she attempted so many years ago. She's very keen for me to try it again. That's the other reason I can't let you live. I was certain you'd try to stop me and you may be the only person who could. However, once I've taken care of that eventuality I stand to profit quite heavily from my actions."

Doc began to collect twigs and logs to start a fire. He piled them up and put a match to them. As the moon came up and the flames lit the shell of the old house, Brigitte's eyes darted to a figure who stepped out of the shadows.

"I think you remember Vincenzo," said Doc. "He used to be your rival for the head of the Ounfó. Only his liking for secret Petro rituals and his traffic with malevolent Loa got him exiled to Haiti. I invited him back and offered him a very good position in my new organisation. He's going to assist me in disposing of you." Doc turned to Vincenzo. "You got what I asked you for?"

Vincenzo handed him another pouch, Doc looked inside. It was filled with ground human bones. Doc emptied them into the snakeskin pouch then tossed it on the fire.

What are you doing? What was in that pouch?

"Ground human bones," said Doc. "To seal the paralysis spell."

There's more to it than that. What are you up to?

"A simple rite to sever the connection with an ancestor who's plaguing you. You grind the ancestor's bones to a fine powder and then you burn them.

You what!?

"You didn't think we could find your grave did you? It has no marker and your bones don't lie in any cemetery, but the Loa told Vincenzo where your remains were buried. He dug you up and ground your bones for me."

Why?

"I'm afraid I don't have room for partners in this new venture and you simply don't have the vision to understand it. The market has moved on too much since your day. So I'm dissolving our merger as of this moment."

The temperature in the ruined house dropped in spite of the fire. There was a sound like a huge wind rushing by and Mary Papamal was dragged back to the afterlife.

She let out a bitter scream of fury. Even Vincenzo and Brigitte heard. The flames of the fire leapt as it roared with her anger and frustration.

Then she was gone.

"Well she certainly had spirit," said Doc. "If you'll pardon the pun. Mary's grave, did you dig it deep enough to house Brigitte?"

"I did," said Vincenzo. "Do we bury her tonight?"

"We do." Doc turned and spoke to Brigitte. "After incapacitating you in the house of your ancestor's bitter enemy we're going to inter you in her grave. I hope you appreciate all the trouble we've gone to on your behalf.

"Do we move her now Doc?"

"Don't call me Doc. As of this moment that's no longer my name."

"What should I call you? Doctor Emil?"

"Doc Papamal perhaps. No that doesn't sound right. Doc Papa that's who I've become. Call me Doc Papa."

CHAPTER THIRTY-EIGHT

Tatyana jumped as gunshots sounded outside the metal door. The Zombies around her became aware of her heart beating faster. Tatyana backed slowly away from them.

She joined Benjamin with his ear pressed up against the door.

"What's happening?" she said.

"I think some of the guards have arrived," Benjamin said. "They told the guests to get out of the way, but the guests weren't budging. They're too desperate to get their hands on the Zombies. That must have been when they opened fire."

"Did they shoot anyone?"

"I don't know. I didn't hear any screams. They're probably just firing into the air to scare them."

Tatyana put her ear against the door but couldn't hear anything. "What do you think is happening?"

"I don't know. It's gone quiet now. I heard footsteps and some cries. That might have been the guests moving. They were more bothered about grabbing a Zombie than getting shot. I don't understand it."

"They're changing," said Brigitte. "The longer their Gros Bon Ange goes without a proper vessel, the closer they get to being one of the Zombies. It's what happens when you tear the soul out of something."

"And you knew this when you sabotaged all the Pot-tets?" said Tatyana.

Brigitte looked affronted. "Yes I did. Is it any more than they deserve? You've seen what they're capable of doing. They studied so hard to be like Zombies and now their wish has been granted. I don't see how you can judge me. I recall seeing you sink to murder with the rest of them."

Tatyana dropped Brigitte's gaze and stared at the floor in shame. The memory of the man she had helped to kill stung her to the very core.

"I'm sorry," said Brigitte. "That was a low blow."

"You're right though," said Tatyana. "I wasn't being judgmental. I was just surprised. It's not like you to do something that would harm someone else. When everyone was tearing that poor man apart for instance, you used your Voodoo to hide yourself so no-one could see you weren't joining in."

"You could see that?" Brigitte was astonished.

"Erm, well yeah. You made me forget didn't you. But it just came back. It's happened before as well. You made me forget in the lecture hall, but then I felt this presence and the memory came back. I hope you don't mind but I followed you when you left the lecture theatre. Your field has this, like, blind spot. I hid in it so no-one saw me, not even you. That's how I knew where the secret entrance to the compound was."

"That's where you went," said Benjamin. "Why didn't you tell me?"

"I don't know. It just seemed like something that I shouldn't talk about. It was all kind of strange. I thought you might not believe me. I'd always thought I was this sceptical atheist, and then I start to see and experience all these weird things."

"Sceptical atheist?" said Benjamin. "You came here to take part in Voodoo rituals and free Zombies. How sceptical is that?"

"Okay, when you put it like that, I don't sound too sceptical, but that seemed different somehow. I don't think I really believed in any of it except for the Zombies. Now I'm not so sure though."

"The Loa are calling you my child," said Brigitte. "You have a gift and a feeling for this. You might pretend to be a sceptic, but your soul knows different. It is hungry and it calls for sustenance."

"We have to feed our souls?" said Tatyana.

"Of course we do. How else will they grow?"

"How do you feed your soul?"

"With prayer, and devotion to God, with pure thoughts and deeds and with service to the Loa. That's why you're right about what I did to the guests and their Pot-tets. That will impoverish my soul, not feed it. When we die our Gros Bon Ange has to argue our case before God and that action will not go in my favour."

"Well I don't know about my soul," said Benjamin. "But my stomach is famished. I haven't had anything to eat since yesterday morning."

Before she could say anything Tatyana was knocked off her feet. The ground shook and the metal door buckled as something exploded outside it.

"What the hell was that?" Tatyana said.

"A grenade I think," said Benjamin, picking himself up. "Or a rocket or something. I don't think we should wait around to find out."

"No," said Brigitte helping a rotund male Zombie get to its feet. "They'll be through that door any moment. We'll have to go further into the mines to escape them."

As she spoke Tatyana heard the guards start battering the badly buckled door. They were minutes from getting inside.

"Follow me," Brigitte said.

She led them down a darkened tunnel carrying the lamp. At the end of the tunnel was an old electric lift that could hold about twenty or thirty people. Brigitte threw a switch to get the power on then started up the lift and sent it down without anyone inside.

"What did you do that for?" said Benjamin. "How are we going to get down now?"

"There's a steep tunnel just along from here," said Brigitte. "I want them to think we've taken the lift. That way they'll descend to a different network of tunnels."

"Oh right," said Benjamin. "Good plan."

As they entered the tunnel Tatyana heard the door give way. This was followed by sounds of gunfire and shouted commands. She prayed they had enough of a lead to evade the guards.

Prayed, did she really just think that? Maybe Brigitte was right. Perhaps her fascination really was a hunger. But there wasn't time to think on this.

CHAPTER THIRTY-NINE

Palmer had gotten out of the dot com bubble before it burst. He'd dumped his shares in both Enron and Bear Stearns before the scandals broke. He was damned if he wasn't going to get out of St Ignatius before it all turned to shit.

"Damned is the right word," said his soul.

"What?" shouted Palmer. The jeep's engine was making an awful racket and the black goat tethered in the back was bleating its head off, probably sensing its impending death.

"I said 'damned' is the right word," said his soul. "Unless you get off this island, repent your ways and start making amends."

Palmer glanced from the dirt track ahead of him to the lady-boy Zombie that housed his soul. It was wearing that sanctimonious expression that infuriated him.

"You know what?" Palmer said. "You are one almighty pain in the ass. That's what you are. An almighty pain in the ass."

"That's all I've ever been to you. A tiny wizened appendage, like a stunted Siamese twin you couldn't wait to have removed and pickled in a jar."

"I thought I had removed you."

"You did indeed. Then fate took a hand and suddenly you're forced to confront me and every terrible crime that I know about. Do you think you'll be able to ignore me if you do manage to reunite us?"

"Well I've been fairly successful so far, if you're to be believed."

"Of course I'm to be believed. I don't lie to you Samuel. I know every lie you've ever told yourself and others, but I never repeat or believe them. That's why I'm so valuable to you."

"Don't flatter yourself. You're only valuable to me because I don't want to become like that thing you're currently inside."

"What this old thing?" said his soul in a mocking tone. "Why Samuel you picked this out specially for me. Don't tell me you've gone off my outfit."

"It's strictly last season," said Palmer pulling up right next to the hidden glade. "And it's time to slip into something more comfortable – namely me."

Palmer climbed out of the jeep, untied the goat and lifted the bamboo cage with the black hen inside it. "Grab that bag in the back and come with me. I want you inside me, as soon as possible."

Palmer led the goat and the Zombie into the glade. It contained seven citron trees which were sacred to Baron Samedi, the head of the Gédé, the Loa of the dead. It was also right next to an abandoned burial ground, which made it ideal for the ceremony Palmer wanted to perform.

He tied the goat to a tree, put the cage down and took the bag off the Zombie. He pulled some flour and a diagram of a Vèvè out of the bag. Then he tried to draw the Vèvè on the ground with the flour.

"Does that look anything like this to you?" he said, holding the diagram up to his soul when he was done.

His soul shook the Zombie's head. "Not a bit I'm afraid. I don't think this is your forté."

"Thanks for the encouragement."

"I said I'd never lie to you Samuel. I'm the only presence in your life that won't."

"Never mind, it's the best I can do."

"Are you sure you want to go ahead with this? These are ancient, primal forces. The Houngans and Mambos who commune with them train for years before summoning one."

"This is the only way," Palmer said, lighting the black candles he'd got from the bag. "I'm running out of time and I haven't got anyone else to do this for me. Besides I've watched Doc Papa and Vincenzo do this enough times. How difficult can it be?"

Palmer opened the bamboo cage and took the black hen out. It immediately tried to fly away. When Palmer stopped it, the bird tried to attack him. He held it at arms length and lifted it up to what he hoped were the four points of the compass, muttering the incantations he'd memorised.

Now how did this go? That's right he had to break its neck first, then the wings, then the legs. Every time he reached for the bird's neck it pecked at him. In his annoyance he squeezed it until it ribcage cracked. The bird squawked in pain but he was finally able to despatch it in the way he intended.

Now he had to bite its head off. Palmer put the limp head in his mouth and bit down. His stomach turned over as its spine cracked and he choked on blood and feathers. He spat the head out onto the *Vèvè* he'd drawn and dropped the body next to it.

He produced a hip flask and poured rum over the hen as he picked the feathers out of his teeth. Next he took a knife from the bag and cut the rope tethering the goat. He grabbed the goat by the horns but it could sense what he was up to and it dug its heels in.

It started to bleat and kick. Palmer put his arm around the goat's neck and tried to drag it back.

"A little help wouldn't go amiss."

"Trust me," said his soul. "In the long run you will not appreciate my help with this."

"Well in the short term you can go fuck yourself. Ow!" Palmer cried out as the goat bit him. Without thinking he rammed the knife into its eyeball. It stopped kicking and started to spasm.

Palmer dragged the dying goat over to the Vèvè and slit its throat. It's blood gushed onto the ground soaking the badly drawn symbol and splashing his handmade leather shoes. He uttered the last of the invocations to Baron Samedi and waited.

Nothing happened.

The flames of the black candles guttered. The glade was still and silent. Palmer felt an intense anti-climax.

Why was nothing easy today? Why wouldn't anything go his way? Once, just once, couldn't he catch a fucking break?

Unable to control his anger, he kicked the goat. Then he kicked it again and again in a blind fury.

"Cock sucking, motherfucking asshole!" he shouted waving his fists at the empty air. "Why didn't you come you asshole? Why didn't you fucking come?!" Palmer turned to the Zombie. He was panting and his shoulders were slumped with defeat. "Go on then, aren't you going to say it you sanctimonious bastard? Aren't you going to say I told you so?"

Palmer's soul didn't say anything. In fact it didn't seem to be inside the Zombie anymore. The smug pitying look had been replaced with a vacant stare. Palmer didn't know why, but he was suddenly quite nervous.

The Zombie began to shake and twitch. Then its face burst into a huge lascivious grin. It started to gyrate its hips then threw back it's head and let out a raucous laugh.

"Baron Samedi," said Palmer. "Is that you? Look, I'm sorry about calling you a... I mean about what I said. I'm sort of new to this and I didn't know, you know, how long I should wait or if you were coming or anything."

"You certainly are new to this, and quite terrible judging from the mess you made of the ceremony," said the Zombie. It didn't sound like Baron Samedi, the voice was deep and husky but exceptionally feminine.

"Err, you are Baron Samedi aren't you?"

"No my dear, you got his wife Le Gran Brigitte. I told you you were terrible at this didn't I? Nonetheless I've been waiting to speak to you for a long time."

"You have?" Now he felt really nervous.

"Oh yes, I've been receiving a lot of complaints from my daughters about your activities."

"Your daughters?"

"The dead my dear, I'm like a mother to all of them. Especially those who feel they've been wronged. Who can't protect themselves and want retribution."

"I don't know what you're talking about."

"Oh don't be ridiculous you foolish little man. You don't think you can hide anything from the dead do you? Most of them have nothing better to do than watch the living all day. They know everything that goes on. Particularly when it concerns their newly dead bodies and what happens to them. Just because they're dead doesn't mean they've granted you consent you know. It's still rape my dear."

"Look, if it's a question of money..."

"Money my silly little darling, and pray tell me what would we do with money where we live? Buy ourselves a new house or some expensive jewelry. Invest it in the stock market perhaps? I don't think so. You can't buy your way out of this little problem."

"If you don't want me to pay then what do you want?"

"Oh I want you to pay my sweet, but not with money."

"I don't understand."

"You've wronged so many of my daughters. Violated their bodies over and over again while they were forced to watch, unable to do anything. You've visited grieving families and gloated over what you were going to do to the loved one they'd lost. Now you must be punished."

Palmer picked up the sacrificial knife and held it out in front of him. "I'm warning you. Don't come any closer."

"And just what are you going to do with that my dear? I'm an immortal being inside an animated corpse. Do you think a little bit of sharpened metal is going to hurt me? Incidentally, I don't envy your poor soul having to live inside this little thing. She's a bit far gone isn't she? Should I use the word she? Isn't that how they like to be referred to? Transsexuals that is, not walking corpses. Anyway she's been out in the wild rather a long time hasn't she? Her flesh is crawling with maggots. But that rather suits my purpose."

Palmer glanced back at the jeep, wondering if he could outrun the Loa.

"Don't even think it sweetie," said Gran Brigitte. "It doesn't work that way."

A bony hand broke though the earth by Palmer's foot and grasped his ankle. It dug it's fleshless fingers into him. He howled in pain and tried to pry the fingers apart but he couldn't.

"This is a burial ground or did you forget?" Gran Brigitte said. "This is where I hold dominion. I control everything here, and not just the dead. Death has a gravity you see. It draws everything to it eventually. If I increase that gravity I can accelerate life cycles. Take the maggots squirming inside this corpse. I can turn them into flies in an instant."

Palmer watched as the maggots began to writhe and thrash under the skin of the lady-boy Zombie. Then, to his horror, he saw them burrow out and turn into a swarm of flies. The flies swirled around the Zombie like a buzzing black aura.

"I can snatch their tiny souls," Gran Brigitte said clicking her fingers. The flies dropped out of the air and formed a carpet of tiny corpses at her feet. "And I can reanimate them as undead insects under my control."

The flies began to wave their legs in the air. Then, gradually, they flipped themselves over and took to the air around the Zombie again, making an ominous drone with the beating of their wings. There was something unnatural, almost otherworldly, about the sound they made.

"Why are you doing this? What are you playing at?"

"Well seeing as you like raping corpses so much my sweet, I thought you might like to find out what it's like from the other side."

The undead flies landed on the Zombie's midriff and began to crawl back under its rotting skin. The Zombie's abdomen bulged as they forced their way inside it. Gran Brigitte lifted the Zombie's tattered skirt to reveal where all the reanimated flies were going.

The Zombie's gargantuan member no longer hung flaccid between its legs. It was standing stiff and proud with all the undead insects burrowing into it. The glans bulged and rippled quite obscenely from the zombified flies crawling about inside.

Palmer tried once again to free his leg from the skeletal grasp of the dead hand. Before he could get anywhere the Zombie was on him. It knocked him, face first, to the ground and placed a rotting hand between his shoulders. He struggled as hard as he could but he couldn't shake it off.

"What was it you called your soul when it was in this body?" said Gran Brigitte. "Oh yes, that's right, an 'almighty pain in the ass'. Well honey you don't know the half of it."

"Stop it! What are you doing?"

Palmer felt the Zombie's fingers slip down the back of his trousers and take hold of the belt and the waist band. With one unnaturally strong tug and his trousers were torn off.

Gran Brigitte let out a throaty chuckle. "You did say it's time to slip into something more comfortable – namely you."

"Please... Oh God no, please..."

"Oh come now Samuel. You just said you wanted it inside you, as soon as possible."

Palmer's soul drifted back to the Zombie it had been inhabiting. Gran Brigitte was long gone. Palmer was still on the ground at the Zombie's feet. He was lying in a pool of blood and faeces with what was left of his trousers round his ankles, sobbing quietly.

Palmer's soul couldn't think of anything to say to comfort its owner. To be truthful, which was its nature, it didn't really want to comfort him.

The soul looked down at the mangled remains of the Zombie's penis. It hung in tatters like the fraying dress it wore. The flies of the living dead had left it. They'd swarmed into Palmer on the point of climax.

Palmer suddenly jerked and held his stomach, writhing in pain. He coughed and a trickle of blood spilled down his chin. His eyes were full of pain and fear.

"The flies. They're inside me. They're trying to get out. They're... oh God they're feeding on me!"

Palmer screamed with unimaginable agony as a thousand ravenous little mouths consuming his innards.

Palmer's soul shook the Zombie's head in contradiction.

"Not flies Palmer, guilt. You see that's the thing about guilt, sooner or later it eats you all up inside."

CHAPTER FORTY

"I have to attack her from the inside," said Doc Papa. "Her magical defences are primed for an external attack. She still thinks I don't know who she is. So she won't expect me to get up close and personal. She won't have shielded her core, at least not where I intend to strike."

"What if her astral form gets loose?" said Vincenzo drawing the last of the protection charms around Doc Papa in fine ground bone dust and gunpowder.

"It won't, that's what the binding spell is for."

Doc Papa was lying on the floor of his ceremony room. It was hidden behind his office on the top floor of Mangrove Hall. He'd had it specially built when he'd renovated the estate. Only he and a handful of his acolytes knew about it.

It was everything his office wasn't. The magical Id to the Super Ego that was his place of work. Taken as a whole, the two rooms symbolised the duality of his nature as a successful businessman and a powerful Houngan. The office displayed the trappings of his wealth to show the scale of his success, the ceremony room betrayed the strength of his Voodoo and the degree to which the Loa favoured him.

The ceremony room was not a traditional space like the Ounfó. Doc Papa had brought his vast resources to bear on it, creating a modern, technological approach to the mysteries of the Loa. He was taking Voodoo into the twenty-first century.

Instead of a bare earthen floor, Doc Papa was lying on a toughened LCD screen. It generated a series of holographic symbols that combined to make a living Vévé which could alter and adapt itself to the exact nature of the ritual at any moment. The precision this gave Doc Papa's psychic will, combined with the traditional charms Vincenzo had drawn, made it an impenetrable magical barrier.

The speaker system played a series of pre-programmed ceremonial drumbeats, each one looped and intercut with the others to intensify its powerful rhythm. The hi-tech speaker system provided a surround sound that utilised the walls and floor as a series of sub woofers, with the result that the listener could bathe in the sonic waves of the Voodoo rhythms.

To bind Brigitte's astral form Doc Papa had prepared a black bottle lamp. Hanging from the ceiling was an antique glass bottle filled with castor oil, piment-chien, Guinea-pepper, powdered lizard, the powder of a decomposed corpse, and soot. Tied to the wick was a tiny bag containing samples of Brigitte's hair, a tooth she'd lost and a snipping from her dress.

Doc Papa had gathered these last items from the old hut by the shore where Brigitte used to live. No-one had been back there since the night they buried her alive. The place was exactly as she left it. It woke long suppressed feelings in him.

The tooth he had taken from an old charm he had found over a door. The dress clipping from her closet. And the hair he'd collected from the bed where they had lain. It lay on sheets they'd stained with their passions and marked with their scent. In another lifetime when they were other people.

He knew her true name and he had touched her essence. She was his helpless prey. He would trap her spirit and he would wrest the Gateway of the Souls from her.

Doc Papa let the life go from his body. The rhythm of the drums bathed his whole being. The living holographic Vévé pulsed and shifted in accordance with his soul's vibrations. He released his astral form and shuffled off his mortal body.

Doc Papa was just orienting himself and preparing to leave the room in search of Brigitte when Vincenzo surprised him. He rubbed away two of the powder-drawn charms with his foot. Then he dropped another wick into the black bottle lamp and lit it. That wick also had a tiny pouch tied to it. Doc Papa knew exactly whose personal effects were in the pouch.

Vincenzo was trying to trap him. Thanks to the new wick in the black bottle lamp Doc Papa's astral form was now bound to the room. His body was seemingly defenceless. He would have to wait to see how this one played out.

He didn't have to wait long. Vincenzo opened the secret door that connected the ceremony room to his office and the five shareholders walked in with their Zombie soul vessels.

So that was his game.

"Now you're sure this cock sucker's out cold?" said O'Shaugnessey. "He can't hurt us?"

"His astral form has left his body and I hold it captive," said Vincenzo. "He is powerless against us."

"Is he here in the room?" said Walden Truffet. "Can he hear us?"

"Yes," said Vincenzo. "He can hear."

Doc Papa watched as O'Shaugnessey walked over to his body and prodded it with his toe.

"Sorry feller," said O'Shaugnessey. "But we're mounting a hostile takeover. It's not that we don't appreciate everything you've given the corporation, we just don't trust you to run it for us anymore. You have to admit that your recent actions haven't done much to inspire confidence in your decision making."

"You've lost control," said Lyons. "And the whole thing has fallen to shit. So you're out of the picture as of now."

So that was their game. Doc Papa's suspicions were right, which was why he'd taken precautions. Of course they'd waited till he was vulnerable before they struck. Which was only good tactical sense. They weren't totally incompetent, he'd give them that.

Vincenzo had impressed him. It was a shame that his cunning and deviousness would have to be punished. Doc Papa nearly admired them.

Vincenzo's major failing however, was his arrogance. He thought himself invulnerable to attack. While he was shielding himself from Doc Papa's astral form he hadn't covered his Mettet, the invisible route by which his Patron Loa could enter his body and ride him. Before he had time to realise this Doc Papa struck.

He shot into Vincenzo's body and Vincenzo shook violently.

"What's happening?" said Frank Evans. "Is he meant to be doing that?"

"No," said O'Shaugnessey. "I don't think he is and I don't think I like what it portends."

"I wouldn't if I was you," said Doc Papa, taking full control of Vincenzo.

"That's not Vincenzo," said Walden "Why does he sound like that? Who is it?

"Can't you guess? I'm afraid Vincenzo is a little indisposed at the moment. You'll have to go through me instead."

"Doc Papa?" said O'Shaugnessey. "Now wait a minute, let's not do anything hasty. This is business after all. No-one's getting personal here. If you've got a counter offer then we're prepared to listen to it."

"The only offer I'm going to make you is a quick but painful death."

Doc Papa walked over to the black bottle lamp and removed the still burning wick. Then he took a small paper disk with some markings on it out of glass jar on the altar.

The shareholders were muttering amongst themselves the whole while. One of their souls inside a Zombie was trying to make itself heard.

"You pipe down or you'll get worse than last time," Lyons threatened. Then he turned to Doc Papa.

"Now look here Papa. Don't think you can intimidate us with

all your Hoodoo bullshit. We put good money into your operation and in the last couple of days all you've done is put our lives and our fortunes at risk. We're taking control of this outfit for everyone's benefit, and there's nothing you can do to stop us."

"I wouldn't be so sure of that," said Doc Papa setting light to the disk of paper. "You see I anticipated that you might attempt a little coup, so I took some precautions."

As one the Zombies began to scream. Their flesh began to liquefy and drip off them in great, foul smelling gobs.

"What have you done?" said O'Shaugnessey.

"I've activated the necrotising spell that I put on your Bakas," said Doc Papa. O'Shaugnessey stared at him non-plussed. "The what?"

"Necrotising spell. You see the Bakas I gave you were corrupted. If you think of them as a portal and your souls as information, then you'll understand the dangers inherent into downloading them into new machines, in this case the Zombies. I impregnated your Bakas with a magical virus that rode into the Zombies on the backs of your souls. When I burnt that paper I activated the virus. It causes the Zombies to rot away to nothing in a mater of minutes."

The Zombies were now little more than skeletons standing in puddles of rancid flesh.

"As you are linked to the Zombies via your souls the virus will also affect you," Doc Papa said. "Taking effect almost immediately."

The shareholders tried pleading, threatening and bargaining with him. It did them no good. In no time they just looked just like the Zombies. All of them ran together into a fetid pool of bubbling flesh.

Doc Papa lamented what it was going to cost him to clean this up. He was going to have to get rid of the carpet, take up the floorboards and get the whole room refitted. And that was after he'd had the place fumigated. Still that was for later. There were more pressing things to deal with.

Doc Papa used Vincenzo's fingers to redraw the protection charms around his still motionless body. Then he took a large sacrificial dagger off the wall. Held the dagger over Vincenzo's left breast. Some distance away he was aware of Vincenzo's Gros Bon Ange pleading with him not to strike. He ignored it.

Doc Papa plunged the dagger into Vincenzo's heart. As his body fell to the floor Doc Papa discarded it like an old set of clothes. His astral form hovered in the air and looked down at Vincenzo, lying next to the putrid slop that had once been the shareholders and their Zombies. Blood was pouring out of Vincenzo's chest where the dagger had pierced it. More cleaning bills to think of, this had been an expensive exercise in maintaining power.

Doc Papa put this out of his mind however and returned to the matter at hand. He still had to get Brigitte to give up the Gateway of the Souls. He concentrated on the rhythm of the drums and tried to forget that all the melted flesh was deadening the sound.

He pictured Brigitte at her most intimate and vulnerable, then he reached out with his mind and went looking for her.

CHAPTER FORTY-ONE

Benjamin was looking for Brigitte. He'd stopped to look at an arrangement of skulls in the wall and they'd turned a corner and left him.

After trying to feel his way along the tunnel in pitch darkness Benjamin keyed into the Zombies' group mind and followed them. He was slowly working his way to the front of the group where Tatyana and Brigitte were. This wasn't easy though.

He had to sidestep and slip past the Zombies in the pitch dark. One wrong move and they might pounce on him. He couldn't see Brigitte's lamp up ahead so she probably wasn't close enough to save him if the Zombies did decide to start feeding.

In the distance he heard the insistent tramp of the guards' feet getting closer. They'd never quite lost the guards. They'd come close several times but the guards always seemed to pick up their trail.

To throw the guards off, Brigitte had led them into a series of natural tunnels connected to the mine. She told them the whole island was crisscrossed with underground caves and catacombs. Most of them were naturally occurring but a few had been specially excavated by the natives. Like the ossuary where they now found themselves.

The walls and ceilings of these long tunnels were entirely covered with human bones. Skulls mainly, but there were also intricate arrangements of other bones embedded in the stone walls. This was where the islanders had come to honour their dead and commune with their ancestors.

Benjamin hoped the ancestors would look out for the Zombies as the guards got closer. He tried not to think about how slow the Zombie's dead muscles and atrophied limbs made them. Or how fast the guards could move.

He had to fight his rising panic all the time. If he didn't his heart would start racing, he'd break out in a sweat and begin hyperventilating. Any one of those things would give him away to the Zombies.

He'd been in fear of his life for so long now he couldn't imagine not being in a state of constant terror. His old life of comfort and privilege seemed so far away. He couldn't imagine what it would be like to do simple things anymore, like fixing a snack, watching cable or just calling up friends.

He clung to the Rules of Interaction like a lifeline. Each one had become like a mantra to him. He repeated them over and over in his mind. It was the only way to ensure his survival. They felt like a series of spells designed to ensure he would come out of this ordeal alive.

It doesn't matter and you don't care.

Master yourself and nothing can threaten you.

He wished he had enough mastery over himself for that rule to be true right now.

Finally he saw a glimmer of light up ahead as he drew closer to Brigitte and Tatyana. The lamp Brigitte was carrying lit up the ceiling above her. A host of skulls stared down. Their sockets wide with terror, their jaws open in a silent cry of warning.

Benjamin was getting really close to the other two, but the Zombies directly in front of him were too tightly packed together to squeeze past. He could almost tap Brigitte on the shoulder but he didn't want to risk it in case he accidentally hit a Zombie and his fingers were bitten off.

They stopped at a crossroads. The tunnel directly ahead of them led out of the ossuary. It wasn't covered with bones but the roads to their left and right were. The Zombies started milling about as Brigitte deliberated over which way to go. Benjamin was able to slip past them and grab hold of Tatyana's hand.

She turned to him with a look of relief and squeezed his hand to show she was pleased to see him. There was comfort and reassurance in their physical closeness but there was no longer any passion. It seemed like their fear had chased all that away.

It also felt like they were learning too much about themselves and each other to carry on as before. They just couldn't live inside the dreams that had propped up their relationship before they came here.

"Which way now?" said Tatyana.

Brigitte seemed indecisive. "The route ahead of us comes out near the crossroads where I have to take my people. That's where I can open the invisible crossroads between the three worlds of the Loa and our own. Their souls are held captive there. "

"Well let's go," said Tatyana. "We don't have much time."

"But I don't want to lead the guards there. We need to shake them before we can get there. It'll be too dangerous otherwise."

"How long have we got?"

"Until sunrise."

"Guys, I don't want to worry you," said Benjamin. "But we haven't got until sunrise until those guards catch us. We've got five minutes or less. We need to make a decision now. Do we stay underground or try and lose them in the jungle above?"

Before Brigitte could answer she shuddered and almost lost control of her body. Benjamin caught her to stop her falling and Tatyana took the lamp.

"What's the matter?" Tatyana said.

Brigitte was rolling her eyes. "I carry a great weight inside me. I was given it by my ancestor for safe keeping. I need it to help my people but the burden is too great. He wants it. He wants it so badly. He's inside me looking for it."

"Who?' said Tatyana. "Who is it?"

"I can't fight him," said Brigitte. She looked as though she was struggling to stay conscious. "You've got to protect them. Please look after them."

Brigitte's face went blank. Her eyes rolled up into her head and her body went limp. Benjamin struggled to hold her up.

"What's up with her?" said Tatyana. "Is she still alive?"

"She's still breathing. But she's gone into some kind of coma."

"What are we going to do?"

"Well we can't stay here."

"Can you carry her?"

"I don't think so. I'm going to have to put her down."

"We can't just leave her here for the guards to find. We're completely lost without her."

Just how lost became apparent when the Zombies around them started to notice their presence. Their hearts were beating faster from the shock of seeing Brigitte keel over. The Zombies could smell this.

A young female Zombie reached out and ran her fingers along Benjamin's cheek. She put her fingers unsteadily in her mouth and ran them along her dried up tongue. She could taste Benjamin's sweat on the tips.

Tatyana started to back away. She didn't see the rotund male Zombie come up behind her. She backed right into him and only just managed to get away before he closed his arms about her. She dropped the lamp as she dodged him and it went out.

Rule Number One, Benjamin heard in his head. *Show no signs of life.* They'd already blown that. Now Rule Number Two – *move in slow motion* – seemed totally inappropriate too. All Benjamin wanted to do was get away as fast as he could.

In the distance he heard a voice call out: "Boys, hey boys, over here. Donovan they're over here."

The guards had finally caught up to them.

He and Tatyana were trapped underground, in the pitch dark

with an uncontrollable horde of the living dead. The only person who could keep them alive had fallen into a coma. They had to avoid being torn apart and eaten long enough to keep the Zombies safe from the guards, who were also coming to kill them.

There didn't seem to be a way out.

CHAPTER FORTY-TWO

Brigitte couldn't find a way out. She was trapped. Her astral form had been plucked from her body and she wasn't able to return.

She was on the second astral plane of the Loas. All around her planetary forces, expressed in strange geometries, intersected with one another to create shapes her earthly eyes couldn't understand and her earthly brain couldn't process.

She hadn't entered this astral plane voluntarily and she wasn't prepared for the shock of being here. That was what a ritual was for, to prepare the initiate to experience this kind of heightened reality. Without that vital preparation she was reeling from the shock of finding herself in a space that wasn't anything like the reality she was used to.

She knew who'd brought her here. She'd been so careful to fly under his radar, to remain undetected inside Miriam's body. Nevertheless it was inevitable that he would discover who she really was. She'd hoped he wouldn't realise until she'd gotten all the islanders to the crossroads and returned their souls. But, as her grandmother used to say, "the Loa teach us more through the hopes they deny than the desires they grant."

As soon as she thought of Doc Papa he appeared. Thought had greater properties on this plane. He came in the body of a serpent with a human head, wearing a top hat that had the eight of spades tucked into the brim. She felt his coils wrap themselves around her before she saw him. He slithered round her and thrust his face into hers.

Remembering how to alter her form in this space, she transformed herself into the golden apple of Erzulie. This had repelled Ogou Fer when he took the serpent form in Eden, which was why he had Eve pick it for him. As soon as she shifted into this shape Doc Papa was himself repelled and shot away.

He reverted into the human shape of his Ti Bon Ange and so did Brigitte. Strangely, though she knew his physical body, had explored every inch of it with her own, she had never seen the astral body of his Ti Bon Ange.

Even under the circumstances, she still felt a huge desire for him. She could tell that he felt it too. It crackled though his astral body like a flame and it sang in the resonant vibrations it was giving off.

"I'm impressed," he said. "You threw me off quicker than I anticipated. I should know not to underestimate you."

"Something you do at your peril."

"Yes, as I learned when I unearthed your grave. But you were tricked so easily when I put you there, I was quite surprised. I became complacent. I didn't think you'd escape."

"Seems I'm not the only one who's easily tricked. But it wasn't your complacency that undid you, it was your arrogance. You didn't think anyone could circumvent your magic."

"For old times sake, as one magician to another, tell me how you managed to escape? I'm guessing you possessed one of the Zombies and dug yourself up. But how did your soul get past all the spells I set to keep it trapped with your corporeal form?"

"As I said, it was your arrogance that undid you. You forgot that magic, especially in Voodoo, is all about the letter of the law. You have to specify the outcome you want and allow for all possible interpretations. This means, unless you allow for everything that could happen, one spell can always get around another. You set the traps to catch my dead soul, not my living one. So as long as I was still alive in the coffin the traps wouldn't catch my soul."

Doc Papa tilted his top hat to her. "Exceptional. I am ashamed to say I hadn't thought of that. You won't escape so easily this time however. You know what I want. The location of the Gateway of the Souls."

"As I told you two years ago, it's safe. That's all you need to know."

"I'm afraid that's nowhere near what I need to know. I am only giving you the opportunity to tell me out of sentimentality. I'm quite prepared to take it from you."

"I assume that's what this is all about."

"Of course."

"It still doesn't have to be this way you know?"

"Oh really? Are you still suggesting we can love it all better? That a two hundred year old blood curse can be brushed aside by simply holding hands and gazing into each other's eyes? I've come too far to throw it all away now. I stand on the verge of dominating the entire planet. Do you think I'm just going to throw my hands in the air and say: 'You know what, you're right. Let's have a big hug and kiss it all better'?"

"I've seen things just as miraculous."

"Not with me you haven't."

"You've been lusting after the Gateway of the Souls since I first mentioned it," said Brigitte. "Why are you so fascinated with such a dangerous artefact?"

"Because of the power it will bring."

"It's a portal for drawing souls from one place into another, often against their will. How is that going to bring you power?"

"You expect me to reveal my whole plan to you, like some bad movie villain in the last reel?"

"Humour me. What can I do about it? I'm not going anywhere, you've seen to that."

"I have on St Ignatius the most precious possessions of the most rich and powerful people in the world."

"You're talking about their souls."

"I am. Having them in my possession gives me a great deal of leverage with these people, but not as much as I want. If I take the Gateway of the Souls inside me, as your ancestor did, and then open it, I will have complete and utter dominion over them. I will be the receptacle for their souls. I will own their single most valuable commodities. They will be a part of me. If anything happens to me, their eternal futures will be void. They'll have no choice but to put my wellbeing and survival above their own. I will be like a god to them and they will have to do everything I tell them. They control nine tenths of the world's resources and I will control them."

Brigitte was aghast. "You know there's no way I can tell you where the Gateway to the Souls is now you've told me that."

"There's no way you can avoid telling me," Doc Papa said. He shifted shape again.

The second astral plane of the Loa's was where everything that had been born on the first plane found its shape, prior to being given form on the third plane. Shape was everything here. To think something was to become it. The shapes that held the most power were those that mirrored the divine mysteries of the Loa.

Doc Papa became a serpent once more but a different Loa, Dambala Wédo, whose serpentine form represents the path of descent taken by the gift of life and secrets of the Holy Spirit as they come from God down to man. Because of his great age, Dambala never speaks and so is the great confessor to whom all secrets are confided.

Brigitte could not afford to confess the secret of the Gateway's location to Doc Papa. As he prepared to strike she became the rainbow of Ayida Wédo. The heavenly form through which the gifts that Dambala brings are dispersed and distributed to the world.

Doc Papa's energies were dispersed and disempowered as he struck, like the rays of the sun refracted by the rain. He slid harmlessly down her rainbow but found no pot of gold at the end.

"Well played," Doc Papa said. "But you realise you are simply delaying the inevitable. The best you can hope for is a quick demise."

"That remains to be seen. I have much of your work to undo and I can't afford a quick demise."

"Then you'll have to settle for a painful one." Doc Papa took the shape of Baron Zaraguin, Scorpion Loa whose insect body is impermeable metal and expands across unimaginable dimensions. He arched his tail ready to sting and reached for her with his unbreakable claws. Brigitte became Sim'bi d'l'eau, countering his unyielding and relentless form with the fluid permeability of water. She trickled through his claws and ran down his spine, rusting them as she went, which brought him to a halt.

In a move Brigitte would never have anticipated Doc Papa became simply a Govi. A clay pot used for holding otherworldly spirits. As Sim'bi d'l'eau she spilled into the container and he brought a stopper down on the top. She was trapped.

"This is your last chance to die with a little dignity," Doc Papa said.

He began to alter the shape of the Govi. As Brigitte was trapped inside his shape she couldn't do anything to stop him. The earthenware Govi became a clear glass container in the shape of a heart. Doc Papa manifested a giant dagger above her. He was becoming the sacred attribute of Erzulie Zandor – a bloodied heart pierced with the dagger of the Ogou.

As Brigitte was inside him she was at his heart, so the dagger would pierce her Ti Bon Ange and slowly kill her. From out of nowhere she heard a voice say: "Stop, if your pierce me you harm the Gateway." It sounded exactly like her voice but she hadn't said those words or even thought them. They came from somewhere else, but where?

Doc Papa chuckled. "Of course," he said. "Toussaint would have hidden it in the one place I wouldn't think to look. Inside his own ancestor. You have been carrying it inside you all this time. He passed it on to you. He knew that if I thought you dead I would never suspect that the Gateway lay inside you."

"You'll have to cut it out of me to get it," said the voice that sounded like hers.

How had he coaxed her to say that? How could she have given away the location of the Gateway? How was she able to speak without even realising it?

Shh, little sister it wasn't you it was me.

Toussaint? How was her ancestor able to speak to her here?

It's Erzulie Zandor's doing. As soon as Doc Papa took her shape he gave her the power to place me inside here. It's time for me to take back what I gave you for safe keeping.

"Cut it out of you," said Doc Papa. "What an excellent idea."

Brigitte felt Toussaint reach into her and take the burden from her core. He was reclaiming the Gateway of the Souls. He was taking it to safety before she died.

No little sister, you will not die. I am taking your place and I am sending you back to help our people.

But that meant Doc Papa would kill Toussaint.

Just as he is supposed to. I am taking your place just as I took your great, great grandmother's.

Doc Papa would take the Gateway of the Souls if Toussaint did that.

Exactly as I plan him to, this is my curse coming to fruition.

But how would Brigitte help her people without the Gateway? How would she draw them back from the crossroads as Toussaint had done if she couldn't open it. She felt her astral form begin to flow out of the great glass heart as Toussaint's spirit poured in to take its place.

Hush little sister, you already have the solution. You just applied it to the wrong problem.

What did that mean? There wasn't time for Toussaint to answer as the last of Brigitte left the heart and the dagger descended. She heard Toussaint scream as he died a second time at the hands of a Papamal. Even in death beyond death, Toussaint disguised his voice to sound like hers. *That's what I would sound like if I were murdered*, she thought.

Brigitte felt herself pulled back to her body along a path Doc Papa couldn't see. She could still see him though.

She watched as he sliced the Gateway of the Souls out of Toussaint, without ever realising who he had truly killed. He held up the Gateway and let out a bitter laugh of victory. The Gateway was almost too bright to look at. It had an immense gravity that bent everything around it and seemed to refract both time and space.

Doc Papa took the Gateway of Souls and disappeared back to his body.

He had won, completely and irrevocably.

CHAPTER FORTY-THREE

They were lost, completely and irrevocably. Tatyana couldn't get her breathing and heart beat under control and the Zombies had noticed. They were shambling towards her. Her eyes had adjusted to the dark and she could see a little. She wished she couldn't.

"Benjamin," she called out. She needed him close to her. She didn't want to die alone.

He was struggling with Brigitte's body. "Here, give me a hand." He propped the body up on its feet and huddled behind it, pulling Tatyana to him.

The Zombies stopped advancing. Some vestigial memory inside them still responded to the sight of Brigitte.

"We're going to drag her to the tunnel behind us," Benjamin said pulling Brigitte towards the tunnel that led to the surface.

Further down the tunnel Tatyana could hear the guards approaching. "We're going to die aren't we?" she said. "It's all over."

"Do you hear the fat lady singing?"

"No," Tatyana had no idea what he was talking about.

"Neither do I. And that means it's far from over."

"What are we going to do?"

"We're going to take the fight to the guards."

"But they've got guns and rockets and God knows what."

"Yeah, and we've got an army of Zombies. I know who I'd put my money on."

"An army of Zombies that's about to eat us."

"No it's not," said Benjamin. She'd never seen him like this before. So focused and determined. "Look Tatyana, I know it's all over between us but I still love you, I always will and I'm not going to let you die like this, down here in this tunnel on some foreign island. We can do this. It's time to stop hiding behind Brigitte. Okay, so she stopped them from attacking us once before. But we rounded them up for her. We've spent longer in the company of blood-thirsty, flesh eating Zombies than probably any human who's ever lived and we're still alive. That's not just Brigitte. It's also us. We're good at this.

"What's gotten into you?" said Tatyana. "I've never seen you like this before."

"Maybe I've been backed into too many corners not to come out fighting."

Tatyana put her arms round him and pulled him close. She couldn't keep the tears out of her eyes, however soppy that made her feel. Was he right about it being over between them? She hadn't thought about it till now. He was being so brave and mature about it and she wasn't sure if she wanted to let him go yet. Even if he was right.

Benjamin took hold of her by the shoulders and looked her straight in the eyes. God he had beautiful eyes. Even in the pitch dark they sparkled.

"Listen to me," he said. "We're going to use ourselves as bait and lure the Zombies back down the tunnel on the right. It leads down to another crossroads at the start of the ossuary I'm sure of it."

"What good will that do?"

"They're expecting to take the Zombies from the rear. They won't anticipate the Zombies coming up behind them. They'll be caught in a... what do you call it? A pincer movement. They'll be trapped in the tunnel and they'll have to fight on both sides. They won't have a chance."

"But what if they outnumber the Zombies?"

"I've been listening to the footsteps of the guards chasing us. I was at the back of the Zombies for quite a while don't forget. I'm sure there's only about seven or eight of them on our tail. That means the Zombies outnumber them by more than twenty to one."

"What about Brigitte?"

"We can't carry her, she's too heavy. She'll be safe if we leave her here. No-one's going to look for her in this tunnel. We can come back for her later." Benjamin took Tatyana's hand and squeezed it. "Look. You're one of the coolest and most together people I know. I can't do this without you. Are you with me?"

"Of course." She wiped the tears from her eyes and brought his hand up to her lips. His beautiful fingers were interlaced with hers. She kissed each one. "Just say the word."

Benjamin sat Brigitte up against the wall of the tunnel, tucked behind a convenient outcrop.

"The word," he said and ran back out to the crossroads. "Hey over here," Benjamin called out to the Zombies. "Look it's a moving buffet." He motioned to Tatyana to follow him. "All you can eat so long as you catch me."

Tatyana ran out and stood behind him. The rotund male Zombie and the female Zombie who'd tasted his sweat were lumbering after him, followed by another female Zombie dressed in a maid's outfit. They were gnashing their decayed teeth and grabbing for him with their rotten fingers.

More Zombies began to follow as Benjamin led them down the tunnel which, just as he guessed, began to curve round so it ran parallel to the tunnel they'd left. Tatyana stayed behind Benjamin as he taunted the Zombies. He'd put himself almost within their reach and then jump back as they lunged for him.

If Benjamin put one foot wrong he'd be dead. They'd both seen what the Zombies could do to a person. Hell, they'd even tried to copy it. It took a lot of guts to do what he was doing.

She'd been about to go to pieces back there at the crossroads. Hunger, lack of sleep and too much stress had gotten the better of her. Benjamin had really stepped up to the mark just when she needed him. He was probably right about them being over, but right now she wanted to think of him as her man. Her big, brave man who was looking out for her.

As they walked backwards down the tunnel Tatyana could hear the guards more clearly.

"Listen," Benjamin said. "I want you to start your Zombie breathing now, get your heartbeat down too. As soon as we get to the crossroads we've got to drop back into Zombie mode and hang back. Can you do that?"

"I think so."

"Brilliant."

They hit the crossroads and did just that. Tatyana ducked around a corner to get out of the way and compose herself. Benjamin backed right into the guard on point. The guard swung round but Benjamin took the initiative. He pushed the guard right into the hands of the Zombies chasing them.

Tatyana saw at least six pairs of undead hands and teeth latch onto the guard before he had time to react. His screams brought two more guards running down to the crossroads. They were met with a mass of starving Zombies lurching round the corner of the tunnel. The guards tried to run back up the tunnel. One of them made it, the other was too slow. He went down under the tide of ravenous undead.

The guards were now trapped between two flanks of Zombies. There were several burst of gunfire. Two bullets struck the wall inches from Tatyana's head, showering her with shards of bone and rock. She flinched and fought to keep her heart rate under control.

"Don't shoot you fucking idiots!" shouted one of the guards. "You'll just damage the merchandise. Besides it doesn't stop them, use the fucking flamethrower!"

"The piece of shit flamethrower's not working."

"Where's my talisman thing? Oh shit, I've dropped it. Can I get a light over here?"

"There's too many of them, we can't pull out."

"What do we do now eh, Donovan? C'mon, you got us into this, what do we do now?"

The question went unanswered as the Zombies overwhelmed them. Tatyana stood very still and hardly breathed. She concentrated on reducing her vital signs. All to block out the sounds of the guard's screams and curses.

She tried not to think about their suffering, or whether they had wives and children who'd mourn them but never recover or bury their remains. She tried especially hard not to think about her part in their death or the other deaths in which she was complicit.

She wondered how she was going to atone for all the things she'd done. One of the main things that fascinated her about religion was the opportunity it offered for absolution.

If the Loa were calling her, as Brigitte said, should she answer the call? Would that be her opportunity to make good for all the bad things she'd done?

CHAPTER FORTY-FOUR

Doc Papa was about to make good on everything he'd done since founding the Way of the Barefoot Zombie. He'd returned to his ceremony room and was hovering above his body. It was still lying on the floor surrounded by the living Vévé.

He held up the Gateway of the Souls and savoured his victory. It was an artefact of rare and unimaginable beauty. Fashioned from a perfect blend of solar energy and dark mass it had an undeniable gravity about it, even when closed as it was now.

The Gateway was to the soul what a black hole was to light, inescapable. Even in his astral form he could feel his soul beating at his body's breast to be free to enter it. What a burden it must have been to Brigitte to have carried it within her all this time. Yet she put up such a fight to hang on to it.

The living Vévé shifted into a new shape so that Doc Papa could return to his body with the Gateway. He descended with exceptional care into his corporeal form. It felt like clambering down a gigantic pile of broken glass carrying several pounds of live gelignite. One wrong move and his mind, body and soul would be torn to pieces.

He marveled again at the brilliance and ingenuity of Brigitte's ancestor for not only opening the Gateway, but finding a way to carry it inside himself and later to hide it in Brigitte. He was relieved to be free of the curse that Toussaint had placed on his bloodline.

Doc Papa's astral form finally found its way carefully back inside his body and brought the Gateway with it. He came back to consciousness with a start. He sat bolt upright and vomited. He emptied the entire contents of his stomach over Vincenzo's still cooling corpse. That was something else that would have to be cleaned up in the morning.

Still, he shouldn't focus on tiny details like that at such an auspicious moment. He got to his feet but couldn't stop himself from swaying. He felt drained and unsteady. He didn't want to admit it, but the battle with Brigitte had taken more out of him than he realised.

The Gateway was also having an effect on him. He could feel an immense inward pull at the centre of himself that was contracting his whole being. So much power and so little time left to use it.

Doc Papa reached inside himself and opened the Gateway.

It felt like an infinite unfolding, taking place forever and in the space of one moment. The finite nature of his being was now host to an endlessly expanding opening that it shouldn't be able to accommodate but was.

As the Gateway opened he started to feel its pull. A huge vortex was unleashed within him. It hollowed him out inside and drew every untethered human soul to him.

He felt the first of them dragged to him, mewling and afraid. George Griffin the investment banker and the real estate tycoon Arthur Sonnenfeldt. More followed. He enveloped them as they entered him in a confused and vulnerable state. They were totally prone to his dominant consciousness. He had never had such power over other humans. It was beyond intoxicating.

Every part of their essential being belonged to him. Within an instant he knew every guilty secret they harboured, every weakness they hid. Their whole being was annexed to his. Like a small pool of water that meets a larger one, they were engulfed by him.

He was swollen by them as their thoughts, hopes and fears swam through him and became his to command. This was domination beyond the dreams of any despot. It was subjugation to which no police state could ever aspire. No implanted micro-chip, twenty-four hour CCTV coverage or illegal wire tap had ever stripped a citizen of this much privacy or individuality.

And still more souls flooded into him. Everyone who'd ever entrusted their soul to his bank was drawn into him. He glutted himself on their greed and lusts, their needs and hunger, all of them his now, all of them part of him.

He became the central nexus point for all the souls. They could have no desperate longing, no vengeful urge or boiling hatred that didn't run through him first.

Every whim or desire he had was filtered down to the hundreds of souls under his dominion and would bring hundreds of responses as the other souls processed it. His tiniest impulse brought a wall of feedback that was almost too much to take in.

He was surrounded by a symphony of being. He had hundreds of other consciousnesses to consider, hundreds of desperate clingy appetites grasping at his attention. There was no longer any separation between his own will and that of every other will he'd married to him.

The barriers between himself and the others began to crumble. There were too many of them in too little space. It was too much to bear. He couldn't find himself any more. Stripped of their uniqueness and identity none of the souls could tell themselves apart and neither could Doc Papa.

Who was who? Who was he? What was his anymore? Was this his thought or theirs? Was it his confusion or theirs? Who were they, weren't they him now? Where was he?

Didn't he own them? Didn't he? All of them his. All of them on top of him. Needing. Wanting. Taking. Taking. Taking.

Stop. Stop it. Stop them. Who them? Them or us? Isn't them us? I am them but who is I? They are here but where is me. What am I? I am Legion...

... and lost...

stifled

suffocated

drowning.

Wait, get a grip. A grip on this. How to stop this? What caused this? The Gateway. Yes, the Gateway! Got to close it. Got to remember how to close it. But how? So many memories to go through, so many memories that are now his. Which one holds what's needed?

Can't think. Can't stop thinking. Too much thinking. Move. Get out. Fresh air, we all need fresh air. Take me out. Take me out to the ball game.

Ball game, there's a ball game?

No stupid, it's a song.

Who are you calling stupid?

I don't know, who are you?

Don't you know?

Doesn't who know?

Who's in charge here?

Who has hold of the reins?

Reins, are there any?

Where are we going?

Out to the ballgame.

This is a whole new ballgame.

This is madness.

This is

This

From the furthest reaches of the afterlife, the last remnants of the man who was Toussaint looked down on Doc Papa, the last of the Papamals, as he ran from that hateful house he'd rebuilt.

Doc Papa screamed as he ran. He laughed and gibbered and cried. He tore his clothes and he pulled his hair. He scraped his skin and he bit his tongue till they both bled. But nothing he did would silence the clamour inside him. Nothing would get them all out.

This was just as Toussaint had planned it. It was all playing out as he knew it would. The curse had come to fruition. Erzulie Zandor had granted Doc Papa's wish. As she had said, it would be a lesson to many. Toussaint could rest now.

CHAPTER FORTY-FIVE

Brigitte couldn't rest now, though she desperately longed to. Her body ached and her soul was weary. It had been a long route back from the astral plane to her body. Or at least it felt that way.

She came to in complete darkness. She was sitting up against the jagged wall of a tunnel. In the distance she could hear the sound of shuffling feet and flesh being rent as bodies were torn apart and chewed by lifeless jaws.

Oh God, she hoped that wasn't Benjamin and Tatyana. Brigitte tried to get to her feet. She banged her elbow on the wall and fell back down. The sound of shuffling got closer and she felt something bump against her leg. There was a scuffle and the sound of someone falling.

"Ouch," said a voice. "I think I've found her." It was Tatyana. Legba be praised she was alive.

"Are you alright?" said another voice, Benjamin's. "Let me give you a hand."

"I could do with a hand as well," said Brigitte. She heard Tatyana gasp in surprise.

"You're okay," said Tatyana. "Thank goodness."

"I was thinking the same thing," said Miriam as they helped her to her feet. "What happened to the guards?"

"The err... Zombies got them," said Benjamin. He sounded contrite.

"Oh," said Brigitte unable to hide the disappointment in her voice.

"You asked us to look after them for you," said Benjamin. "It was the only way we could stop the guards from capturing them and killing us."

"I'm sure it was," said Brigitte, sighing with tiredness. "It's just that they've been used as violent monsters for so long I get upset when it happens again. I take it that's the guards they're feeding on?"

"Yes," said Tatyana. "I'm sorry, we couldn't stop them."

"No I don't suppose you could. But it makes them harder to control when they've tasted blood. Where are they?"

"They're in the tunnel just down here," said Tatyana. "We'll lead you if you like. Our eyes have kind of got used to the dark now."

"I thought we had a lamp."

"Yeah, that got broke when I dropped it sorry. I was avoiding one of the Zombies.

"It was trying to eat her," Benjamin said by way of explanation.

"Do you mind us calling them Zombies?" said Tatyana. "I mean I know that's what they are, but they're your friends and relations aren't they? Should we call them by their names or something?"

"That's okay. You can call them Zombies if you like. I don't like to think of them as monsters, but I don't want to think of them as the people they were. Not when they're in this state."

Benjamin and Tatyana led Brigitte to the crossroads in the tunnel. She readied herself to take control of the Zombies one last time. She reached out with her mind and pieced together a group mind for them. Teasing out each tiny piece of consciousness they possessed and weaving it into a collective mind. One that she could communicate with and instruct.

It was harder after they had just killed. There was little to them but savage instinct and it took a bit of effort to get them all to focus on her. Especially as they hadn't been fed in a while and there was plenty of fresh meat left on the guards. She was tired and hungry and hardly had the strength for the extra effort. She pushed herself all the same.

Eventually they all came round. She felt light headed from expending so much energy. She swayed and nearly lost her footing. Benjamin caught her and stopped her from falling.

"Are you okay?" he said. "Do you want to sit down and rest?"

"There isn't time. It'll be sunrise in just under an hour and then the Festival of the Gédé will have passed. We can't afford to wait another year for this chance."

As her islanders stood and chewed over the bones or other scraps they'd torn from the guards' bodies Benjamin pointed to several beams of light on the floor.

"Hey look," he said. "They had those torch things on their helmets There's one for each of us."

Brigitte led them out of the ossuary and along the tunnel that took them back to the surface. They came out of a cave entrance that her ancestors had carved to look like a skull. In times gone past they would light candles in the eyes and leave offerings to Baron Samedi and Le Gran Brigitte during the Festival of the Gédé.

A short walk from the cave entrance was the crossroads. When they arrived Brigitte arranged the islanders around the crossroads in a circle. This took some doing. Some of them were still vicious and savage from the blood they'd tasted and needed coaxing. When she had them all in position she led Benjamin and Tatyana into the centre of the crossroads with her.

"This crossroads sits at the very centre of St Ignatius," Brigitte said. "For that reason it is a very sacred site. This is where I'm going to open a portal to the Celestial Crossroads that lies between the three worlds of the Loa and the world of the humans. When you pass on, your soul comes to the Celestial Crossroads. A soul can also be sent to the Celestial Crossroads by a powerful Houngan or Mambo while its owner is still alive. When you arrive you can choose to follow the roads to eternal damnation or eternal salvation, to re-enter the cycle of birth and death in another life or even to return to the life you've just left."

"Hold on a minute," said Tatyana. "Didn't you say that when you died your Gros Bon Ange argued your case before God and that's how He decided what was going to happen to your soul? But now you seem to be saying that we can just choose, how can that be?"

"Sooner or later you'll meet God on the road you've chosen to follow. That is when your Gros Bon Ange will argue your case. Ultimately however it is God's decision whether your choice of road is the correct one and if it will lead you where you want to go."

"Wow."

"Indeed," said Brigitte. "Sometimes a Houngan can trap a soul at the Celestial Crossroads so they can't choose a road. When a person's soul is no longer part of their body and unable to move to the next life, then they're no longer alive but they can't properly die either."

"They become a Zombie," said Benjamin, as the penny dropped. "That's what happened to your islanders. And it's also what's happening to the other guests."

"Exactly," said Brigitte. "I need to open a portal to the Celestial Crossroads so that I can free my people from the spell they're under and give them the opportunity to make the choice they've been denied all this time."

"How are you going to do that?"

"To be honest," said Brigitte. "I'm not entirely sure. I'm going to have to wing it. I was given a magical artefact that my ancestor used to free his people from the crossroads. But Doc Papa stole it from me when I was out of my body. It's very powerful and I'm afraid of what he'll do with it. We have to free my people before he tries to stop us."

"What do you need us to do?" said Tatyana.

"More than anything I need you to believe. The world only continues to be the way it is, and operate according to certain laws, because we believe it will. This goes for everything from gravity to money or the rules of high finance. Magic within Voodoo is the same. We only get the outcome we want because we *believe* the Loa will grant it. If you want to alter reality, your belief in this change has to be stronger than the belief of everyone who's keeping reality the way it currently is. You need to defy their belief in order to change the way things are. Do you understand what I'm saying?"

"I think so," said Tatyana.

"Opening this portal involves strong magic because it goes against most people's view of what reality is. If you have any scepticism or doubt about the outcome it could jeopardise the whole spell. I'm hoping that after everything you've seen this won't be the case but I need to know you believe in what I'm about to do?"

"I want to believe in this more than anything in the world," said Tatyana. "In fact I need to."

"I thought that might be the case," said Brigitte. She turned to Benjamin. "How about you, do you have faith?"

"Yeah, you know what, I do have faith."

"Good, because we need to invoke Papa Legba, the most powerful of all the Loa, to make this work, and he demands complete faith from his servants."

"Who is Papa Legba?"

"Papa Legba is the Master of the Crossroads and the Gatekeeper between the worlds. It is only through his permission that the other Loa are allowed to cross over into our world. That's why he's the first Loa to be invoked at the beginning of every ceremony. Only he can open the portal and lift the spell on my people."

"Is there anything we need to do?"

"Usually it would take a big ceremony with a sacrifice to summon him. We don't have the time or the tools for that though. So I'm going to improvise. Kick off your shoes then join me in the circle."

Brigitte held out her hands to Tatyana and Benjamin. She reached out to the group mind of her people and sent an impulse out to all of them. They all lifted their left leg and brought it down. Then, concentrating hard, she got them to do the same with their right leg. Most of them did this in unison. She got them to repeat the actions, stamping first their left foot then their right until they had a workable rhythm going.

"We don't have any drums," said Brigitte. "So we're going to use our feet instead. We're each going to take a ritual drum and stamp out the part ourselves. Tatyana, I want you to be the Ka-Tha-Bou drum. I'm going to stamp out your part then I want you to repeat it." Brigitte stamped it out for her and Tatyana tried to copy the rhythm. After two attempts she got it right.

"Benjamin, you're going to be the Manman drum. This is your part." Benjamin got it first time and stamped in counterpoint to Tatyana's rhythm. "I'm going to be the Grondez drum."

The whole ground shook to the slap and the stomp of living and undead feet. "As I can't draw a Vévé we're going to have to picture Papa Legba in our minds. You can visualise him as a crooked old man with a walking stick and a small pipe. Or you can think of him as St Peter carrying a holy book and a set of keys. This is the Catholic saint he's associated with. He is very charming but a great trickster, so be careful in his presence."

Brigitte closed her eyes and pictured herself drawing Papa Legba's Vévé on the floor of her Ounfó. Then she summoned up every time she had ever encountered the Master of the Crossroad from her memory. She put together a composite picture from these memories and she overlaid it on the Vévé she had drawn in her mind.

"Now I want you to sing this invocation with me." Brigitte sang them the invocation line by line and after a few attempts they were word perfect. They repeated the invocation over and over again, singing:

"Papa Legba ouvri bayè-a pou mwen

"Pou mwen pase

"Lè ma tounen, ma salyié Loa yo."

The moon was low in the sky but a sudden shaft of her light

fell on Tatyana. She began to shake and flail as Papa Legba entered her. Tatyana let go of their hands as though she had been dragged away. Her limbs and back began to twist and bend into the posture of an old, old man.

"Greetings to you Papa Legba," said Brigitte. "I didn't expect you to honour us with your presence."

"Ah no," said Papa Legba. "You expected me to hear you treaties from afar and grant your request. It's always the same. I'm the first up and the last to bed. Opening the way so the younger ones can rush out and mount their horses while I wait patiently at the gate."

"I have a request Papa Legba."

"I know, I know, you always have requests. No-one calls me up just to chew the fat, or ask me how my day went. No-one offers me a glass of rum or a comfortable seat by the fire. No, no it's always 'can you put my name on the guest list? Can I get a backstage pass? Which Loas are playing tonight, could you introduce me?' It's a wonder I ever leave my bed."

"Papa Legba if I have offended you ..."

"You'd be wearing your innards as a necklace little sister. I am having fun with you. There's no need for this sobriety."

"But there's every need for care."

"Indeed little sister, watch where you tread. I am old but not toothless."

"If I may ask of you a favour...?"

"Ah yes your request, don't waste your breath little sister I know what you want. Quite a few of the Loa have been watching your progress. I had already decided if you got this far you would earn my favour."

"Papa Legba I don't know what to say."

"Oh hush, shush, you haven't heard my conditions yet. I like this horse that I'm riding. She is fine and supple and bends well beneath me. I will have her stay here on the island and I will be her Met-tet. You will train her and teach her to serve the Loa."

"What if she doesn't want to stay?"

"Oh *Pshaw!* I think we both know what she is secretly planning to do, even if she hasn't admitted it to herself yet."

"Then you'll grant my request?"

"Step aside little sister, your people are coming home."

Normal space seemed to warp around Papa Legba as the Loa reached out much further than Tatyana's arm should ever stretch and took hold of the night sky like a curtain. With a movement that defied human anatomy, he pulled aside the fabric of this world to reveal the worlds beyond.

From the corner of her eye Brigitte saw Benjamin shake his head as his mind tried to deny what he was seeing. She placed a hand on his shoulder. "Don't close yourself off from what you're seeing. Allow yourself to believe this and you will grow in more ways than you can imagine."

Brigitte saw the Celestial Crossroads and she saw her people at the centre of it. They looked beaten, dejected and oppressed. They were huddled together in such a tight space Brigitte was reminded of a picture she had once seen in a book that showed prisoners jammed into a cattle truck. She reached out to them with her soul but as she got close she ran into the force that was holding them captive.

It was the essence of barbed wire and steel bayonets. It was powered by the force that inspires concentrations camps, detention centres and secret military prisons for terrorist suspects. Brigitte recoiled in pain and fear.

"Oh come now little sister," said Papa Legba. "Are you going to let the residue of a defeated Houngan's spell deter you?"

Defeated Houngan? But Brigitte had been beaten by Doc Papa. She had seen him snatch the Gateway of the Souls from Toussaint's dead breast. Was Papa Legba playing a trick on her? Or had Toussaint played one on Doc Papa?

Brigitte put that from her mind. What mattered right now was freeing her people. What was it Toussaint had said? She already had the solution. She'd just applied it to the wrong problem. Was he talking about the curse? She'd tried to beat that with love and the consequences had been disastrous.

Would love be any more effective now?

"Love is how you beat hate and dispel dark Voodoo" she'd told Doc Papa. This spell he'd cast was the worst sort of dark, hateful Voodoo. She had to try it.

She reached out to the force that held her people and she tried to find some love for it. She concentrated on the things she loved about Doc Papa, the man who had tried to condemn her and all the islanders to a living death. But she needn't be beaten by that.

She thought of the things she loved about him. She loved his hands and the way they'd touched her. And his mind, so quick and brilliant, she loved that too. She loved the taste of his skin, especially when it was speckled with sweat from the sun. She loved the expression on his face when he came.

She took this love and she sent it into the dark force around her people. All at once the pain and fear were banished. The barbed wire wilted and the barriers crumbled. Her people were captive no longer.

They could hardly believe they were free. They didn't dare move. Then a few of the bravest tested the ground around them and found there was nothing holding them in place. When the others saw this they were overjoyed.

"Brothers and sisters," Brigitte said to the souls at the Celestial Crossroads. "Your ordeal is over. It is time to come home or continue into the next life."

The souls didn't know how to react to this news. They looked out from the Crossroads at their empty, shambling bodies.

The youngest souls were the first to venture back to the world they had left. Other souls looked with dismay at the state of their bodies and the things they must have done and decided they could no longer live inside them. They turned with a heavy heart and followed the road to the next life. Most chose salvation, a tiny few judged their sins too great and took the road to damnation.

Brigitte was surprised to see that one of these was the guest whose soul she had sent to the crossroads when he broke into the mine.

Still others searched in vain for their bodies. They looked from face to face among the Zombies and never found their own. Having nowhere else to go they too eventually turned and went with reluctance along another road.

When the last of the souls had chosen a road, the portal closed and the Celestial Crossroads faded from view. It felt like waking from a dream that has just slipped your mind.

Papa Legba let out a wild laugh and disappeared. Tatyana dropped to the floor. Benjamin rushed over to her. All around them the islanders were having convulsions, throwing up or shuddering uncontrollably. After spending two years outside of their bodies they were now having difficulty adjusting to being flesh and bone once again.

Brigitte never found it a pleasant experience when her soul returned to her body after she'd sent it out. It felt like putting on clothes caked with blood and filth after stepping out of a warm cleansing bath. And that was returning to a live body after only a few hours. She could only imagine the horror and revulsion the islanders must be feeling returning to bodies that had been walking corpses for two years.

Benjamin was supporting Tatyana in his lap and cradling her head as she came round. "What happened?" she said. "God, my arms and legs ache."

"Aw man it was awesome," said Benjamin. "I wish you could have seen it. You were possessed by Papa Legba. He was old and really funny, but kind of wise and dangerous with it. He parted the night sky like a curtain and showed this other world underneath, and Brigitte freed all the souls there. And hey, he also said that you..."

Brigitte put her hand gently on Benjamin's shoulder to stop him. "Wait. That's something she has to come to herself."

"Oh, so now you're both going to go all cryptic on me," said Tatyana. "It worked though right? The ceremony I mean."

"Yes it worked," said Brigitte. "Thanks be to Papa Legba."

"So what now?"

"Now we begin rebuilding our lives," said Brigitte. "But first we must find out what's happening with the guests and the others who have lost their souls. For that we must find Doc Papa."

CHAPTER FORTY-SIX

Must find Doc Papa. Him have their souls. Him suck them all up like greedy belly. Bessie join others in hunt him.

Bessie get worse and worse now. Legs not work good no more. Brain not think right no more. Everything not work good no more. Others not good neither. Look like Zombies and stink bad. They all hunt Doc Papa now. His fault they not work good.

Doc Papa try run away from them but them feel where him is. Empty hole in all of them feel where Doc Papa is. Empty hole aches from no soul. Souls in Doc Papa now. Pull them to him. Doc Papa no escape them.

Them all go into grounds of big house now. Doc Papa try hide there. No good. Empty soul holes feel him out.

Them nearly catch Doc Papa earlier. Him on road, run from big house. Them come for him. Him scream like him laughing at them and laugh like him screaming. Him pull his trousers off and try piss at them.

Then him do shit and throw at them. When them not stop coming for Doc Papa, him smear shit on him body. Him not want them eat him. Him think shit make him taste bad and them not eat him.

Them not mind. Them have no taste no more. Them have no feelings no more. Bessie fall on steps when she come up to big house. Her leg go smack. Her bone go crack and poke through skin. Little blood come out. Her no bleed much no more.

Bessie no feel thing. Leg no walk right no more. Bessie stop and look at leg. George Griffin stop too. Him look at Bessie's leg. Him sniff Bessie's leg. Them still smell good even if them no feel.

George want eat Bessie's leg. Him lick Bessie's blood then try bite leg. Bessie hit George and hit him again. George's nose go crack. Bessie's knuckle go pop. George stop trying to eat Bessie's leg. Bessie's hand not work good now with knuckle popped.

Bessie walk slower as them come into big house. Bessie's leg keep slipping and Bessie fall lots. Others over take her as them go in door. Them get better morsels than Bessie.

Bessie feel so hungry as she get close to Doc Papa. Soul hole ache like Bessie been stabbed. Bessie feel soul calling to her from Doc Papa's body. Soul crying like little baby in trouble. Soul dying in there. Soul go rotten like Bessie's body.

Doc Papa on stairs as them find him. Him want run from them but their souls inside him want back in their bodies. Bessie see Doc Papa have fight with himself. Him argue with himself, then plead then burst out laughing and shout. Bessie try get closer to him on stairs but fall down when leg slip. Stupid leg! Bessie angry. Bessie hit leg and then fall down again.

First of them get hold of Doc Papa on stairs. Him swear at them and tell them him will choke and kill them if them eat him. Bessie get more hungry when him talk of eating. She try stand on stupid leg again. She walk five steps without falling. That good record for stupid leg. Bessie not hit it so hard when her fall this time.

Doc Papa start screaming as them get their teeth in him. Them feel hungry for their souls too. Bessie feel her teeth start chewing by themselves her get so hungry at thought of eating Doc Papa.

Bessie try get closer as them start to chew on him whole body. Him blood start to pour down stairs like red waterfall. Bessie stop to look at blood. Her think it pretty till she skid in it as she try get at Doc Papa. Then she fall in it. Blood on her hand. Bessie lick him blood and want more.

Many others have big mouthfulls of him, with blood drip down them chin. Bessie is jealous and wants mouthful too when she sees them chins with blood on. She starts to push through others to get near him and others push back. Them start to fight over him when not all of them can have bite of him flesh.

Doc Papa him scream and scream with pain as them eat him and fight. Some of them start to pull on him arms like a tug of war. Doc Papa shouts at them as him arms come off and some blood hits Bessie in her face. Bessie licks blood and her stomach growls.

Some of them grab for the arms and push each other to get bite of them. Others pull at Doc Papa's head and legs. Doc Papa's head comes off but still him scream and shout even when one man bite him tongue out. Him legs split apart and him guts fall out on stairs with wet splat sound.

Bessie like that. Her grab for guts and get him liver. Moira Jacobs try and take liver from her. Bessie put hand on Moira Jacobs' head and smash her face into stairs. Moira Jacobs teeth come out and her leave Bessie alone.

Bessie bite warm liver. Taste good. Bessie hear liver scream. Bessie feel it in teeth as her chew him liver. Liver scream as it go down Bessie's throat and into Bessie's stomach.

Doc Papa so full of souls that every part of him alive. Him not die when them tore him into pieces. Every piece still feel pain. Every piece scream and scream and scream. All them hear it and feel good to make Doc Papa scream.

Him feel it as they chew him guts and bite him flesh and crack him bones and lick him marrow. Even him marrow feel the pain and scream. Him screams are closest Bessie come to feel her soul again.

Souls them going now. No more left of Doc Papa to keep them in. With them souls gone them not have life now. Them stop breath and heart stop beat.

Bessie feel tired. Others start lie down and not get up. Others fall down with him screaming blood dribbling from them mouths. Them bodies not work no more. Some twitch, some kick, some don't.

Bessie stop think.

Body stop move.

Bessie sto...

CHAPTER FORTY-SEVEN

A WEEK LATER

Tatyana found another spot on the stair. She sprayed it with the stain remover and scrubbed it with the brush, trying not to think how it got there in the first place.

"Only another forty steps to go," said Brigitte coming down the stairs.

Tatyana grinned. "Are you sure this is an essential part of my spiritual training?"

"Anything your Mambo tells you to do is an essential part of your training. Besides I need all the slave labour I can get to clean this mess up."

"It feels kind of weird though. I'm not being funny but when I scrub at a patch of blood that's still kind of fresh, it feels like it's... well it almost sounds like it's..."

"Screaming?"

"Yeah, how'd you know?"

"It's still alive."

"It is? Oh my God that's gross. How can it be alive if it's week-old blood?"

"Every part of Doc Papa was alive. When he opened the Gateway of Souls inside himself he became suffused with all the souls that were loose. That was more than anyone could accommodate or even bear. The souls couldn't all reside in his core so they spread out and filled every part of his body. It would most probably have driven him mad. I didn't realise it at the time, but that's why my ancestor Toussaint gave him the Gateway."

"And the guests tore him apart and ate him?"

"They would have been trying to get their souls back I imagine. They would have been more or less Zombies at that point."

"So if every part of him was alive from the souls inside him would he still have felt it even after they tore him apart?"

"Every shred of his flesh and bone would have been in unimaginable pain throughout the whole ordeal."

"Gross."

"It was Toussaint's curse coming to pass. Mary Papamal's descendant died a hideous and bloody death at the hands of a Laveau. It just wasn't the Laveau I imagined."

Tatyana heard a clatter behind her. She turned to see Benjamin dropping his spade as he tried to lean it against the wall. He'd been helping to bury the guest's bodies. He was in his vest. His muscles were taught and firm from all the digging he'd been doing. His skin had a sheen of sweat from working in the sun and his arms were smeared with dried mud.

Tatyana felt a pang of desire and loss at the same time. She loved Benjamin and she still found him attractive but she'd chosen a different future for herself.

"That's pretty much the last of them done," he said.

"You made certain they marked every grave with the right name didn't you?" said Brigitte. "Because at some point their families are going to want to come and dig them up again."

"I checked every name against the register and whatever ID we found in their wallets."

"What are we going to do when the authorities start asking

questions about what happened?" said Tatyana.

"My guess is, the people who set up the course were so connected to everyone in power that the authorities will want the whole thing covered up," said Brigitte. "Too many of them would be embarrassed if it all came out."

"What about you and the islanders?" said Benjamin.

"We're going to carry on rebuilding our lives."

That's pretty much what they'd all been doing since they came to Mangrove Hall and found the bodies of the dead guests on the stairs. Everyone was trying to find a bit of normality after the bloodshed. The horror was over and they had to pick themselves up and deal with the business of everyday life.

Tatyana found it rather comforting to worry about mundane things again. Like what she was going to have for breakfast and where she was going to be sleeping from now on. That's why she didn't mind scrubbing the stairs. It felt good to do a household chore. Something that wouldn't lead to a violent death if she didn't keep her wits about her. It was a far cry from the privileged lifestyle she was used to, but it felt more honest and real.

While she and Benjamin helped clear away the bodies and clean up the hall, the rest of the islanders repaired their old homes and started looking for food and other necessities. There was a sense of optimism in everyone in spite of what they'd been through. The very worst had happened but they'd survived and were getting on with their lives.

Faces that had been blank and feral, now wore smiles and winked at Tatyana. Hands she once feared might tear her apart, patted her on the back and helped her whenever they could. Suddenly the islanders were people again. With personalities and memories and opinions. They weren't some monstrous threat anymore.

In many ways, she thought, that's what a Zombie represented. A faceless human threat. It was the enemy. It was any country, organisation or group of people you were against.

They were people you couldn't identify with, so they weren't human. If your opponent's not human then it doesn't feel so wrong to hurt or kill them. That's probably what Doc Papa intended when he started preaching the Way of the Barefoot Zombie. That's what turning people into Zombies was all about.

"So you're really going to stay and join the Ounfó then?" said Benjamin, joining her on the stairs.

Tatyana nodded and made sure he didn't get dirt on her clean step. "Yes I am. In fact I'm kind of honoured they've accepted me, seeing as I don't come from the island or anything."

"I don't think we had any choice about accepting you," said Brigitte sitting on the step above them. "As servants of the Loa we have to heed their wishes, and Papa Legba was pretty adamant that you stay. You have a talent for this and you might not realise but you've had the calling for a long time."

"Who'd have thought?" said Benjamin.

"Yeah," said Tatyana. "But I think I've been looking for something to believe in my whole life. That's probably what drew me to the ZLF. I wanted to have faith in something and I thought taking up a cause would give me that. Of course there were other things that attracted me too." She took Benjamin's hand as she said that. He squeezed it in a friendly fashion and let go. He was withdrawing from her emotionally. She knew he had to, but she missed being close to him. And she missed the sex. She was probably going to have to go without it for a while.

"I know what you mean about the ZLF," Benjamin said. "I think we all hoped the cause would give us something we were looking for."

"What were you looking for Benjamin?" Brigitte said.

"I think I was looking for somewhere to belong. And I think I was really trying to piss my step dad off."

"That's the first time I ever heard you call Richard your step dad," said Tatyana,

"I know. I guess that's what he is though. I need to accept that if I'm going to get on better with him and my Mom."

"This is a really mature side that you're showing," said Tatyana. "I rather like it."

"Thanks," said Benjamin. "Coming here has put a lot of things into perspective for me. Doing this course showed me how much I wanted to belong and the things I was capable of doing to feel I belonged. I think that's what my fascination with Zombie movies was all about."

"Really?" said Tatyana.

"Yeah. It was the tension between being an individual or fitting in. The human survivors in these movies were like the individuals resisting the mindless herd of the Zombie conformists. I always identified with them at the beginning of the movie but towards the end when they all start becoming Zombies I couldn't help thinking it would be easier to just lie down and get it over with. To get bitten, become a Zombie and then they couldn't hurt you anymore."

"So you secretly always wanted to conform," said Brigitte. "That's why you identified with the Zombie."

"Exactly, even though all the dressing up and stuff made me stand out."

"I find the West's fascination with Zombies quite baffling actually," said Brigitte. "Is that what it's all about, being an individual or conforming to some sort of mass cultural stereotype?"

"Not entirely," said Benjamin. "I think the Zombie is sort of how we secretly see ourselves and our society. Our culture's all about mindlessly consuming material things, a bit like a Zombie. We're devouring the world's resources and any other culture that gets in our way. Trying to turn them into mindless consumers like us. Modern Zombie films are always about the breakdown of society due to some calamity that brings the dead back to life. And we don't want to admit it, but we know that if we carry on this way our society's going to break down and that's the kind of world we'll be living in."

"Wow," said Tatyana. "You have been getting things into perspective haven't you?"

"Yeah I guess I have. You know I'm reminded of something my granddad once told me. He wasn't my real granddad, he was Richard's dad but he's the closest I ever got to a real granddad. He was a broker during the stock market crash of 1929. He saw all his money wiped out in one afternoon. The only thing he could think of doing was to open the window of his top floor office and walk out onto the ledge. When he got out there he just froze. He couldn't get back inside and he couldn't jump. He was trapped there for eight hours until the fire fighters got him down.

"While he was up there, facing death, he said his whole life suddenly fell into perspective. He saw all the wrong choices he'd made, like cheating on his wife and lying to his bosses. He saw the reasons why he'd made those choices and the things he could do to put things right. When it looked as though his life was over he saw all the ways that he could fix it."

"I know exactly what you mean," said Tatyana. "That's totally what we've been going through."

"Isn't it though?"

"God yes. It just cuts through all the bullshit. Being so close to death for so long has convinced me that there's got to be something else beyond it. I'm not entirely certain what that is but I'd like to learn more about it. I know this probably sounds a bit strange coming from a former atheist, but Voodoo just makes sense of the way that I've always experienced the world. Do you know what I mean?"

"Yeah, I think I do. And trust me, nothing sounds strange after what we've just been through"

"I've always known there was this other invisible world going on all around us but I never wanted to admit it. Mainly because of my father I guess. I mean he told me and my mother we were atheists and so we were. I was too frightened of him to argue. I was frightened of being disloyal to him. That if I started believing in things he didn't, then I'd stop loving him, which I don't want to do, in spite of all his faults. I think I was also afraid that if I started to believe in religion it would take over my life and I'd stop being the person I was. Now, of course, I realise that having a faith allows me to be the person I really am."

"Now look who's getting some perspective." Benjamin said.

"So you understand then, why I'm doing this I mean? And you're not mad at me?"

Benjamin shook his head and rolled his eyes in mock exasperation. "Are you kidding? I'm so impressed by what you're doing. Why would I be mad?"

"Well, you know, because of you and me, and the way things have turned out."

"Listen, we've grown up loads together and now I guess we've gotten to a stage where we going to have to grow some more apart from each other. I won't stop loving you though, no matter what happens."

"I can see what you saw in him now," said Brigitte.

Tatyana put her hand on Benjamin's knee. "He's lovely isn't he?"

"And what about you Benjamin?" said Brigitte. "What are you going to do next?"

"Well first I'm going to grab a shower, get my stuff together and catch the launch this afternoon," he said. The islanders had got a boat together to take all the people left alive who'd worked for Doc Papa over to Haiti. Benjamin was joining them.

"After that," Benjamin continued. "I think as soon as I get home I'm going to have to get in touch with the families of our friends and explain what happened to them here."

"Are you okay to do that?" Tatyana said.

Benjamin shrugged. "Someone's got to and I guess it ought to be me. I got them involved in the first place so I suppose it's my fault." Tatyana and Benjamin's mood suddenly dropped as they thought about the friends they'd lost.

Brigitte put her hand on Benjamin's shoulder."What you did was foolish, ill considered and reckless, but you can't hold yourself responsible for what happened to your friends. I've been holding myself responsible for what happened to my fellow islanders since I left the island two years ago. I realise now that I was wrong to do that. There's only one person who's ultimately responsible and he paid the ultimate price."

"Yeah, I still get creeped out when I think about what happened to him," said Benjamin. "I guess your ancestor really knew how to place a curse."

"Yes. He certainly did."

"So you're really going to try and get on better with your folks?" said Tatyana.

"Well my Mom mainly. But Richard too I guess. First I've got to face the music and explain what happened to Richard's yacht and the five million he put up for me to come here."

"How do you think they'll take it?"

"Richard will be a dick. My Mom will play peacemaker and I'll have to eat a lot of shit and make a lot of compromises to get back in with them. But I figure it'll be worth it to patch things up with my Mom."

"That's kind of a big step for you."

"It is, but out in the jungle, when Brigitte did that Voodoo healing on me, it lifted so much anger off me. I see now how so much of it came from my relationship with my Mom. We both miss each other and the way it used to be between us. I want to put that right now. I never properly thanked you for that Brigitte."

"No thanks are needed," said Brigitte. "In fact I should really be thanking you."

"You should?"

"Yes, you've made me realise how important the bond between a mother and a son is. I haven't told anyone, but before I came back here I gave birth to a son. It was part of the agreement I had with Miriam and Oliver Chevalier. I carried him for nine months but I told myself that he wasn't my child. I was inhabiting another woman's body and the baby inside me belonged to Miriam and his father not me. I felt so guilty about what happened to everyone on St Ignatius that I was fixated on getting back here and doing what I thought was my duty to them. I forgot about my duty to my son. He might not have been conceived in the womb I was born with, but I'm still the only mother he has. I need to become the mother he deserves."

"How are things with your own Mom?" said Tatyana.

"They've been worse," said Brigitte. "At least she's talking to me now."

"Cos she's forgiven you or cos she's not a Zombie anymore?" said Benjamin.

"Probably the latter."

"This is incredible," said Tatyana. "The past week or so I've been more intimate with you guys than anyone else in my life.

But I've learned more about you in the last thirty minutes than the whole time I've known you. It's like we're suddenly spilling our guts."

"That's what happens when you think you might not see someone for a long while," said Benjamin. "You suddenly think of all the things you want to tell them before you go. That reminds me, I need to shower and pack."

Tatyana stood on the jetty and waved goodbye. Benjamin was fooling around at the back of the boat, pulling faces to stop her from crying. It didn't work. The tears ran down her cheeks.

She'd pulled Benjamin to her for one last kiss just before the boat left. He was a little surprised and hesitant at first but she wasn't going to let him go without one. That meeting of lips spoke more about how they felt than they'd said in their whole awkward farewells.

She watched until the boat disappeared over the horizon, taking all those people away to carry on with the rest of their lives. While she stayed here to continue hers.

Is this where the adventure ends? thought Tatyana. She remembered Benjamin telling her his Uncle Brian once said that there were no beginnings or endings in real life. Just a sequence of events from which we draw our own significance.

Tatyana was sure of one thing, no sequence of events would ever hold more significance than those she'd just lived through.

THE END

JASPER BARK is a novelist, children's author and script writer specialising in comics and graphic novels. He's written three previous novels, *A Fistful of Strontium* (Black Flame, 2005 with Steve Lyons) *Sniper Elite: Spear of Destiny* (Abaddon, 2006) and *The Afterblight Chronicles: Dawn Over Doomsday* (Abaddon, 2008). His all-ages book, *Inventions, Leonardo Da Vinci*, has been translated into five different languages and his *Battle Cries* series of graphic novels are used in schools throughout to improve literacy for 12 to 16 year old readers. He's written comics for just about every publisher in the British comics industry, from *2000 AD* to *The Beano*, and an increasing number of American and international publishers. Prior to this he worked as a film journalist and cable TV presenter by day and a stand-up poet and playwright by night. In 1993 he released an anthology of poetry and a spoken word album both called *Bark Bites*. In 1999 he was awarded a Fringe First at the Edinburgh International Festival.

CHAPTER ONE

Katja

The rising of the dead was the best luck I'd had in years. A godsend, even. I was lucky to survive, of course; my owners showed exactly how they valued me when they left me locked in a Cheetham Hill brothel to drown. I was lucky they kept me upstairs; I heard the women on the ground floor. I heard them die. Heard their screams of panic, heard them choked off as they drowned.

At least, at the time I thought they had drowned. Hours later, clinging to a rooftop, holding a gun with one bullet left in it and trying to decide which of us to use it on, I wasn't so sure.

My name is Katja Wencewska. Although my family is Polish, I grew up in Romania. It's a long story, none of it relevant to this. I will tell you what is relevant.

I am twenty-seven years old. My father was a military officer. Special forces. A good, brave man, always very calm. Tall, as well. A tree of a man. An oak. My mother, in contrast, was like a tiny bird – very bright, excitable. I loved them both dearly. I was their only child. They were proud of me; in school I won prizes in Literature, the Arts and Gymnastics. I have two degrees.

None of that helped when they died. A stupid man, driving drunk, late one night. Their car went off the road, into a ravine. My father died instantly; my mother took several hours. The idiot responsible was cut out of the wreckage with barely a scratch. I wanted to kill him, and could have. Papa had often shown me how. He knew the world is full of predators, and taught me to protect myself against them.

I was studying for a PhD at the time, but of course that had to be abandoned. Bills had to be paid, but there was no work to be found. Then I heard of a job in England. For a fee, strings would be pulled, things arranged. A teaching job.

I spoke good English. I thought I would work hard, make money. Eventually I planned to come home – when things were better there, when I had money saved.

I thought I was so clever. I was well-educated and, I thought, streetwise. I could kill with a blow after all, if I was forced to. But the thought never crossed my mind. I had heard of people trafficking of course, but you never think it will be you. Predators would be so easily dealt with if they came to us as predators.

I was a fool.

You can guess the rest. My passport was taken. There was no teaching job. I was to service men for money. When I refused, I was beaten and raped. Worse than rape. Other things were done to me. I will not talk about those things: they are not relevant, you have no need to know. After this I felt defiled and wretched. I did not refuse again. It was made clear to me – to us all – that if we were too much trouble we would be killed. We were expendable; easily disposed of, easily replaced.

I was kept at a brothel in London at first. After six months they moved me to another, in Manchester. I spent the next eight months there. Being able to kill with a blow means little when there are always more of them, when the doors are always locked, the windows always barred, when you have nowhere to go.

I think that is all I need to say about myself.

I was woken that morning by screams and blaring horns.

I got to the window and squinted through the bars. On Cheetham Hill Road, people were leaping onto the roadway to avoid something pouring over the pavement. At first I thought it was water – dark, filthy water – but when I pushed the net curtains aside I could see it flowed uphill. And over the screams and traffic noise, even the horns, I heard it squealing.

I realised they were swarming rats.

It was raining heavily; water gushed down the pavements and the road into the gutters. There'd been a lot of that lately.

There were rats on the road too – all on one side, the lane for city bound traffic, which was deserted. The road out of Manchester, on the other hand, was jammed solid. I could see the people in the cars – wild, terrified faces, fright and fury mixed, fists pounding windows, dashboards, steering wheels, making their horns blare and blare and blare.

The rain intensified until the road blurred. I stepped back from the window, let the curtains fall back into place. My stomach felt hollow and tight.

We had a television there, but I hadn't seen the news in months. We weren't allowed, and besides, we only wanted to watch things that would take our minds off our lives. I had no idea what had, or was, happening, only that something was very wrong.

Soon, I heard banging on the brothel's front door. I looked outside. It was Ilir, our owner. One of his sons came out of the door; he'd been left in charge. Ilir's black BMW was in the traffic jam, doors open. Ilir dragged his son to it. They slammed the doors; Ilir pounded the horn, but the traffic didn't budge. After a minute, they pulled into the deserted city bound lane. Other cars started following their example, and for a short time the traffic moved forward, but then locked up again. So many people, all trying to leave. Some of the other girls had started screaming, pounding on the doors. They'd abandoned us. They hadn't even turned us loose, just left us here.

People were running along the pavement, clutching their belongings, their children. Their eyes were wild.

An hour or so after Ilir and his son left, the answers started coming. Below Cheetham Hill are the Irwell and the Irk, two of the three rivers that run through Manchester. None are very deep; all have high banks. But water was washing *up* the street. Lapping up in slow, relentless waves.

Even then, I didn't really get it. It only really sank in when people started abandoning their cars.

It happened very quickly after that. Water washed round the wheels of the cars and rose higher. It lapped round their skirts. It poured over the pavements. Across the street, water flooded under the front door of the kebab house and across the floor. People were wading the torrents, then began climbing on top of the cars.

For a few minutes, I just watched. None of it felt real. It was like watching some bizarre art-house film. But nothing had felt real in that place for a long time. You couldn't let it, if you wanted to stay sane.

The water now started pouring over the crest of Cheetham Hill, and the rising waters now became a surge. A middle-aged Asian man fell over and was swept along, screaming for help. His arms flailed, and a toupee slipped off his head. I heard myself giggle; it was a jagged, ugly sound. I clapped a hand over my mouth. He went under and didn't come up.

Then I heard the girls downstairs begin screaming in earnest, and I realised the waters were entering the brothel.

We were all locked in our rooms overnight. Each one had an *en-suite* sink and toilet – for convenience, not comfort. The windows were all barred, so there was no escape. Even if the waters didn't flood the upper floors, I could still look forward to starvation.

My father had shown me how to pick a lock. I could've escaped my room easily enough on several occasions. The difficult part had always been what I would do then. There were two front doors, inner and outer, the inner triple-locked. And even if I'd got clear of that, where would I go with no papers, no passport, no way of getting a legitimate job?

But now the rules had changed.

I started searching, trying to find something I could use. The women downstairs were screaming. People on the street were screaming. I blocked it out. It didn't help me to hear it, wouldn't help me do this faster.

I tipped up the wastepaper basket. There were used condoms in it, slimy to the touch.

Ignore them, Papa said.

At last I found a paper clip.

I knelt by the door and set to work. It was a slow job. Trial and error. My fingers got sweaty and slipped on the metal.

Suddenly I realised something.

The girls downstairs had stopped screaming. All but one. Then suddenly, that too was choked off. And there was only silence from the ground floor.

Outside the street was silent. I went to the window. Stopped, and stared.

Most of it was underwater. Brown, dirty water had covered almost all the cars. The roofs of a few vehicles showed. There was a double-decker bus opposite, the top deck still above water. A dozen people were there, slack-skinned faces gazing into mine. Here and there, on the water, I saw reddish stains, dispersing slowly in the current.

There were two other women upstairs in the brothel – Marianna, who was about my age, was praying over and over in the next room. Marta, the youngest of the girls, was sobbing helplessly across the landing. She was only fifteen. A child. Tiny. Dark. Like my mother had been.

I ran back to the door, back to the lock. My fingers shook. I took a deep breath.

Panic is a choice, Papa used to say. *You can decide not to be scared, not to panic. You can decide who's in charge.*

So I chose to stay calm. I could still hear the rain pelting down outside, but I didn't look to see if the waters were still rising. I couldn't think about that. I had to act as if time was not a factor. I just kept working. Even when the thin carpet I knelt on grew cold and wet.

Marta was sobbing and screaming as well now. From next door, Marianna's prayers had blurred into a rising jumble of sound, fast turning into a wail.

The tumblers clicked.

I got the door open. Water filmed the landing, welling up from the flooded staircase. There was a fire extinguisher on the wall. I could smash the locks on the other girls' doors.

Then there were fresh screams. From outside.

I don't know why, but I went back to the window. I suppose I thought the worst of it was past. The door was open. I had time. Or, perhaps, there was something about the screams that alerted me.

When I look back, I believe going to the window probably saved my life. It forewarned me – just a little, but enough. Even so, as with much else, I wish I hadn't seen what I saw.

It was the double-decker. The waters were still rising, but the top windows and the people inside remained visible. They were scrambling away to the back end of the bus.

Someone was standing up in the water at the front end, near the staircase. At first I thought he was just fat. Then another figure rose up out of the water and I almost screamed. The bus passengers weren't so restrained. I could hear them from where I stood.

The second shape – its flesh resembled well-cooked meat, falling off the bone. I could see the bone of one arm showing through, and when the thing swivelled sideways for a second, showing its back, I saw the flesh coming away from the spine on each side, baring it like a moth's body when its wings are spread. Then it turned my way. *God. God almighty. That face.* Grinning because so much of the flesh was falling from the skull. And looking at me. The sockets of its eyes were empty. They glared; a greenish-yellow glow, bright. It started forward, the fat shape following – I saw now it wasn't fat, just bloated, from its drowning. And then a third figure rose up into view, climbing up the bus's flooded stairwell, and a fourth... all with those glowing eyes.

The passengers were still. There wasn't really anywhere to go in any case. The rotting thing seized one of them, a woman in her twenties, and bit into her neck. I heard her scream. The bloated figure grabbed her too and they pulled her down; blood sprayed up and splattered the windows.

It was over for them very quickly after that. Sometimes I think they were the lucky ones.

I just wish, before I turned away, I hadn't seen the child, hands and face against the glass, screaming...

But there was nothing I could do.

I grabbed the extinguisher off the wall and smashed the lock on Marta's door. She stumbled out, then shrieked again as she saw the flooded stairwell.

"What are we going to do?" It came out in a wail.

I pointed to the hatch in the ceiling. "Get into the loft, then out onto the roof."

Luckily I didn't have to tell her everything; she clambered onto the landing rail and I caught her legs, boosted her up. She pushed the hatch up, grabbed the edges and started wriggling up into the loft. I ran to Marianna's door and smashed the lock there too.

Marianna was on her knees praying. I dragged her to her feet and out onto the landing. The water there was ankle deep now.

"Climb!" I shouted to Marianna, and started clambering onto the banister. Marta reached down to grip my hands. Then her gaze drifted past me and her eyes widened.

I looked.

Wished I hadn't.

Down in the dark water, in the flooded stairwell, I could see movement. And lights. Pairs of yellow-green lights, rising towards the surface. And then I could see their faces.